AMERICA for BEGINNERS

AMERICA for BEGINNERS

Leah Franqui

WM

WILLIAM MORROW

An Imprint of HarperCollins*Publishers*

P.S.™ is a trademark of HarperCollins Publishers.

AMERICA FOR BEGINNERS. Copyright © 2018 by Leah Franqui. All rights reserved. Printed in the United States of America. No part of this book may be used or reproduced in any manner whatsoever without written permission except in the case of brief quotations embodied in critical articles and reviews. For information address HarperCollins Publishers, 195 Broadway, New York, NY 10007.

HarperCollins books may be purchased for educational, business, or sales promotional use. For information please email the Special Markets Department at SPsales@harpercollins.com.

A hardcover edition of this book was published in 2018 by William Morrow, an imprint of HarperCollins Publishers.

FIRST WILLIAM MORROW PAPERBACK EDITION PUBLISHED 2019.

Designed by Bonni Leon-Berman

Library of Congress Cataloging-in-Publication Data has been applied for.

ISBN 978-0-06-266876-9

19 20 21 22 23   LSC   10 9 8 7 6 5 4 3 2

For Rohan, who told me I should

and

for my family, who always knew I could

Flying toward thankfulness, you become

the rare bird with one wing made of fear,

and one of hope. In autumn,

a rose crawling along the ground in the cold wind.

Rain on the roof runs down and out by the spout

as fast as it can.

Talking is pain. Lie down and rest,

now that you've found a friend to be with.

—Rabindranath Tagore

AMERICA for BEGINNERS

1

"You're going to get violated, madam, that's all I have to say on the matter."

Given that her maid, Tanvi, had been lecturing her for over an hour, talking as the other servants of the house had come and gone, Pival Sengupta was quite certain that this was *not* all the maid had to say about the matter. It was irrelevant that Pival had told Tanvi that she was visiting family, that she would be perfectly safe in America. Beyond being scandalized that she was traveling a mere three months after her husband Ram's death, no one believed that she would survive the trip.

Perhaps their suspicion came from Bollywood, from movie after movie where women on their own in foreign lands were constantly propositioned. Or more likely it came from the thousand lectures that girls from India's villages received about how travel of any kind led to rape. It was amazing, Pival thought, that so many village girls came to Kolkata to work if their families were all so concerned about losing their honor. If anything, Pival had assured her servants, America would be safer than India. It had to be. But they refused to listen.

All of the servants had shown their disapproval in their own ways, from Suraj, her yoga instructor, who told her as he stretched out her calves that the prospect of the trip was altering her breathing and negatively affecting her chakras, to Pinky, the cook, no more than eighteen years old and already scowling at Pival like an old village woman. Even the milkman had taken a few moments out of his busy early morning schedule to warn her about the dangers of traveling anywhere, particularly alone.

All of them she could patiently ignore, except Tanvi. Her voice was the loudest, a never-ending fount of dire warnings and forebodings that barely stopped even as the maid chewed and spat paan, her words bubbling out with red spit around the mouthful of leaves. Her lips were stained bright red, which was the point. Pival knew she and the other maids chewed the stuff for its lipstick-like qualities. Pival would catch them admiring their crimson mouths in the mirror, humming songs from the latest Shah Rukh Khan movie. She knew she should scold them for their laziness, but she could never bring herself to do so. They hid their stained red teeth with closed-mouth smiles, but when they laughed it looked to Pival like their mouths were full of blood.

"Such things happen in America, every day. Nice people go on trips abroad and come back violated. And, it's expensive. Huh! Lakhs and lakhs for a pair of shoes. What is the point, I ask you? Shoes are here. Why go somewhere to get violated for shoes? Visiting relatives is all well and good but decent people should be coming here to comfort you, not this leaving and begging-for-family nonsense."

Sarya, the other maid in the room, nodded as she received Tanvi's wisdom and the white garment Tanvi had folded. It was a perfect square. As Tanvi grew upset, her folding became increasingly precise and perfect, until you could have cut onions with the razor-sharp corners of the sari silk.

Pival had never liked Tanvi. Her husband, Ram, had employed the girl when they first married, presenting a child of fifteen to his twenty-year-old bride before the maid had the chance to wipe the dust from her village off her shoes, before his bride's wedding henna had begun to fade. Pival wanted to keep her own maid, but Ram insisted that young Tanvi would be easier to train. At the time Pival had accepted the new servant as an indulgence, one of the many Ram, then so generous, lavished on her. As Tanvi grew from Pival's maid into a kind of housekeeper, directing all the servants around her with an iron fist, she wondered if Ram had known even then that his wife would be lacking in authority and had found a servant who could act as a substitute. That, too, she had seen as a kind of kindness, a thoughtfulness on Ram's part, making up for her deficits, anticipating her flaws. It wasn't until years later that Pival realized Ram didn't want a servant more loyal to Pival and her family than to him. He had built himself an ally, who would turn against Pival when needed.

Of course, Pival didn't allow herself to think such things about her husband until much later, after they'd had Rahi and lost him, before he lived and gave her life light and then darkened it again.

The maids continued with their packing and dividing. Pival never knew she had so many clothes until she saw them pass through the hands of so many people. She could not help; she would not be permitted to do so. They would be silently furious with her if she tried, more angry than they were now, even, and Tanvi would sigh and recite the wages they paid each woman, an unsubtle commentary meant to remind her that any labor she performed was a waste of her own money.

Pival looked at Ram's photo in its permanent shrine, warping slightly under the weight of the faded marigold wreaths and lit by small lamps whose ghee was refilled daily. The combined scent of flowers and ghee made her feel slightly sick. Still, she liked the flickering lights, the cotton wicks, the way the fire swayed and gave things a golden glow. She was obligated, she knew, to treat Ram's picture as a sacred object, to give it offerings like she would an idol. He didn't deserve such a place in anyone's home; perhaps that was what made her feel ill, and not the smell at all.

Looking around, Pival realized that the maids had started unpacking the carefully sorted trunks and boxes. At her gasp, Sarya looked up, her large eyes wide.

"It's bad business. Best not to do it. What will people say?"

Tanvi shook her head in agreement, clucking like a chicken.

"Going to such places? Begging old relatives to take you in? You will lower yourself, madam. What would sir think? Who does such a thing?"

"And what are you saying, either of you? How would you know what people do? Living in the same ten streets all your life, what do you know but the tread of your shoes? Close your drooling mouths and pack my things!"

Tanvi stared at Pival, her mouth wide in surprise. Sarya had already begun to cry, her childish wails filling the air between them. Pival had shocked even herself. She was never so articulate in Bengali, and she never got angry. While Ram Sengupta might have raised his voice at the servants, Pival rarely spoke above a soft tone, making most people strain toward her when she talked. It was one of her husband's many criticisms of her. He had called her with disdain a little squeaky mouse.

Pival had tried to speak louder. She had gone to a breathing seminar taught by a prestigious doctor turned guru to improve her lung capacity and diaphragm control. She had even seen a throat and larynx specialist, who informed her that what she lacked was not strength of voice but strength of confidence. Pival had known then that it was a lost cause. Whatever confidence she had once had was now a withered thing, dead on the vine.

A cacophony of wailing, like a funeral procession, brought Pival back to the present. She gazed dispassionately at the faces of her sobbing maids. She said nothing as Sarya and then Tanvi left her room. Sarya fled like a deer, but Tanvi made a more leisurely departure, waiting for Pival to call her back and apologize. As the older maid waddled away, Pival couldn't help but think of the thin child she'd met all those years ago and looked for her in Tanvi's plump frame. She couldn't find her, couldn't see that girl who had pressed her lips together with happiness when she first ate a piece of chocolate, trying to keep it in her mouth forever.

Pival turned, shaking her head. Why should she care what Tanvi and Sarya and all the rest of them thought? Pival looked at herself in the mirror. She had been avoiding mirrors since Ram's death, afraid she would look too old, too unhappy, or worse, too happy. She couldn't find her younger self in her own face anymore either. The room around her was richly appointed, filled with beautiful and expensive things. They reflected behind her in the mirror, overwhelming her thin, faded face, leaving her feeling ugly next to their glow. She had been overwhelmed and buried by her own life. And now, unable to dig herself out, she was going to leave it all behind.

Pival rubbed at her wrists gently, an old habit to comfort herself. She didn't like that she had yelled at the servants. She may not have liked the maids but that was no excuse for cruelty. Since Ram had died, all their help had been so devastated, mourning much more deeply than Pival could herself. She should have had sympathy for those who loved her husband more than she had.

She rubbed her wrist again, looking at it. She had always been fascinated by the skin on her wrists, the thinness of it, the way she could see blue veins popping up through it like tunnels. She had thought of ending her life this way, with a shard of glass to the wrist, the way women did in the Bollywood movies she would sneak off to watch alone when Ram was at work. Other women in the theaters cried and sighed at every twist and turn, but for her, the only parts that interested her were the mothers, the ones who martyred themselves for their sons. As a young woman she had found this ridiculous. Now she found it shaming. She watched them slice through their veins with a kind of envy, but she hadn't thought she could bear cutting through her own skin. She had tried it once, when Ram had told Rahi he could never come home again, and there was a small dip in the skin of her left wrist as evidence of her failure. She had cleaned up and bandaged her wrist and hid it from Ram under her bangles. Besides, after Rahi was banished Ram stopped looking at her at all. She checked now for that little dent, rubbing at it gently, pressing her pinkie into the pucker as her thumb caressed the rest of her wrist.

"This is not done, madam." Tanvi's formal declaration interrupted Pival's thoughts and she hid her hands behind her quickly, like a little girl. It was always this way with Tanvi, like Pival was the servant and the maid the master. She forced herself to bring her hands back to her sides, pressing her sweaty palms into the skirts of her white sari. "You have hurt Sarya. She is threatening to leave."

"She should, then. It's time for her to marry, anyway. Soon she will be too old."

Pival was amazed by how quickly the words sprang to her lips. Tanvi had never married. The maid looked like she had been slapped.

"This is not doing what sahib would have wanted. Leaving home like this."

"I have no home, Tanvi," Pival said, looking toward the wall at a large family photo of the Senguptas taken thirty years ago, at Rahi's first birthday.

Pival knew this was blasphemy to the maid, who had left her village of one-room houses and well water and now lived in the luxury of the Senguptas' apartment, with a maid's quarters she barely had to share and fresh milk delivered daily. Pival was lucky, she knew. In another age, in another family, she would have been banished to a wing of the house, forced to live as a pariah for her widowhood. In villages outside of Kolkata these things still happened. Perhaps where Tanvi was from, even. She knew that she, Pival, was privileged, for being so free, for having so much when most people around her had less than nothing. She saw the maid's eyes dip to the jewelry sitting in a box. She felt her face hardening.

"Please repack my things. I've already told you, you can take whatever you like. You needn't worry about your salary, Tanvi. I told you, I will pay everyone through to the new year. So you may stop pretending to be concerned about me now. You can have everything you need. Do you understand?"

Tanvi began to cry again, angrily this time, and stomped from the room, though not, Pival observed, without a trailing handful of sari silks streaming from the pocket of her apron. Good. Tanvi should take such things from her. For Tanvi they were riches. For Pival they were fetters, caging in her life. Tanvi could keep them all. Pival only hoped Tanvi would share them with the other maids, who were even now peeking out from their quarters, watching their leader return.

She decided to call her travel agent. She slipped a disposable cell phone she'd bought on the street out of her pocket. It took a long time for a phone call to reach America. Pival wondered how it would be for her, when even the phone seemed afraid to let its call leave India. The phone rang and rang and then the now-familiar voice of her travel agent, a nasal drone, began, inviting her to leave a message in three languages. She left her message softly and carefully, merely asking him to call her back without explaining in either English or Bengali what she really needed, because she wasn't sure herself. Assurance, maybe, that America was a real place.

Carefully removing the drying flower garland, she opened up the back of Ram's photograph, smiling gently to think of the appropriateness of this as her hiding place. Between the back of the frame and the benevolent, falsely smiling image of her husband was all her trip information. Her itinerary, her ticket, her passport with its crisp new tourist visa, everything she would need. It was far worse than her servant could have possibly imagined. Pival wasn't going to meet anyone at all in America. She had no family to meet there, no matter what she had told the maids. At least, not in the way they thought.

Ram had had a large family, many of whom still lived in Kolkata, all of whom had been quick to guide Pival through the rituals of death and widowhood with a speed and sense of authority that left her breathless. While they might not have been true dyed-in-the-wool Brahmins, they acted that way when interacting with the world and expected her to do so as well. This was why it was essential for her trip to happen soon, and silently, while the noise of the massive Durga Puja festival left them distracted. She would escape from her life and take a tour, a cross-country trip of America. It would give her a chance to see the country her son had known and loved, the place he had refused to leave, even for her. It would bring her to Los Angeles. She would have time to prepare, time to make herself ready to meet *him,* the person who had taken her son away.

Pival looked back at the family portrait, her hands in the shot around a plump and grinning version of Rahi, theirs the only two smiling faces in a sea of familial disapproval and stern Bengali brows. She walked up to it and traced Rahi's tiny face with her pinkie. She then dipped her pinkie back into the depression left by her half-hearted suicide attempt of the previous fall. November would mark a year since Ram had told her Rahi died. She wondered as she stared into the fat baby face, not for the first time, if it was really true. Surely her son couldn't have died while she still lived. She refused to accept a universe in which Rahi had died. She knew she would have felt his death like a blow to her own body. She didn't care what had been said, what had been told to her. Everyone could be lying. Ram had always tried to control the way she saw the world, not lying, exactly, but forcing reality to fit his desires. He might have told her Rahi was dead because he was already dead to Ram. It could have been something he had told people so often he really started to believe it himself. She had to go to America and find Rahi, alive and whole or dead and gone. She had to be sure. And if he was gone? Well, then it was her time, too.

Ram had declared their son dead so often by the time the phone call came from America that afterward Pival was never sure if the phone had really rung or not. While she had always nodded along with Ram in public, in private she had never agreed that their son was dead, and that had, she knew, troubled Ram. When she looked up that day and watched him put down the phone, she realized that she hadn't heard the ringing. That was not surprising; she lived in such a dream world in those days. Ram said, "It's done. He's gone," and Pival had believed him in that moment. But now, months later, she couldn't decide if Ram had really heard news from across the world or if he couldn't stand her continued love for the son who had so dishonored him. Things were so blurry, even now. She had to find the truth, even if it stabbed at her heart.

Pival Sengupta was going to America to find her son or his lover. And to kill herself.

2

Halfway around the world, Ronnie Munshi was, most unprofessionally, avoiding Pival's calls. Perhaps if he had known about her dramatic intentions he might have been more eager to speak to her, but it was doubtful. Suicide is awfully bad for business.

Ronnie Munshi had a policy. He would answer his phone before a tour was booked, but never afterward. His usual strategy with customers was to woo them with relentless passion, but once he booked them he cut off all communication until their trip, to give them no opportunities to back out once he had received their deposit. He was terrified of such an occurrence, and not without reason. Indians, Ronnie thought, with complacent derision, were notoriously unreliable, especially when presented with the bill.

It would have come as a surprise to many that the First Class India USA Destination Vacation Tour Company was, in fact, run by Bangladeshis. The fact that this surprise would have been essentially unpleasant, or at the very least awkward, for his clients made it information that Ronnie was careful to hide. He had heard that Indian-Bangladeshi relationships had improved since his departure from his native land, but he suspected strongly this only applied to wealthy people, who were all the same anyway, wherever you went.

In his fifteen years in America, Ronnie had transformed from a skinny adolescent dishwasher at his distant uncle's Curry Hill kebab joint to a plump and prosperous owner of his own business. He had also learned enough to understand that that business came at the cost of being Bangladeshi. So for all intents and purposes, publicly, at least, he wasn't. To the best of his ability, that is. It's very difficult to pretend to be from a country you dislike while living in another country that doesn't know that the country you dislike and the country you are from are actually two distinct and separate places. Still, Ronnie had managed thus far, and he had no intention of letting Mrs. Sengupta, an uppity Bengali widow, interfere with his performance. Her calls, however, were not doing wonderful things for his heartburn.

Ronnie reached into a drawer on his desk and pulled out a jumbo-sized container of Tums, or rather, an off-brand knockoff guaranteed to get him the same results. His deceit, although carefully calculated and developed over many years, coupled with his avoidance policies, gave him digestive issues, and the right half of his desk was devoted to medicines, be they Ayurvedic or pharmaceutical, to aid his ever-aching stomach. As he chewed the chalky mouthful of pink and yellow tablets, he tried to remember the last day he had gone through without stomach pain.

Ronnie had arrived in America at the age of eighteen with four hundred dollars in his pocket, fifty of which were rapidly stolen by a cabdriver who could see that the frightened foreigner had no concept of United States currency, and a letter of introduction to his uncle and uncle's family.

His uncle, Pritviraj Munshi, actually a third cousin of his late father, introduced himself to his trembling relative as Raj, informing him that this name was easier for Americans to understand. This introduction confused Ronnie, then Rosni, because surely his uncle could count on a relative to understand his real name, even if these strange white people couldn't. But Rosni was too tired and overwhelmed to question his uncle, who had, after all, not only survived for some twenty years in the United States but prospered. Pritviraj had left Bangladesh after the revolution and somehow had made it in America, and that made him a hero in Rosni's exhausted eyes.

Recovering from his jet lag, Rosni presented himself at his uncle's Manhattan business the following day to start working. He realized to his horror that his uncle, a proud Bangladeshi man, had set up an Indian restaurant. Instead of mustard-scented fish curries and coconut mutton chops served with plain rice, his uncle was doing good business selling people kebabs and dals and naan in a cramped but cheerful place with large color-enhanced photos of the Taj Mahal all over the walls and sitar music twanging in the background. There was a tandoori section of the menu, but no tandoor in the kitchen, and nothing was the way he had thought it would be. Confused, and less recovered from his flight than he had thought, Rosni almost fainted on the spot.

Ronnie crunched another handful of Tums, his stomach rebelling at the thought of this, the first lesson in America for beginners. His uncle, sensing his complete disorientation and despair, hastily sat his nephew down and, making sure the place was locked, as business had not yet started for the day, explained that most Americans were not aware of Bangladesh as a concept. They were, however, aware of India, made popular by a band called the Beatles in the past, and they had, at least in New York, developed a taste for North Indian food, and so North Indian food is what Raj gave them. Ronnie, who had never cooked a day in his life, could start on the dishwashers and, if he showed promise, work his way up to a cook. Ronnie agreed, reluctantly, because what else could he do? Working his way dejectedly through a plate of sweet butter chicken, which coated his mouth with viscous sauce, he knew his mother's chicken curry with mustard seeds and curry leaves was highly superior, but they could only afford chicken a few times a month at home. Here, it might have been bland, soaked in butter and too sweet, but he could have it every day. If it hurt his nationalist sensibilities to work in a place that pretended to be Indian, well, he was hungrier than he was patriotic.

Ronnie did not, in fact, show any promise in food service whatsoever, for though he ate the food he still disapproved of it. He quit, and
soon found himself selling tickets to Circle Line boat tours around
the island of Manhattan. If America had quickly lost its glamour for
Ronnie, there was no reason, he thought, that this experience should
be the same for others. He was eager to give people insider tips about
America and steer them, should they seem interested, back to his
uncle's restaurant, because family is family after all and besides, Ronnie still lived with them.

When one particularly satisfied Ohio-based family turned to Ronnie, who had urged them onto the boat, off the boat, and over to
the restaurant with a smooth professional air, and told him that he
really ought to give his own tours, he listened. But the competition
for American tourists was fierce, and Ronnie's English, while much
improved over his five years in the United States, was far from perfect, making him an unsafe bet for many Midwestern and Southern
sightseers who did not appreciate accents other than their own. Ronnie was on the verge of throwing in the towel and returning to the
Circle Line when a rare stroke of luck came in the form of a family
from California but originally from West Bengal. Though Indian, the
family was so relieved to find someone who spoke Bengali that they
overlooked Ronnie's Bangladeshi roots. It was while showing these
people New York and commiserating on the difficulties of this New
World living that Ronnie realized it wasn't his idea that was wrong, it
was his client base. Once he began to advertise himself as an Indian
guide for Indian people (his gut clenched at this, but he soldiered
on), the tourists poured in, first from the United States and Canada
and soon, as phone lines and Internet connections grew, all over the
world.

He looked out onto the office. It was empty now, true, but it had
fifteen desks in it, each one for one of his guides. Ronnie ran his tour

company from the third floor of a building in Astoria, a cheap space for a growing business, although if anyone asked they were located "in the heart of Manhattan exactly." Of course clients didn't ask, they asked about the Grand Canyon and where to buy the cheapest imitation designer bags. He tended to lie about such things, as he had no idea. Ronnie saw no irony in sending his clients all over a land he had barely seen. He had taken exactly two trips since his arrival to New York, one back home to Bangladesh after the careful acquisition of his green card, to pick up his arranged and mother-approved bride, Anita, and one for their honeymoon to Wisconsin, land of cheese.

The thought of cheese pushed his fragile internal life to the limit. Ronnie reached for his trash can and vomited all the Tums, and then, mechanically, reached for the container and stuffed another handful in his mouth. He knew he shouldn't feel so stressed. This was not his only client who expected a Bengali guide. *All* Ronnie's clients harbored strong expectations of a Bengali tour guide of decent birth and background, but once they arrived in America they were perfectly happy to be stuck with a courteous, helpful, cheerful, Bengali-speaking tour guide who had been well trained in downplaying his Bangladeshi patriotism; concealing his Islamic faith, should any such exist; and flatteringly expressing a strong desire to be re-included in either the Indian or the Pakistani state, depending on the audience.

Picking out Mrs. Sengupta's guide would be extremely difficult, Ronnie thought, nodding his head in grim agreement with his own mind. *Who shall I give her?* There was Vikrum, a burly fellow with gold teeth who made guests feel safe in this strange country, and serenaded them with early Bollywood tunes and village chants in his surprisingly melodic tenor. There was Ashwin, a mild-mannered guide whose ability to rattle off statistics made him very popular with visiting engineers and the like. There was even Puli, a consummate foodie who had mapped out the finest Indian cuisine possible in all fifty states. The man could find rice in a pasta store. But were any of them right for this widow? Besides, they were booked already. All that was really left was the new boy, Satya, a recent addition to the team.

Ronnie paused his volley of thoughts and considered that prospect. It might be possible. Perhaps Mrs. Sengupta would want a guide who felt like the son who *should* have been taking care of her? It wasn't a bad idea, that.

Mrs. Sengupta was traveling scandalously alone, without a husband or gaggle of women her own age. This was something that had shocked Ronnie, and he had feared his horror during the initial phone-call inquiry would lose him Mrs. Sengupta as a client. She certainly hadn't seemed very assertive in that first conversation, saying little, asking few questions, and hanging up as soon as she learned about the packages. He had thought it was just another Indian auntie with empty days indulging in a long-distance phone call for a thrill. But she did call back, and accepted Ronnie's laughably expensive packaged "deal" without even a token attempt at bargaining. This saddened Ronnie, who always enjoyed a good back-and-forth over his absurdly padded prices, but money was money, and he swallowed his disappointment along with the fee.

Mrs. Sengupta, understanding that she would be getting a male tour guide—Ronnie didn't hire women for fear that they might distract his employees and male clients—requested that Ronnie provide a female companion/travel partner, for an appropriate extra charge, of course. In short, Mrs. Sengupta was looking to hire someone to be her friend. Ronnie, who had no friends himself, was unsure about hiring one for someone else. He wished, not for the first time in his life, that *escort* meant just that, and not a woman who pretended to be one's girlfriend.

Ronnie's first instinct was to enlist his wife, Anita. It had seemed

like the perfect solution, he remembered, munching glumly on a handful of dried peppermint leaves. He liked to switch between remedies
for his stomach, hoping together they might work. Ronnie shook his
head as he remembered proudly presenting his plan to Anita at dinner,
Thai for her, stomach soothers for him. He had stirred his yogurt with
a resigned sigh as Anita happily devoured a papaya salad, comforting
himself with his brilliant idea. He was just leaning back in satisfaction
when Anita surprised him by laughing her large braying laugh.

"Oh, absolutely not, Big Nose!" Anita's favorite pet name for Ronnie was one he hated. "Surely you must make joke. No way, no how,
nowhere. Over my ashes, as they say."

Ronnie, stunned, said nothing, not even correcting her English, an
opportunity he rarely passed up. They had agreed to speak English
to each other for at least an hour a day, using it as a chance to try out
new words and idioms that they might have been fearful to try out on
strangers. Ronnie loved to assume an air of superiority, having been
in America for so much longer than Anita, but the truth was, she was
a far faster learner than he.

He realized, sighing through his peppermint leaves, that he should
have expected this from his wife, but at the time, almost a month
ago, he was flabbergasted. It sometimes troubled him how Anita was
nothing like what she was supposed to have been. He had specifically
asked for a wife who would be, like the families he guided, enrap-
tured with his intellect and his knowledge. Instead, he had gotten
Anita.

Although he enjoyed the freedoms of America, when Ronnie had
decided to get married, he looked for his bride in Bangladesh. He had
met nice Bangladeshi girls in America through his uncle and the growing network of Bangladeshi friends and neighbors who had flooded
into Jackson Heights in the years since Ronnie had arrived. However,
he had found the women raised between Bangladesh and America to

be too much of everything. They were bold, these girls; they looked him directly in the eyes, they ventured to touch his shoulder when he made them laugh, and they sat too close at movies and meals. It made him uncomfortable. He would never be the authority with a girl like that. He had to look to the old country.

He called his mother, who was initially annoyed to be disturbed during her favorite soap opera but forgave all when she heard his reason for doing so. She nodded constantly through the conversation, because she had never really understood that her face wasn't visible across the phone line. After hearing Ronnie's careful stipulations, she concluded that she had just the girl in mind, her friend's sister's daughter's niece, Anita Das. Anita would do very nicely for Ronnie; she spent her days in her home helping her mother, who was, by all accounts, an excellent cook, which meant that Anita herself must have inherited this ability.

For her part, Anita was not actually consulted at any level, but if she had been, she would have been thrilled by the new match. Not because Ronnie Munshi, a skinny child she could barely remember from the village school years ago, seemed to be any great prize, but because marrying him would be a one-way ticket to America. Anita would have consented to an Indian husband, a Pakistani husband, even a Chinese husband, had one presented himself, because they would have all meant the same thing to her: escape. Her family was not an unhappy one: she was not beaten any more than was deemed strictly necessary by her parents; she had been allowed to complete several years at the local school, and even took classes and received a junior degree from a two-year college in the nearest city. Still, Anita had been born, she had been told, looking up at the world, emerging from the birth canal with her eyes open and unblinking. Ever since then, she hadn't been able to stop looking for something better or deeper or just more.

She had been considering her own escape seriously, hoarding little bits of money in a hole in the ground in a corner outside of her father's house, when the offer from Ronnie finally reached her, relayed through a series of long-distance interactions. This was two weeks after Ronnie had first contacted his mother, but eventually her mother deigned to explain to Anita that she had, at long last, found a husband, despite her tanned skin and disinterest in domestic duties. Her dance of joy was interrupted by her mother's reminder that now would be an excellent time to learn to cook. Her major selling point had been her cooking abilities, passed down, it had been assured, from her mother. Anita merely laughed. Her mother slapped her hard, but that rebellious giggle was worth it. Her mother didn't matter anymore. Anita was already far away.

Though Ronnie had been certain that his delicate country-bred bride might find the US of A overwhelming, the reality was that Anita took to America like a fish to water. Initially, she had been worried about only two things. One was the food, and the other was the bedroom. However, Ronnie, who had never been with a real live woman, lasted all of twenty seconds after entering his virginal bride for the first time, and it would take him several years to improve on this performance. While not exactly a pleasant experience, it was, for Anita, a mercifully short one that seemed to give her new husband pleasure and, more importantly, a deep sleep.

As for the food issue, Anita very quickly discovered takeout by means of Chinese food menus that were slipped under their apartment door, and that was that.

While Ronnie had carried an expatriate's love of home and hearth, Anita had spent her childhood and adolescence in the Bangladesh of reality, rather than the lovely and lush country village of Ronnie's imagination. Initially confused and disappointed in his wife, Ronnie sought the advice of his aunt and uncle, hoping to find someone to dictate Anita's behavior more effectively than he had managed to do. But Ronnie was out of luck, for Anita, with her quick mind, respectful disposition, and easy laughter, was seen as brave, funny, and adaptable. Instead of Anita's changing, it was Ronnie who grew to see his wife's abilities and interests as, if not attractive, then certainly rather useful at work.

But not this time, apparently. He begged, he implored, but Anita stood firm.

"You are thinking this madam will be so thrilled to see a nice brown female face she will dance for joyousness, yes?"

Ronnie nodded slowly. He had, indeed, been thinking along those lines.

"You are ten kinds of an idiot. This Kolkata auntie will take one look at me and swim back home. Look at me!"

Ronnie surveyed his wife. She looked very nice in her hot-pink spandex leggings and teal polyester tunic, he thought. Her bangles, all neon plastic, provided a nice contrast to the two other elements, and her sneakers were bright silver and purple.

"Even for dinner with Uncle I don't wear sari nonsense. This memsahib will expect someone from another century. I can't do it, Ronnie baby, just haven't the wardrobe!" Anita licked her fingers. "And besides. Two weeks traveling around dull towns with an Indian auntie judging my every movement? It's been too long for me, nah, I'm too USA now for such things. No thank you."

Anita raised her trim body up and gave her disappointed spouse a peck on the cheek.

"Sorry, Big Nose. It's not for me."

Ronnie knew better than to try to convince her, or worse, order her. Ronnie was no match for his wife, a village flower with an iron will. He would have to think of something soon. Mrs. Sengupta was one client, but that's how it began. Disappoint one person, and the rest stop giving you the chance to do so. He could not afford for his business to fail. He could not be one of those men who clung on to life and thought about what they used to be. He would have to accommodate the widow, if that meant forcing Anita on to the trip with his bare hands.

3

Pival sighed with frustration as yet another call to Mr. Munshi went to voice mail. She looked over her balcony rail to the busy street below. Since her dramatic confrontation with her maids the previous afternoon, the house had been silent, punctuated only by the tread of the servants' feet. Pival had never understood how the maids managed to make their walk reflect their mood, but they had a footfall for every emotion, and their steps sounded accusatory. Pival wished she could serve herself tea, instead of waiting for Sarya to do so, but that would never be allowed. It was strange, she knew, that she was more restricted by her servants than served. If she had married someone poorer she could have served herself her entire life, and probably would have longed for help. Now she was jailed by her waitstaff, unable to do anything on her own. She grimaced at the thought. She was ungrateful, she knew, to resent being so wealthy that she was expected to use help. Still, she wished she could make herself tea. It had been so long, she could barely remember how anymore.

She heard Sarya coming from the kitchen, her light footsteps distinguishing her from Tanvi and the male servants. The maid's feet tapped out an unhappy rhythm as she carried the tray. Pival felt rather than saw the maid's gaze when she entered Pival's room and set down the tray with a thud, but Pival didn't turn around, keeping her eyes fixed on the street and the people below. It was easier to look out the window than to face her servants. She longed to begin her trip, to find her ending. Every moment before that felt like a waste of time.

She heard a cough. "Thank you, Sarya, you can go." Her voice had wavered but held firm, she thought to herself with no small amount of satisfaction. She heard Sarya sob petulantly behind her, and she knew this would be another piece of gossip for the servants' quarters, the cruelty of madam, her refusal to even look them in the face.

Once Pival was sure that the girl was gone, she allowed herself to turn back and look at the meal she had been given. She noted that the cook had left her tea and a light repast of digestive biscuits, but no sugar or cream. They must not have thought she deserved those luxuries.

The quiet of the apartment felt strange. Normally it was a hive of activity, or it had been during Ram's life. A host of people began to arrive as early as six in the morning, starting with the milkman who brought their milk daily, delivering to them first as the result of a few well-timed extra rupees each year. Then there was her breathing instructor, who arrived at seven; the yoga instructor, at eight; and at least three times a week a priest would arrive at nine to lead them in prayers and bless their shrine. Ram's departure for work at ten would empty things out a bit but soon a stream of people delivering things would begin again, and then, of course, the visiting hours, the memory of which made her shiver despite the steam rising up from the cup of tea in front of her. The clock struck two, which meant teatime was upon her. Small wonder she felt uneasy, she thought, her mouth twisting. Although she had eliminated teatime the day Ram died, memories of it haunted her still. She looked around her, reassuring herself that she was alone.

When Ram had been alive tea had not been a beverage. Tea had been an event. Although Ram was rarely home at that hour, the timing of tea was strictly maintained in his absence. From two P.M. to five thirty P.M. a daily stream of visitors poured through the door, a stark contrast to the workers who entered in the mornings. They would include all the cousins, aunts, distant acquaintances, and close friends, implicitly demanding drinks and snacks and, most importantly, conversation. If not quite the cream of Bengali society, it was the richest milk of it, wealthy and well educated, and if not quite Brahmins, trying to make up for it at every turn. Ram, a barrister in Kolkata's high court, was not expected to be present. In fact, his absence was a point of pride for his many female admirers, who beamed and remarked happily, "So busy he is with his work!" Between the countless cups of weakly brewed, milky tea and the vast amounts of commentary, Pival often felt like she was drowning in a caffeinated sea. She wished Ram would return home at two, at first because she missed him, and later because when he was there she could retreat and be permitted some relief and stillness.

She took a sip of her tea, savoring the simplicity of the liquid and the pure silence filling the room. She couldn't help but think of all the teatimes that had felt endless, when she had watched the clock from the corner of her eye and groaned inwardly when the eagle-eyed gaze of disapproving relatives seemed to pin her in place.

Pival's parents had raised her with gentle curation, like the caretakers of a small private museum. Her parents' strict rationality and disdain for superstition had made them disapprove of blind adherence to any custom that could not be explained logically. Pival had grown up trusting herself and her own judgment, and it had come as an unpleasant surprise to find out that her husband and his large and ever-present family did not.

When they spoke to her, offering what they considered to be deeply helpful ways to improve her life, they did so with the assumption that she would already know their expectations, which left her confused, them disappointed, and Ram derisive. Her husband's frustration at her inquiries about these rituals and habits, which seemed so natural and self-explanatory to him, submerged Pival further into silence.

The quieter she became, the more he chastised her. Seeing how her husband treated her, his family followed suit. After a daily serving of their disdain, swallowed with her own snacks at teatime, Pival's confidence had faded and died, replaced by a reserved meekness and deep inner pain.

And then there had been Ram, who had isolated her with his judgments. No one was ever good enough to be their friend, so now she had none. Who could measure up to the Sengupta standards? It had been easier not to argue, easier to just quit. Her brother had died in an accident when he was twenty-seven, so when her parents passed away, her last ties to anyone outside of the Sengupta clan had been effectively severed. Now, she realized, she knew no one else.

Pival took another sip of her tea, trying to force that pale shadow of herself back into the past. *Stop haunting my living room,* she told it in her mind. Today she was alone. She no longer had to bend and mold herself into the shapes others had left for her to fill.

After Ram's death, many of her former visitors had maintained their teatime arrivals to comfort her in her time of need. At least, that was what they said they were doing, but Pival had been aware that their real goal was to ensure that her grief followed the prescribed paths set out for her by the Senguptas. Carefully they observed her, as if she were an animal at the zoo. Even in mourning there was a host of customs for Pival to neglect and perform incorrectly. *That must give them a great deal of happiness,* Pival thought, finishing her tea. Pival sometimes found herself speaking to her husband in her mind in a way she never could have in life. *At least I'm good for something, Ram.*

A crash and then the sound of angry protests floated up to her window. She returned to the balcony and looked down below. A car had collided into a cart full of supplies to decorate the goddess, and now brightly colored paper and paints and flowers filled the narrow road. The owner of the cart screamed at the driver, demanding compensation for his damaged goods. The driver, on the other hand, was furious at the injury to the car, which seemed to have suffered no ill effects that Pival could see, other than a few splatters of paint and a shower of flower petals. Certainly his vehicle would face more such damage during the festival itself, which flooded the city with people and left cars covered in its decorations for days.

Inside the car, the passenger was rapping loudly at the window, and the screaming driver's face shifted instantly from angry to servile. He bowed to the car's occupant, who had rolled down the window an inch or two and was slipping a slim handful of rupees rolled into a neat cylinder into the cart owner's hand. The man accepted the compensation happily as the driver grumbled and spat a large stream of paan right at the cart owner's feet. The driver resumed his position within the car, and the cart owner dragged his cart, now with a cracked wheel, in the other direction. The small street was silent once more, with only the spattered remains of the decorations as evidence that anything had happened. A flicker of movement caught her eye. There was a child crouched in the gutter, begging. She hadn't even noticed.

When she was young, Pival had loved Durga Puja, but as an adult all the joy of the holiday had died for her the day that Rahi left. Without him in the house, her celebrations felt hollow. Rahi had always loved to take his lantern and dance in front of the goddess, thanking her for her triumph over the evil demon and imploring her for her grace. Ram would watch, disapproving of his son's dancing but unable to say anything because it was traditional. Once Rahi was gone they didn't decorate their house or their shrine; instead they visited with others during the holiest days of the event, leaving their own house empty and allowing the servants time off.

She had thought she had nothing to thank the goddess for this year, but as she watched the empty street she realized Durga Puja was giving her the opportunity to escape. It would be like the child in the road. People would be so distracted by the festival that they would never see her slip away. She watched the child scratch at his scabs and made a mental note to send down some food from the kitchen if there was extra. The cook had yet to learn how to prepare meals for Pival alone, and they always had too much. The child would have something to eat that night, at least.

Why had Mr. Munshi not returned her calls? Was there some problem with the guide, or worse, the companion? Mr. Munshi, whom Pival would not want to insult but who sounded vaguely Bangladeshi to her, had assured her, "All is possible, probably, prepared, madam!" Now she feared that this was not the case. Her tickets had been booked. She left in a week, at the height of the festival. What would she do if there were no tour guide and companion waiting? She hated to admit it but Tanvi's dire warning echoed in her brain.

She wished she had kept more of herself whole throughout her long marriage. She could have used her youthful boldness now, but it was gone. In its place was fear, and what could that help her now? She thought about Rahi. Why had he left her all alone? What had he found in America?

4

Jacob Schwartz fell in love for the first time sitting in a traffic jam on the way back from the airport and it was only because of the horrible congestion of the Los Angeles freeway that he realized it. If he had lived in another kind of place, who knows what might have been possible? But he looked over at the face next to him, the strong jaw, the straight nose, the smooth tanned skin, and the mouth stretched wide as Bhim belted out a power ballad from the early nineties, and there it was. Love. They were two miles from their exit and in the half an hour it took to travel that distance Jake had convinced Bhim to kiss him back, and by the time they reached Jake's apartment their inhibitions were long gone, as were their shirts.

For as long as he could remember, Jake's life had been dictated by traffic. He had grown up in Los Angeles, so commuting had been a way of life. His mother, a divorcée and part-time yoga teacher living in Venice Beach, had carted him from school to guitar lessons to soccer practice to the mall to movies and finally, three nights a week, to his father's condo in East Hollywood for awkward meals from nearby Chinese food takeout joints. Together he and his father would eat moo shu chicken in silence, with his father's tentative overtures met with surly rebuffs. What they talked about, because they couldn't talk about anything else, was traffic. How to get where, what route they had taken that day, what its potential benefits and downsides were. Traffic was the language of neutrality in Los Angeles and Jake learned it young.

The early years after his parents' separation, which occurred just after his tenth birthday, had been filled to the brim with activities, as if his life could be made too full for him to notice the difference. Jake, as he had been called by everyone in his life but Bhim, had observed his parents carefully after they split up, like a scientist monitoring a long-term experiment, noting changes and constants, variations and radical outliers. He kept a diary with carefully maintained charts, as he was, according to all his teachers, a visual learner. His ultimate conclusion, after several years, was that in fact the best situation for them all was this, for his parents to live in two separate bubbles, with Jake as the only connection between them. This hadn't stopped Jake from craving a partner, however, though it did make him wary about finding one.

Like many children of divorce, Jake was so good at telling the story of his family that by the time he was an adult he could gauge which detail would amuse his listener the most and play to it. When he had first met Bhim through mutual friends at a bar outside of San Francisco called Bangers and Mash, which served neither, their conversation had eventually shifted from hours of discussion on the nature of monotheism, marine life, and architecture to Jake's family. When Jake had cheerfully described the divorce, wringing it for the kind of humor he thought this quiet Indian graduate student might enjoy, Bhim had turned pale and quite seriously apologized to Jake for his "broken home." Jake, having never heard that phrase outside of Lifetime original movies, laughed hysterically. His home was far from broken, he gently explained to Bhim. The other man looked at him with such compassion in his eyes, and Jake had to admit, he couldn't help but lean into it, hoping it might turn into something more.

There was something about Bhim that was completely hidden from Jake, and although it should have driven him insane, he loved it. Right off the bat, Jake could tell that Bhim had the gift of real empathy, something Jake always worried he lacked. Bhim could put himself in the shoes of any person; he could get complete strangers to speak to him about their lives, their fears, what lived in their hearts, all without sharing anything of himself. He had perfected the art of imitating a deep conversation, all without the other participant's ever realizing that it was entirely one-sided.

To Jake, right from that first conversation, Bhim seemed so apart from things, his own island. He was unexplored territory, and Jake wanted to be the explorer.

Bhim had never dated a man before. In fact, he had never dated anyone before. Although men were what he wanted, or rather, what his heart desired, as he told Jake in his serious way, it felt wrong to him, because he knew, as he had been taught, that it was unnatural to feel this way. As the bar lights flickered around them and the once-roars of the crowd turned to the murmurs of a handful of other patrons, Bhim told him that while he wanted Jake, he knew that this was because he had lost his morality under the influence of America, and he didn't want to become corrupt for his whole life, the way Jake was. He put his hand on Jake's knee and Jake felt the warmth of his palm radiate through his body as Bhim asked him if he would be with him for one night only, so that Bhim would know what it was like before he agreed to marry a woman.

The scent and feel of this man so close was intoxicating to Jake. He had been with others before, but something about Bhim resonated with him in ways no one else ever had. Perhaps it was the fact that this was the first crack in Bhim's reserve, the first spark of emotion he had displayed. Or perhaps it was the way Bhim said such horrible things in such beautiful ways, the smooth tenor of his voice and slurring affect of his accent making bigotry sexy. He could almost forget what was being said and concentrate solely on the mouth that was saying it.

Jake had been more than a little afraid to come out to his parents. It wasn't that Jake's parents had ever expressed the opinion that homosexuality was in any way negative. They had gay friends, knew gay couples, described gay people in their lives with the same adjectives and nouns they would have used for anyone else. Nevertheless, Jake had no idea what their reactions would be when they heard it from their own child. He had never dared displease his parents in any respect during his entire young life. He had had a Bar Mitzvah for his father, and spent vacations in spas devoted to raw foods and meditation with his mother. He was the poster child for a happy product of an unhappy union. What would they think of him now?

But it turned out what they thought of him was exactly the same as it always had been. And from the day he came out, life was fairly simple. Jake was what he was, and anyone who didn't like it could go to hell, including those who remained closeted themselves.

The first time he had ever even questioned that was when he met Bhim, the boy in the bar in Berkeley. Jake wanted to give Bhim what he wanted. He wanted to do it for his younger self, the child of wealthy liberals who nevertheless was petrified of being an outcast. He knew what it was to wish you were something different even when it was the thing that made you yourself.

But he also knew even in those first moments that one night wouldn't be enough. He wanted possession, to have Bhim totally, and that could never happen if it was just an experiment, a way for a closeted man to tell himself he was over his youthful folly.

So when Bhim, drowsy and bold, with the scent of a mojito on his breath, asked him if he would be with him for that night and that night alone, Jake removed Bhim's warm hand on his thigh and shook his head. He walked away from the handsome young Indian man with the soul of a guru and the eyes of a supplicant, and forced himself not to look back.

After he had returned to Los Angeles, Jake thought about Bhim often. He saw Bhim's face in his daily runs and during his drive each day to work, as he sketched blueprints and researched indigenous plant varieties. He could not rid himself of Bhim's eyes; they floated in Jake's mind as he tried to sleep, dark and enticing. They blinked at him, big, widely set, lushly fringed cow's eyes, and he thought he could see tears in their corners and woke up crying himself for no reason. When he checked his email several weeks after his trip to San Francisco and saw a message from a Bhim Sengupta he was thrilled, and terrified. Bhim was sorry; he had begged for Jake's email from the friend who had introduced them (who, when Jake interrogated him later, admitted that he had always thought Bhim, closeted though he was, would be a good fit for Jake) and just wanted to apologize. No, more than that, he wanted to be friends. Jake felt sick. He responded anyway, thinking himself an idiot and not caring.

They began by emailing, once or twice a week, then daily. In writing, Bhim was freer than he had been in person, giving little glimpses into his thoughts, displaying new things in each message: a wicked yet silly sense of humor, a love of nature, a fear of snakes. The communication came in waves, inundating Jake with information, with questions, with thrills up and down his spine. Soon came texts and phone calls, and before long they were wishing each other good night and sending each other photos in increasing states of undress. Jake had started it, being the bolder one of the pair, but Bhim surprised him with his own images, his responses, and his tentative innovation.

Then, as suddenly as it had begun, it stopped. It was as if Jake had been an imaginary friend that Bhim had played with for a while but no longer needed. Jake tried not to care, he tried to remember that Bhim was from a different culture, that he was closeted and racked with self-hatred, and that they hadn't been dating, they hadn't been anything, really. But it hurt. It hurt everywhere, like sleeping on a sunburn. Jake started agreeing to dates with anyone who even thought about asking. After one, a brunch in downtown Los Angeles, Jake was driving home, cursing the traffic, when he got a call from Bhim, who was at the airport, waiting for Jake to pick him up.

When Jake saw Bhim on the sidewalk by Arrivals, Bhim's face was as stiff as a mask. Jake looked at him for a moment, waiting for his eyes to flicker with affection, recognition, anything. It was like watching a statue come to life, the way expression poured into Bhim's face as he saw Jake. Jake wondered if this was why he liked Bhim so much, the way he felt like maybe Bhim was coming to life just for him.

They didn't say much to each other in the car. There were many smiles, tentative and deeply aware. There were no apologies or explanations. Bhim had a small bag, and he informed Jake that he would be spending the weekend with him. There was nothing more to say. Instead, Bhim sang along with the radio. It was the second time they'd met in person, and Jake knew it was love.

Bhim had never had sex with anyone before, man or woman, which he confessed once they had survived the Los Angeles traffic and were standing in Jake's immaculate bedroom, with its coordinating shades of blue and gray. Jake had lowered the blinds and curtained the windows, but Bhim still looked at them like they might let the whole world in to see him. Jake thought of his first times, his drunken nights in college dorms and his pain afterward, and he vowed to himself that he would make this good for Bhim, that they would go slow and enjoy everything. Bhim lasted all of five minutes into their naked foreplay before he spent himself on Jake's coverlet. They spent the rest of the evening doing laundry and eating Chinese food and trying again, and again, until it was good, for both of them, better than good, it was perfect. Jake bit back the words he wanted to say and enjoyed sleeping next to someone, but he couldn't help but think about the way Bhim had looked at the airport before he had seen Jake, like a dead person, like someone who was already gone.

5

Pival always blamed herself for her marriage, for the way it became and the way it began. Pival had been the first one to say hello, in a fashion. Ram Sengupta had been sitting in the canteen, reading her university newspaper. It was very much *her* university newspaper, as Pival was the editor, a fact that her delighted father would recount to anyone he could force to listen. Ram Sengupta, then thirty years old and somehow, to the grave distress of his family, unmarried, had picked up a copy of the *Calcutta College Courier* with amusement as he waited for his friend Charlie Roy, a professor teaching at the school, who was always late.

Pival, young and alive with purpose, watched this tall, slim, yet commanding stranger sneer at her paper and saw red. Who was this man? What did he know of journalism? She could not stand by and watch him scorn her hard work, her long nights of setting type and editing articles. A closer look revealed that this stranger, handsome as he was, was laughing at her own article, a piece she'd been quite proud of, detailing the city's architecture as a troubling metaphor for the continued influence of British colonialism on Indian mentality and cultural consciousness. Her article was cautiously tinged with Naxalite rigor, coated in intellectual argument, and she was deeply proud of it. Pival was not one to stand by while her work was being impugned in such a cavalier manner. She marched up to this strange man and asked him in polite and careful English:

"What, exactly, is so very funny?"

Ram Sengupta looked up at this serious young woman, with her dark eyes glinting, and asked her to join him for tea. Pival was so flustered that she sat down without another word. When Charlie Roy finally showed up some thirty minutes later, he found his friend, a confirmed bachelor, assessing his future wife.

The two fused into a unit almost immediately. Ram's authority destroyed Pival's own sense of herself and replaced it with a version that Ram created, a version she liked better, for a time. For Pival's part she had never met a man who looked at her with such a mix of calculation and interest, and she mistook his manipulative speculation for a deep true love. So, for that matter, did he. They were engaged within a month.

Looking back on her excitement at the time, Pival cursed herself for being ten times a fool. She had thought Ram would be the antidote to the loneliness and longing she had begun to feel. Instead, he became the cause of both. She had thought for a while that her marriage was normal, no worse than many, better than most. But it had proved weak, and in the end, rotten to the core.

But Ram was gone now. And she could have her son back, just as soon as she could wrench him from the grasp of the man in California. They could be together. And if he was really gone, if it hadn't been, as she hoped, a kindly meant act that pierced her heart with its cruelty, she could die with Rahi. Even if she couldn't live with him.

6

The morning after Jake and Bhim had slept together for the first time, Jake, as he had done every morning for the last twelve years, took a run. His lifetime of waiting in traffic had bred in him a need for movement. He had run through college, through his early twenties, and even now, curled up in the arms of a man he wanted and hadn't known he could have, his muscles still tensed and prepared themselves. He shifted carefully in Bhim's embrace, inching out of it in slow degrees, and then, grabbing his shorts and his phone, he escaped the room and was gone, his feet pounding the pavement as he moved with tireless joy through the morning haze of the city.

On his daily runs, Jake would often see remnants of the Los Angeles nightlife haunting the city and wincing in the harsh light of the sunrise. What hurt their eyes made his glow; he loved the mornings. Jake worked for a large architecture firm located in downtown L.A., which catered to the elite and the effete, as his bosses liked to joke. The firm included both landscape architecture and residential and commercial work, and often attracted clients interested in combined design, updating or creating new spaces that integrated natural design as well as buildings. Jake worked in the landscape department. He enjoyed any work that took him outside, that had him under the sun for hours on end. He loved the smell of dirt and the way plants anchored into it.

After college, Jake had floated for a bit, uncertain what he wanted to do next. He had enjoyed working on Brown's organic farm so he got a job at the New York Botanical Garden as a researcher. But he soon realized that biology wasn't as interesting to him as space, and the way plants and buildings could fill it. He enrolled in architecture school the following fall. Within two years he had his master's and, weary of the East Coast winters, chose a job in Los Angeles, to the delight of his parents, and started working at Space Solutions. Once he settled into that it seemed that he settled into everything. Life became pleasant, compartmentalized, and predictable. The job was good, the people were nice, the high school friends who like him had come back were happy to reconnect, the guys he met were fit and a little dim, but open and friendly and never hard to catch or lose. His apartment was spacious, his world was small.

Now someone had joined him, and the apartment no longer was empty. Suddenly he wondered why he was running away from home, not toward it. What would Bhim say, when he woke up? Would he regret this? Jake's breath caught in his chest. This had been one of the best moments of his life, the first time he had felt truly with someone else, in sync with him. What if Bhim hated what they had done, what if he woke up horrified with Jake and with himself? He tried to shake off these thoughts, to run again, but his feet had turned to lead. He walked home, dragging his body the few blocks back to his apartment, and opened the door with dread.

Bhim was still in the bed, sleeping. His lashes formed spiky uneven crescents on his cheeks and Jake felt a sense of relief that there was something in Bhim's face that wasn't perfect. He watched him sleep deeply and got into the shower. Jake washed himself off briskly, trying to ignore the fear that had struck his heart. *What if, what if, what if* resounded in his brain and he wished he could drown out the noise of his worries. He almost wanted to wake Bhim up, to face his judgment and his disgust sooner rather than later, but each moment gave him more time to feel like they were together.

He struggled to clean his back, working to reach the space where his hand refused to reach, right underneath his shoulder blades and above his tailbone. Suddenly he felt a hand joining his, washing that area for him, spreading the soap gently up and down his spine. He held his body perfectly still, not wanting the moment to end. He felt a handful of water spill down his back, washing away the soap.

"Feeling dirty?" he asked, his voice a strange croaking sound. He closed his eyes, regretting the stupid innuendo of the question, although he wanted a genuine answer. He wanted to know if Bhim felt unclean after what they had done but had sheepishly used a line from a teen drama.

"Maybe." Bhim's voice whispered the response in his ear. "Help me wash?" Jake turned to see Bhim's face, earnest, smiling, cautious, and amused. Hopeful. He kissed him, and fell in love all over again.

Later, he tried to get Bhim to run with him, but Bhim hated it. Bhim could manage only a few blocks at a panting, halting stride before giving up, claiming that his heart would explode. It was a relief to find something Bhim was so bad at, something that ruffled his serenity. Still, it was disappointing. Jake knew that with Bhim he would have a future of running alone. He tried to accept that, he did, but he realized that his routes became circles, wider and wider, but always pulling him back to the same place. Whenever Bhim came to stay with him his runs were short and left him with that same fear, that if he went too far or stayed away too long Bhim would be gone, that he would return home to an empty house and a vacant life. Jake could run well only when Bhim returned to Berkeley and he was alone. He ignored that, though, refusing to examine the fact that the two things that made him feel best were mutually exclusive. He tried to stop feeling afraid whenever Bhim left, but he couldn't hide it from his dreams. In his dreams Bhim ran, and he outpaced Jake, even, getting farther and farther away forever.

7

The last time Satya Roy had been able to look himself in the eye it was in the small cracked mirror that hung in the communal bathroom of his old Sunset Park apartment. He did not know it was his last time, although if he had been asked, he would not have said he minded. Before moving to the United States he hadn't seen his own face very much. The bathroom in the apartment in which he had grown up in Bangladesh, in the city of Sylhet, was a tiny one, with a squatting toilet. He had always bathed outside near the waterspout, rubbing his body with mustard oil, when he could afford it, and rinsing it off with a bucket while the others in his apartment complex waited nearby, eager to use the facilities. These did not include a mirror. His grandmother, with whom he had grown up, had a small hand mirror, which she had used to let him check his hair from the back when she had cut it on the second Sunday of every third month. Otherwise, he saw mirrors only in shops. Once he moved to America, he looked at himself in a mirror every day. He showered in a ceramic tub, and the water was always there in the pipes, waiting for him. The toilet had been difficult to manage but he had figured it out, eventually, by perching awkwardly over it in a spindly squat. In his first two months in America, Satya had realized that his favorite thing about the country was his own bathroom.

There had been a repeated knocking at the door. Satya didn't realize it at first; he thought that this was just the throbbing of his head.

"Just a minute!" He heard a muffled response in a language he didn't understand. Satya shrugged and looked at himself again, patting his cheeks and wondering when he would have enough hair to shave.

The apartment was his because he paid four hundred dollars a month, an amount he couldn't afford, to live there, but it also belonged to the four other immigrants who called the minuscule two-bedroom home. Two of them were Mexican, Juan and Ernesto, and after they returned home from their job at a restaurant, they split their bounty of leftovers with each other over beers and hushed conversation in Spanish. All of the sounds seemed to Satya at once nasal and soft, like a sweet-sour pudding of a language. They stuck together, mostly, always quietly speaking with each other, but when they had extra food they always shared it with everyone, meticulously dividing each dish with almost surgical precision to ensure fairness in distribution.

One of the other residents, Kosi, was from Ghana, and though he had been an engineer in Africa, now he worked at an auto parts shop in the neighborhood. His voice reminded Satya of a thick stew with chunks of meat and bone in it. Satya, who prided himself on his fluid command of English, both the proper construction as taught to him in school and the slang he'd learned from the MTV videos he viewed in electronics stores, couldn't understand a word his African housemate said. Satya decided that the poor man must be struggling to learn, and he generously tried to teach Kosi in between his own searches for work. Thus far these lessons had not progressed well. At times it seemed that Kosi thought that he was teaching Satya instead.

The last roommate was Satya's only real friend, in America and in the world, Ravi Hafiz, his fellow immigrant from Bangladesh, the man who slept near him nightly on the floor of the kitchen and shared his dreams. They had been friends since they were six years old. They had snuck into America together. They had made a pact to help each other survive. And that morning, Satya was going to steal Ravi's job.

Ravi and Satya had grown up together in Sylhet, which sat on the northeast corner of Bangladesh, very near the Indian border. They were not friends because of a shared religion, or even a shared language. Satya was Hindu, one of the small population still left in Bangladesh, and Ravi was Muslim, one of the overwhelming majority. They had gone to different schools and lived in different neighborhoods, and they had very little in common in background or family life. And yet, they had been thick as thieves—and sometimes they were thieves—since the day they met. They were friends because they were a part of the same club, and it was a terrible club indeed. They were both the sons of Bangladeshi war babies, inadvertent heirs of their country's shame.

As Satya had learned in school, along with every other Bangladeshi child, the revolution of 1971 had been met with an immediate Pakistani invasion and the wide-scale systematic rape of hundreds of thousands of Bangladeshi women. Those rapes had, approximately nine months or so after the army came through, led to the emergence of pale-skinned babies from the bodies of their darker mothers. Though fairer had always been lovelier in Bangladesh, these butter-skinned children were a visible reminder of the revolution and the generation of women who should, as they were so often told, have fought harder. Despite the departure of the Pakistani army, the seeds they had spread were already growing into people.

Ravi and Satya knew on the day that they met that no matter how different they were, they had both come from the same place. Both boys had become used to being targeted on account of their paler faces. Satya had run, as was his habit, and hidden behind a row of parked rickshaws until the bigger boys got tired of calling him a whore's cur and throwing stones at him and left him alone. He was settling into a corner formed by the wheels of several vehicles when a pair of running feet flashed in front of his eyes. He reached out and grabbed the back of the running boy's neck and pulled him down, furious that this idiot might give away his spot. Ravi was panting loudly and Satya had to throw his hand over Ravi's mouth to stop his unseemly noise. It turned out that Ravi was not as accustomed to this treatment as Satya, and had in fact run almost a mile from his own schoolyard before being pulled into Satya's hiding hole. Satya, all of nine, surveyed the Muslim boy and sighed, figuring that it was just his luck to be saddled with this idiot. Although he could not have explained why, Satya knew as he walked Ravi home that their time together would stretch on because they knew each other, as few others ever had. They shared something that made them disgusting to the people around them. They would have to be friends. They already had too many enemies.

They started teaming up in small ways, stealing coins from beggars and using them at the local cinemas, coaxing extra rotis out of Satya's grandmother, who raised him, or candies from Ravi's father's store. But their world was changing; it seemed that it had never stopped changing, never staying in one place for long. No sooner did India become East Pakistan become Bangladesh than it became something else entirely. As Satya and Ravi grew up, images of American pop stars and British singers emerged on walls of shops and buildings, hung side by side with Bollywood vixens and images of Lord Shiva. America was everywhere, with people moving and writing and calling and even, eventually, emailing home. Ravi and Satya watched any movie with an American in it, imitating the accents and pretending to shoot each other. Soon even these pleasures weren't enough, and the boys discovered beer, junk food, and music, steps on the bridge that took them piece by piece from their home. Poor but smart, well cared for but careless, the boys were sick of being the dirty secret of their nation's sad and violent history, sick of Bangladesh and its poverty and its corruption and its crime and the ways that their own pasts seemed inescapable.

When Satya's grandmother finally passed away, unable to live through another difficult year in an impossible place, the last tie to Bangladesh was severed for Satya. His mother had died in childbirth, and his father, a wealthy businessman who had seduced and abandoned her, had never known of Satya's existence. Satya's grandmother, who despite her own bloody and brutal experiences, the worst of which had led to the birth of her child, was far sturdier than her fragile daughter. She had raised Satya herself, telling him the best of his mother and leaving him to speculate on the worst. He had nothing to tie him down to Sylhet, nothing to cling to. He decided to move on. And when Satya found a way to sneak onto a freighter departing to New York, he invited Ravi to come along with him, and Ravi said yes.

And so they came to America and moved to their tiny shared place in Sunset Park and searched for jobs and watched their money fall from their hands like sand. Both boys, now almost men, had planned to send riches back home to Ravi's parents and now they worried they might have to beg for funds from their already overtaxed families, or in Satya's case, from Ravi. Both of them had thought they spoke English like natives but somehow had to constantly repeat themselves. Ravi, a Muslim whose beard and prayer beads hanging at his waist made him as visible in New York as they had made him invisible at home, found himself even further from acceptance. Satya, a Hindu who looked Indian enough, was familiar looking in New York, acceptable to deli owners and store managers, who, if they didn't hire him, at least rarely treated him like a threat.

Their friendship, which had been so unified at home, had begun to splinter under the weight of hunger and fear. Ravi called his family constantly, while Satya envied him the comfort of relatives. He began to resent having to share everything, the food he bought, the information he found: he worried that Ravi wasn't sharing equally with him even as he plotted how to hide things from his friend.

And when Ravi told Satya that he had a strong lead on a job at a tourism company run by Bangladeshi Hindus, Satya knew that he could do the job as well as Ravi, if not better. He wasn't sure how to be a guide, but he knew how to be a Hindu. Ravi had come home delighted by the prospect, with an interview set up for the next day, and Satya hated him. Ravi was his friend, but he had a father and a mother and now a job, and besides, he was better looking and always smoother with girls. Satya had his grandmother, now gone, and a pimple-marked face that women overlooked. Fueled by months of rejection, hunger, and fear, and a lifetime of feeling worthless, Satya sat down with a bottle of cheap scotch and got his best friend drunk. It was a celebration, he said, of this new job, this new life. And Ravi trusted him, as he had since they met.

Ravi snored in the next room as Satya prepared for the interview Ravi had planned to have. He had dressed himself in his best clothing, a bright red-and-purple collared shirt emblazoned with stars at the breast pocket and his most expensive pair of jeans, stylishly faded with seams running diagonally and up and down his legs. He slicked his hair and applied copious amounts of cologne carefully, looking, he thought, like the most successful of the shop boys and hawkers he'd seen at home. It was all perfect, except Satya noticed as he combed his hair that he couldn't meet his own eyes in the mirror, but what did that matter? He didn't have to look at himself. Only other people had to do that.

Satya arrived at the First Class India USA Destination Vacation Tour Company a full half an hour before Ravi's scheduled interview and, because of the slowness of the day, was seen immediately. Satya was thrilled; he wasn't exactly sure that Ravi wouldn't wake up and make his own way there through some survival instinct. As he sat in front of Ronnie Munshi, on the very edge of his chair, he smiled nervously. The man looked at him and sighed, a strange expression in his eyes that Satya couldn't read. The boss looked resigned, somehow. As soon as Satya tried to open his mouth to speak Ronnie waved his hand to cut him off and grimly informed him that the job was his, and sent him off to talk to another guide about how to work. And that was that. Satya finally had something to hold on to in America. He would tell Ravi when he returned home, and Ravi would be happy. It would be both of theirs, like everything was, and Satya could stop resenting that now that it was his first. They would share the profits until Ravi got his own job. This was for the best, for both of them. Ravi would understand.

But when Satya came home that day, Ravi was gone. No forwarding address. No way to find him. Vanished. Now that he didn't have to share a thing, Satya wished he could.

Two months went by, and Satya heard nothing from Ravi. He had no official status in the United States, like Satya, so inquiries were impossible, although Satya tried. He could have tried harder, he knew, but he pushed that thought out of his mind like the memory of a bad dream. He couldn't look backward. He had too much to do. Still, he wondered on the edges of his mind where Ravi was, what he was doing, what had become of him. He couldn't tell if he felt free or alone.

And then one day, in the mail, Satya received a letter, his first in America. It was from Ravi's mother. She had written to ask how he was, knowing that no one else from home ever would. She told him that she had not heard from Ravi, but she knew that Satya would be there to keep him safe. He read it over and over again until he wept and knew what he felt wasn't freedom at all.

Ronnie paid his guides a monthly salary, low but livable. It was one kindness he extended to his workers, something to live off of between guiding jobs, for which they received a set fee. It was more money than Satya had ever seen in his life, and it let him move into a

new place, with two roommates instead of four. It bought him clothing and decent food. It left him secure, this job, and filled with the
purpose that had been so lacking in his life up until now, but it also
felt empty. He showered every evening, washing the city off his skin,
still feeling dirty. Nothing would erase the sense of continued shame.

He distracted himself, studying maps and guidebooks every day,
and after two months he got a call from his boss, Mr. Munshi, on
the brand-new pre-owned phone Mr. Munshi had given him. There
was a job for him. He would be leaving New York soon and traveling across the country with a Bengali widow and a female American
companion, one Mr. Munshi was looking for even now. Ravi would
have laughed to hear it, but he wasn't there, and when Satya pretended to tell him one night in the bathroom, he still couldn't look at
himself in the mirror. He wondered if he ever would again.

8

Rebecca Elliot woke up to the sound of snoring. This wasn't the first time Max's nasal trumpeting had disturbed her but it would be the last, she told herself as she stared up at the ceiling. A headache from last night's whiskey pounded at her temples. She had met this one, like many before him, at a bar, after another failed audition a few weeks ago where the casting director had eyed her breasts but not her performance and sent her on her way with a limp "Great work."

Rebecca habitually used her combined salary from part-time jobs in a coffee shop and a small map store to buy cheap drinks at the place around the corner from her apartment, a Chinese restaurant that became a dive bar after five. It attracted odd people, which is why Rebecca liked it. This boy, Max, had joined her that night, and together they'd washed away her desperation with alcohol, only here it was again, as always, waiting for her as the man beside her slept.

Yesterday's audition, the third she had drunk her way toward forgetting since she met Max, had been particularly painful. It was for the role of Anya in *The Cherry Orchard*. Rebecca loved that role; she had wanted to play it since college. It was a prestigious director and it was a huge production and it was *Anya*. But when she had entered the room, the casting director had looked her up and down and frowned, explaining that they would be doing the readings for Varya, Anya's older sister by seven years, the following day. Rebecca had blinked back her tears and explained that she was there for Anya and everyone had laughed and joked and pretended it was fine. Rebecca had auditioned and tried to "use it" but the damage was done. She left shaking, wishing she could throw up, wishing she had the kind of mom she could call for sympathy.

Rebecca had grown up in Washington, DC, the only daughter of well-educated, well-bred American Jews. Her father, Morris Elliot, ran a small law firm specializing in divorce, which was a prosperous business given his discretion and the instability of many political marriages. Rebecca's mother, Cynthia Greenbaum, taught economics at Georgetown University, where she delighted in sparring with her Catholic coworkers. They had raised Rebecca with strong assurances that she could be anything she wanted to be, and then, like so many American parents, were surprised and dismayed when she believed them.

She had attended Columbia University because her parents, alumni of the school, approved, and since they were the people footing the bill, that was important. To her, it didn't matter where she went, just as long as it was in New York. She had dreamed of the city since she had been a child. She'd done well, but she hadn't made friends, holding herself apart from everyone but the theater crowd and acting in every role for which someone cast her. It seemed for a time that it would even be easy. She couldn't imagine failure. Who can, before it's actually happening?

Rebecca graduated with a flurry of acting accolades and enough flashbulb photos snapped by her proud parents to cause a seizure in a susceptible person. But once the world of acting was no longer confined to her pool of fellow students, Rebecca realized for the first time that acting was a form of begging, and all you could have was what people decided to give you.

She had gotten a few roles, a few commercials, a lot of promises of things that were going to be "the thing that launched her," and nothing had. So, after the early difficult years following college, Rebecca found herself performing in her own life. When she met someone new they would transform in her mind to an audience, and Rebecca would go to work. Her body would grow languid and pliable, her breath lifting her chest in trembling motions that held men, and sometimes women, captive. She was sick of this performance, but it kept attracting audiences, and given that almost a year had passed since her last real acting job, she wasn't sure if she *could* actually play another role anymore.

Next to her, Max shifted again, throwing his hand over her breast. It was clammy with sweat. Glancing at her buzzing phone, Rebecca realized that she was late for work at the coffee shop, again, which meant she would be fired, again. She supposed she should be unhappy, but she only felt annoyed. Every job but the map store was disposable and yet she was always surprised when she discovered her employers felt the same way about her.

"Turn that off, would you?" the guy, Max, asked groggily. It was one in the afternoon. Rebecca's phone buzzed again, a voice mail this time. She deleted it, already knowing what it said.

"Thanks." Max coughed, and reached down to his pants, which were lying in a heap on the floor of Rebecca's otherwise neat apartment. He took out a pack of cigarettes and fumbled around his pocket for a lighter.

"What are you doing?" Rebecca didn't mind smokers. She even had the occasional cigarette herself, when drunk or stressed or devastated or all three at once, which happened more and more these days. But no one smoked in her apartment. Not that he was asking, this near stranger, this idiot poser who claimed to want to make music but really just spent his time getting high in the Williamsburg apartment his parents had purchased for him after he graduated from the Berklee College of Music without a record deal or a clue.

The strength of Rebecca's sudden hatred surprised her. She had enjoyed Max, his banter, his faux self-deprecation and real self-satisfaction. She even liked him in bed, finding his confidence and his rich vocabulary welcome. Now, sitting naked, blowing smoke in her face, with last evening's drinks seeping out of his pores and sweating onto her sheets, he disgusted her.

"I have to go. I have work." Rebecca stood and walked into the bathroom. In her studio apartment, the walk wasn't long. Avoiding her own gaze in the mirror, she ran the shower, soaping up briskly, tempted to linger in the hopes that Max would leave and never return and that would be the end of it.

"I'm making us breakfast!" His cheerful call echoed through the apartment. *Damn it,* Rebecca thought. He was trying to be nice. He was trying to be the "good guy." There had been ones like him in the past, ones who had thought they liked her for her no-strings declarations, somehow thinking they were a lure and a challenge, not statements of fact. They rushed in to claim her in some way, but this quickly moved from amusing to disturbing. They took such pride in being good, these men, in being what they assumed she must want based solely on her insistence that she didn't.

Rebecca rushed out of the bathroom in a manufactured hurry.

"I'm late! Sorry, sorry, so sweet of you, sorry, but I have to run. Sorry!"

She pulled on clothing quickly, tying up her wet hair and hopping into jeans as Max, standing with a bowl of half-beaten eggs in his hands, looked on, concerned.

"You should eat something, Beck. It's important."

He had a nickname for her? Rebecca's mouth twisted with disgust.

"No time! Sorry! Had *such* a good time I didn't even remember my stupid job. Really gotta go! That smells great. Please, eat it, obviously, and let yourself out when you go. The door locks behind you, okay?"

And she was gone, closing the door on his protest. Her phone beeped.

Last night was great. Miss you already, sexy. Get some breakfast on your way.

It was perfectly constructed, a neatly packaged mix of flirt and feeling. Rebecca closed her eyes, her head pounding even harder.

Thanks, she responded. *Please don't smoke in my apartment.* She turned off her phone, and, with nothing else to do, she headed north, to the map store.

Maps on St. Mark's was a small dusty place owned and operated by its founder, Rasheed Ghazi, who first opened the store in 1980. Mr. Ghazi, as everyone, including Rebecca, now called him, had been a philosophy professor in his native Tehran before his disagreements over matters such as freedom of speech and other trifles ran him afoul of the ayatollah and he was forced to depart. In Tehran, Professor Ghazi had specialized in giving people complicated answers designed specifically to provoke more complicated questions, but now he ran a dusty tiny store selling maps in the East Village, and specialized in giving people large pieces of paper designed to tell them simply where to go. The irony was not lost on him, or Rebecca, who had learned his life story over their many long afternoons together, watching the tourists outside of the store's one window drift by.

Mr. Ghazi referred to Iran by its older title, Persia, as the only act of rebellion left to an expat unable to return to his homeland. Not that he would have wanted to. The country he had known and loved was gone, its current incarnation bearing little resemblance to what he thought of as home. With his family either displaced throughout America or slaughtered, and unwilling to put old friends in danger by contacting them, Mr. Ghazi contented himself with the small older Persian population he could scrape together in New York. However, he did not limit himself to their numbers alone. He found he had a kind of affinity with many immigrants, especially Middle Eastern and Southeast Asian ones. They shared spices and rices, and the whispers of a destroyed but still missed home buzzed in all their ears. Mr. Ghazi felt comfortable with these men, these Pakistani cab drivers and Lebanese convenience store owners, much to the consternation of his wife, Sheedah, who felt that he was lowering himself in spending time with uneducated foreigners. Rebecca heard them arguing about it some days, for the Ghazis lived over the store. Personally she enjoyed the strange men who came to greet Mr. Ghazi and bring him rose-scented pastries and bags dripping with grease. She always got the leftovers.

Mr. Ghazi had bought his tiny apartment and the store below it twenty years ago when the East Village was still a wild no-man's-land. Back then it had been all he and his wife could afford. Now he and Sheedah were immune to astronomical rent raises and were, in fact, sitting on a gold mine. Sheedah, whose only interest in American events was reading the local real estate news, begged him to sell so they could buy a condo and retire in suburban New Jersey, but he refused. For this, Rebecca would be eternally grateful, as the work was easy, the pay was enough, and the stability of the store was the only thing keeping her vaguely sane.

Mr. Ghazi was a creature of habit. He opened the shop each day at ten A.M. exactly. He ate lunch, a curry from a local place that delivered, along with a fruit salad (for health) and strong black coffee, every day, closing the shop from twelve thirty P.M. to one thirty P.M. to enjoy his lunch in peace. Anyone who knew him knew this. Rebecca assumed he would be surprised to see his only employee knocking tentatively on the door at one twenty-five that Friday afternoon.

She didn't need to knock, being in possession of a key, but she did so anyway out of respect. Rebecca made her own hours but always told him what those hours would be, and she felt a twinge of guilt at not calling to tell him she was coming. After all, he barely needed her at all, even when she was scheduled to work.

Mr. Ghazi had hired Rebecca seven years ago after he had broken his ankle due to a fall reaching for an atlas from 1498 describing the geography of medieval Europe. He needed help while he healed. At twenty-one Rebecca was kind, responsible, and cheerful, and in need of part-time work. She competently ran the shop as he recuperated. Once he had fully healed, however, he couldn't bear to fire this bright young actress, and he kept her on to assist him, to keep him company, to charm customers and browsing friends, and to give Sheedah someone to foist lamb dishes and pastries on. Sheedah, who usually hated American women with their bare arms and their loud voices, took an instant liking to Rebecca for no particular reason other than her once-mentioned interest in Persian rugs. It was done. Rebecca became a permanent fixture in the shop.

Rebecca smiled tentatively as she entered the shop, savoring the scents of old paper and dust and curry from Mr. Ghazi's lunch. The needs reflected in the eyes of her recent bed partner were mercifully banished by Mr. Ghazi's familiar smiling gaze, though it did hold a hint of worry.

"Do I look that bad?" Rebecca patted her still-damp hair self-consciously.

"I have never understood how you leave your home with hair still dripping. My mother would have had fits."

Rebecca smiled as Mr. Ghazi scolded her. "So would mine." She stepped around Mr. Ghazi and headed to the minuscule back room to put her bag down and try to do something presentable with her wet, bedraggled hair. Catching sight of herself in the mirror, her eyes smudged with last night's eye makeup, she sighed.

"I *do* look that bad," she called out to him.

"These are your words, not mine." Rebecca smiled. Her boss was a sweet man. "It was a bad night?" Rebecca was wiping off her eye makeup and almost missed the question. She paused for a moment, as she often did before responding to Mr. Ghazi's probes into her personal life. It wasn't that she didn't trust him, but Rebecca was careful with her candor, because Mr. Ghazi, while liberal in many respects, was still a Muslim immigrant from Iran, and Rebecca was never sure what would shock. It was safer to test the waters with little moments than to reveal her entire life to him. Rebecca didn't want to lose her tentative Persian family, so she made her life fit into what she perceived to be their scope of understanding and morality.

But something about the morning, with its crushing panic, and her immediate reaction of escaping and fleeing to the map store, made her feel that if she did not tell Mr. Ghazi in some small way that she was suffocating she would start to cry, and she didn't want to do that in front of him.

"It was a bad night." She finished washing her face and stepped back into the main room of the store, where Mr. Ghazi's inquiring eyes made tears spring from her own. *Damn,* she thought, *there I go.*

"What is it, Rebecca? What makes you so sad?" Mr. Ghazi gestured for Rebecca to sit, keeping a formal distance. He had always been awkward around emotional females, his wife included, but he considered it an honor that Rebecca had admitted her pain, which she so often kept tucked away like a handkerchief. Watching her in the seven years she had been in his employ, he had seen her early enthusiasm become a hardened fear, and he worried for her.

Rebecca struggled to contain herself, but it felt so futile. What was the point of holding herself back? What was she containing her feelings for, anyway? A politeness? A vague social expectation that she wasn't supposed to feel anything at all? The way everyone kept saying that they were fine until the point where the word lost all meaning? She wasn't fine. She hadn't been for years.

"There was this boy—" she started.

"Did someone hurt you?" Mr. Ghazi looked both disturbed and in some way relieved. If it was a love affair gone wrong, this was at least familiar territory. There were platitudes he could express, soothing words he could say. He waited.

"He's not important. I just feel like I am slipping. It's harder than I thought anything could be and I'm so tired. I need someone to give me the chance. I hate that. Why can't I choose, instead of wanting to be chosen?"

She felt pathetic. He looked at her with pity and she wanted to hide.

"I'm sorry. I'm being stupid." Rebecca's voice pierced the air as she apologized for herself, brushing aside her feelings in a bid to return to normalcy. She should have claimed it was women's troubles and let it be.

"You are not stupid, Rebecca. But if this is your life, you must change it. If this is the world you live in, one that confronts you with a feeling that you are not worth being chosen, then it is a stupid world."

He didn't understand. He was kind, but he didn't understand anything.

"Unless I can change the things I want, how can I change the way my life is?"

Mr. Ghazi had no answers. Maybe that was the cure for pain. It was to stop wanting anything at all.

9

Ronnie woke up to the sound of a buzzing phone. He often woke up this way. His life was ruled by buzzing. He received texts from tour guides reporting on the nature of their tours and complaining about the Indian food in Iowa, a state where it was impossible to find decent paneer, and clients alternately praising him and berating him for some new trial or tribulation, and sometimes even his mother informing him of the latest developments in her soap operas, which Ronnie followed religiously without ever seeing a single minute of any of them.

It was five A.M. in Queens, which meant it was two P.M. in Kolkata, just around the time that most people, people of means, at least, took their tea. Ronnie sighed and glanced at the screen, where his suspicions about his caller were confirmed. It was Mrs. Sengupta making another bid to contact him and check, he assumed, on the progress of her tour arrangements.

Ronnie usually placated his clients with a mixture of obsequious flattery, gentle intimidation, and well-placed xenophobic warnings, a cocktail that always left them putty in his soft ring-bedecked hands. But none of those tactics seemed to be working on Mrs. Sengupta, not his soothing tones nor his invocations to trust in fate, destiny, the stars, and his own authority as a World-Class Number One Best Tour Guide. Didn't she know that he was a busy man?

In the twin bed three feet from Ronnie's own, Anita snored and snorted in her sleep as if she were laughing at him. Ronnie looked over at her with disgust. Ronnie had felt deeply betrayed by Anita's refusal to cooperate with his brilliant plan. He should have known better than to ask her. Ronnie watched Anita shift in her sleep, marveling at her ability to fall asleep anywhere and sleep through anything. Here he was tearing what was left of his hair out, tormented by clients, and she simply turned over, enjoying her dreams, in the bed he had paid for, in the apartment he had bought.

He leaned back on his pillow and, unable to sleep, for he was not a good sleeper under the best of conditions, played a game in his mind of counting objects. This often helped him sleep, at least briefly. He had heard that the American equivalent of this was called counting sheep, but attempts to count lamb-based dishes had made him hungry, not tired. It was no use. Once the buzzing began he was up.

Anita slept on. Eventually, if they ever wanted to start a family, as his mother and hers constantly urged them to, he would probably be the one waking up at the baby's screams as his wife dreamed blissfully. That, more than anything else, held him back from suggesting they start trying. The business was his child, and it was already keeping him up. Why add something else to disturb him?

Walking from the subway later that morning, Ronnie decided that instead of sending a lackey to fetch his monthly supply of maps, which he kept in large supplies for all his guides and clients, he would fetch the things himself. Thinking of lamb, he had hopes that the trip to Manhattan and subsequent diverse lunch options it would entail might clear his head and give him an idea for Mrs. Sengupta's companion.

He had asked each of his guides for options, but the women they presented, sisters and cousins from their own families, were all either too traditional or too wild for his liking. This companion must be someone who could aid Mrs. Sengupta in her trip, a respectful, intelligent, and interesting person without a personal agenda or an interest in flirting with Satya Roy, the guide. Green as the boy was, this was an easy job in theory, with only one guest to corral and a companion to aid him. Ronnie thought this would be the perfect introduction for Satya to cross-country guiding, a task he wanted to train Satya to do. It was simply unfortunate that as the boy had worked for Ronnie and gotten large helpings of good food and long walks shadowing guides for day-trippers, his emaciated form had started to fill out and Ronnie now had a rather handsome guide on his hands, despite his oily skin and crooked smile. The boy had inspired breathy sighs on the part of the interviewees for companion-hood, good Bangladeshi girls who were supposed to be the perfect companions for Mrs. Sengupta. Instead, their love-struck giggles ruled them all out instantly. If only they had seen him when he had just arrived, thought Ronnie ruefully, all this nonsense could have been avoided.

Ronnie then placed an advertisement on Craigslist, with Anita's help, but that disaster of emails and calls from most unsuitable candidates was best never thought of again. So now he would visit his friend Mr. Ghazi, the owner of the map store. Then he would think the problem over again in a new environment over a plate of kebabs from a nearby Pakistani deli. What he needed was someone who would have no interest in Satya. Perhaps he was going down the wrong road interviewing Bangladeshi girls? If he found someone white, they would surely have no interest in this Bangla boy, he thought as he boarded the subway.

He was considering his lunch order when he walked into Maps on St. Mark's and almost tripped over a set of cartographer's charts from the sixteenth century.

"Ah, I'm sorry, Mr. Munshi! I've been meaning to put those away." Mr. Ghazi cheerfully greeted Ronnie from the other side of his small counter, enjoying a cup of black coffee, his fifth at least. Mr. Ghazi was always meaning to put things away and never doing it. The shop was only in any kind of state for visitors on the days his employee came, a girl Ronnie had spotted once reorganizing travel guides in their small section in the corner. Mr. Ghazi did not approve of selling travel guides because of the ways they chopped maps up into small pieces and isolated them from each other, but he had to admit, travel guides sold well.

"How are you today, Mr. Ghazi?" Ronnie asked politely as Mr. Ghazi disappeared into the back room to retrieve Ronnie's standing order.

"Very well! Very well. This time of year is quite invigorating, don't you think?" The weather had just started turning brisk, something Ronnie dreaded.

"Invigorating. That is a word for it, yes."

Mr. Ghazi smiled. "What can I say, it keeps my brain fresh, being on ice!" He laughed at his own joke, looking up when he realized Ronnie wasn't joining him.

"I'm sorry, Mr. Ghazi, I have a trouble on my mind and not ices. It's very funny, yes, I am just not in a laughing way today."

As Ronnie explained his problem, he realized that Mr. Ghazi's expression had changed from displaying the interest of a concerned friend to showing a certain level of calculation, a strange expression for his usually guileless face.

"So there you have it. I need to find her, and soon, or this whole job is kaput. She's willing to pay double, you see, which is no small amount. And these Bengalis always have so many friends and relatives who they will tell if the trip is not good. Real problem, no?"

Mr. Ghazi looked at Ronnie for a moment and then looked away, his lips moving slightly.

"I might have a solution for you, Mr. Munshi. Of course, it all depends, obviously and completely, but if it works, it might be the best solution for everyone."

"Everyone?"

The doorbell chimed as the shopgirl entered the small store, smiling.

"Everyone."

10

The First Class India USA Destination Vacation Tour Company was housed in an office building in Queens exactly four blocks from the second-to-last stop on the N train, a trip that took Satya two hours each way from Brooklyn. He rode almost the entire length of the N train daily, boarding at Eighteenth Avenue, six stops from the end of the line in Brooklyn. He had, more than once, ridden the train to each of its ends, falling asleep on his way to or from his job and waking up to see the train turning itself around. But this hadn't bothered him; in fact, he enjoyed these subway rides, watching the entire line in motion and the change in customers from one end of the route to the other. It was the people in the middle who were the most strange to him, loud people who looked too wealthy to be on a subway at all, and gaping tourists whose teeth chattered from the movement of the train from Fourteenth Street to Times Square. But most of his fellow travelers on either end were people like himself, exhausted but determined, their eyes locked on the floor of the train car.

He had never seen so many kinds of people in his life before he had moved to America. At home, everyone looked the same, or if they looked different, like he did, like Ravi had, everyone had known why. Skin tones varied within a limited spectrum; hair ranged from blue-black to the hennaed red that old men dyed their beards, hoping to look younger but never succeeding.

Here, everyone looked like combinations of people, more colors and shapes and bodies than he had known possible. The irony was that everyone dressed in the same colors, somber blacks and grays, while back at home the monotony of people's faces had been obscured by the violent rainbow of their clothing, printed cottons as far as the eye could see, swathing women in their saris or draping playfully around them in a salwar kameez. Sometimes a flash of color caught in the corner of his eye, or he saw a Muslim prayer cap, and he thought it might be Ravi, but it never was. They had both brought only Western clothing with them, anyway. Ravi's mother had promised to keep their kurtas safe for them at home. Satya wished he had burned his instead. He thought about writing her and asking her to do so, but he knew that would raise too many questions. He still hadn't responded to her letter. So instead he looked for Ravi on trains, and wondered what he was doing, and what he thought of all the different kinds of people who lived in America.

One morning Satya took his normal ride, leaving Brooklyn at six in the morning to arrive just past eight at the agency. No one else ever showed up at this hour, so he sometimes treated himself to a cup of tea from a street vendor who let him have it at half the price, leaning against the building and waiting for Ronnie to let him in. Satya supposed that he could actually leave Brooklyn at a later time, but what was the point of staying in his dingy apartment and listening to his new roommates snore?

Ronnie was particularly late that morning. Satya waited, making his tea last for a full hour until Vikrum arrived, producing his own copy of the building key. Satya found September already quite chilly, although no one around him seemed to share that feeling, as the people passing him by wore short sleeves like it was high summer.

"It's lucky this isn't the winter, eh? You would have frozen to death, brother." Vikrum grinned at Satya with his golden smile.

"It can't get that cold, can it?" Vikrum only laughed in response. Satya watched the burly man putter about with surprisingly elegant gestures, preparing a pot of coffee for the office.

"Make yourself useful, then, take the messages." Satya shot up to do the older guide's bidding. Gentle as Vikrum was, Satya was a bit afraid of him. He was the kind of man who was hired by criminals back home to intimidate shop owners and scare people. If Vikrum had been an actor in Bollywood he would have been cast as a goon, but he was a very good guide, and a deeply kind person. He often divided some portion of his lunch to share with Satya. He arrived before most other guides, and so Satya had grown accustomed to spending quiet mornings with Ronnie's snorts and scowls, Vikrum's placid whistling, and his own thoughts. Ravi would have made fun of Vikrum, Satya knew, for his large size and easy smile, and Satya would have laughed, agreeing. Satya frowned; the thought tasted bitter in his head.

He listened to the messages, dutifully recording the names and numbers of potential clients. Ronnie encouraged most of his Indian and Pakistani clients to speak English, claiming it was good for them to practice before they arrived, but that was really to mask his own accented Hindi, which could give him away as a Bangladeshi. If they were Bengali, however, he didn't bother. For Hindi-speaking tourists, Ronnie had two guides who spent most of their time practicing by watching Indian films from the 1950s and '60s to get the cleanest and most proper accent they could. In general, however, he encouraged English as much as possible, even in the office, and while many of his guides resented it, the reality was it helped them more than most of them ever acknowledged. Ronnie had never forgotten the sour feeling in his stomach when he had learned how much that cab-driver had ripped him off on his first day in America. He understood, even if his guides didn't, that not understanding English was something recent immigrants could rarely afford.

As a result of this policy, most of the messages left were in English. Satya had a hard time with recorded messages, but he knew he needed the practice. He would listen to each message five or six times before he was confident that he had gotten the information correct. There was a rather shrill message in Bengali from a woman in Kolkata, which he listened to ten times that morning. Although he spoke the language, the emotion in her voice made it hard to understand, but also the sound of a woman speaking Bengali reminded him of home. His grandmother had visited Kolkata once and described it to Satya. He wondered who would guide this woman and wished, for a moment, that he could meet her, and ask her if the stories his grandmother had told him about the city were true.

That afternoon, sitting in the small break room, Satya looked up from his lunch, a pile of roti he had burned into hard black disks and sour, undercooked dal made of a mixture of lentils and kidney beans. Ronnie had arrived, followed by a slim white woman. Vikrum was out for the afternoon and hadn't offered Satya anything to eat before he left. Satya had never cooked much before arriving in America, and his early attempts had not been particularly successful. He grimaced, his mouth full of unhappy tastes, as he watched the woman's body sway.

He wasn't the only one staring. It was a rare occurrence to see any white person, or any nonemployee in general, enter the office. Almost everyone working that day, studying maps, categorizing invoices, or fighting with Ranjit, the bookkeeper, over receipts accumulated during tours, raised their eyes from their work to watch the girl go by. Satya lifted his nose to sniff, trying to catch any hint of her scent in the air.

Satya could smell nothing, he realized sadly as the woman went by. Ravi had told him that you could smell it when a woman was ready for a man, and since then he had tried to surreptitiously sniff around when he saw a new woman, but it had never worked. Maybe Ravi had been lying to him, he thought. The notion comforted him. How could Ravi have known about things like that?

Both boys had left Bangladesh virgins, at least as far as Satya knew. And yet, it had never occurred to him before to question this knowledge. He was annoyed with himself. Why had he trusted Ravi with something so important?

Satya's time in America had already exposed him to many women and had given him a new understanding of what it meant for women to be so on display. At home in Sylhet, women's bodies were largely shaded from the male gaze, and their faces, with their downcast eyes, held no invitations. America, however, was completely different, in ways he never could have anticipated.

Each of the guides around Satya was looking at the girl like a dog watching hanging chickens in a butcher shop. It was a profound comfort to Satya to know that these men also watched women with a single-minded focus. Together they made a detailed study of the strange girl's body (slim, but with nicely shaped breasts and sweetly curving hips), which was covered with a floating thin top that was somehow longer in the back than in the front, an issue with the manufacturing, Satya assumed. Her legs were clad in tight-fitting gray pants that ended at her ankles, and small shoes that looked like slippers fit her feet, with an anklet gently gracing her right ankle like a ribbon around a present. When he finally found the time to examine her face, Satya found it to be a pale heart-shaped one surrounded by light brown and honey-tinted wavy wisps of hair. Large brown eyes sat widely over a substantial but not overwhelming nose, and plump pink lips pursed, he realized, in an expression of concern. She did not, he suddenly understood, enjoy being stared at by a roomful of strange men. She hesitated once, shrinking into herself against so many concentrated gazes, but then walked on, and for a moment Satya admired her.

He turned back to his terrible lunch and his studying. Whatever was going on with this woman and Boss, it was certainly no concern of his. His grandmother, he knew, would have been happy with him for averting his eyes. Ravi would have mocked him, calling him an idiot. But Ravi wasn't there. Satya was not sure if what he felt was guilt or relief. His eyes looked at a passage from his tour book on the Grand Canyon, describing the Hopi people and their devotion to the canyon as a religious site. He tried to lose himself in the book, but the image of the canyon swirled in front of his eyes, becoming at once Ravi's smile and this strange woman's face, shrinking and pinched with discomfort. *If she had had a dupatta on,* he thought, *I never would have known.*

11

Rebecca sat, ramrod straight, in front of the strange man who Mr. Ghazi had assured her was far less dodgy than he seemed.

The plump, small figure in front of her had on the most gold jewelry that she had ever seen on any man. He wore three gold chains around his neck, the longest of which dipped into the hairy V formed by the undone top buttons of his collared shirt. The shirt itself was a violent shade of puce, a color Rebecca had never actually seen in real life and was surprised to find looked exactly the way it sounded, like something toxic.

He had several bracelets around his pudgy wrists, which were exposed by his shirtsleeves. His stomach wasn't grossly large, but it extended gently over the top of his black pants. He wore gold rings with gemstones on each of his fingers, except for his thumbs, whose rings instead held large golden structures that looked to Rebecca like Aztec temples. The effect was finished off by what smelled like a potpourri shop of men's fragrances, from sandalwood to Axe body spray, undercut slightly by the smell of antacids. Opening his mouth, Mr. Munshi revealed a tongue coated in light pink, and he ate a handful of Tums like candy, crunching loudly.

Mr. Munshi was sweating profusely, his armpits showing deeper shades of puce whenever he lifted his hands. A cold cup of tea sat next to his elbow and Rebecca worried vaguely that his enthusiastic hand gestures might send it tipping all over his desk at any moment.

Mr. Ghazi had explained that Mr. Munshi's business catered mostly to Indian tourists. At first she had thought he was merely sharing a tidbit of information with her, but the urgency in his gaze and the blatant hope on the face of the other man, who introduced himself with a sweaty handshake and the words "Ronnie Munshi, madam, very pleased, impressed, and happy to meet you," had convinced Rebecca that something else was going on.

Mr. Ghazi took the long way around when explaining things, a quality that Rebecca had initially found frustrating but now enjoyed, understanding that this was simply his way of being polite, sidling up to an important or difficult subject without tackling it right away. Mr. Ghazi began this particular explanation by contextualizing Mr. Munshi, describing briefly Bangladesh and his own experience with the country, which was nonexistent, and mentioning Mr. Munshi's wife, Anita, and the circumstances of their relationship. He then moved on to Mr. Munshi's work, its evolution out of his time on the Circle Line, and Mr. Ghazi's own feelings on boats and their attractions, and then settled upon this new client of Mr. Munshi's, who, Rebecca realized by Mr. Munshi's sudden interest in the conversation, had been the point all along.

When Mr. Ghazi had mentioned Rebecca as a potential companion for the trip she had immediately started shaking her head no. She could miss auditions. It would be insane to leave town, no matter what they were willing to pay her, no matter how much she could use the money. She simply couldn't leave New York for something that wasn't an acting job.

However, Mr. Ghazi had looked her in the eye and asked her to think about it, and so she had agreed to do so, while privately feeling that her decision had already been made.

When she got home, though, she couldn't get Mr. Ghazi or Mr. Munshi out of her mind. She thought about his stumbling description of this widow languishing in Kolkata, and his heartfelt and circuitous explanations of how this trip would make the widow's life worth living.

She thought of *Time* magazine photos she had seen of women in white saris weeping while tossing the ashes of their husbands into the Ganges. One image had stayed with her, a woman, mouth open, tossing the ashes into the water. She wondered if she should, in fact, take the job. After all, it wasn't like anyone would cast her for anything anyway. She scolded herself for her self-pity, but the damage was already done, and she thought more seriously about this trip, now considering it less a death sentence for her career and more an escape from her dull and unrewarding life.

Rebecca decided to call her mother, who she knew might give her good advice by virtue of recommending the thing Rebecca least wanted to do. Arguments with her mother solidified Rebecca's resolve on a number of issues and she looked forward to them as a kind of reinforcement against her own fears.

The phone rang twice.

"Yes?" Cynthia barked, her usual greeting. This alternately amused and annoyed Rebecca, depending on her mood. Today, she found it soothing.

"Hey, Mom." Rebecca heard an audible sigh from her mother.

"Well, it's good to know you are alive, Rebecca," her mother said briskly, her words clipped, "although I wish I received proof more often."

"Sorry, Mom. I've been busy."

"You got a thing? Some show or something?"

Rebecca gritted her teeth.

"Not quite."

"Ah. So what do you have to be busy about?"

Rebecca counted to five slowly, a trick some daytime talk show had implied was good for uncontrollable rage. It never worked.

"Rebecca? Are you still there? It's gone quiet. Stupid phone. I keep telling Morris—"

"Yeah, I'm here, Mom. Listen, I have something I want to talk to you about. You remember my boss?"

"You have a job?" Rebecca gritted her teeth again at this and waited. "Oh, the map store. Yes. Right. He's Saudi, right?"

"Persian. Anyway, look, through him, it doesn't matter how, basically someone needs a companion for a cross-country trip, and he asked me if I would want to do it. And I'm just wondering what you think."

"A companion? Is that like, what is that?"

Rebecca smiled at her mother's worried tone, realizing what she feared this job might entail. "It's not an escort thing. It's not, like, sexual. The person who needs the companion is a woman—"

"That doesn't preclude sexuality, Rebecca."

"Mom, she's an Indian widow from Kolkata so even if she swings that way I think it's going to be pretty latent. She wants to go on a tour, and she has a guide, but he's a man, so she wants a woman to come along for, I guess, modesty? Safety? I don't know. It's all expenses paid and it's three thousand dollars in my pocket. Two weeks, cross-country, New York to L.A."

Rebecca waited for her mother's opinion, sure that it would come pouring out of Cynthia like a geyser.

"Why isn't she going to San Francisco?"

"What?"

"Indians love San Francisco. She should go. Your dad had these Indian clients—they lived here, obviously, but both from India—and that was their favorite place to go."

"But they got a divorce, obviously, right?"

"Yes. But they still loved it. She should go."

Rebecca held the phone away from her face for a moment and

hissed. She would have screamed but her apartment was too small and the phone too good at picking up her voice. She had few ways to express her frustration with her mother, and she had found that hissing was satisfying, in the absence of a good scream.

"What was that? Did you get a cat?"

"No, Mom, maybe something outside. Listen. What do you think I should do?"

"Don't get a cat, that apartment is too small, you will never stop smelling litter."

"About. The. Trip." Rebecca wished her mother didn't drive her to such rage but she always did. It was why Rebecca didn't call.

"Ah. There's no need to shout. We were talking about cats." Rebecca had started thinking about how to end the phone call when her mother surprised her by asking:

"What do you want to do? Really want, not just what you think you should do. Because, Becky, you've never been across the country. She sounds a little bit amazing, this widow, traveling like this alone after her husband's death, wanting to see the world. It might be worth it to go, get out of New York, clear your head, think about things, but only if it's what you want to do. So what do you want?"

This thoughtful response from her mother startled Rebecca, and tears sprang to her eyes. She couldn't remember the last time her mother had acknowledged that what she wanted mattered. She knew her mother loved her, and wanted what she considered to be best for her, she did, it was only that what her mother considered best and what she considered best often lived in two separate worlds, and Rebecca could never seem to connect the two.

"I did something like this once," said her mother, interrupting Rebecca's thoughts. "There wasn't the whole widow thing, but I took a trip across the country alone to visit your father when he was at Stanford for law school. I had the summer off at Princeton, I had a car and some money saved from whatever job I was working to pay my rent, and I thought, *Screw it*. I got lost so many times and ended up in so many places that by the time I got to Palo Alto I had to turn right back around and go home. But it was great. I hated every minute of it, and it was great."

Rebecca smiled, imagining her organized and compulsive mother as a young hippie on the road alone.

"If you want to do this, do it. It's a few weeks of your life. Why not?" Rebecca couldn't think of a single reason.

And so, the next day in Ronnie Munshi's office, his sweat dripping off the end of his nose, his staff craning their necks to see her, she agreed to accompany Mrs. Sengupta across the country. The happiness in his eyes briefly obliterated her doubts. She knew that the doubts would return, furiously pinching at her mind through the night, but for now, she would bask in the sense of relief this would give her bank account and the knowledge that Mr. Ghazi would be pleased.

Rebecca watched Mr. Munshi leave Mrs. Sengupta a message in a strange mix of English and what she assumed had to be Bengali, informing her that everything was all prepared and the trip would begin with its three New York City days as soon as she arrived. That gave Rebecca three days to prepare and one perfect excuse to politely end things with Max. Part of her was terrified, her doubts already rising like mosquitoes out of a swamp, but the time for dithering was over. She had wanted something in her life to change, and now, albeit briefly, it would. Besides, at least it was another role to play.

12

After escorting Rebecca out of the building, Ronnie had decided to take a trip to the Ganesh Temple in Flushing to make an offering thanking the gods for her agreement and the end of his worries over this whole mess. In order to reach the temple, Ronnie had to take the 7 train out to its final stop and then walk for thirty minutes, which was thirty minutes more than Ronnie was accustomed to walking on any given day. The idea of this much exercise made his heart hurt in anticipation, but he was determined to do it, because the gods had answered his prayers.

Smelling soy sauce and rotting garbage in the air, he girded himself for the journey as the train pulled into the final stop on Flushing's Main Street. As he walked up the stairs of the subway his knees creaked in protest, but he refused to listen to them, keeping his divine mission on his mind. Emerging into the sun, however, Ronnie was distracted by the lusciously spicy smells coming from a noodle house on Roosevelt Avenue. His stomach growling, he realized that in the anticipation of his interview with Rebecca he had forgotten to eat. This was an indication of the toll this issue had taken on Ronnie's life, as the concept of forgetting to eat was an utterly foreign one to him.

The smells around him made his mouth drip with saliva. He looked at the many food shops and restaurants. All the writing was in Chinese and he could not tell what would be the best lunch possible. He decided to go where the people seemed the happiest, and soon sat down in front of a small cup of weakly brewed tea at the Happy Frog

Noodle Café. Ronnie settled in for a large lunch as compensation for his stress. To order, he simply started pointing at other people's meals, which the waiter correctly interpreted as desire, and he was delivered plate after plate of pork. He ate them with mingled glee and wonder, for the meat still felt like a novelty to Ronnie after his childhood in a country of halal butchers.

When all the meat was gone, Ronnie washed down his last bite of sweet bean buns with the weak tea that had grown no stronger from its steeping. It was already three thirty in the afternoon. It would take him at least half an hour to reach the temple and he really ought to be getting back to work. The guides became utterly useless without his careful eye observing them. He decided to forgo the gods and contented his need to leave an offering by leaving a large tip for his waiter instead. He was sure the man would be thrilled by the two extra dollars he'd included to accompany his fifteen-dollar meal. And money was a kind of sacrifice, wasn't it? Besides, the girl, Rebecca, was white, so he probably shouldn't be thanking Hindu gods for her anyway.

Satisfied with his logic, he ground his fortune cookie into dust, and feeling settled, Ronnie returned to his office, softly humming a Sanskrit hymn. He called Satya into his office and explained to the boy that not only had he given the untried youth the magnificent opportunity of a cross-country tour, but, benevolent boss that he was, he was also gracing his life with a companion—in fact, the young woman who had visited the office earlier. She would be invaluable in helping manage the elderly madam. Satya would be in charge, of course, and should report to Ronnie daily, but— And here Ronnie broke off because Satya looked as though he had seen a ghost. His eyes were glazed over and he didn't seem to be listening to a word out of Ronnie's mouth.

"Now is no time to be doing daydreaming!" Ronnie yelled, incensed.

Satya shook his head several times to clear it, his hands stretched out in front of him in a gesture of begging pardon. Ronnie was slightly mollified at what he took to be an apology. He repeated himself in Bengali to Satya, just to be sure he understood everything clearly. Then, switching back to English, he continued:

"Companion is very nice girl. American. Be respectfully of modesty. No hanky or panky. No ideas. Right hand is there for a reason. Understand?"

Satya closed his mouth and blushed bright beet red.

"Is this clear or no?"

Satya nodded briskly, pleasing Ronnie. He liked to think of himself as a beloved boss, tough but fair. He was happy when his employees responded as if this was the case.

"Excellent. Well done. Day after next madam comes. She has three days here, then you leave. Are you packed?"

Satya nodded, less certainly this time, his eyes shifting away from Ronnie's gaze. Ronnie sighed, reaching for more Tums.

He had seen that look before. He remembered his own beginnings, with his pitifully few possessions, the denim coat that didn't last the first winter. He was sure this boy had nothing, a comb, a few changes of clothing, a pot or pan perhaps where he made his terrible meals. Far too many of the Bangladeshis Ronnie had met in America lived the most barren existence possible—not, Ronnie had discovered, because they were as incompetent with housework as he had been, but because they didn't know how to accumulate anything. When Ronnie could help, he did, as much as possible. He considered it a good investment, and the only act of charity he could justify doing. For the sake of his guides, Ronnie kept a store of shirts in different sizes in the office, along with belts and shoes, and whenever he observed one of his boys, as he thought of them, struggling, he made a point of helping. Pride was all well and good, but New York was painful for those without socks.

Standing, he took three hundred dollars out of his wallet.

"Here. Trip bonus. Buy more things. Better things. Something warm. Yes? It will be cold in some places. Hot in others. Best to be prepared."

Satya took the money, stunned.

"Close your mouth, idiot. Going to catch flies. And remember, guides are *always* . . . ?"

"Experts!"

"Excellent. See you on Friday to meet madam. Come in ironed shirt and with permanent wide smile. Good breath. Buy toothbrush, pastes, and gum. Go!"

Satya bowed his way out of Ronnie's office. Ronnie watched him go, frowning. It wasn't that he didn't think the boy would do well. Many of his guides had taken Indian tourists all over the country with far less time to prepare or willingness to learn than Satya had displayed. People believed what they were told. As long as his guides spoke with some authority and a manufactured command of English, it was fine. Ronnie was quite careful to pair tour guides with tourists whose experience traveling and understanding of English were at least two levels below that of the guide. Most mistakes, therefore, could be blamed on others, and most navigational errors could be packaged as surprises. Many an Indian came home showing friends and relatives this famous rest stop or that significant mountain named by the guide after a local star or an Indian deity. He wasn't sure about the widow—her English was very good—but since she had never traveled before he was confident that Satya would be able to take command.

No, it wasn't his guiding abilities that worried Ronnie about Satya. It was the look of abject terror that had struck the boy when Ronnie had mentioned Rebecca. Ronnie couldn't remember ever being scared of women. Aroused, yes. Scared? No. Rebecca, as pretty a girl as she was, didn't disconcert or interest him. She was an employee like any other. Satya, however, seemed to view women as an alien species. Would he last two weeks traveling with two such creatures? He would have to.

13

Despite Ronnie's commands, Satya did not spend the time before his trip in a state of total preparation. Instead, he spent his two precious days off searching for Ravi. It was a frustrating and futile enterprise, but he did it, because he didn't know what else to do. The letter from Ravi's mother had haunted Satya, and he reread it often. Why hadn't Ravi contacted his mother? Had something happened to him? Satya conjured up visions of kidnapping, or worse. But who would kidnap him? Ravi was worth nothing to a kidnapper; neither of them was. Satya knew he should write to her, tell her the truth, but what could he say? She would hate him as much as Ravi must have, and right now, she was someone who knew him from his other life who thought well of him. He clung to that, false as it was.

The boys had never been apart for this long in their lives, not since they had met. Whenever they hadn't been together in Sylhet, spending the days with their families, or when Ravi spent the long nights of Ramadan feasting with his community, at least Satya had been aware of Ravi, known what he was doing, could picture his friend's life in his own mind.

The main problem with trying to find Ravi was that he had no idea where to start. It wasn't as if he didn't know the city, at least on paper. He had been spending his days examining maps and guidebooks of New York and other American cities. He knew where to take those seeking cheesecake or "authentic" pizza or those who were *Sex and the City* aficionados (though he'd never seen the show). He even knew how many stories there were in the Empire State Building. He knew about George Washington and Lafayette, strange names he'd swallowed like milk, and he could tell you which bridge or tunnel to take to New Jersey. He knew which musicals were good for kids and which hot dog vendors were halal.

Yes, Satya could show New York to others but he didn't know where to find anything or anyone for himself. And Ravi had simply disappeared, leaving no trace of himself behind for Satya to track.

Worse still, Satya had no resources with which to find his friend. Ronnie was helping Satya with his legal residency, fabricating a family connection and securing him a work visa, but Ravi had nothing like that, a fact that Satya knew to be his own fault. They had both secured tourist visas to reach the States but those had run out. There was no official way for Ravi to be found if he didn't want Satya to locate him. Satya couldn't go to the authorities, not that he would have trusted them anyway. He couldn't hire a detective, not that he would have had the money. He couldn't ask Ravi's relatives because that would reveal too much. He couldn't infiltrate the Muslim community, because there were so many Muslims from so many different countries, and how did he even know if Ravi, apathetic about religion at best, would reach out to other Muslims?

Having no logical way to search, Satya woke at dawn and set out walking, hoping for inspiration. He sought out delis and cafés, spice shops and garages, anywhere that he saw Bangladeshi faces or heard Bengali. He walked around Brooklyn for hours, shuddering at the September winds, which felt cold to him. He made it all the way to Coney Island, where he recognized the amusement park from a movie he had seen. Sitting on a bench, he watched the ocean sweep toward the shore. He wished he could swim, and for one mad moment he wondered if Ravi had drowned himself. That would have been stupid, he thought. Ravi wasn't sad; he was.

The worst thing about looking for Ravi was that as he walked, he couldn't help but think about what Ravi would be saying, thinking, how he would react to the world around him. Would he, as Satya did, love the spray of the sea on his face? Would he want to try the chicken and rice at this stall or that one? Would he have thought the blonde was prettier than the redhead on the train, would he have wondered about the color of their underwear like Satya did?

As he walked, Satya realized Ronnie had been right, he did need something more to wear. He wondered if it would get much colder than it was. He trudged back to the train station and warmed himself on the long ride to Manhattan by rubbing his hands together, which he soon realized was useless. He got off at Canal Street, for once grateful for the press of people around him who made the streets warmer with their claustrophobic presence. Walking up Broadway, he stepped into a large store where everything was bright and cheap and looked decent enough. He found shirts in a warm soft flannel, on special for seven dollars each, and he bought four in various plaids, along with two sweatshirts and a wool cloth jacket. The labels informed him that the shirts were made in Bangladesh, which made him smile. He put one of the shirts on before he left the store, not caring that the tags were hanging off him, and felt an instant comfort enfold him.

Back on the street, carrying his other purchases carefully, Satya became aware that he was hungry, as the popcorn he had hurriedly stuffed in his mouth in Coney Island was proving unsubstantial as a meal. Looking around for something cheap, Satya spotted a cart that looked familiar. At first he ignored the thought, reminding himself that all carts look familiar after any amount of time in New York. But something caught his eye about the cartoon donut dancing on the outside of the silver box. Was it? Yes!

When they had moved to New York, he and Ravi had stopped there and eaten egg sandwiches with a turkey bacon that the owner,

also from Bangladesh, had assured them was halal. Satya had laughed
at Ravi for this, for enjoying all the other things prohibited by Islam
with gusto but maintaining the dietary restrictions to the letter. That
was the kind of person Ravi was; he possessed his own sense of the
world, he made his own rules. It was something he'd learned from
Satya, who was always the braver one, the one who hit the boys first
before they could call him a Paki bastard.

Satya quickly walked over to the cart and stood in line.

"Sir, may I speak to you? I think you know my friend."

Satya was so sure it was him, but the man looked at him blankly.

"I know no friends. We closed now. Closed for the day."

Satya's protests fell on deaf ears as the man started sliding down
the metal shutters of the cart. He knew it was him! Why didn't the
man recognize him? He had to get a message to Ravi.

"Please, tell him I'm sorry! Tell him it's Satya, tell him please. Tell
him his mother wrote to me! She doesn't know where he is, he must
write to her, tell her he's safe! Tell him I can give him a job, please,
tell him, you have to—"

Satya screamed in Bengali, pounding on the cart as it closed. His
shopping bag fell on the ground, his shirts mingling with the dirt and
debris of the city as he kicked one of the cart's wheels in frustration
and pain.

"Is there a problem here?"

Satya looked up and realized people were staring, including a
policeman. His heart jumped to his throat.

"There's a lot more carts out there, buddy. Try one of them, okay?"

Satya nodded as the people around him laughed obediently at the
policeman's joke. His features became frozen in a pained grimace,
the way they would when he was confronted by the police in his own
country. He carefully picked up his bag of clothing and walked away,
his heart pumping wildly. He thought the officer would watch him

as he went, to make sure he didn't abuse any more carts on his way, but looking behind himself he realized that everyone had already lost interest. And the cart was gone.

At home that night, Satya carefully washed his new shirts and sweatshirts in the bathtub of his apartment. In Bangladesh whenever he would wash something the dyes would gently run off the material, like a puff of colored smoke in the water. But these things held fast, their colors staying put on the material. Satya watched in vain for something to happen, for these to feel familiar in some way, for the colors to dull and for the shirts to look like something that would remind him of home. His grandmother would have loved these things, with their brightness refusing to change. It would have cheered her, and she would have declared them to be survivors, just like herself.

He wondered what his grandmother would think of him now, of his life, of the way he had lost his only friend, and he paused in his washing, trying to hear her voice in his ears. She would probably just tell him to hang up the wash, so he did just that, carefully spreading out each piece of clothing so it would dry well. He missed the laundry lines of home that stretched from window to window and held his shirts as the sun dried them. Now he draped things over chairs and opened windows to try to stave off mildew, shivering as the evening air blew in. His grandmother would have worried about the cold, he knew.

In the months after her death he had heard her every day, yelling at him for not brushing his teeth for long enough or wearing a dirty shirt or not offering to help an older woman if he saw one, not that she would have ever accepted help herself. But with time her voice had grown softer and less precise, and he hated it. It was like losing her all over again. No one cared about him enough to yell at him now. No one existed who would bother. If he didn't go to work, Mr.

Munshi might be irritated, but really, what was one tour guide more or less?

He shut the window, choosing mildew over illness. His grandmother would not want him to be sick. He imagined her scolding him now for feeling sorry for himself, for thinking foolish and negative thoughts, for not *making* people care about him. He almost smiled. Only she would believe someone could be made to care. She had cared about everyone she knew so deeply the idea of apathy would never have occurred to her. It was because of this that the nature of her death, cancer that ate through her bones and left her weak and frail, had been such an injustice.

She had urged him to see the best in people, to forgive them their evils and forgive himself. He didn't blame himself, he'd told her, but he'd lied. He had been able to do nothing in the face of her needs. He could only watch as his healthy body grew and her sick frame faded away.

Satya hoped Ravi would write to his mother. He thought about the day he had had and pretended that Ravi had been there with him. Then, barely stopping to think, he picked up a pen and paper and began to write. *Dear Mrs. Hafiz . . .*

14

Her laptop open and reflecting the weather of several American cities, including Washington, DC; Niagara Falls; New Orleans; Phoenix; Las Vegas; and Los Angeles, Rebecca surveyed her clothing, spread out on her bed in neat piles. Her mother had always made her pack this way, with categories and layers and constant cross-referencing between her choices and the weather reports, and now she couldn't stop.

Rebecca's thoughts turned to the widow, a woman who wanted a tour of America by an Indian tour guide. Ronnie had explained that the widow thought Satya was Indian, although he was Bangladeshi, and there was no reason to correct her assumption unless she explicitly asked, and if that happened would Rebecca please phone him immediately and as soon as possible? Ronnie had a habit of being oddly redundant with his commands, but Rebecca had nodded, smiling. Rebecca honestly didn't know the difference between Indian and Bangladeshi. She knew, of course, that they were different countries, and neighbors, but South Asian history wasn't her strong suit.

After she'd agreed to take the job, a bit of Wikipedia-ing had revealed that there was quite a history between the countries, whose back-and-forth border shifts and conflicts with Pakistan confused her. She realized she didn't understand enough about the cultural differences between Indo-Pakistani ethnic groups vis-à-vis Bangladesh to really know why it would be a problem for their guide to be Bangladeshi and not Bengali. She hadn't really known what Bengali was, to be honest, or that it applied to anything other than tigers.

It embarrassed Rebecca that she knew so little, that so much of the world was a mystery to her and that she hadn't bothered to find out more. She read the paper, or at least select articles from the *New York Times* digital edition. She read books. She clicked on Facebook links about Syria and Darfur, genocides and terrorist attacks, trying to understand what was happening in other places, thinking herself lucky for the safety and security of her own life. She thought she was keeping up with things. How had her world become so small? She loved New York, and more and more she had become seduced by the idea that nothing important happened anywhere else. Ten million Bangladeshi immigrants displaced in the 1970s seemed like it should have been more important to her. At the very least, she supposed it would have to be now.

She wondered what Mrs. Sengupta thought about all this, if she had strong feelings about Bangladesh. She wondered if the guide, Satya, hated India, hated serving as a guide to Indian people. And what would they think of her? Would they take pity on her and tell her their versions of their countries' histories, or just laugh at her American stupidity and arrogance? She wished she spoke another language or had ever lived abroad. She had traveled, yes, to Paris for a summer, to London to see plays, to Mexico for the beaches and the tequila, to Israel with Birthright, but those were vacations from her life. She had never lived in a place where no one spoke her language, never lived anywhere but the East Coast of the United States, in fact. She didn't know much about India beyond what she ordered at restaurants and what she'd read in a few Salman Rushdie novels.

The description of her duties that Ronnie had given her, which had seemed so clear in his office, now seemed vague. She reminded herself that the most important part of the job wasn't about her, it was about this woman, making her happy, making sure she was enjoying herself. For two weeks, all she really had to do was focus on someone else.

Opening up her suitcase, she started to pack in earnest. For the three days they would be in New York she would be staying with Mrs. Sengupta and Satya in a hotel, not in her own apartment as she had requested. She supposed that was to preserve Mrs. Sengupta's modesty, or sense of security, but still, it was deeply annoying. She hated tourists in New York, and now she would be forced to be one of them. She sighed, thinking of the money, and continued packing.

Once done, she looked at the itinerary for the umpteenth time. It was so strange, she thought, what people who came to this country seemed to think was important to see. Mrs. Sengupta had booked a very elaborate cross-country trip, with all the American greatest hits on the menu. In New York they would spend half of the first day taking the deluxe Circle Line, a tour boat that circled Manhattan. The second half of the day would be spent at the Statue of Liberty, with a climb up to the top that Rebecca couldn't imagine their elderly widow would be eager to attempt. Day two included a tour of the 9/11 Memorial, an Indian lunch in Curry Hill, and sojourns to the Empire State Building and Times Square. Day three started with a bus ride to Woodbury Common, a shopping outlet outside of New York that was recommended on every tour for foreigners Rebecca had found in her quick Google search of "tours for non-Americans of America." There were no museums, no parks, nothing that held any interest for Rebecca, just sights filled with bright neon lights and too many people.

Returning to her suitcase, Rebecca surveyed her work. Her travel wardrobe looked back at her, its sensible layers and pale colors reminding her of department stores her grandmother had taken her to as a child. That's what she had been hired to be, the background color.

As she zipped up her suitcase, Rebecca realized that her hand was shaking. She finished her zipping and stepped back, watching it move. She felt a sense of total disconnect. She could see it shaking.

She could feel it. But she couldn't make herself care. *This ought to be important,* she thought. Maybe she had simply lost control of her body, the same way she had lost control of her life. She wondered if this was a sign about her trip, and then reminded herself that she didn't believe in signs. Perhaps this was a symptom of a serious illness and she would die with these strangers and her parents would have to come get her body and take it home.

The image of their looking at her dead body in some nameless American town knocked her out of her trance, and she sat, suddenly, resting her shaking hand on the bedspread gently. She felt the shuddering of her hand run through her body and out of her left foot, and it was gone. What had it been? Something else to be afraid of.

Rebecca shook off her self-loathing and fear with a shrug, twisting her neck and rotating her shoulders to try to ease the knots that had migrated to her upper back.

She hoped Mr. Ghazi would be all right at the map store. All those years ago, after his ankle had healed, it was painfully obvious to her how little he needed her. She had waited each day for him to let her go, given that there was barely enough for him to do to maintain the tiny ill-frequented shop, let alone her. But as the months, then years, passed, and their association had deepened from her fetching him tea and dusting to her reorganizing the books and reframing maps, one day she looked up and saw that Mr. Ghazi had lightened in some strange way. Perhaps giving up his tasks in the name of keeping her busy had freed him. Either way, the change had suited him, she thought, and she hoped in her absence his life wouldn't grow heavy again. He had been so thrilled that he had facilitated something she'd sought that Rebecca worried he was happy to see the back of her. Would anyone notice or care that she was gone? Perhaps her real fear in leaving New York was that once she did, she would cease to matter to anyone there.

Her phone buzzed. A text from Max again. Always Max. Rebecca sighed, exhausted with packing and worrying, and did a stupid thing. She responded.

Twenty minutes later, she looked at the ice melting in her whiskey with an expression that was, she could feel, quickly turning from manufactured interest to thinly veiled disgust. The knots in her back were throbbing now, tightening her neck under the still-prickling skin. Next to her, his body thrumming with energy, Max was vibrating with eager need. He touched her constantly, rubbing her arm and smoothing his fingers along the small of her back, laying claim to her in little ways. His hands felt cloying, sticky with eagerness.

She swallowed the watery whiskey in one mouthful and motioned for another.

"That's my girl."

She almost visibly winced, but caught herself in time and transformed the motion into the post-drink shudder so favored by college students.

"It's good whiskey, right?"

It was fine, a brand she'd had many times before Max and would have many times after him. She smiled and nodded, though, her eyes the right degree of wide, her smile the right shades of grateful and admiring.

She slipped back into the person who had so entranced this stupid boy. Whiskey had loosened him, made his need for her even keener and more painfully clear. The part of her brain that always stayed outside of any role she played observed his slackened mouth and brightened eyes with dull anticipation. He was predictable, and she scolded him for his lack of showmanship. He opened his mouth to speak and she knew what would emerge, and began preparing her response.

"Where have you been? I missed you. You avoiding me?"

There it was, her cue. She smiled gently, projecting bohemian busy, the flaky but fascinating girl he wanted her to be.

"I'm so sorry, Max, things have just been crazy. I kept wishing I could see you but I didn't want to involve you in my whirlwind. I just wanted to get through it all and see you on the other side. You know?"

Inwardly she frowned. Had she gone too far? But then he smiled, content, accepting happily that she was the kind of girl who contained her problems, who didn't lean, depend, cling, or demand. Rebecca read this in his face and accepted her new whiskey from the bartender with a nod.

She would sleep with him tonight. The knowledge resigned her, robbing her of some of the sparkle that pretending to be someone else had given her. She drank her whiskey and smiled, letting her eyes go soft and liquid in the low light and thinking of the luggage in her apartment and the places she would be going soon.

Later, in his apartment, she lay underneath him as he pumped into her, moving her body, trying to find something for herself in the act, a tremor of pleasure, something to make her feel like she was really there. She clenched her trembling hands in the sheet and waited for him to finish.

When he fell asleep she went home. The trip would begin in the morning. She was grateful now for the hotel, though she had resented it just hours before. It would be good, she thought, to get away and leave this person behind. She didn't know whether she meant Max or herself.

15

Pival didn't sleep the night before her flight to America. She was haunted by the fear that she would oversleep and miss her flight, coupled with the vague suspicion that the maids would refuse to wake her. She imagined the servants running around the house turning all the clocks back and forward so that Pival would be confused but then dismissed the thought, reminding herself that most of them were far too lazy for that. The most likely to do it would be Tanvi, and she couldn't tell time.

Nevertheless, her fantasies could not be banished. They morphed into other things, and she imagined crowds of Sengupta aunties and uncles barricading the doors, screaming at her and shaming her for her disrespect to the memory of their beloved Ram. She imagined a vision of Ram himself, in the form of an incarnation of Vishnu, emerging from the heavens, his hand raised up to keep her from her flight, his crown blinding her with its brilliance, forcing her body into a crouched bow on the ground. Another Ram sprang forth and began to insult her, calling her a weak little mouse, a nothing. She had heard the words so often toward the end of his life that she had no trouble remembering them now, giving this ghost-fantasy the worst of them, the ones that would emerge from Ram's mouth after late nights at his club when he would come home smelling like alcohol and angry that she still existed. He would burst into her room on those nights, wild-eyed and rough, railing at her as she huddled beneath her quilts and coverlets, calling her a curse, blaming her for everything wrong, telling her the world would be better without her in it. Strange, then, that he had been the first to die.

It hadn't always been that way, she reminded herself. Their marriage had become that only after they found out about Rahi, after Rahi called them and told them what he was.

Ram had left the house as soon as the words were out of Rahi's mouth, throwing the phone at her, leaving Pival to sob against its hard plastic. He came back at five in the morning, reeking of alcohol and towering in his rage. He had broken everything in Pival's room except the bed, and slurred at her that their son's deficiencies and perversions were her fault, that she was a black smear on the world for allowing such a piece of filth to emerge from her body. He told her that she had ruined him, destroyed their son, perverted him, that her influence and their closeness had made their son the disgusting thing he now claimed to be. Pival kept waiting for Ram to hit her, until he left and she realized she wasn't worth the effort. The next morning Ram delivered a stiff apology and claimed to have no memory of whatever he'd done or said. Pival nodded weakly and let every word play over and over in her head until they formed a barrier around her heart. And in her mind she thanked him, for teaching her to be strong.

Ram had told her that Rahi was not welcome in their home, that he was not their son any longer. She had not known how to disobey him, not understood what she could do, so she had agreed by not disagreeing. Pival had not spoken to Rahi since. And that was her fault, she knew. But she could fix that, now, once she got there. She had exiled her own son. She could talk to Rahi, conversing with him in her mind in every city she visited; she could understand his life by understanding the country she had lost him to; she could find him, if he was alive, and bring him back with her. She could heal him, restore him to his unperverted self. She knew she could. She just had to make it to the flight.

At three in the morning Pival got up from her bed and checked for the thousandth time that she had everything she needed. Her bags were in order; her passport was right there in her purse, along with her wallet, stuffed with American currency, and a book of poetry by the Bengali writer Rabindranath Tagore. She had never read his work before. Everyone else she knew had, and now she couldn't say anything, couldn't admit her ignorance. His songs and poems were everywhere—she knew the verses to a few—but she had never sat down and read anything he had actually written. She didn't know if Ram had, either. It was just one of those things he had insisted on having in the house and displaying when guests came, a declaration, *Look, we are all Bengali, we are all well-read, aren't you impressed?* Pival didn't think it meant anything if you hadn't actually read the work. For all his anti-British declarations, Ram only really enjoyed Western spy novels, his secret shame. But she would take this on her trip, as a genuine act of Bengali pride, and see what she thought. She should read one of the books she had lived with before she died.

She performed her morning puja in her pajamas, praying to the goddess Durga first, apologizing for missing her festival. She begged each of the gods in front of her, Lakshmi, Parvati, Vishnu, Ganesh, Krishna, Kali, for protection, for care and guidance. She did not apologize to them, nor did she try to explain her journey. She simply asked them for their help and thanked them for their kindness. From her purse she drew out a photograph, crumpled and creased. It was a photo of Rahi, the only one she had for herself. Ram had destroyed all the others in a small bonfire in their courtyard, ordering a weeping Tanvi to find any reminders of their son and bring them to be incinerated. Tanvi might have cried but she did it anyway, and Pival would never forgive her for that. She had managed to save two photographs, the family portrait with Rahi as a baby that now hung in her room—she argued that it would cause comment and be a bad omen to destroy a photo of their entire extended family—and one she'd concealed from Tanvi and Ram both, a snapshot Rahi had sent her from America, in which he looked calm and so happy.

She placed his image next to Ganesh and prayed to them both, both the sons of fathers eager to reject them. She then slipped the photograph back into her purse, with more reverence than she could give any god. Whoever the photographer was, Rahi must have loved him, for he looked at the camera with such adoration in his eyes. Pival felt a sudden rage at this person for owning even an iota of her son's affection, and told herself that Rahi was looking at her instead.

16

Waiting for his weekends with Bhim transformed Jake from a solemn landscape architect into a giddy teenager. He hadn't even felt like this when he *was* a teenager, he realized, grinning as he broke his pencil lead for the fifth consecutive time, ruining his drafting. He reached for another and simultaneously checked his phone. There was no new text or email, but that was all right, he told himself, Bhim was busy. He would see him soon, in two weeks, as they had agreed. He had wished Bhim a pleasant flight a full week ago, dropping him off at the airport on his way to work, and he had spent the rest of the ride alternately beaming and on the verge of tears. He had never felt this mix of elation and despair, felt so addicted to someone else's skin and scent and voice. In the week that followed he felt like he was going through a mental breakdown at least four times a day, with his mood shifting from happiness to anxiety to lust to sadness. He talked to Bhim daily, before bed, and was tormented with dreams of him until the morning. His work had always distracted him from any consuming feeling, but now that respite was gone, and he could only see the curves and angles of Bhim's body in his slide rule.

He stood up, shaking out his cramping hands and looking dolefully at his botched plans. He had, he realized, drawn Bhim's face into a model of a tree. He traced it with his finger, blurring the pencil strokes.

"Who is she?" Morgan, one of the partners, was standing in Jake's doorway, observing his distraction with a faint smile.

Jake grimaced. "He," he said firmly. Morgan was a senior partner in his seventies, and he knew that Jake was gay but continued to ask him about the women in his life. Jake knew that the man didn't mean anything by it, that he was just one of those people who couldn't get their head around changing the pronoun, but Jake corrected him every time.

"He, she. You're running around like a putz, Jake. What is that? Some kind of sculpture garden? Modern art?" Morgan gestured to the garden plan, which did look like something more for a museum than the private home of tax accountants to the stars.

"I apologize, I've been distracted," Jake stiffly said, rolling up the tracing paper. "I'll redo this, I don't mind staying late."

"You could stay all night, I don't think you'll do better. You can't think with two parts of your body at once," Morgan wryly observed. "Go home, Schwartz."

Morgan was in coach mode, revved up to dispense advice. Jake sighed and shrugged, but he was happy to leave. The office, which had long been his sanctuary, had become claustrophobic. On the way out the door he began Googling flights to San Francisco, calculating how many sick days he had, wondering if he could afford to leave tonight, to take the rest of the week off. He turned back around and walked into the office, catching Morgan as the older man was sitting down to look over blueprints of a new community center, their one charity project amid all their high-profile work.

"I'm going to be out for the rest of the week," Jake announced.

"Must be quite a boy," Morgan said, surprising him with the appropriate gender.

"I think so," Jake said, but his tone must have conveyed something of his longing, because Morgan looked almost embarrassed, and he looked down from Jake's grinning face, sorting the papers on his desk with lined and worn hands. Morgan had the hands of a master builder, scarred and ink stained, which always looked strange to Jake as they emerged from his expensive shirts and well-tailored suits.

"I see. Well. Be in on Monday, and I want a better plan for the Sykeses' garden by Tuesday. Not everyone wants to look out on your boyfriend's face in their trees every morning, understand?"

Jake saluted. He wasn't offended. He ceased to care about Morgan as soon as he was out the door. Now it was only about the destination, the person he would see in Berkeley, the person he needed to be near. Two weeks was too long. He drove straight to the airport and boarded the first flight he could. He had nothing with him but his work bag, a leather messenger stuffed with notebooks and gum. He read the in-flight magazine cover to cover twice and tried to contain his excitement, the rolling pit of his stomach that worried about what might happen when he arrived. Would Bhim be excited? He had quietly admitted that he missed Jake on the phone the night before, and Bhim had tried to cover it with a laugh. Surely he would be happy?

He arrived at the airport and called Bhim, his phone battery dangerously low.

"I'm here," he said, tentative.

"Everyone is somewhere," Bhim replied, playful, not understanding.

"I'm in San Francisco," Jake said, holding his breath. There was a long silence.

"Why?"

Jake felt as though he had been punched in the stomach. "I came to see you."

"We said in two weeks—"

"I couldn't wait," Jake said, fighting to keep his voice from wavering. He would not apologize for this, for wanting something and trying to have it. There was more silence. Then, a sigh. Jake wondered if this was it, if it ended here before it had begun.

"I'm glad," Bhim said simply, and Jake could hear it in his voice now, pure happiness, echoing Jake's own. "When will you be in Berkeley?"

"Soon."

"Good." And Bhim gave him the address, and hung up the phone. Jake did not remember the rest of the cab ride, which was long and horribly expensive. He only remembered arriving and being in Bhim's arms as soon as they had entered his tiny apartment, a cramped and messy space that Jake barely registered before their clothing was off and their bodies were open to each other. Bhim held him like a lifeline, drinking him in, and as they kissed Bhim whispered *I missed you* into Jake's skin, as if he could infuse his pores with gratitude.

But afterward when Jake, tentative and a little self-conscious after his big sitcom romantic gesture, asked Bhim if he was happy that Jake had come, almost as a joke, Bhim said of course, lightly, without any weight behind it, and told him it was time to sleep.

The next morning he watched Bhim shave with a straight razor, the first time he had ever seen anyone do that. His father, growing up, had tamed his bushy, rough hair with an electric razor, and when it had come time for Jake to begin shaving he had found that the genes for his mother's fair, thin locks had been outmatched by his father's Semitic ones, and he too would have to shave daily to avoid looking like a lumberjack. He remembered his father singing to his little black hairs as they rinsed down the drain, "Run free, into the sea, a little piece of me, run free!" He could hear it even now when he shaved.

It took eight more weekends, stretched over six more months, before Bhim would consent to meet Jake's father. Jake tried hard not to be hurt by this. He returned to Los Angeles, corrected the Sykeses' mangled garden plans, and learned to remain focused at work once again. He tried to contain his joy for the conversations he and Bhim shared over the phone, and the precious hours they had together once or twice a month, but it was difficult not to feel that Bhim did not care enough about his life, did not really want to be a part of it, no matter how often Bhim insisted that he did. He knew that Bhim was afraid, that Bhim did not really believe anyone could truly find their relationship acceptable, especially Jake's father.

Bhim rarely mentioned his own family, or his childhood, or anything that had happened before California. It was as if he had been born on a plane and walked off fully formed, without a past. Jake tried to compensate by telling story after story about his parents, his hippie mother, his East Coast intellectual father, his "broken home," his college years, anything he could think of, but while Bhim drank them up like wine, asking copious questions, remembering every detail months later, he didn't respond with similar memories.

Bhim was good with people, and people liked Bhim, but there was no one close to him. Partly that made Jake feel special, and partly it troubled him. Jake would have worried about the apparent emptiness of Bhim's life, but wherever there may have been a gap, Bhim filled it with work. Jake understood, since this was the bedrock upon which most of their commonality stood. They both were passionate about what they did.

If Bhim's work had seemed boring to other people, it had always fascinated Jake even as the conversations about mollusks and mud qualities confused him. Likewise, Bhim enjoyed Jake's long lectures on light and space, on man's relationship to architecture and to the land. Wasn't Bhim himself immersed in the study of how these snails made their own homes, created a space for themselves to shield their tender bodies from the harsh world? Jake had asked once if he was the snail, building spaces to shelter himself and others, re-creating the world around him with structure and artificial boundaries, if his buildings and gardens were like shells. Bhim had replied of course, you are just like the snail, and that is why I must study you! And he had spent his time discovering Jake's body like a scientist, testing each part until neither of them could stand the exploration.

Once Jake asked Bhim how he had become interested in the ocean and the snails that made it their home. Bhim had explained that in Kolkata, the river that ran through the city was always on its way out to sea, and when he was a little boy his mother would take him to watch it flow away and he would wonder what lure the ocean held over the river that it ran to it so eagerly. From then on, he had been hooked on the ocean, and he couldn't wait to explore it.

The details of Bhim's life, when he chose to reveal them, excited Jake, but they also made him sad in their limitations. He wanted a shared life, and his desire for it was starting to overtake his desire for Bhim alone.

One night, as Bhim began to touch him in bed, Jake found himself for the first time unresponsive.

"What happened?" Bhim asked. He was always asking that, *What happened,* when Jake's face would change or his eyes would drift away. Bhim spoke about emotions as if they were events, passing storms. Well, for Bhim they were, clouds passing over his otherwise calm serenity.

"Will you meet my father?" And something hard and hurt must have flashed in Jake's eyes, because without trying to argue him out of it Bhim closed his own and murmured *yes.* Later, Jake wondered if he had manipulated Bhim, used his body and its lack of response to force his inexperienced lover to do something he wasn't ready for. But Jake was too overjoyed to seriously consider the thought, and he made the plans, ignoring Bhim's discomfort. On the evening of the meal they dressed carefully, and Jake once again watched Bhim shave, scared of the blade that came so close to his neck and the look of resignation in Bhim's eyes.

They met Jake's father, David, at a Japanese restaurant in the Valley and Jake, high on the moment and a little tipsy from the sake, begged his father to sing the shaving song, which David did. Bhim, who had barely said a word, watched in amazement as Jake joined in, his baritone warbling with David's bass.

Bhim had never heard his own father sing anything, not even a Sanskrit hymn, and to watch these two Schwartz men engaged in a duet to discarded hair, over sushi and tempura, with the full knowledge that David knew who and what Bhim was and had wanted to meet him, overwhelmed him. Everything about the meal was anathema to Bhim, the intimacy displayed in public, drinking alcohol in front of and with a parent, the way Jake touched his arm. He tried not to feel startled at the little touches, but they were icy cold to him. His face pinched with longing. He had always tried to want as little as possible but now he was flooded with need, drowning in it. He couldn't breathe.

Jake somehow understood this as he watched his boyfriend shrink into himself more and more as the dinner went on, and he cursed how casual he'd been, blaming the song in particular. He should have held back, should have pushed his father away somehow, picked a fight about something meaningless, like the menu, tried to show Bhim that he wasn't alone, that Jake was on his side. But he hadn't, and he couldn't pretend to hate his father any more than Bhim could pretend to care for his own.

Thinking more about it, Jake grew suddenly angry at Bhim, angry that he so clearly resented Jake's bond with his father, and even more frustrated that Bhim would never even admit it. It was the way Bhim hid things that most angered Jake, hid how he felt in the folds of a calm that was, Jake knew now, just a mask.

Why were there so many moments like that between them, with Jake looking for something that Bhim refused to show him? Jake had dared to hope that this was changing: Bhim had agreed to this dinner, coerced though he may have been, but now Jake felt that by the simple fact of his closeness with his father he had dug another abyss.

That night, arriving at Jake's home, Bhim said that he wouldn't be coming in, that he needed to be alone for a while, that he would stay with friends. Jake nodded, of course, desperate to show that he was okay, eager to prove to Bhim how relaxed he could be about things, how understanding. Inside Jake wondered if something had broken. Bhim must have seen more in Jake's face than Jake thought he would, because he cupped Jake's cheek and kissed him, lightly.

"Go shave," he ordered softly, "your father's beard is growing on your face."

Jake had drunk a glass of wine instead, waiting for Bhim to call, waiting for something to happen. But it didn't.

At breakfast with his father the next morning, Jake had been wary, touchy, provoking the argument he should have had the evening before, only without Bhim there to witness it there was no point. David had watched his son flail and nitpick for almost a full hour, finding nothing appealing on the menu and scowling over the excellent coffee, before he finally said something.

"I liked him. The guy from last night."

Looking up furiously, Jake saw his father's slight smile and deflated.

"Yeah. Me too."

"You can't make someone happy, Jake, you know that, right? You can't *make* someone anything."

Jake looked away from his father, out the window, onto the bucolic Los Angeles suburbs around them. Everyone looked happy outside. What had made them that way?

"He seems to care about you, though."

"How do you figure?"

"He doesn't mind that you're a terrible singer, for one." David returned to his eggs happily, humming the hair song in between bites.

Returning home that afternoon, Jake pulled into a parking spot near his apartment and standing by his front door was Bhim, with a box in his hands.

"May I come in?"

Jake opened the door, looking at the box curiously.

"Later," Bhim said. "What will we eat?"

Over dinner, a meal of Mexican takeout, as Bhim could barely toast bread unsupervised, Jake's eyes returned to the box over and over again. Bhim caught him, and smiled at him as if he were a spoiled child.

"It's a present."

Bhim had never given Jake anything before. He had explained that he hated the concept of presents, and it had led them to what was almost an argument, something they had been avoiding, having never had one and having hoped they would be one of those miraculous couples who never fought. Jake was careful of fights—he'd hated them from the days of his childhood—and this state of zero conflict with Bhim had seemed vital to preserve, so he had not pushed the issue. He had been very careful not to give Bhim anything as a gift. And now Bhim was giving him something instead.

Opening the box, Jake was confronted with an old-fashioned set of shaving implements. He stared at them, confused.

"Do you know what it is?"

"Of course. I've seen *Sweeney Todd*." Bhim's face wrinkled the way it always did when Jake made a reference he didn't understand. Jake made a "move on" gesture with his hand, unwilling to dive into such a loaded subject as Stephen Sondheim.

"It is a shaving kit. My father, I never saw him shave because he didn't shave himself, he had it done for him. When I moved here I realized that this wasn't customary here, that I would have to shave myself, and I bought a kit like this. I thought you might like one, too."

Jake smiled. "I've never had someone shave me. It seems like an easy way to die. You sneeze and there you go."

Bhim grinned. "It's not like that. I'll teach you. Come on. Your afternoon hair is already coming in. I don't want to feel that tonight."

And just like that Jake knew that Bhim would be staying, that the alone time was over, that they were back to the intimacy he so craved. Since then he had shaved each night before bed, for Bhim, to make sure Bhim felt what he wanted to feel, his bare face and nothing else.

Lying in bed, Jake asked him about his father.

"I don't want to talk about my father," Bhim said, gently, to diffuse the sting.

Jake thought for a moment. "What about your mother, then?"

Bhim smiled, a smile Jake had never seen before. It was a gentle spreading of his lips, soft and smooth. His face suffused with light, like he was thinking of something wonderful. "My mother is the reason that I love you," Bhim said simply. "She is the reason I know what love is."

Jake stared at Bhim, transfixed.

"I wish that you could meet her," Bhim said. "You would like her very much."

"We can go to India—" Jake said, surprising himself with the suddenness of his thought, but Bhim was already shaking his head. He turned to Jake, his face serious and sad. He wet his lips and whispered softly.

"I can never go back. I have told my father what I am. I have told him today."

Silence hung between them like a noose. Blood rushed to Jake's face—he heard it in his ears—and Bhim reached out, comforting him. The absurdity made Jake laugh a little, a hysterical bubble foaming out of his mouth. Bhim smiled sadly.

"When I saw you with your father, I realized, there is nothing at home for me. I will not marry. I will not be that way. And if I cannot be that way, they do not want me at all. So you see, I can never go to India with you. And you will never meet my mother. I am sorry. I would have loved for you to meet her. For her to meet you. I wish they would sing about my beard with me and we could sit at a table and just look at each other and be happy. But at least I will have that with you. And that will be enough. Won't it?"

Jake couldn't answer. He held Bhim's head as he sank it into Jake's lap. He watched as the bedspread turned darker with Bhim's tears, and he decided he did not care about these people. If they could turn their backs on a person like Bhim, then he simply could not care less about them. He would think of Bhim as someone who did, in fact, come off a plane fully formed; he would forget that Bhim had a family and a past, because it was only their time together, and their future, that mattered.

Still, he wondered about the smile on Bhim's face at the thought of his mother. Her, he would have liked to thank, at least, for the gift of her son. Bhim's words echoed in Jake's ears as he cried himself to sleep and Jake watched him, keeping guard over him through the night, as if by protecting him from future evils he could erase the pain of the past.

She is the reason I know what love is.

Jake did not even know her name.

17

Pival left the house at four thirty in the morning, just as the city was waking up. The apartment was silent in the haze. As Pival crept through her own home she felt like a thief, sure she was about to be accused of stealing her own luggage. She left two envelopes full of rupees, one for the cook and the maids and one for the driver, which she hoped would make it into his hands and not the maids' pockets. She had paid for the milk through the end of the month and settled up with the yoga instructor at her last session. She left her wedding ring, which had always felt a little too tight on her finger. It was a Western affectation. Ram, who had been so against such things, had insisted that she wear it so foreigners would know that Pival was married. Not that she ever met any foreigners. She would now, she realized, and she would meet them unmarried. Ram would hate that, she thought with a broad smile. The maids could pawn it for all Pival cared. She thought of what Ram would think about someone else walking around in her ring, some poor couple enjoying her gold, which they would, no doubt, if Tanvi pawned it. She almost started laughing at the idea but she bit her lip and swallowed the sound. She walked out of the house just as the sun began to glint through the windows, and in her mind she said, *Good-bye.*

The street was already creeping with life. The milkman bustled and servants and workers and early risers made their ways across the pavement, busy and uninterested in her. She was anonymous in her own city and it was glorious. She spotted the beggar she had seen days before; this must be his spot. The debris from the accident was long gone and new preparations for Durga Puja were sweeping through the city. By noon the streets would be flooded with people. This was the first Durga Puja she wouldn't be there to see.

Pival had spent her entire life in Kolkata. The city's borders were the boundaries of her own existence. Her parents, the Banerjees, had no relatives to visit in other cities. Ram had never taken her anywhere. Indeed, he himself had only been to England, and had vowed never to return after his schooling in London was through. It was the rare thing the Senguptas had agreed on, the fact that they had no interest in the world outside of their own.

It had amazed both of them, Rahi's desire to leave Kolkata. Pival had wondered if the meaning of his name, "wanderer," had dictated his fate in some way. She had always been uninterested in leaving the small world she had been thrust into, much as she disliked it, much as it seemed to dislike her. But now she, like Rahi, was escaping her only home, possibly never to see it, or India, again.

Though several young men tried to help her, she waved them away with a smile and hailed her own cab and carried her own luggage. She hadn't done either of those things in years and it made her feel vital and alive. She watched the city go by as the cab swept through it, the dirty fading glory of Kolkata crumbling under the weight of modern life. The cab moved in fits and starts, sometimes inching through the swarms of people already gathering to worship the goddess, sometimes zipping through empty streets devoid of shrines. She had left early to ensure that she would make it on time despite the murderous traffic the Durga Puja would inevitably cause in Kolkata, traffic she had heard about but never experienced. Every year since her marriage she and Ram had gone no farther than five blocks in any direction from their home.

She glimpsed the river now and again as the cab barreled through the streets. Pival had often watched the Hooghly, a tributary of the

Ganges, pump through the city and wondered if it was sad when it left India, the holiest of rivers becoming mortal as it reached the larger sea. She probed her own mind as she watched the waters rush away and could feel only readiness and anticipation building in her stomach. She decided that the water was happy to leave India, eager to continue its route and become part of something larger.

Was this what Rahi had felt? Was this the sensation that drove him from coast to coast and world to world? Pival thrilled at the thought that she might have a moment of closeness with him even now, solely through her imagination.

Arriving at the airport, she was bewildered by the signs and people and activity. But she had prepared herself, she had read guides on how to go through the airport, what to do, and Mr. Munshi had, rather kindly, included a list of things to know upon traveling. She wondered if he gave that to all his clients or if he could sense her inexperience over the phone. Mr. Munshi had told her that just as she would never accept less than first class taking an Indian Railways train, she ought to follow that rule when booking the flight. It was frightfully expensive, but she couldn't argue with his logic, and she had felt a little thrill at how appalled Ram would have been at the price. How appalled she herself was. They had always been thrifty, despite their relative comfort. Conspicuous wealth was for newly moneyed peoples, flashy Punjabis and Marwaris, not the elegant refined Bengalis that they were proud to be. She hoped she was sitting near a Marwari on the plane. Ram would, if he could, die a second time.

As she had been instructed to do, she checked her bags and endured the strange security rituals that made people feel safe in airports, handing over her purse, pushing her body through a metal detector, allowing the hanging folds of her sari to be examined by a female security guard.

They touched her all over her body and Pival realized that it had been a long time since she had been touched. She supposed she should have felt violated by the search, but instead it warmed her. It was contact. It reminded her that this was real.

She had vastly overestimated the time she would need. She was early. She looked around, clutching her purse to her and wondering what to do. There were cafés and stores everywhere; the airport was like a little mall. She knew what to do in malls.

Settling down at a café with a cup of chai cooling beside her, Pival exhaled. She had been half holding her breath since she had left her apartment. Now she felt her lungs expand in her chest. It was over. She had escaped. There was no one left to stop her because there was no one left to care.

It had just been much easier than Pival thought it would be. That was, in some indefinable way, troubling. She might never see Kolkata again. She might never walk by the Victoria Memorial or her mother's old school, she might never suffer through the New Market or stroll down Park Street. Her small treasure trove of good memories with Ram flashed through her mind. There was their wedding, where he had looked so handsome; the wedding night, when she had been so afraid, hating her ignorance, the way he had soothed her fears and given her appreciation, if not pleasure, and at least a kind of security that the job had been done; the early excitements and rare tenderness; the day she had given birth; the shared love of Rahi as they watched him stumble through the places of their lives. All of that was in the past now. She waited to cry. Nothing happened.

Her equilibrium surprised her, worried her, and made her feel like she was perhaps already dead. She wasn't ready yet, not in this country; she still needed to feel something, to be angry, to confront the pervert who caused her son's death, if Rahi was really dead, and to cause her own. She was too used to compressing things within herself. Looking through the steam of her tea she vowed she would try harder. She would practice feeling something again. She would never make it to Los Angeles otherwise.

Pival boarded the plane at eight in the morning and left India as the sun shone bright over the country and spread its rays over her city like a blanket. It would take her almost a full day to reach the United States, but that couldn't have felt longer than the lifetime it had taken her to reach the airport that morning. As she boarded, she felt like the stale air of the plane was a benediction, sweeping away her old world and bringing her somewhere new.

She had never been on a plane before, never traveled anywhere. Now the plush seats of first class held her body comfortably as a kind woman brought her a glass of water. Behind her the rows and rows of seats for the other classes of tickets belied Mr. Munshi's information, but she didn't mind. The plane was exactly like she thought it would be from the movies, and nothing like it at all. She held on to her purse as they prepared to take off. She thought of screaming, telling them this had all been a big mistake, getting off the plane, going home, living her life the way it had always been lived. She did nothing.

All the servants must be up by now, Pival thought as she watched the plane's wheels lift off the tarmac. Her stomach lurched and she was grateful she had only had some tea. Trying to take her mind off her protesting body, which was disturbed by the motion of the flight, Pival forced herself to wonder what the maids had done upon finding their mistress missing. She felt a wave of affection for Tanvi, who had always seemed to her like a watchdog of Ram's desires, but now appeared as a sad and lonely figure in Pival's mind. Tanvi had never married, never had children of her own. She had viewed the Senguptas as her family, as both her owners and her possessions. Now she had been abandoned by both of them. The other servants were mostly young. Pival was convinced they would easily find other positions, marry, have their own lives. Tanvi would not.

But Pival couldn't feel any guilt, though it would have been appropriate; all she felt was relief. It was a strange feeling, a slight loosening she could sense around her body, a creeping suspicion that she could stop feeling that she was choosing the wrong thing. She could still hear Ram's voice in her head, scolding and scowling and demanding things of her. But it was growing fainter.

Looking out the window of the plane as it sailed smoothly through the sky, she wondered about the companion that Mr. Munshi had secured for her. It was, perhaps, a waste of money to have a companion, but then again what did she care? What kind of girl would take this job? she wondered. What would she be like? Would she be Indian? Would she like her? Would it matter?

These questions buzzing around in her head, her body exhausted as the plane jolted through the sky, Pival finally slept, and dreamed at last, of nothing at all.

Pival's first night in New York City was like discovering, too late, that she was inside a fireworks display.

She had arrived at John F. Kennedy International Airport a full twenty hours after she had departed from Kolkata. When she had booked the flight she hadn't been sure what seat to reserve, but people in movies always seemed to want the window, and so that's what she had chosen. She had thought she would be terrified of flying, having never done it before, but it was simple: all she had to do was sit there and watch the sky.

The plane landed with a jolt against the runway, and everyone clapped, so Pival did, too. The airport was a blurred maze of customs and baggage claims and fluorescent lights in sterile bathrooms. Pival was pleased to find them so clean. It was true, what people said. Everything was so clean in America.

The taxi service—*specially arranged, madam, all part of the fees but tip is required, strange custom but when you are being in Rome, as it were, you pay Roman fees. Have you been to Rome? Very nice place, my wife says. Do leave tip!* warned Ronnie Munshi—had dropped her off at the Courtyard Manhattan Times Square, a hotel that was, she had been assured, right in the heart of New York City.

The lights around her were blinding as she stepped out of the cab, and the crush of people moving quickly in every direction baffled her. She came from a busy city herself, it wasn't as though Kolkata was some dusty village, but the sheer variety of people was over-whelming. They moved around in all colors and clothing styles, jeans and sweatshirts, yes, which she had expected, but also head scarves and dupattas, women in full saris layered with denim jackets herd-ing their children in T-shirts and shorts, tall African women with brightly printed dresses and hair piled up into what looked to Pival something like Sikh turbans, Chinese tourists and women in abayas. She was blinded by all the movement and she swayed gently against the taxi as the driver unloaded her two large bags.

"Is everything like this?"

The driver looked at her, surprised. Pival had been silent through-out the trip. He did not respond. Pival frowned; her English was excellent, she knew, she had always been complimented on it, and Ram had preferred it to her Bengali, which he had never felt sounded good enough, classical enough, for his ears.

"Excuse me. I have asked you a question. Please respond. Is every-thing like this? Is everything like this here?"

The driver shrugged.

"Surely you must know. You live here."

"I don't live here. I live in Queens. And Queens is not like this," said the driver, his accent pouring thickly out of his mouth, through his brilliantly white teeth.

"Where do you come from?" asked Pival, curious now. She had been afraid to speak to him at first. She had never met a black person before. She had clutched her purse the entire time and closed her eyes, breathing deeply in the cab, reminding herself over and over again that Ronnie Munshi would not have hired this man had he not trusted him not to rape and kill his clients. Now, having safely arrived, standing under the bright lights of this strange place, she wondered what all that fear had been for.

"I am from Nigeria. You are from India."

"How did you know?"

The driver smiled.

"Indian women are always like you. You are alone here?"

Pival nodded. It was embarrassing that he knew she had been afraid. She was not, she knew, as fearful as so many of the people she had known at home. She had always hated the way Ram talked about skin color, about the shades of people's bodies as corresponding to the worthiness of their hearts, and of their lives. She knew if she had been even a touch darker, Ram would not have married her. Her parents had not raised her to view skin tone so zealously. Her brother Arjun had been several shades darker than either of her parents, and they had laughed and teased and wondered if he had been touched by some deity, or if he blushed so much in the womb he came out browner. Arjun's darkness had embarrassed Ram, though, and Ram had limited Pival's contact with her brother when she was pregnant, worried that he might contaminate their baby somehow, darkening its skin by touching Pival's own. Pival had pointed out to Ram that this was quite the opposite of his own insistence *on science and logic supplanting the superstitious Indian nonsense that has arrested us in a state of backwater mentality for so many years,* but he had told her she knew nothing about anything, and when Rahi had been born so pale and fair, Ram insisted that he had been correct.

"Good for you. Good to be alone."

Pival nodded again. She tipped him generously, because it would have made Ram mad, and gave him a smile. He smiled back broadly and drove away. Pival entered the hotel, received her room key, and was directed to her tiny suite by one of the cleaners, Pival supposed, as the woman had a cartful of cleaning supplies and an apron. She asked the girl if she would be her maid throughout her stay, but she didn't seem to understand, so Pival let herself in, with difficulty, wondering why the key was like a credit card and not a key at all, and surveyed her room. It was a simple place, and clean. It felt a little claustrophobic, and she fought the panic that rose in her throat and threatened to strangle her. She breathed deeply.

She sat on the bed, staring out the lone window onto the large streets below, where the people looked like ants struggling to build something together and failing. The lights were so bright and blinding, bouncing off every surface. They hurt her eyes, but she couldn't look away.

It was strange to be with all strangers, although it was what she had wanted. It was like being in costume, and no one knew who she was. For the first time in months, years, really, no one was pitying her, no one was sorry for her loss.

The first wave of pity had come with Rahi. Ram had never shared Rahi's excommunication from their family with the outside world, preferring to maintain the fiction of their happy family with their smart son working away in the United States who was doing so well and would be coming back to make a match with a pretty Bengali girl next year, always next year. Then suddenly Ram had announced that Rahi was dead, after a brief phone call from someone in America that Ram would not acknowledge. She hadn't even heard the news herself, and she didn't know if it was true or another way for Ram to punish her. He told her that Rahi had died of a heart attack in California, and Pival knew, just knew, that if it was true it was because his heart had broken when they would not let him come home.

It wasn't until months later when Ram died that Pival wondered at the speed and ease with which everything had happened. For Rahi there had been no paperwork, nothing to sign; Ram hadn't visited any government agencies or registered Rahi's death, at least not to Pival's knowledge. She hadn't seen a death certificate. For Ram there had been so much work, so much to do; how could there have been nothing for Rahi? It just didn't add up to her. She began to feel the most dangerous of feelings, hope, and she couldn't help but be grateful to Ram for dying. If he hadn't passed away so quickly after Rahi's death, she might never have wondered if Rahi was dead at all.

The Senguptas had explained away the lack of ashes with a vague story about a car crash, and the implied messiness of the fictional incident scared off all but the most persistent questioner. To those pernicious people who wanted to discuss, at length, the terrible pain they must have felt at not being able to spread their own son's ashes in the Ganges, they nodded and frowned, until a more polite and sympathetic witness changed the subject delicately. Pival appreciated the concern, but the loss of her son so far outweighed the absence of his ashes that she couldn't understand why that wasn't obvious to everyone, why that wasn't all they could focus on as well.

When Ram had died the process had begun all over again, although many comforted her with the fact that *this* time all the demands of their religion could be met. Pival had carefully anointed his feet with ghee and sandalwood, tender and loving in her ministrations, the very picture of a Hindu widow, serene but profoundly sad. For once, in the matter of Ram's funeral, she had been approved of by all. They did not know that the only way she had been able to stomach any part of the event was to pretend that Ram's body was Rahi's, that she was helping her beloved son move on to the next life and not her husband, who had caused her so much pain.

Now, here in New York, no one knew about Ram and Rahi. No one had looked askance at her as she had walked alone through the lobby, or as she had picked up her key to her room for one. No one looked at her at all. It felt wonderful, and it felt strange. She had always been someone's something, someone's daughter, someone's wife, and then someone's widow. At the front desk, all the clerk had wanted to know was her name. She regretted telling Ronnie that she was a widow. She should have lied.

Later that night, bathed and in fresh pajamas, she picked over a meal from room service. She had been informed this meal was not included in her tour package and found that she did not care. The lights of the city still invaded her window, while the sounds of the world below seemed to be directed straight at her ears. Blazing neon stretched out in every direction, blasting into her eyes so strongly that even when she closed them she felt dazed, the violent colors raging on the inside of her eyelids. The hotel wasn't well soundproofed, she realized, for she could hear the hawkers on the street below, imploring people to come to events or trying to sell them something, she couldn't tell what; the sounds were loud but the words were blurred together, indistinct.

Peering out of her window, she watched as a large figure in an extremely fluffy red suit, which covered his entire body, complete with a giant fuzzy head, attempted to hug a passerby. She couldn't be sure, but he looked like the children's character of Elmo. She remembered the creature, who had featured in a movie Rahi had loved. Ram had allowed it, despite its not being based in an Indian myth, as all Rahi's other childhood entertainment had been, because it was in American English and could be useful in the development of his language skills.

But Rahi had loved the characters who had spoken English the worst, that is, this Elmo fellow and a sweets-obsessed monster with a lazy eye. Pival had always thought it was strange that the animal, Elmo, spoke in the third person, but she found herself smiling at it now. She felt like Elmo as she watched the giant version of him try to find people to hug in the busy light-flooded square, which was really a triangle, she saw. *Pival is watching,* she thought, *Pival has escaped life and Pival is walking in another world. And now, Pival is tired.*

This would be her only night alone in the hotel, as after this the woman, Rebecca, and the guide, Satya, would be joining her in adjacent rooms. Rebecca would be between Pival and Satya, as a kind of barrier to her virtue, Pival supposed, although that didn't exactly leave Rebecca in a safe position, but perhaps Ronnie Munshi had thought that as an American girl she could take care of herself. Or that she was more disposable, virtue-wise.

Pival smiled at the thought. Would she be a loose girl, this Rebecca, the way American girls always were in the movies? Pival knew she should disapprove, and she did, in a way, having never been with anyone but Ram, but part of her hoped that if indeed this companion was a little on the dirtier side of the laundry pile she might tell Pival something about it.

She sat, listening to the people around her through the walls of the hotel room, wondering if any of them were having sex right now. Growing up, she had heard women moaning in what seemed like a combination of pain and pleasure. She had lived in a small apartment building where the paper-thin walls left little of their neighbor's sexual relations to the imagination. She herself had never uttered more than a squeak or two of pain when Ram had visited her room on those rare occasions. Sometimes she wondered how she ever had gotten pregnant, he came to her so infrequently.

Unable to sleep or even rest, with the lights outside and the buzzing in her own head, Pival turned once again to her itinerary, as though it were some kind of holy text. She had practiced saying each city on the map she had been given, rolling the letters of each name in her mouth like fennel seeds, splitting them with her teeth and swallowing them down to try to absorb them, to be prepared. What would they be like, these American cities? What would she find in them that Rahi had left behind? She wasn't sure where he had visited or what he had seen during his time in America. Perhaps she would be walking the streets he had walked, or perhaps she was searching in vain. Perhaps he really was dead or perhaps he would be there in the end, waiting for her, and he would leave the strange man who had enslaved him with desire and run away with her.

Her son would be thirty now. She had been thirty the year that she had had him, so late, so many people thought she would never have a baby, had wondered what curse the Senguptas had taken on that the greatness of Ram Sengupta wouldn't be passed along to the next generation, and then, there he was. Rahi. Their gift.

Pival put away her itinerary and turned off her lamp. The curtains tried their best, but light still poured through the edges of them, spilling around the cracks. She lay in the blinking low colorful room and waited for the morning to come.

18

After Bhim came out to his parents, Jake had assumed that his rules about public behavior would shift a bit, but if anything they grew worse. This confused Jake, but when he asked Bhim about it, he would simply say it was how he had been raised, that it would have been the same with a woman. Jake did not believe this, but as he had no evidence to the contrary he had to take it as truth. Privately he thought that Bhim was determined to live in a way his parents would approve of, despite the fact that they would never know it.

For Bhim, this was his only connection to his family, but for Jake, it was a new rejection every day. Indoors, in his comfortable apartment or Bhim's tiny rooms in Berkeley, Bhim would cling to him with desperation, but out on the street they were friends, nothing more. Bhim would try, clumsily, laughing at himself, telling jokes, attempting to make it funny, and Jake would laugh, when he could, but most of Bhim's attempts just made him sad. Bhim called himself "the ice queen," which he thought was unbearably clever. He performed exaggerated flinches when Jake tried to touch him and pounced on Jake when they came home, desperately trying to make up for his public deficits with private affection.

Jake wanted to respect Bhim's needs, but he hated that the person he loved, the person who loved him, refused to touch him in front of other people. It made Jake feel cold, and he found himself smiling brightly at passersby and waiters, craving the public display of affection that Bhim refused to give him.

Bhim sensed his hurt once as they sat together in a darkened movie theater, and he carefully put his hand on Jake's knee when the lights went down, after looking around to make sure no one could see. Jake was disgusted. Bhim was placating him with a half-hearted grope in a darkened theater as if they were teenagers. He shook off Bhim's hand and angrily stormed out of the theater, not caring about the scene he was making, wanting to be far away. He looked back once. Bhim was still staring at the screen, trying to look normal. Jake wanted to scream.

Jake did not smoke. He knew it was bad for him, and besides it was criminally expensive and he hated the smell that clung to his hands and his hair. He would proudly tell anyone he met that he was a *non*smoker. But when he felt anything so deeply that it hurt, the only cure for him would be a cigarette. The numbing feeling of the nicotine and the slight lightheadedness it caused calmed him and made him feel balanced. He had tried to break this rare habit many times, but he could not. Instead he would, when very upset, buy a pack of cigarettes and allow himself a single one, and then leave the packet and matches out for a homeless person to find.

Bhim caught up to him just as he was inhaling the last puff of a burned-down cigarette. Bhim's eyes widened, and Jake realized Bhim had never seen him smoke before. Bhim sat down next to him on the pavement and reached for the pack, taking a cigarette for himself and lighting it up with matches taken from Jake's limp fingers.

"I've never seen you smoke before," Jake said.

"I'm sorry," Bhim said.

"Why?" Jake was curious. Would Bhim be sorry for the right thing?

"For the way I am." Bhim said it simply, shrugging. Jake looked at him.

"I love who you are," Jake said, his voice cracking slightly.

Bhim smiled again, sadly. "I was not raised watching people touch. I was not raised watching men love each other. Some things are for public and some things aren't. My parents—"

"I don't want to hear about your parents," Jake said calmly. "They are not here. I am."

Bhim looked at him, his eyes dark and glistening with tears. "I know." And then he began to cry in earnest, finally unrestrained in a public space. Jake held him. Bhim was stiff in Jake's arms, but Jake didn't care. It was better than nothing.

Jake knew that Bhim might never be as physical as he wanted him to be. But something had shifted, and he knew that the charade of public denial was done. Perhaps this had been how Bhim mourned, and after the mourning was the moving on.

Jake lay in bed that night, watching Bhim, who was a deeper sleeper, snore, and wondered if he could stand to be with someone who might never be okay with his own life, who would always feel that what they were doing and what they wanted from each other was wrong. He loved Bhim completely, with a force that often terrified him, but he also loved himself. How long could both loves survive?

Jake closed his eyes, but all he could think about was smoking a cigarette.

19

Although it was unusual for him, Ronnie had decided that he would accompany Satya and Rebecca on their first day with Mrs. Sengupta. As it was Satya's first tour, and Rebecca's first experience with the company, he told himself that he was being a responsible boss, but in reality he was excited to be back on the Circle Line. It was the one tourist activity he actually enjoyed. Looking at himself in the bathroom that morning, he giggled in anticipation as he combed his thinning hair. It was six thirty but he had to leave soon if he was to be there at eight forty-five, his customary fifteen minutes early for clients.

Getting out of the train, Ronnie followed a slim but round pair of buttocks up the subway stairs and out into the sea of people that was Times Square. He liked following women up the stairs, especially when the weather was nice and their bodies weren't restricted by bulky coats. He enjoyed the denim-clad view for a full two minutes before realizing that the person he was following was none other than his newest employee, Rebecca. She struggled to roll her two suitcases down the crowded sidewalks of Times Square, and Ronnie rushed up to help her, almost receiving a smack in the face with her purse as thanks for his pains.

"Mr. Munshi! I'm so sorry, I thought someone was trying to steal my stuff."

Ronnie reeled back, hurt. He recovered quickly.

"You're right on time, I see," he said approvingly.

Rebecca knew she was in fact early, but she felt it wise not to argue the point. Instead she smiled and nodded. "I like to be prompt. Is Satya with you?"

Ronnie shook his head. They arrived at the hotel and stepped into the lobby. Ronnie didn't see Satya anywhere. He had repeated his injunction that the guide be early at least five times when they had spoken the previous day, and he had also mentioned that he himself would be accompanying them on their first day of excursions, which should have been an indicator that the boy should be on his best behavior. As he looked around the lobby there was no sign of Satya, no one who appeared to be remotely Bangladeshi, just a few Mexican people cleaning.

"I know it's too early for me to check in, but do you have a place where I can store my luggage?" Ronnie opened his mouth to respond but realized that Rebecca was talking to the person at reception, who helped her lock up her bags and place them in their luggage room. Ronnie checked his watch. It was 8:50. By his calculations, Mrs. Sengupta would have finished her breakfast by now and was, presumably, checking on her appearance before making her first entrance in front of her awaiting audience. For all their claims to modesty and simplicity, he found these Indian aunties by and large to be a vain lot, always conscious of their need to make an entrance, of their gold jewelry and their fine purses, and he felt it part of his job to accommodate them, exclaiming over their smooth skin and dark hair, which he knew owed more to dye than to youth.

"Mr. Munshi?"

A quiet voice behind them made both Rebecca and Ronnie turn, catching their first glimpse of Mrs. Sengupta. The plainly dressed Indian woman in a simple white sari, no jewelry and no makeup, surprised Ronnie, but he had no time to register his surprise because he was too upset that Satya himself had yet to appear. It was unconscionable for the guest to have arrived before the guide. If he could, he would have wanted to give the impression that Satya had been waiting in the lobby since the previous evening, standing at attention in anticipation of Mrs. Sengupta's every whim. This was not a good start, not a good start at all. Ronnie fumed, internally, while presenting Mrs. Sengupta with a slightly oily smile and bending over to touch her feet respectfully. He then stepped back, indicating Rebecca as if he were a game-show host.

"Your companion!"

"Hello. I'm Rebecca Elliot. It's very nice to meet you, Mrs. Sengupta," Rebecca said, formally but with a nice degree of warmth. She held out her hand to be shaken. Mrs. Sengupta seemed surprised but happy. She opened her mouth to reply but was cut off by Ronnie.

"Greetings, distinguished auntie and wonderful madam, and welcome yourself to America! I trust you have had a night of extreme comfort and luxury here in the very heart and center of the great city of New York, the biggest of apples, though I of course prefer the highly superior Alphonso mango. I am Ronnie Munshi, you are recognizing my voice from the phone, I am sure and certain. Guide has been delayed by life-threatening illness, very serious but I am sure completely fine very soon, so we will start the tour together, as of course planned, in approximately and exactly four minutes, which should give you this time to use the WC, as it is called, water closet or loo, of course, should you need to do so at any time in this time. Guide will of course be here quite soon but in the meantime you will be pleased to accept personal attention from myself—"

"But the guide *is* here, Mr. Munshi." Mrs. Sengupta's voice was as soft in person as it had been on the phone. Ronnie and Rebecca had to lean forward a bit to hear her, which made the woman shrink back.

"What is this, madam?" Ronnie looked around for Satya again, wondering if Mrs. Sengupta was one of those spiritualists who had been speaking in a religious sense, that is, the presence of all people was always around and that sort of nonsense. Ronnie hated that kind of thinking but he would adapt, of course, to the needs of his client, and perhaps they could stop by a psychic reading along the way to the boat or after, really, because of the timing—

"Here it is, Mrs. Sengupta." Satya ran up and handed Mrs. Sengupta a purse.

"I forgot my purse in the breakfast room. Mr. Roy very kindly went back to get it for me. He arrived here at eight, and accompanied me at breakfast. He doesn't *look* sick, Mr. Munshi." Ronnie's face reddened to the shade of a ripe cherry at Mrs. Sengupta's faintly curious tone. She didn't appear to be mocking him but Ronnie wasn't sure. He had to regain control of the situation, fast.

"No, yes, no, not him, another guide, I am very sorry, all apologies, forgot which one I was speaking to, business is doing so well I have too many guides now! All apologies." Ronnie glared at Satya. A full hour early? He would have admired it if it hadn't been so presumptuous.

"Shall we go then?" Mrs. Sengupta inquired.

Ronnie nodded, all smiles. "Your adventure awaits!"

Mrs. Sengupta paused as she passed Ronnie, making sure Satya was well on his way out.

"He doesn't look sick at all, Mr. Munshi. He doesn't look *Indian*, either."

This was not a good start. The boat ride, which he had been anticipating with such joy, now seemed like a prison sentence. He would remind Satya to be as Indian as possible when he got a moment alone with him, and reprimand him for this one-hour-early trick. And, he thought, make it mandatory for all his guides from now on.

Looking out over the side of the boat onto the rippling waters of the Hudson River, Satya felt his insides twist like candy floss. He hadn't been on many boats in his life, and something about watching the Circle Line boat, a large ungainly thing slugging through the dark oily water, made him feel dizzy.

He had been early to pick up Mrs. Sengupta, as instructed over and over again by his employer. He had been polite and watched his Bengali diction carefully, trying to smoothly erase any geographical markers from his inflection and accent. He had bowed, touched her feet, explained that he was honored, debased himself completely in deference to her age and social status—in short, he did everything Ronnie had ever told him to do and then some. But Boss was refusing to look at him now, and though he was jovial and enthusiastic, this was, to Satya's eye, for Mrs. Sengupta's benefit.

"Boats leave right on time, here, you see, madam? Neither too early nor too late. It is an excellent rule for life, as well, is it not, Satya?" Ronnie's voice had a strange edge as he continued speaking. "Too early can be as bad as too late, can it not, madam?"

"Can it, Mr. Munshi? How?"

The widow's calm response stumped Ronnie, who opened his mouth like a fish and sputtered, gasping for air.

"Well, it is an obvious fact, isn't it?"

"Not at all," Rebecca broke in. Satya didn't know what was happening but he resented Rebecca's intrusion. Rebecca shrank under Ronnie and Satya's dark looks, but she kept her eyes on them, unblinking. The staring contest seemed to progress for ages, until Ronnie finally pretended that some spot of water from the ocean had irritated his eye, and he ducked his head.

"People can die too soon."

Mrs. Sengupta pronounced this as calmly as if she were stating the price of onions. Everything froze, and exactly ten seconds after she had said it Ronnie began nodding his head, smiling, frowning, almost crying, apologizing for her recent loss with a fervor that amazed Rebecca, Satya could see. He himself was used to this sort of thing from his boss, but he always enjoyed the performance. Ronnie took on the mantle of mourning this stranger as if he were Ronnie's own father, praying to Mrs. Sengupta's husband, asking for his blessing. Satya looked around and saw Rebecca's eyes, round and yet somehow skeptical, and despite his own understanding of the doubt in her gaze, he felt the need to defend his boss, and so he joined in, sobbing and sighing for a man he would never know. Really he should thank the man, he knew, for allowing the widow her trip, which let him be her guide. Still, he felt a loyalty to Ronnie, so he moaned and groaned along with him as the widow watched, her face a blank slate.

"Isn't that nice?" It was Rebecca's voice again, and Satya cracked open one eye, ready to scream at her for her lack of proper respect for the important mourning rituals of the widow's world, when he realized that she was pointing out Ellis Island, an important sight on the tour and a vital part of Understanding America, which was one of Ronnie's major points of guiding. *Have Fun, Stay Safe, Buy Gifts, and Understand America.* Satya realized he was falling behind in his guiding duties and rushed to catch up.

"It's where people used to have to stop and be examined before they entered the USA," Satya remarked helpfully.

"Yes. I know. My grandparents came through there." Rebecca said the words absently, but they left Satya amazed. This was something he had read about. To meet someone who actually had been a part of this was astounding. Bangladesh only dated back to 1971. Rebecca's family had come to Ellis Island before his country had even existed.

"They used to change people's names," Rebecca explained, "to make them more American. You would come in a Scarolla and leave a Smith."

"Just like that?"

Rebecca nodded. Satya gritted his teeth. He should have been explaining that fact, and if he had known it, he would have. But the widow seemed interested.

"Do they still do that?"

"I don't think so. Not if the immigrants don't want to," Rebecca replied. The widow nodded and looked at the island until it was too far behind them to see.

After Ellis Island floated away into the distance, the group quieted, each retreating to their thoughts as the boat guide droned on endlessly about the 9/11 Memorial and why New Jersey wasn't as bad as people might think.

As the tour continued, Satya observed his little group from the corner of his eye as he breathed deeply to calm his churning stomach. The day was cool and mildly drizzling, but Mrs. Sengupta didn't seem to mind. She sat with a scarf around her head, observing the cityscape as it slowly drifted past. Unlike so many of the tourists on the boat, she didn't take a single photo. Her abstinence was more than compensated for by the small Japanese tour group sitting in front of her, who hadn't stopped recording the journey with phones and video cameras since the moment they stepped onto the boat. They weren't alone. Everyone on board was obsessed with documentation except them. Teenagers took selfies, constantly comparing them, while a couple had a friend take endless photos of the two of them, the girl's large engagement ring prominently displayed. Even Ronnie had snapped a few shots.

Sitting beside Satya, Rebecca read from a tour book. This surprised Satya; she had lived in New York for a long time, why would she need a book about it? But she was absorbed, ducking her head over the pages to protect them from the moisture in the air. Satya hoped she didn't have aspirations of guiding the tour herself; with Boss being as oddly angry as he was, she might supplant Satya, and then where would he be?

Satya yawned deeply. He hadn't been able to sleep the night before. He was nervous about guiding, and it felt strange to be leaving New York without knowing where Ravi was. What if Mrs. Hafiz sent him another letter? He had stopped by his first apartment just to check, but there had been neither mail nor news of his friend. When he wrote to her he had sent a new address, but the letter had gone out only the day before; it would take weeks to arrive and weeks for a return letter, if there even was one. And Ravi was nowhere to be found, although Satya had pretended in the letter that they had been together. By the time the lie reached Mrs. Hafiz, he hoped it would be true.

As the ship plowed through the waters, it reminded him of the trip over, of watching the ocean with Ravi and looking for fish in the grimy depths. He felt suddenly fragile as the boat listed heavily in the water, and grew even dizzier, almost faint. Satya scowled at his physical weakness. He knew he had been the one in the wrong, stealing something that wasn't his, but wasn't that what they had always done? When they were children they had had a tradition of stealing the food off each other's plates. And then there had been the real things, the actual thefts, the money stolen from Satya's grandmother to pay for Ravi's fancy sneakers, leaving the Roys without milk for the whole month, or the pilfering of one of Ravi's mother's bangles to pawn in exchange for movie money. Theirs had been a friendship based on robbery, running out of food stalls together to avoid paying for steaming plates of fish curry and rice, or stealing girls' underwear off the washing lines to sniff them in their beds at night. Was this so different?

The boat guide on the loudspeaker tore through his reverie, alerting the passengers for the tenth time at least to the 9/11 Memorial, which was, at this point, approximately 1.5 miles away. Satya frowned, wondering if this man was so adamant because he saw a small group of brown people on board. Looking around, he saw Rebecca rolling her eyes and Mrs. Sengupta looking confused. Only Ronnie seemed happy about the constant repetition of the information, smiling and nodding as if this man was doing a magnificent job, giving constant updates as to their proximity to the site of the tragedy.

"Never, never, never, never, never forget. If you haven't been, as soon as you leave this boat today, I want you to make your way down there. It's just a short five-block-and-two-avenue walk to the train, right there at Times Square, yes, with the lights, and then you just take the E train right on down. Discounts are available at our Circle Line ticket booths but really, for something like this, can't you splurge? September eleventh. If you remember nothing else in your life, remember that day."

Mrs. Sengupta was looking increasingly puzzled. Was the widow so out of touch? Even in Bangladesh he had heard about the event, though admittedly, some members of his class had cheered when they saw the news, thinking it was a publicity stunt for a movie. That had seemed very funny at the time, he remembered.

Satya leaned forward, ready to impart his limited knowledge about the subject, which included planes, Arab terrorism, firefighters, and a movie with his personal American hero, Nicolas Cage.

"Madam, September eleventh was—"

"I know what he is talking about, Mr. Roy, I simply don't know what it has to do with the United Nations. We are passing it on our left, aren't we? I have seen pictures of it, but I don't know if they are the same building."

Satya looked over. It did indeed seem to be that building, although he couldn't be sure; just like the photos Mrs. Sengupta had mentioned, the photos from his guidebook had shown only the front, not the rear. Ronnie was watching him, however, and he remembered that the first rule of guiding was that you always know the answer, even when you don't. He nodded, smiling brightly.

"Absolutely, madam! First-rate observation. Very United. United States!"

Rebecca snorted. Satya looked at her quickly, but her face went completely blank.

"I simply do not understand why he is repeating this information about the 9/11 incident so often. I understand it was a terrible thing, but I had thought it was a single location in New York. Was it everywhere?"

Ronnie opened his mouth, his self-important smile neatly in place. He himself had given many a talk on the subject, and felt ready to explain to Mrs. Sengupta the importance it had to Americans and why, in fact, should she be interested in a slight detour to the memorial earlier than planned, dinner at the first Indian restaurant on her itinerary could be moved back an hour, as he happened to know the owner of the restaurant in question, an uncle, of course, hence the very reasonable price for such exquisite food—

But before Ronnie had a chance, Rebecca's voice rang out.

"They have some deal with the memorial. Or they think you don't get the news in other countries. For some reason, it's really important for guys like this to make sure that tourists like you really acknowledge how awful it was. They feel like it's their duty."

Satya held his breath. She *was* trying to guide! He would put a stop to that, or perhaps the widow would be so offended that she would request a change. But Mrs. Sengupta looked at Rebecca for a long moment and then nodded, dismissing the subject. She looked out on the bow and asked about another building along the river, one on the Brooklyn side. As Satya rushed to explain how the boroughs of Manhattan worked and Rebecca returned to her guidebook, Ronnie deflated, sinking into his folding chair and slumping down against the boat's movement.

The precipitation had gotten neither better nor worse, but stayed an unmitigated drizzle, and Ronnie's face and glasses were beaded with tiny droplets. Satya looked over at him and followed the direction of his gaze, to where the Circle Line ticket sellers were enjoying a nice cup of coffee and chatting underneath the deck. Both Satya and Ronnie had taken one look up at the dull, bruised sky and recommended to the ladies that they observe the tour from inside the boat, but Mrs. Sengupta wouldn't hear of it, proclaiming proudly that she was not made of salt. The small widow seemed rather fragile, though, and Satya fretted about her taking ill, but Rebecca had smiled in support and told her that *here we say sugar*. Ronnie and Satya had immediately contributed with a chorus of why salt was better, and with that they had ended up on the upper deck, getting spat on by the sky.

"What is that?" Mrs. Sengupta was pointing to a large sign on the Brooklyn side of the river, which was on their opposite side now, as the boat had turned around, halfway through its journey and ready to make the slow return to the dock. There was a large sign on the shore facing the left side of the boat that said in proud letters WATCHTOWER. Rebecca started laughing, while Ronnie looked momentarily puzzled, unable to see it, Satya guessed. Satya thought fast, wondering what lie would be the most easily swallowed about a building that he had never seen before in his life.

"Madam, it is what it says it is, a watchtower, making sure that sea vessels and things of that like are suitably safe in the water. In the northern parts of this coast they call such things lighthouses, but here the lights are not necessary as the city is already so well lit, as I'm sure you observed last night on first night in USA, so here they just have watchtowers. For the ships."

Satya was suddenly sweating, despite the chill. Ronnie was looking at him with approval for the first time that day, however, which made the stress of inventing this quick-thinking explanation worth it. Rebecca looked at Satya with her eyes wide and her lips pursed. Satya assumed this was her look of admiration for his prowess as a guide, and he smiled at her. Rebecca frowned and opened her mouth, then quickly closed it, looking away. The boat plowed on through the waves, and Satya relaxed, enjoying the chilly breeze as it cooled him, soothing him, congratulating him on his first real test as a guide. He had passed, he knew, and whatever Ronnie had been angered by earlier, it seemed to be gone now.

The rest of the day went quickly, from the pizza lunch in midtown that Rebecca picked through as Ronnie explained the importance of pizza in America; to the Statue of Liberty, which Mrs. Sengupta refused to climb, deciding she enjoyed the view outside more than she would the one from the middle; to dinner at Ronnie's uncle's restaurant, where Ronnie himself served them and over dal and naan described his brief and calamitous career in the food industry. There was one fragile moment in which Mrs. Sengupta complimented the food as the best Indian food a Bangladeshi could make, and the bottom of Satya's stomach dropped out, but Ronnie laughed and no one seemed mad. Ronnie told Satya and Rebecca when the widow went to the bathroom that Satya didn't have to pretend to be Indian anymore, which was a relief in a way, because Satya didn't know how to be Indian in the first place, even if everyone already assumed he was.

By the time they delivered Mrs. Sengupta safely to her room, she was yawning widely but smiled faintly as well, which Satya realized might be her way of showing happiness. She didn't smile much, which was perhaps to be expected of her, given she was in mourning, but she seemed to have enjoyed herself, or at least, she hadn't complained. Ronnie had told Satya of many a customer who had sent back food, demanded that the subways should be cleaner, and found the sights and sounds of New York subpar, asking for their money back on account of their disappointment.

Satya shivered. He thought of what Rebecca had said, about changing your name at Ellis Island. You could, it seemed, walk into a building in America one thing and then out another. After all, he himself was now a newly baptized un-Bengali Bangladeshi, all over again.

That night Satya showered, trying to ignore his deep sense of disquiet, his dread at leaving the city without knowing he had gotten word to Ravi, and, Ronnie's warnings about the minibar in mind, ate three of the large candy bars he had smuggled in with him. Satya lay on his bed and looked around, unable to stop himself from enjoying the room, so much more luxurious than his own at home, with air-conditioning and heating controlled by a dial, soft clean towels sitting in piles in the bathroom, and even a painting on the wall. The television had one hundred channels and the bed felt soft and plush. Satya had slept in many places—buses, trains, the storeroom of the boat, his desk at school—but his bedrooms had always consisted of a mattress on the floor. Often they had not been bedrooms at all; in his grandmother's apartment he'd just slept in a space where he would not be in the way. Now he had a whole room to himself, not just in this hotel but there in New York. He did not have to share a thing with anyone.

Satya ate a fourth candy bar and felt calm. Perhaps not being Bangladeshi agreed with him, he thought sadly, and despite the rush from the sugar he put his head on the pillow and went right to sleep.

20

Rebecca knew that the guide's far-fetched story about the Watch-tower building shouldn't have made her so angry. Why should she care if this guide was an idiot? Why should it matter if this Indian woman never learned about Jehovah's Witnesses? But it did, some-how, matter to her, or at least, it mattered that Satya had lied.

Rebecca had taken only one trip with a guide before in her life. It was a Birthright trip to Israel and she had loathed every minute of being controlled by a man on a bus with a microphone. She tuned him out whenever possible, but seeing Jerusalem, drinking arak, and letting an Israeli soldier slip his hand under her bra had eventually made it worth it. She had, however, done tours of individual places with a guide, and she had always appreciated those experiences. She loved feeling like she was learning something. It was what she enjoyed most about traveling.

She remembered a fact about Notre Dame in Paris she had learned on one tour, that the magnificent church had been saved from destruction by Hitler's army because one soldier, an art lover, had stayed behind as the army marched on and cut the fuses to the explosives that would have rendered the building a pile of rubble. She had been repeating that story for years. Was it a lie?

She hadn't thought of herself as a patriot, but something about the idea of this Indian woman getting a false image of the United States aggravated Rebecca. Why bother going anywhere if you were simply going to be deceived? Who was Satya to make up stories about the

US? She wasn't making up anything about Bangladesh. She barely even knew where it was.

Rebecca smacked the hotel pillow. The tiny room smelled dank and musty, and she knew there must be mold behind the beige and green wallpaper. The lights of Times Square were clear through the one small window, and the water, when it had emerged from the groaning tap, had been yellow for five minutes until it turned clear. Shivering, she had sat naked in the bathroom, waiting to take a shower. The night was clear and cool and when they'd been out walking she could smell the dried-leaf crispness of fall in the air, but not near Times Square, where it smelled only like hot dogs and burnt pretzels and garbage.

Having showered, she figured out a way to draw the blinds on the window and block out the obnoxious neon lights, but she still couldn't sleep. The blankets felt heavy on her body and she kicked them off, sweating.

Rebecca didn't spend much time angry, as a rule. She avoided dwelling. But now she was angry, irritable for no real reason whatsoever, except that the guide had been wrong and hadn't cared. He had presented the lie with such an air of confidence and pride, so assured and clear, that she had almost found herself nodding along.

She wouldn't stay silent next time, she resolved. She would correct Satya, at least once Ronnie was gone. She didn't want to jeopardize her position—she was already counting on that money for the next month's rent and a new set of head shots—but once they left New York she would assume control if it seemed that Satya was incompetently explaining America to this woman. Comforted by her decision, her body temperature returning to normal, she pulled the blankets back up and finally slept.

The next few days in New York were a whirlwind for Rebecca,

filled to the brim with things she had never wanted to do as their little group joined thousands of other tourists at the Empire State Building, Madame Tussauds wax museum, the Brooklyn Bridge, and Central Park. They had changed the itinerary when Mrs. Sengupta shockingly had no interest in shopping.

The park particularly seemed to confuse Mrs. Sengupta, which made sense to everyone but Rebecca, and so she asked about it as they sat on a wooden bench watching fat ducks become fatter off park concessions. Mrs. Sengupta explained that she had never been in a park that wasn't flat before. This amazed Rebecca, and she asked them all to explain what parks were like where they were from.

"Well, miss, there are no parks in Bangladesh, unlike India," explained Ronnie, to which Satya reacted by rearing back angrily. Their pretense of being Indian had been dropped, which relieved Rebecca, as she hadn't understood it in the first place.

"Excuse me, sir, but perhaps you did not experience parks but in my experience parks are there. Bangladesh is not such a place that there are no parks there," Satya sputtered, his tone respectful but his eyes blazing. Ronnie met Satya's gaze and frowned, but this time Satya didn't grow subservient or humble. On the contrary, his look withered Ronnie, making him duck his head down slightly, almost as if he was ashamed.

Rebecca watched them curiously. She had seen the two men clash in slight ways over the three days in New York, as Ronnie was unable to let go after the Circle Line tour. He clearly missed being a tour guide; everything from the way he directed the route they took to the fact that he insisted on ordering for everyone, using his most precise and descriptive English, peeking back at Mrs. Sengupta the entire time to make certain she was observing his abilities, screamed "guide."

"Parks in Kolkata are flat. And I have never been outside of Kolkata before." The simplicity of Mrs. Sengupta's statement caught Rebecca off guard and interrupted Ronnie and Satya's silent sparring match.

"I had assumed parks were flat," the widow continued. "Isn't it nicer that way?"

Ronnie and Satya rushed to agree, yes, madam, highly superior, but Rebecca shook her head, considering her words carefully.

"I think it depends what you are looking for in a park, really. That is, what your philosophy is. This park was designed so that when you were inside of it, you wouldn't feel like you were in a city anymore. You would feel like you were in nature. I don't know if that really worked, but that's why it's hilly and so full of trees, so that you don't see the city around you. It's an escape."

"How should a park have a designer?" Satya asked skeptically.

"This one did." Rebecca closed her eyes, searching her mind for the name. She had been told about him during her Columbia orientation. "Olmsted. Frederick Law Olmsted."

"I have never heard of this man," said Ronnie, frowning. Rebecca thumbed through the pages of her guidebook and showed Ronnie and Satya the section on the park. As they looked over it, their heads bowed together, Rebecca wondered if she had made a mistake, upstaging them. But when Ronnie's face lifted from the page, it was bright with determined happiness.

"You see? Nothing but the best for you, Mrs. Sengupta. Even companion is a kind of guide!"

"It is an interesting idea. Designing a park. I wonder if people do this in India. I did not know that this was something a person could do with their lives. As old as I am, I did not know this."

Ronnie and Satya instantly jumped in with another chorus of denials that Mrs. Sengupta was old. Mrs. Sengupta seemed uninterested in their token protests, however, and she continued looking out at the park as two ducks fought for a particularly large chunk of bread floating through the murky pond. She seemed content to simply sit and observe the world around her.

Over the past three days, Rebecca had accumulated more than a few questions about the widow. Was Mrs. Sengupta usually such a passive observer? If so, why had she decided to take this trip, to be so confronted by so many unfamiliar and unknown things? In the face of her tragedy, instead of sinking into what she knew, she had come to a new and strange place where the parks were hilly.

One of the ducks had waddled out of the water and was now begging for scraps up on the walkway, looking at Mrs. Sengupta expectantly. The widow smiled and shook her head at the animal.

"Always on the lookout," the widow said. "Greedy things."

But she spoke with a fondness. The park loomed around them, a vast forest in the city. Mrs. Sengupta seemed more at ease now, in this park that wasn't flat.

Rebecca resolved to ask Mrs. Sengupta more about herself as soon as they were free from Ronnie's watchful eye. Ronnie had explained to Rebecca in rather severe terms that Indian women did not like to talk about themselves because it was immodest and un-Hindu. Rebecca, however, couldn't believe there was anyone in the world who didn't like to talk about themselves. After all, Ronnie himself was now declaiming once again about his experience of New York City, explaining that now that Mrs. Sengupta had seen everything of value there, they should be ready to depart for Niagara Falls first thing in the morning. If, of course, she was still tired from her flight, the van procured for the purpose and driven by Saurish, a very good friend and very reliable driver, would be a very comfortable place to sleep on the eight-hour trip.

Mrs. Sengupta nodded and declared herself rather tired at this very moment, in fact, and could they skip dinner that night at yet another Curry Hill establishment? Ronnie looked deeply saddened by this prospect and tried to convince the widow that she really ought not to miss this particular dal, despite the fact that they had eaten dal at the majority of their meals so far. Mrs. Sengupta was not one to be persuaded of anything, Rebecca understood, as she watched the woman smile politely and patently ignore each of Ronnie's justifications, maintaining that she would really prefer room service, despite her acknowledgment that this was not, in fact, included in the price of the tour.

Once Ronnie had made sure that she did indeed understand this salient point at least five times, he shrugged, still baffled that she would choose to pay for an extra meal. At this point, Mrs. Sengupta gently suggested that perhaps this meal should not go to waste, and nothing would please her more than Ronnie and Satya and Rebecca's enjoying the meal themselves. Rebecca quickly excused herself and then pointed out that the loss of two dinner guests meant that the men would receive twice as much food, an idea that deeply intrigued both of them. After a few half-hearted protests, Ronnie and Satya agreed.

Sitting in her hotel room later, having been abandoned by the men as they pursued their Curry Hill bounty, Rebecca wondered if Mrs. Sengupta was content with room service, whose menu Rebecca disdained as overpriced and bland. Maybe she might like to try something new? The idea had only just formed in Rebecca's head when she found herself knocking on the door next to hers, surprising herself with her own eagerness.

Mrs. Sengupta answered the door in her pajamas, a sort of loose tunic that reached her knees with slits up the sides almost to the waist, and soft-looking billowy trousers. Her graying hair, usually confined to a neat bun, hung in a long braid, almost to her hip. She looked inquiringly at Rebecca, who smiled nervously back.

"I was thinking of opting for takeout instead of room service. Would you like to join me?"

"Opting for?"

Rebecca smiled. As excellent as the widow's English was, Rebecca had found quickly that colloquialisms were totally lost on her in any form. Mrs. Sengupta spoke like someone from a book, one from the 1950s, perhaps, with a formal precision that amused Rebecca. Satya and Ronnie peppered their speech with Americanisms and short overused phrases, but though Mrs. Sengupta's English was clearly more fluent, her expressions were slightly dated.

"I'm choosing to get some food delivered," Rebecca rephrased. Mrs. Sengupta nodded, and Rebecca realized the room service menu was in her hand. "Oh, have you already ordered?"

Mrs. Sengupta shook her head slightly. "No, not yet. I had just been observing my opportunities. They seem limited. I do not eat meat of any kind, which seems to be a rarity here. Almost all these dishes include some degree of flesh."

Rebecca nodded. "Have you ever had Thai food? It's an excellent choice for vegetarians." It also had a variety of curries and rice dishes, thought Rebecca, which might ease Mrs. Sengupta into non-Indian options slowly and comfortably. Mrs. Sengupta wiggled her head from side to side, confusing Rebecca. She had seen, in the last three days, each of the other members of the group employ this head-wiggling motion, but she couldn't tell what it meant. As far as she had understood, it could mean anything, or nothing.

"I have eaten Thai food twice. There is one excellent place in Kolkata and I finished my shopping early on two occasions and indulged in lunch alone. It was very nice. I would like to join you, if you do not mind. Please, order for me. I enjoy many things. No meat, or fish, or eggs, please." Rebecca had turned away to order when she heard the widow clearing her throat. She turned back. Mrs. Sengupta seemed almost shy, but the widow opened her mouth again to speak with determination.

"Would you eat with me please? I have had Thai food only alone. It would be a nice change, to share it with you."

Thirty minutes later, sitting on a chair in Mrs. Sengupta's suite, Rebecca opened up a steaming plastic container of red curry with tofu and offered it to Mrs. Sengupta, who sniffed the fragrant steam with delight. Rebecca also opened a small packet of vegetable spring rolls and set them on a paper plate, along with their sweet, sticky sauce, and finally she unveiled her own entrée, a heaping mound of vegetarian pad thai. Mrs. Sengupta seemed about to protest as Rebecca offered her this, too, so Rebecca quickly explained.

"I thought we could share. This way you can try more dishes, if you like. I requested that everything was meat- and egg-free, and—oh!" Rebecca broke off, standing quickly and making for the door.

"Where are you going?"

"I have something else to add."

Rebecca left the room and returned a few minutes later with a bottle of wine in her hands.

"Here! It's white, so it goes perfectly with Thai food. I know I should switch to red, with the fall, but I'm not quite ready to make that transition yet. I'll grab the glasses from the bathroom. Did you try it yet? I hope it's good."

Rebecca spoke nonstop as she collected two glasses; unscrewed the bottle, internally congratulating herself on picking a screw top; and poured a healthy measure for both herself and Mrs. Sengupta, before opening a small white rice box. Mrs. Sengupta looked at the glass as if it were a snake that might bite her.

"I have never had alcohol before."

"Oh, I'm sorry, I had thought that was Muslims, I didn't know that—"

"What was Muslims?"

"Uh. Muslims have a religious law against drinking. Don't they?"

Mrs. Sengupta nodded.

"I didn't know that Hindus did, too."

"We don't. Not formally. My husband drank. It's only that, women aren't supposed to drink. There are women who drink, but it's . . . it's bad."

"Really?"

"Yes. Very bad, those women are."

Rebecca smiled.

"That must make me a terrible woman then." She raised her glass and tipped it at Mrs. Sengupta, and took a swallow of her wine.

"Have you . . . have you drunk with others?"

Rebecca could have sworn that the woman looked eager.

"I don't understand."

"That is, do you drink with . . . with men?"

"Sometimes. If they pay!" Rebecca joked.

"Of course, things are so different here." Rebecca noticed that Mrs. Sengupta was not smiling as she said this.

"Does that apply to everyone in India?" Rebecca asked.

"I don't know. Everyone I know, at least. But I don't know so many people."

"I'm sorry. You don't have to drink it, of course. I'm happy to have yours."

Mrs. Sengupta looked at her glass and wiggled her head slowly.

"I hope you don't think less of me, because I'm having wine. I was just kidding, before. I'm not bad. At least, I don't think so."

Mrs. Sengupta wiggled her head again. Rebecca sighed internally and twirled noodles around her fork. She wasn't sure what to make of this conversation. Perhaps Mrs. Sengupta *did* think less of her now. Who could tell with that gesture? And really, did it even matter? Would she be less fit as a companion now in Mrs. Sengupta's eyes?

Rebecca had no sense of alcohol as a moral issue. She had never been one for addiction of any kind, except, apparently, to failure.

"This is very nice."

Rebecca looked up to see Mrs. Sengupta enjoying the tofu with a small forkful of white rice. Rebecca smiled. "I'm glad you like it. It makes a nice change, doesn't it?"

"All of this is a change. It is very nice, to change, sometimes."

Mrs. Sengupta wrinkled her brow in determination and lifted her glass. Rebecca watched, amazed, as the widow took a small sip of her wine. Her face stayed wrinkled, and she handed the glass to Rebecca.

"This is not for me. Still, I thank you. A nice change." Rebecca smiled and added the portion of wine to her own glass.

"You are not a terrible woman," Mrs. Sengupta told her seriously, and took a bite of the curried tofu, her eyes closing in delight.

"Thank you," Rebecca said, equally seriously. As she watched, the widow savored each bite like it was the finest meal she had ever had. Perhaps it was.

21

The trip to Niagara Falls had been a good idea, Pival thought as she stared into the mountain of water gushing toward her. She hadn't thought that it could have been worth the arduous drive, but it was. Every bump in the road and stall in the traffic had felt like torture but now, seeing the massive falls pour their sheets and sheets of water so close to her that she could feel the spray, she knew it was only the torture that comes before joy.

It had been a pilgrimage, she realized, thinking of her shrine at home, and now she was seeing the divinity in store for her. Astounding rainbows exploded off the edges of the waterfall. When Pival closed her eyes she could almost feel their colors on her face. Her body encased in a bright blue plastic poncho, she leaned off the edge of the deck into the spray of the falls, trying to crane her body as close to the water as possible.

Around her, a surprising number of Indians jostled with each other for space on the deck, pushing and shoving and muttering rude comments as their phones and cameras rose above the crowd, snapping a never-ending series of photos of the same exact view. *Just like home*, Pival thought, watching her countrymen elbow each other out of the way and berate each other for their rudeness. "Are there many Indians here?" she asked Satya, who looked startled at the question.

"There are Indians everywhere," Rebecca said, adjusting her slicker so it would cover her hair completely. Pival wondered if that was really true. Certainly everyone she knew at home had sent someone to America. But they usually came back. Where had all these people come from? What was life here like for them? Had Rahi been here? Had he seen the falls, crashing on and on and on?

Amid the crowd, one man took his small son—Pival judged him at three or four—and raised the boy over the water, dangling him off the side of the boat, and the child kicked and squealed with delight, making his dangerous position even more precarious.

Pival gasped in horror at the man's tenuous grip on the wildly bucking child. The man was thin and reedy, struggling under the weight of the boy, and the more the child's body squirmed the more likely it seemed that he would be dropped into the cold and fast-moving waters below. One of the attendants who had outfitted them with slickers and warned them about the water was blowing a whistle, and next to her, Rebecca and Satya seemed not to notice.

"Put your son down!" Pival realized it was her own voice, calling out in Bengali. The man ignored her, or maybe he didn't understand, so she repeated it in Hindi and finally in English, straining her quiet voice uselessly against the pounding of the falls. A gentle hand touched her arm, making her jump. It was Rebecca.

"You might startle him, Mrs. Sengupta. And see? He's finished."

The girl was right. The man was already bringing his laughing son back down, letting his little legs hit the safety of the deck even as a plump woman, her pink sari fold peeking out underneath her raincoat, stormed toward them, scolding and bewailing the man's lack of sense. At least, that's what Pival assumed they were doing; they were speaking Punjabi, a language she did not understand.

Slowly her breathing came back under control. She was amazed she had shouted. Ram would have been appalled. She had been terrified for the father more than for the son, and for the mother most of all. If their child had died, what would they do? She wondered if she would have reacted in such a way to a white child, if she would have cared so deeply had the child not been Indian. She probably wouldn't have; she probably would not have thought it was any of her business. But watching people who looked like her dangle their son out into the arms of death had made her blood run cold, forcing her mouth to open. It was like watching her own life, her own son, dangling off a precipice, and she wasn't sure if he had fallen or been saved.

A wave of disappointed cries from her fellow passengers forced Pival to look up, and she realized that the boat was swinging back to shore. The time on the falls was done.

"Are you all right, madam?" Satya asked. She shook her head slightly and kept her eyes down. She did not want to see the water anymore.

Filing off the boat, Pival caught snippets of Marwari, Tamil, Gujarati, and of course, Hindi, Hindi everywhere, out of the mouths of her fellow passengers.

Now that the boat ride was over, her mind floated back to the trip up to Niagara Falls from New York. The energy of the gorgeous view had faded, leaving only sadness and weariness behind, a hangover of the long car ride and watching a child's brush with danger. It was odd, Pival considered, that they had spent so long getting there to spend less than an hour on the water.

Accidents on the highway had turned their ride into a fourteen-hour trip. At first Pival had tried to ask Satya questions about his life in America, about what it was like here for him. But apparently Satya suffered from carsickness, a fact he had never known, having never spent any similar length of time in a car before. He finally dozed off near an open window, making the car cool with the fall air, waking every so often to dry-heave, apologize, and fall back asleep again, depleted.

Pival herself tried to sleep but found that her body, in a rebellion against the time zone shift, had given up on the concept altogether. She hadn't had a full night's sleep in days. She wondered how long she could go on like this, and why didn't she feel tired? At home she was always tired, napping in the afternoons and going to bed early each night, only to wake up in the midmorning. Now she couldn't close her eyes without wanting to open them again, knowing there was something new to see. Energy coursed through her body, and hope and despair fought battles daily through her mind. Even as they had sped along the monotonous highway toward the falls she had been absorbed with the world outside, unwilling to miss a moment of it. What if she missed a view Rahi had loved?

Rebecca somehow was able to tune everything out by reading a book, *Anna Karenina*, one Pival had heard of but knew nothing about. She was afraid to ask, however, as she felt it was a book she should know, something she should have read.

She liked Rebecca, but something about her disconcerted Pival. She was not used to younger people being more confident than people of her own generation. Though she had felt comfortable with her the evening before, Pival felt uneasy with Rebecca in the light of day. She had never shared a meal with a servant before, and never had wine with anyone. But Rebecca did not act like a servant, even if Satya did, and perhaps that made some kind of difference.

Ram would have hated this self-possessed young woman, who said things in a tone of voice so sure and strong that you started nodding along with her before she even finished her thought. Watching Rebecca read the novel, whose length alone daunted Pival, she couldn't decide if she wanted to be close to the girl, and if such closeness would be possible at all. She so wished she could have asked her more about men, about sex. She was sure the girl had had it. She must have, drinking with men like that. What would it have been like, being with another man? She couldn't imagine it.

Her thoughts had swirled around in her mind throughout the car ride, confusing her, until errant potholes in the road dislodged them and she had to gather them up again. She tried to read from her book of poetry but couldn't focus on the pages without feeling ill herself, so instead she studied the lines on Satya's face as he groaned and slept, and the movements of Rebecca's expression as she read, and wondered when they would arrive. When they finally had, they were swept onto the boat, and now they were being swept off it again, and Pival still was not tired, only deflated, unused to feeling so many things in one day.

After the ride to the falls, families scattered in all directions. Many of them fled to the nearby parking lot, and Pival realized that these people lived close to the falls, or close enough to drive, at least, as large groups piled into large cars and honked their horns at each other, all as desperate to be the first to leave as they had been eager to be the first on the boat. This seemed odd to her, that there were so many of her own kind, and yet not her kind, living in this strange part of the country. She had assumed that America would look totally different from India. She had not anticipated that anything in America would remind her of home.

Pival swayed slightly, the adrenaline leaving her body. Satya declared that it was now time for an hour's rest at the hotel, followed promptly by dinner at Taj Mahal, no substitutions. It seemed that in Ronnie's absence Satya was trying to take on the mantle of all-knowing guide. For the moment, Pival was content to let him do so. Rebecca's lips tightened unhappily, but she said nothing, and together they escorted Pival to her room in the hotel, this time a Comfort Inn, which was not, to Pival's mind, all that comfortable. Everything in the hotel seemed to be a strange shade of mustard, which reminded Pival of Ronnie's ties, which had hung around his neck unfastened, more like scarves than neckpieces.

They had made their good-byes to Ronnie early that morning. *It was strange,* Pival thought, *how sad he was to watch us go.* He had always seemed irritated with her on the phone, and no special bond had formed between them during her time in New York. In fact, Pival had found his servility oppressive and his condescension even more so. More than that, she resented the fact that he had thought he would be able to pass as Indian, and by not objecting outright, she had let him get away with it. It was like her driver at home's announcing he had washed the windows after a rainfall.

She had known from the moment she had met Satya that she had been duped, that he was not Bengali at all. Following closely on the heels of this knowledge was an understanding that forged a bitterness deep in the pit of her stomach, that there were no Bengalis at this company whatsoever, only Bangladeshis trying to fool gullible tourists. She was not against Bangladeshis, at least not strongly, but she did not appreciate being lied to. Looking at the boy's dark face that first moment in the breakfast room of the hotel, Pival had felt whitehot realizing that Ronnie had fooled her, that he thought her so stupid she wouldn't know the difference between her own race and a foreigner, that Ram had been right after all.

She was everything he said she was, and deserved every insult he had hurled at her. She had opened her mouth ready to send the boy away, to cancel the trip, to demand her money back, to book a flight home. She wasn't sure what she would do but this would not work, none of it, she could not execute her plan being dragged along by this Bangladeshi boy. Worst of all she had been as incompetent, gullible, and useless as her husband had always claimed. Obviously she did not deserve to have what she wanted when she had bungled the business right from the start. She would never find Rahi. She could go home to Kolkata and die of shame.

And then the boy smiled at her, his slightly crooked white teeth like tilted sticks in his mouth, a strong jawline and a firm nose foretelling a handsome man somewhere in the future of this skinny boy.

Reaching down, he touched her feet gently with the tips of the fingers of his right hand. The breath caught in Pival's throat. It was a gesture of respect coming from a person whom she would have refused to look in the eye at home, a refugee who would only have come begging to her on the streets. Bengalis seldom encouraged the practice anymore, it was antiquated, demeaning, silly, a North Indian holdover best discarded. But it spoke of respect, regardless of being out of fashion. He honored her in the most menial way possible even as she had been so furious at being so close to him.

When she looked down at his bent head as he lowered himself to touch the dust of her feet, his skull was just like Rahi's. The whorls and spirals of his dark curls seemed identical. That maze of hair had been so familiar to her when Rahi was a child. She had combed it every day after he emerged from the bath, dripping all over like a wet dog. Gently smoothing his snarled knots with amla oil, she had worked a wooden comb carefully through the tangles, freeing him only once she was satisfied that every hair on his head was separated from all the others, that his scalp was fully conditioned. It had been their bath-time ritual, one she had adored until Ram had declared the boy too old for such treatment. He had insisted that she was making Rahi a sissy, a mama's boy, with her affection. Though she had stopped, when she saw his head she always felt a sense of knowledge and of pride. She knew his head better than any other part of him. So odd it was, now, to find her son's head on someone else's body.

She had closed her mouth and smiled as Satya straightened up, swallowing her anger whole. She would take this tour. What did it matter, anyway, that they had deceived her? All that mattered was traveling America to land in California, and if this boy with crooked teeth and her son's hair could take her, what did anything else matter?

Now this young man was leading her gently away from the falling water as the sun began setting above them and a group of attendants began preparing for what Pival assumed was the evening round of trips. She was glad they had made it in time to see the falls in the sun, even if they had left New York at three A.M. to do so. To feel the rainbows so close to her face, to see the light bouncing off the water and refracting to create such vivid streams of color, it had all been worth experiencing.

"I hate how fast the light is going." Satya and Pival both looked at Rebecca, confused. In this way Pival was not so far from Satya, she realized. Both of them were confused by the same turns of phrase, the American accents, the familiar words being used in unfamiliar ways. It was funny that she, a well-educated Bengali woman, could feel as lost as this Bangladeshi boy, but she refused to distance herself from him in her mind. It would not help her understand better anything Rebecca said by pretending to be less like Satya. Besides, Rebecca seemed to sense their mutual incomprehension, because she was already opening her mouth to speak again.

"The way it gets darker earlier in the night, as the winter comes. It's only September but already it's growing darker earlier. It happens every year, but still it surprises me. It's so depressing."

Pival had heard Rebecca use this word several times in the three days she had been with her. *Depressing.* It confused her. People did not speak so much of their inner feelings in Kolkata, and they did not use those terms unless speaking about someone with a serious mental disease. But Rebecca did not seem to suffer from a serious mental disease and threw the term out casually. She wondered if Rebecca felt exposed, saying such things in public. She had never told anyone what she felt, not since Rahi had moved away, and even before then, very rarely and only in moments of extreme pain or joy had she let her son into her mind. Telling people how she felt would be like showing them her naked body. And no one had seen her completely naked since she was ten years old.

She had thought that on her wedding night Ram would take her in his arms, undress her gently, uncover all her secrets. Many had been quick to warn her of the shame of a woman's body growing up, but her parents had not been that way, and as a girl she had heard soft sighs and giggles from her parents' bedroom sometimes at night. She had not expected the violent ecstasy of a romantic movie, but perhaps simple quiet pleasures. A lingering touch, a hidden kiss. But instead, it had been efficient, and fast, so fast she was on her back, her sari bunched up around her hips one moment, and then smoothing herself out while Ram drank a glass of water the next. It was always like that, from that moment on. She wondered what aroused Ram, what made him reach for her. It seemed to have nothing to do with her, her body, at all.

In the beginning of their marriage she had in fact tried to share her thoughts and feelings with Ram, but he had made it clear that this was neither welcome nor appropriate. Her feelings were her responsibility and no one else's. In that way he had done her a kindness, she knew. He had not tried to take anything of her inner self. In the end she knew there had been no malice in her husband, only anger. Whatever it was he had been looking for in their marriage, he soon realized Pival couldn't provide it. He was angry when she challenged him, and he was angry when she didn't. His anger had become cruelty but it had not started out that way, now that she thought about him clearly, from the distance provided by time and oceans. He simply had not wanted to be responsible for anyone's feelings but his own. What an impossible task, she thought, and a futile one.

He had wanted people to be the way he thought they should be, that is, more like him. Contained. Appropriate. Autonomous in every way. He had thought he had found that in Pival when he first met her, and when he understood he hadn't, he blamed himself, and her. He died thinking he had been the best husband and father he could, she knew. She hoped it had made him happy. In a way it was true; he had done the best he could. It was just that they had all deserved so much better.

Rebecca threw around how she felt with a generous carelessness. Pival was unsure whether she was happy or uncomfortable to learn what was in her companion's head. But what she said was true. The loss of the light was *depressing,* she thought, rolling the word around in her mind the way she'd rolled her first taste of wine on her tongue the night before.

"Yes. It is." She was proud of herself for agreeing, for daring to indicate her own feeling in this public space. Rebecca, however, just smiled vaguely, while Satya bobbed his head in another imitation of Ronnie and agreed over and over again, depressing, yes, that's just what it is, madam, absolutely correct, until Rebecca broke in.

"Well, it's not that bad. At least the falls were beautiful, right?"

"Stunning." Pival said it firmly, reverently, and Rebecca smiled. Satya steered them back into the mustard-colored lobby, reminding them that dinner was in one hour and ten minutes approximately and exactly so one hour was theirs. He implored Pival to rest. With that, the little group split apart like the peel of a banana.

Pival used the hour to take a bath instead of nap. She supposed she shouldn't want to get wetter after her time on the water, but she did, in fact, almost as an act of remembering what it had been like. The bathtub spout was a pale imitation, but if she closed her eyes and sank down she could pretend it was the same. When she submerged her head underwater the running tap sounded like thunder, and she smiled. Maybe this would be a way to kill herself, she thought; she could close her eyes and sink away and remember all the light.

She emerged moments later, sputtering, her lungs protesting at the lack of oxygen. Perhaps she would not be able to do it that way, she thought, rubbing soap on her arms briskly. It seemed her lungs wanted to breathe even if her mind didn't want them to. She would have to think of another way. If Rahi was there, of course, it wouldn't matter. The idea of his being alive filled her entire body with a fierce joy. If he wasn't, well, maybe she would just die right there, will herself dead. But if that didn't happen, she would have to think of a backup plan.

Dinner was mediocre but familiar, rice and curries and vegetables that all looked just the same and tasted brown. She thought longingly of her cook's fish curry, a delicate Bengali dish scented with mustard oil that couldn't have been further from this buttery northern mess. It had surprised Pival that Indian food seemed to mean only one thing in the United States when it was so varied at home. That said, of course, she had never known so many *other* kinds of food existed, that the world held so much more. It seemed insurmountable, to know and understand them all. The Thai curry of the evening before had stung her tongue but she had enjoyed it, liked how foreign each bite had felt. After the long day of travel, though, the familiar smells of cumin and cardamom and fennel seed comforted her, even if they weren't quite what she preferred.

The heavy Punjabi cooking reminded her of her childhood, of her parents' Punjabi maid and the dishes she had plunked on the table like large stones.

"Do you cook, Mrs. Sengupta?" Rebecca asked brightly. Pival finally realized what it was that was so disconcerting about the girl. She spoke to everyone as though they were equal, even Pival, whom she was serving. Satya frowned at the direct question, the familiar tone.

"I have always employed someone who cooks for me." Rebecca looked up at her, wide-eyed. Satya looked down. He had clearly anticipated her response. He had expected her to have a cook, she knew.

"Really? You have a cook? That's amazing. Is that normal?" Rebecca asked.

"Is this not normal here?" Pival asked, curious. Had Rahi had a cook? He didn't know how to cook, or at least hadn't in Kolkata. What had he eaten here? Funny, she had never even thought about it before. She just had assumed he had someone cook for him.

"Here most people don't have personal chefs unless they are super rich, like celebrities or politicians, that kind of thing. I'm sorry, I don't mean to be rude. It's just so amazing to me that you have a cook. Wow!" Rebecca spoke quickly.

"Where we are from, people have cooks. People hire people to do everything. People don't need to do things themselves, they can hire people. It's just like that." Satya spoke matter-of-factly, without a hint of bitterness in his tone.

Some part of Pival smarted at his statement, but she couldn't contradict it. She had always had help. Before her marriage it had been more limited, but after her marriage it had been constant. Although she had perhaps used household help poorly, it was certainly something she knew was normal. She had help even now, she knew, this white girl and this brown boy who were only there to serve her. What had Rahi had?

"Where do people get the food they need here? The Indian food?" she asked. Had Rahi lived on Coca-Cola and biscuits?

"They buy it, I guess," Rebecca said. "Or learn to make it."

The thought of Rahi cooking made Pival smile. She watched as Satya tore apart a piece of roti, preferring it to the naan Rebecca seemed to so enjoy. *It must be exotic to him,* Pival thought, *given the way Bangladeshis live on rice alone.* Pival herself had little use for any of the soft puffed Indian breads and preferred Western-style toast. Satya tore his roti into tiny pieces, letting each piece soak in the curry before scooping it up with his fingers and devouring it. Pival and Ram had not eaten with their hands, nor had they taught Rahi to do so, but Pival had seen it daily throughout her life, from her servants to men sitting and eating their daily thalis out on the street. For her generation, it had been one of the many ways they were taught not to be, no matter how delicious it looked, how satisfying it seemed like it would be. Sometimes it felt to Pival that Kolkata Bengalis still bore the brunt of British rule, some sixty years after it was over, desperate to impress their English overlords even now.

It was clear, watching Rebecca's reaction at every meal, that she had never seen people eat with their hands before. Pival was amused. Satya was not Rahi, no matter how much his hair reminded her of Rahi. He was not Ronnie, though he was his employee. He was something else.

At home Bangladeshis had no status. They did the worst jobs, if they had jobs at all. They were illegal immigrants with no rights and no names, just men who melted into the background and women who looked hungry all the time. They were almost never employed for domestic help, those tasks going to the women from nearby villages whose drunk husbands couldn't provide. Pival knew that many Bangladeshi women stood in line in Kolkata's red-light district along with Nepalese immigrants and the most destitute Indian women in the city. Pival was not supposed to know about this, about the women waiting in line for men to pick them out like fruit at the market, but she did; she had seen it on the news one night when Ram had been out at his club. There was an organization that tried to help these women, teaching them to sew bags and to earn money that way instead. It was run by a smiling white woman and Pival had been amazed by her courage, and for a moment had wanted to help, but then Ram came home and she turned off the news and went to bed.

Pival knew a bit about the war in Bangladesh; she remembered the invasion of East Pakistan, as the government had called it then, though she had been a girl when it happened, barely starting primary school. Later, history books called it a civil war, but that hadn't made much sense to her. Now they called it a revolution. After it had gone out of the newspapers she had forgotten about Bangladesh, or rather, forgotten about the war. She remembered that it existed, that people lived there, that many had left or been killed, but beyond that she had stopped thinking about it. It was a poor country with nothing her own nation seemed to want, and despite its origins as a part of the state of Bengal, the border disputes that most interested the people she knew and the papers she read were all with Pakistan. Now that this new country no longer bore the name Pakistan, it had ceased to matter. Her contemporaries were still more concerned with the Partition than the land that bordered theirs, despite the shared language. And she had long ceased to form opinions on political happenings in the world, knowing that Ram didn't want to hear them and Rahi was too far away to care.

"I would love to learn how to cook like this," Rebecca declared, reminding Pival of the original subject, cooking, another ability she did not have.

"So would I," she said, smiling ruefully.

Satya looked up from his meticulous roti and curry concoction. "I can teach you," he said. Stunned, Pival nodded slowly. If they came across a kitchen before they reached Los Angeles, she would remind him. And if they didn't, it didn't matter. The important thing was that he had offered to give her something. And that she had accepted.

22

They soon settled into a rhythm, Jake and Bhim. The conditions and circumstances of their relationship weren't easy for Jake, but Bhim couldn't believe how easy it seemed. He marveled at how comfortable they were, while Jake bit his tongue. Their little heap of shared experiences was too small for him to lose even one of them, so if Bhim thought it was easy, it was easy. They saw each other every other weekend, but once Bhim finished his coursework he spent two weeks a month with Jake, and two on his own in Berkeley, working. Jake offered to come to Berkeley again, but Bhim refused. He told him he preferred the apartment in Los Angeles, but Jake wondered if that was just another way for Bhim to separate their lives.

Bhim was constantly marveling about Jake's ability to keep a house, praising him for the simplest of tasks, like an easy weekday dinner or hanging a piece of art. Now that Bhim was practically living with him, Jake knew why. Bhim had no life skills, a fact he freely admitted with a cheerful shrug. He had never had to do anything for himself in Kolkata, he explained, and now he didn't know how to. Sometimes Jake wasn't sure if they were in a relationship or he was teaching Bhim how to be an adult. Sometimes he would come home to Bhim's standing in front of something like a leaky faucet or a dead lightbulb, studying it like one of his snails. Then, when Jake would fix the problem, Bhim would praise him lavishly, declaring himself unable to live without Jake. And yet he did, up in Berkeley. It made no sense.

Several weeks into their new schedule, Bhim made a comment

about Jake's having many friends. Jake was surprised; he wasn't very social and had a small circle. Most of the people he had known growing up in Los Angeles were elsewhere now. Everyone he had gone to college with back on the East Coast had stayed there. There were a few people from work he liked enough to actually see after office hours, and a few more friends from disastrous attempts at online dating that had birthed friendships, if not boyfriends. But his social circle when he met Bhim was small. If Bhim thought this was a lot, how many did Bhim himself have? Jake wondered.

Living in Los Angeles, Jake had always found it strange to be next to an ocean that he found never warm enough to swim in, given the icy currents of the North Pacific Gyre, which kept the water perpetually cold. When he told that to Bhim, Bhim admitted that this didn't matter much to him, for he couldn't swim at all. Jake had found this hilarious. It was inconceivable to him that Bhim did not know how to swim, not just because he was a marine biologist but because he didn't know anyone at all who couldn't swim. What would happen if he got into the water?

"My work is on the shore. I don't plan on getting into the water any time soon," said Bhim testily. He hated being laughed at.

"But what if you end up on a boat and it sinks and—"

"You are describing that movie with the tiger and the Indian boy."

"It was a book. I didn't see the movie," Jake intoned smugly.

"I don't need to know how to swim."

"*Everyone* needs to know how to swim!" Jake told him cheerfully, echoing his parents' own words to him long ago. To prove this, he enrolled Bhim in a beginner swimming class at the local Y. Bhim had refused to go, categorically, until Jake had dared him, asking him if he was afraid. Bhim bought himself a pair of trunks online that very evening and the next week the lessons began.

Jake dropped Bhim off in the morning like a proud parent, handing him a bag with a change of clothes and a prepacked lunch. Bhim, who had had some time to think about his rash acceptance of Jake's dare, looked gloomy at the prospect.

"I don't like getting my hair wet," he grumbled.

"And to think for a long time you didn't know you were gay," Jake quipped, and promised to pick him up in three hours.

As he waited for Bhim at a local coffee shop, sending out emails and making digital mock-ups of garden plans, he wondered, not for the first time, what things were generally Indian and what things were specifically Bhim. He didn't know much about Indians or India, and Bhim never wanted to talk about either. When pressed, he had admitted to Jake that he was worried that Jake would take Bhim's opinions, his experiences, and use them as facts. This would not be fair to India, Bhim had said. This might have been true, but the policy of silence did not feel very fair to Jake.

The only Indian person Jake knew other than Bhim himself was a lesbian from his softball league, Priya; they had sometimes gone out to dinner with Priya and her revolving door of girlfriends. She was second-generation Indian American, brash and cool with short Bettie Page bangs and a day job as an ADA for Los Angeles County. Her parents had accepted her sexuality because they had no choice, she'd explained. She was their only child and everyone around them had kids who were like her, individualistic and unwilling to bend to anyone's dictates but their own. Bhim had been in awe of Priya, and yet Jake knew that some part of him had looked down on her. He had asked him about it after they had met her and her most recent girlfriend for drinks. Part of Jake wondered if Bhim's disdain was because Priya had been born in America, but Bhim had carefully explained that actually it was because she was ethnically Punjabi, and those people, whatever else they were, were a little trashy. Jake had been amazed that Bhim had carried that stereotype with him out of India, but he said nothing. It was information, something to store away, some part of Bhim he hadn't had before.

Bhim had explained the stereotypes about Punjabi people, making Jake laugh uneasily, unsure whether he should find this funny or not. He lapped up Bhim's descriptions of Punjabi boys he had gone to school with, plump, loud people bursting with practical jokes. Bhim never spoke about people from home.

On the first day of the swimming lessons, Jake picked Bhim up promptly at one. He was careful to be on time at the end of what he assumed had been a negative experience. But when he drove up, Bhim looked tired but happy.

"How was it, slugger?"

"I floated. I felt weightless," Bhim explained, excited.

"Did you learn any strokes?" Jake asked.

"I learned how to float. This way I won't drown. Thank you. It was an excellent gift." Bhim seemed so happy that Jake didn't know how to explain that floating wasn't swimming. And of course it didn't matter, only somehow, it did. If you couldn't swim, how could you move forward? Jake said nothing. He had a surprise planned, something he thought Bhim would like, a reward for the day.

"Would you like to see a movie?"

Jake's surprise was a drag night at a theater that was featuring a Bollywood film from the nineties. South Asian men of all shapes and sizes had shown up dressed as the heroine of the film, with long black wigs and hilariously outrageous saris swishing everywhere as they got up and danced together in each and every one of the ten musical numbers.

Jake thought that Bhim would be delighted, but he soon realized that he was far more entertained than his boyfriend, who was sitting silently beside him, watching the movie with a deep frown of concentration.

It was amazing to see, all the people playing the female lead and not a single male hero in sight dancing the men's parts, just a rush of brightly colored figures running and bobbing away from nothing as the sitar twanged in the background and the high-pitched nasal singing rang in Jake's ears. He loved it, laughing and humming along, although he did not know the tunes, as Bhim beside him grew more withdrawn.

Jake had planned the evening for weeks, ever since he saw the ad on a local gay lifestyle blog. He had bought special Indian snacks at an ethnic market and he had even found a soda Bhim had mentioned that he couldn't find in the States, something that was like Coke but wasn't Coke. He'd thought Bhim would be thrilled. But his face said that he was not. They left long before the four-hour film finished, not that Jake knew what was happening anyway.

On the way home Bhim mused softly about how strange it all had been, how much he had loved that movie as a child, how sad he had felt watching it without his mother, and what a funny feeling it had given him to watch men pretend to be women. He tried to explain how he didn't find it *wrong*, per se, but Jake could only hear the strain in Bhim's voice and the way Jake had failed to make him happy, and he couldn't pay attention. Bhim pleaded with Jake to understand, and he nodded, and looked out onto the streets of the city and let the songs of the movie play in his head, drowning out Bhim's voice.

Bhim left Los Angeles the next day to go back to Berkeley and study his snails, and he was still thrilled that he could float. He kissed Jake tenderly, and thanked him for the swimming lessons, and did not mention the movie. Jake knew they would never see a Bollywood film together again, that some other door had been closed.

He was running out of doors. What would he do when they were all shut, and it was just him and Bhim in a locked room? Would Jake be enough? Would Bhim? Would he ever have the relationship he wanted? Would they ever even live together? Would they get married? Could Bhim even dare to think of such a thing? He tried to put the thoughts out of his head, but when he closed his eyes he saw the bright Bollywood film and Bhim, refusing to see the happiness of the men dancing proud and free.

23

To: boss@americabestnumberonetours.com
To: boss@americabestnumberonetours.com
From: satyaroy57@yahoo.com

Boss, writing from Niagara just now. Hotel has computer room with complimentary internet for two minutes only. Reached falls successfully after minor troubles on road not worry other cars not us. Madam has enjoyed falling water no sickness at boat motion and also aloo gobi at India restaurant. Kind very nice roti. Rebecca companion reads mostly. No gifts purchased at shop. Weather is cold but madam does not yet complain.

Satya

To: boss@americabestnumberonetours.com
From: Rebecca.Elliot.74@gmail.com

Mr. Munshi,

All quiet on the western front! Mrs. Sengupta declared Niagara to be "inspiring" and also declared that the car ride was "bearable." Satya assured her that dinner would be "best possible" but Mrs. Sengupta also seems to enjoy the American continental breakfast. No health issues or affronts to modesty at any time. Satya knows many interesting facts, which he is able to share. We are all eager for the glass museum

tomorrow! A whole museum of glass. What a treat. Mrs. Sengupta is
looking forward to it!
Best,
Rebecca

While the trip to Niagara had seemed an eternity to Satya, the
trip back breezed by. He felt reborn in the early morning light as their
car, with a new driver this time, a Chinese man named John, picked
them up at the Comfort Inn and had them on the road by eight A.M.
Their next destination was Philadelphia, but they would be stopping
on their long ride for a few hours at the Corning Museum of Glass.
Ronnie had carefully explained to Satya that this was an important
stop along the trip, because Satya would receive a small percentage of
whatever his guests spent in the museum shop, and therefore it was
vital in order to maintain this symbiotic relationship between guide
and museum, no matter how little interest his tour group might have
in the destination.

Satya had no problem with this system; in fact, it felt like how
things worked at home. Bargaining with people felt much more comfortable than anything else, and Satya wasn't sure how to feel about
the fact that most things in America had definitive prices, that he
couldn't haggle his way around anything. He wasn't totally comfortable with the idea that prices couldn't shift, wasn't sure he wasn't
being cheated. At least at home he had *known* about the real costs
of things and seen the deception as it was happening. Here he could
only speculate. Sideways had always been the only way to approach
anything. He was not accustomed to front doors.

It wasn't difficult to persuade Mrs. Sengupta to go to the Corning
Museum of Glass, much to his relief. It was Satya himself who had
no interest in the museum, and he wasn't sure how he would have

sold the experience to someone else. He couldn't imagine making an entire museum for glass, and to his mind it spoke to the wastefulness of the United States. Growing up, the only glass thing Satya had known had been windows. He had never drunk from a cup made of glass before his arrival in New York. His grandmother's kitchen had contained metal drinking glasses, small, cool containers that left his mouth with a pleasant metallic taste long after the murky water was gone. He missed that taste in his mouth. In a glass, water just tasted like nothing.

They reached the Corning Museum of Glass within four hours of leaving Niagara Falls, which John assured them was excellent time. After the fits and starts of the journey the day before, it had been a delight to arrive at their destination with no stopping whatsoever. It was not quite fast enough for Satya's bladder, however, as he badly needed to urinate. He would have been happy to do so on the side of the road, but that didn't seem to be common here like it was at home. Hardly taking notice of the museum itself, he waved to the two women and John, and rushed through the entrance to find a bathroom. When he emerged into the large sunlit lobby, he found himself staring up into a green vortex of delicate spiraling light. There seemed to be a plant of some kind growing. Blinking, he realized this was actually a structure fixed to the ground. Stepping back to join Mrs. Sengupta and Rebecca as they marveled at the piece, Satya understood that the thing was made of glass.

It looked like a sea creature, or a wild jungle plant, as he had first thought. It looked alive. He had never seen anything solid look so much like it was in motion, the way the light from the high large windows all around illuminated different parts of the spirals. He wanted to reach out and touch it, but he knew he wasn't allowed. He stared at it for a long time, and when he looked around for his charge and fellow employee he saw that they were gone, only to be replaced with a small group of little children, whose gaping mouths, he realized as he shut his own, had been a mirror image of his.

He barely had noticed the building when he entered, but now he saw that it was a mixture of metal curves and glass plates, bouncing the light around. He had only been inside one museum since he was a small child. Perhaps they all looked like this now. He tried to keep his mouth closed, but he was still amazed, no matter what his face was doing, at the glass and what it could be shaped into. Perhaps this wouldn't be so bad.

He found Mrs. Sengupta and Rebecca waiting in line for tickets, and he quickly joined them, inserting himself in front of both of them so he could arrange for things before they had a chance to try to do so. Rebecca rolled her eyes at this, but Mrs. Sengupta seemed amused, so Satya surged forward, asking for *three passes precisely to all parts of the museum please no exceptions thank you.* The clerk looked at him as if about to object, but Satya held his gaze, giving his bargaining face, eyes implying that he wouldn't stand for any nonsense or conversation. The clerk nodded warily and asked for the fee.

Satya, sure this fee had been slightly lowered for him, smiled at the confused clerk triumphantly and waved at the women to continue onward. He counted out change from the money belt he had strapped on underneath the top layer of the three shirts he was wearing. First was his new flannel, then a lighter cotton shirt from home, and finally a white T-shirt underneath it all. He was terrified of the cold, and while he had been sweating in his layers thus far, he knew he would thank himself for his foresight when they reached a colder state.

He collected their passes from the admissions desk and ushered the women through into the body of the museum.

"Okay, so what do we want to see?" Rebecca chirped.

It was Satya's turn to roll his eyes. "This is a museum for glass. We will look at the glass."

Rebecca sighed and handed Satya a folded pamphlet, which, as Satya realized upon examining it, was a map of the museum. "There are thousands of things to see here. Centuries of glass represented. There is industrial glass, artistic glass, scientific glass, the town of Corning's relationship with glass. It's all glass."

"There is a museum for everything here, I think," Mrs. Sengupta observed.

Satya paged through the map quickly. His own research materials, that is, the guidebook that Ronnie had told him to read, had not included a map of the museum, and now that he looked he realized this museum was so extensive they might not be able to see it all if they had a week, let alone the two and a half hours carefully budgeted for this place, which included a fifteen-minute tea break in the café and, most importantly, the half an hour allotted to the gift shop. He turned to Mrs. Sengupta.

"What kind of glass are you most wanting to notice, madam?"

Mrs. Sengupta looked a bit overwhelmed.

"There is quite a bit to see, yes?" intoned the widow, her voice breathy. Rebecca and Satya confirmed this, nodding. "Then we will start from the beginning, and see what we can do, shall we?"

"The beginning, madam?" Satya had no idea where this museum began or ended.

"The beginning of glass."

Ten minutes and two false turns later, the trio gazed upon a museum display case proudly declaring that it was "glass in nature." Satya had imagined that he would be guiding them through the museum and was now nervously wondering how fast he could read the signs and interpret them before Mrs. Sengupta or Rebecca, for that matter, saw them. But he soon realized that neither woman had any intention of staying together or being guided. Rebecca looked around and after perusing a few of the strange rocky structures behind the display cases, continued on, heading for a display on Roman glassmaking techniques. Satya was about to protest but she waved her hand behind her and called that she would meet them in the gift shop in two hours. He turned to Mrs. Sengupta, only to find that she herself had moved on. He rushed toward her.

"Do you need assistance, madam?"

Mrs. Sengupta smiled at him vaguely. "Are you an authority on glass, Satya?"

"I have been trained to guide you in many things—"

"I believe I can walk through this museum on my own. We have museums in Kolkata, you know. Although not"—and here she paused to look around appreciatively—"as well kept as this one. We do not know how to treat our own history. And then we become angry when others take it away from us. Sometimes I wonder if we deserve anything at all."

Satya couldn't help the spurt of indignation that bubbled up in his chest at this statement. Though Mrs. Sengupta reminded him of his grandmother, making him feel protective of her, when she spoke he remembered that she was Indian, Bengali, and in her own mind, above him. She talked about history because she was lucky enough to have it. It had not been ripped from her by every surrounding country and she had not been left with something bloody and dirty where a legacy should have been.

There were two museums Satya knew of in Sylhet, one for folk art and one celebrating General Osmani, who had led the Bangladeshi army to victory against Pakistan in 1972. Schoolchildren were taken to the one for General Osmani. The one for folk art, the Museum of the Rajas, had been unknown to Satya until his grandmother had dragged him there when he was fourteen and sullen about everything. She had spent the visit to the museum imploring him to be proud of his Bangla heritage, of all the things their people had given to the world. All he saw were dusty artifacts and photographs of dead people he didn't know and didn't care about. And no one else cared about them either, did they? Wasn't that what this museum proved about Bangladesh? That no one cared?

His grandmother had made him promise he would stay after she died, that he would work and study and be part of the new generation of Bangladeshi citizens, the new group of people set to change their country, ready to rebuild it and make it better. He had broken that promise as easily as breathing. Unbidden, the image of Ravi rose up in his mind, Ravi's family, the promises to send something back for them. Would Ravi do that now? Should Satya?

When you had no history, you couldn't be expected to understand it, and if this woman knew anything about what it was like she wouldn't have said a word.

Something must have shown on his face, despite Ronnie's admonitions about being deferential, because Mrs. Sengupta took one small step back. Satya tried to smile, to make it better, but he was just baring his teeth. Mrs. Sengupta looked down, and Satya felt that he had won something, somehow. It was a rare feeling, but it didn't feel as good as he had hoped.

"I will go at my own pace, Satya. I am an old woman, and I need to take things in my own time." Satya nodded once, the comment about her age pulling him back to remember the respect he owed her.

"Rebecca gave me my own map. I promise I will not get lost." Satya nodded again, and Mrs. Sengupta and her funny little smile drifted off in the direction of Glasses of the Islamic World. Satya stayed where he was, in natural glass, looking around at himself reflected in the surfaces of the exhibition cases.

The glass in the exhibit was strange to him, and he did not at first understand how it was glass. There were strange rocks, and some shiny black oval objects that fascinated him. The display card told him these were obsidian tools, carved out of glassy rock and used in the Stone Age. This satisfied him, until he wondered what the Stone Age was.

In his limited Hindu education, which had mostly consisted of his grandmother dragging him to temples to make offerings and drone out prayers, and then listening to her lecturing him all the way home about the perfidy of priests, he had been forced to read a handful of books describing the ages of the world, and positioning him and his life well within Kaliyuga, the age of chaos, of arguments, and of men's irreverence and badness. The other ages were better, as Satya had read, holier, and full of better harmony.

But as he looked at these rocky glass specimens, created from molten lava and lightning crashing against the earth, he wondered if the other ages of life had been any better. He wondered how holy this Stone Age could have been. He could not tear his eyes away from the shiny black of the obsidian. What had it been, a spearhead, maybe? Something that had been used to kill, certainly; it was sharp and carved for violence. There was nothing delicate or artistic about it. He couldn't understand how most of the fragile glass objects around him had survived. But this could survive anything, this black mass of twisting shards and sharp edges.

He looked at it for a long time, and after that, nothing else caught his interest. He had no use for delicate cups and vases, not when he had seen what glass could really do.

Passing through the rest of the displays, Satya caught sight of a glassblowing demonstration. He had never seen glass being blown before, and he wasn't sure exactly what was happening as he watched a man with a long metal pipe inhale deeply and exhale through the pipe down to a small orange bulb at the other end, which slowly began to expand, a syrupy bubble rising by the efforts of the man's lungs. The glass puffed and expanded, a glowing-hot sphere. Satya watched, entranced for a moment, but then walked on. He still preferred a metal cup over anything else.

He had to admit it was a better museum than the two he had seen back home. He hadn't known a museum could be so nice, frankly. If he had come here with Ravi they would have made fun of the informational plaques and probably tried to follow women around without their noticing instead of looking at the glass. He felt a kind of hollow loneliness that made him want to break a fragile display. He walked on, trying not to see anything else as he passed cases by.

Satya found himself a small nook in the corner of the massive and crowded gift shop, and, after a lifetime of being able to sleep anywhere, he soon was dozing off with his cheek against the side of a display case. Sometime later his dream of carving his own glass tools in a glass world as Kali watched him was interrupted by a shadow falling over him. He cracked open his eyes to see John the driver scowling down at him.

"Twenty minutes until we go."

"I have to wait for them to shop—"

"Twenty minutes. We go, I go. I not care. Philadelphia before night. Okay?" And with that, the driver was gone, disappearing out of the store and off into the parking lot. As he rose from his bench, Satya's limbs protested, cramped from their uncomfortable resting position, but he had no time for that as his chest constricted with panic. Where were they? They had promised not to get lost, they had said they would be back there in time for—

"There you are." Satya turned around to find Mrs. Sengupta and Rebecca looking at him.

"We couldn't find you in any of the galleries. You must have looked at them quickly," Rebecca said. She seemed happy, shining as brightly as the glass around them. "This place is amazing, don't you think? I loved it!"

"Very nice," said Mrs. Sengupta in her quiet way. "Are there many places like this?"

Satya didn't know the answer. Did Mrs. Sengupta mean glass museums?

"Do you mean glass museums?" Rebecca asked. Satya scowled.

"Places where things can be studied like this. Things like glass, or, or the sea."

"Oh, yeah. Tons. My dad always said growing up he learned more in museums and libraries than anywhere else."

Satya stared at Rebecca. He supposed it was true; in all the guide-books he had read there were so many museums mentioned, but he had always skipped them, never thinking anyone would want to go to one when there was so much to see outside. "Have you looked around the shop, madam?" he asked. They were running out of time. If he didn't get her to buy something there was no telling what Boss would do.

"We did our shopping, although I did warn Mrs. Sengupta about the insanity of taking glass objects on a cross-country tour." Rebecca held up a small shopping bag.

Mrs. Sengupta frowned, her brow wrinkling with worry. "He said he would wrap them securely. He *insisted*—"

"Hey, if glass can survive the fall of Rome, it can clearly survive America. Satya, that cashier said if we had a guide he would like to speak to you." Rebecca pointed toward the counter. "I'm just going to run to the restroom and then we'll meet you in the car? Can't *wait* to get in a van again, it's been, what, two hours? Oh, how I missed it." And Rebecca was gone. She was like a hurricane, leaving him stunned with her energy. It wasn't only him that Rebecca overwhelmed, Satya realized, seeing his own dazed face reflected in Mrs. Sengupta's slightly shell-shocked expression.

It was so easy for the American girl to be excited about things, strange things.

He wondered at Rebecca, suddenly bubbling with happiness. It confused him. How did it come so easily? He felt a bit disgusted by her. But hadn't he left home to be happy, too? So why was he annoyed by her pleasure?

Picking up Mrs. Sengupta's bag, he took his cut from the cashier, collected Rebecca at the restroom, and led the group to the car.

Sitting in the front seat, Satya opened the window and hung his head out like big dogs he had seen in other cars. As the air hit his face, he enjoyed its chill. It felt like something cutting his face, like glass. He closed his eyes and imagined it was the dark glass of the Stone Age, cutting away the things he loathed about himself. But when he opened his eyes, he was still there, all of him.

They had made good time reaching Philadelphia, pulling into the historic district of the city just as the first stars were blinking above Independence Hall. Rebecca was relieved; she hated being in a van.

The city around her was familiar. When she was growing up in DC, they had taken trips to Philadelphia and Richmond, Virginia, after all the local monuments were exhausted. Rebecca had always preferred going north rather than south. It was closer to New York. Washington's theater scene had only just begun to grow during Rebecca's childhood, and her parents had also taken her on trips to Philadelphia for plays and dance performances. Although it was nothing compared to Broadway, thirteen-year-old Rebecca had announced haughtily after a production of *Hairspray*. Though she had disdained the city as a child, she liked it now, with its cobblestone streets and quaint comfort and cheap drinks. And she'd have killed now to be in a regional production of *Hairspray*.

Ronnie had told her that his tours used to stop in Harrisburg, not Philadelphia, because it was the state capital and closer to Niagara Falls, but too many people had complained about the subpar Indian dining options, so now he routed through Philadelphia. Rebecca was grateful for the change. She had a friend, Stephanie, in a production at a local theater, and she planned to meet her that night for a drink. Now it seemed with their early arrival and Mrs. Sengupta's clear exhaustion, she might be able to sneak away and make the show itself. She dreaded seeing friends in regional productions that paled in comparison to what they had dreamed of in New York, but she could pretend it had been wonderful for a few hours, and besides, it would be an opportunity to dictate her own time.

The trip was already trying, and it was only their second day on the road together. She shouldn't have been annoyed, really. Her duties as companion were minimal. She had to report to Ronnie daily, which she had done so far, sending out emails she was sure he wouldn't actually read. She described the activities and added anecdotes that made her and Satya look good, but there wasn't much to tell, really. All she did was provide female supervision and clarify some American customs as needed.

Her charge, at least, was intelligent and adapted quickly. Once told something, Mrs. Sengupta would close her eyes and mumble it under her breath, and then, in moments of brief confusion, she would do the same thing again, searching back through her mental files, Rebecca supposed, to find the pertinent piece of information. It was like watching someone pray, the way she focused on remembering something. Sometimes Mrs. Sengupta asked things—what was this city like or that one, how many Indians were there, what was it like living there—and Rebecca answered as best she could, but whatever the widow was looking for, she hadn't found it yet, because she always seemed disappointed in the answers. Maybe she hadn't found the right question to ask yet, Rebecca thought.

In the glass museum she had watched Mrs. Sengupta in one of the contemporary glass rooms. Some pieces she had barely glanced at and some had mesmerized her. She had read none of the descriptions.

She had asked Mrs. Sengupta, at one of the moments when they had been in the same gallery, whether she was okay alone. Mrs. Sengupta had smiled at that.

"I love being alone. And I never am. At home, no one ever chooses to be alone, especially not women. It is so nice here, being alone. And so strange."

Rebecca had been shocked. What did that mean, no one was ever alone? Being with people for even an hour could drive Rebecca insane sometimes. How could anyone live that way?

She would have liked to ask Mrs. Sengupta more about her thoughts during her time in the museum, but as soon as they got into the car, the widow had closed her eyes and folded her hands in her lap, a sign that she was trying to sleep. She was content to be dictated to, which disturbed Rebecca, who could not imagine wanting to be told what to do except by a director onstage. She supposed this was the appeal of a tour; you didn't have to think about anything at all.

Satya, too, was unlike anyone else she knew, and Rebecca could not understand him. She was used to sizing up men quickly, but Satya had eluded her usually astute intuition. He did not ogle her, which was good, but he also did not listen when she spoke, which was infuriating. She had found herself speculating on whether this was a cultural handicap—perhaps Satya hadn't been raised to listen to women—but the thought made her feel patronizing and imperialist, so she brushed it aside in search of another explanation. Maybe she had offended him in some way? It shouldn't have mattered any-more, but she was still angry about his fabrication on the Circle Line tour, and now she listened to him attentively, alert to more misinformation.

Rebecca barely noticed when they pulled into the hotel parking lot. This time it was a Comfort Inn on the Delaware River, and she helped Satya with the bags.

The hotel room was as soulless as the others. Rebecca was already tired of these budget hotels, although she nodded her head when Satya praised them. He showed the hotel suites off with the presen-tational skill of a talk-show host, Rebecca thought, as if he had any-thing to do with how they looked or their level of cleanliness.

Mrs. Sengupta barely seemed to notice Satya's talking. She looked dead on her feet. Perhaps the jet lag had finally caught up with her. She stumbled a bit as she walked on the carpeted floor into her room, Rebecca and Satya dragging her bags behind them. She sat on the bed carefully, as if afraid she might fall down.

Satya and Rebecca exchanged a worried glance.

"Madam? Are you feeling tired only? Is some kind of sickness there?"

"When was the last time you had some water?" Rebecca asked. Mrs. Sengupta shrugged listlessly. Rebecca quickly filled a glass in the bathroom and set it in front of the widow, urging her to drink.

"It is from the bathroom?" Mrs. Sengupta asked doubtfully.

"Just drink, please," Rebecca said firmly, ignoring Satya's immedi-ate offer to find bottled water. Compelled by Rebecca's authoritative tone, Mrs. Sengupta drank all her water. Rebecca refilled the glass, and it was dutifully swallowed as Satya glared.

"Are you having hunger, madam?"

Mrs. Sengupta shook her head. Lunch had been pizza at a rest stop and Mrs. Sengupta had managed to eat four entire slices by herself.

"I am still tasting lunch. I want to rest now, only." Both of them said the word *only* more than was necessary, Rebecca observed. Perhaps it made more sense in Bengali. Mrs. Sengupta was making small shooing motions now with her hands.

"Go, go. I want to bathe and rest. I am perfectly safe and sound, I can assure you. Go. We are here two nights. Please, enjoy the city only. You are young, nah? Breakfast can be late tomorrow. We can start at eight." Satya seemed about to protest when Mrs. Sengupta shot him a look. "It is my trip or isn't it?" Apparently the water had done its task. She was herself again, the color restored to her face and her aristocratic tone firm.

Satya bowed his head and nodded as he backed out of the room. Rebecca followed him. Turning from the door as they closed it behind them, Rebecca looked at Satya. She wondered if some of her concerns were ringing in his mind.

"Do you think she's okay?"

Satya shrugged. "She said she wanted resting. So here it is. She will rest."

"She looked sick, didn't she?"

To her surprise, Satya almost snorted at this.

"Sick is different."

Rebecca instantly resented his superior tone.

"Maybe we should have some broth sent up to her."

Satya shrugged. "Why? Bengali women are like this. Weak."

"She doesn't seem that weak to me—"

"Sick is sick. I have seen sick. She is fine."

Rebecca looked at Satya, who was agitated by the conversation. She decided to end it. He knew Indians better than she did, didn't he? Or Bengalis, or whatever. She knew that they were from different parts of the world, but to her, everything they did looked and felt so similar. She wondered if she was just blinded by the accent.

"Okay, well, I'm heading out. Bye, Satya." She looked back and realized Satya was hesitating outside of his own suite. Though he should have been thrilled at the evening off, he seemed a bit lost.

"Listen, you can still have the Indian dinner, Satya—in fact, you can have three."

The boy scowled.

"And what will she eat? You want to get me in trouble? Tell me to eat it all and then run to Ronnie, crying hunger? You want to fire me so you can guide?"

"I'm not going to call Ronnie. That's not what I was saying at all. I don't want your job. It's going to go to waste if you don't . . . you know what? I don't care." Rebecca started to walk back toward her room.

"Please. I did not mean that. I am sorry." Rebecca turned back to see Satya standing in the badly lit hallway, looking miserable.

"It's fine."

"I could not have the meal in anyways. I don't know where it is."

Rebecca sighed. The longing in Satya's voice concerned her. He ate ravenously at every meal, piling on plate after plate of rice and patting his nonexistent stomach after the waiters politely told him, as they had at each place, that he couldn't have any more of the buffet, because he had exceeded what they had imagined "all you can eat" could possibly mean. More than that, though, he looked lonely. She checked her phone. It was seven. She should be able to call a cab, drop him at whatever Taj Mahal or Bombay Grill was tonight's destination, and make it to the play in time to pick up the ticket her friend had put aside for her.

"I'll take you. I'm going out anyway. Come on. Let's go." She waited for him to catch up with her and pressed the elevator button going down.

Fifteen minutes later they were in a cab, another car, Rebecca thought, another backseat, and another opportunity for Satya to be carsick. She thought about suggesting that he take the subway back to the hotel once he had gorged himself on curry after curry, but Philadelphia's terrible public transportation system was one of her least favorite things about visiting. Besides, she didn't know if she could trust him to make it back from the downtown restaurant without his guidebook in hand. Her musings made her grimace. Perhaps she *was* trying to be the guide. Satya was the professional. Shouldn't she let him figure it out on his own?

"Where are you going? Not to the meal?" Satya's question interrupted the ones she was asking of herself. She shook her head to clear it.

"Does your head itch? Is it lice? I know a cure." They amazed her, these questions. Ronnie had asked her several in the same vein, things she would consider highly inappropriate. He had inquired about the timing of her menstrual cycle, as it might affect her moods on the trip, and when she had mentioned her birth control he had probed into how that worked with a fascinated expression and a troubling lack of knowledge of the female reproductive system. Yet when they had passed by a Victoria's Secret in Manhattan both Satya and Ronnie had reddened, coughed, and apologized profusely to Mrs. Sengupta for the wicked, shameless nature of the West. She didn't understand it.

"I don't have lice, Satya. I'm going to a play." Satya frowned. Rebecca had realized that Satya frowned when he was thinking, so she wasn't offended.

"A friend of mine is in it, so, I didn't think I would get to see it, but. Yeah. A play. I act, so. It's nice to see stuff. When I can. In New York, usually, but. Yeah." God, she was babbling. What did she care if he approved? Had he ever even *seen* a play?

"I have not ever seen play." Rebecca started. Had she asked the question out loud or had Satya volunteered the information? She looked at his face, frowning again, and before she knew it she asked:

"Do you want to?"

He wouldn't say yes. He couldn't possibly give up an Indian buffet for a night at the theater, could he?

"Is there food there?"

They were early for the show, which was good, because it allowed Rebecca to purchase the extra ticket for Satya, rebuffing his attempt to pay. She was sure he would hate it. Or not understand it. Or be mad at her for bringing him to it. Or his lack of interest would anger her. Something bad would happen, she knew. After all, what else could occur when she brought her Bangladeshi tour guide to a production of *Three Sisters*? What could the lives of wealthy Russians in the late 1800s mean to Satya? The play had been translated into English, but Rebecca was certain that it might as well be in Russian for all he would understand.

She settled him in with an array of candies, cookies, and chips, the only food available at the theater, and then returned to the concession stand herself, thanking god fervently that this was a modern theater that had adopted the civilized practice of letting its patrons order wine. She conned them into selling her a whole bottle, promising she would keep it discreetly under her chair and only refill her glass in the blackouts between scenes. Rushing back to her seat before the show began, she saw that Satya was almost halfway through the snacks, and she checked her program to make sure there were enough intermissions to keep him fed.

"It's a long play," Rebecca told him worriedly.

He nodded, his mouth smeared lightly with chocolate. "That's good, no? Like two shows for one."

"It's three hours long, at least. Sorry."

Satya just shrugged. Long stories didn't bother him. "Is there a break? To be using the facilities?"

"Yes, three, actually."

"Huh. The actors must get tired, running around up there." Here Satya gestured to the stage and whistled softly between his two front teeth. "In movies all the work has already been done, yes? But here they have to run run run. Phew."

"Maybe they like it," Rebecca said a little bitterly. She would have killed to be up there. She remembered her horrible Anya audition and shuddered.

She opened her playbill and looked at the tiny black-and-white photos of smiling and serious headshots. There was Stephanie; she'd chosen a serious shot for Chekhov, of course. Her eyes looked huge in her face and her slight frown recalled long Russian winters. Rebecca felt a stab of jealousy. It might have been a Philadelphia production but Stephanie was doing it, going onstage and *being* Irina.

"Do you like it?" Rebecca looked up. Satya was now on the last snack. He inhaled food like an anteater. "Do you like running around up there?"

"I love it."

"Do you do it a lot?"

"Not anymore."

"Why—"

Rebecca was happy that the lights were fading so she didn't have to respond. She was afraid it would be a question she didn't have the answer to, or worse, one that made her feel even more terrible about herself than she did in this moment, watching a friend onstage and loathing her for it. Her concerns about Satya's experience were crowded out by her own self-pity. The opening lines of the play rang like a bell and then Stephanie, in a period wig and white gown, stared out into the audience:

"To go back to Moscow. To sell the house, to make an end of everything here, and off to Moscow."

Rebecca had to admit, mollified by wine, that it was really quite a good production. The direction was good, and the cast was strong, including Stephanie, who made Irina seem young but not spoiled, fresh.

The story was so simple, really, she mused as she sipped the wine, which improved from bad to passable as her taste buds numbed under its onslaught. There were people designed to stay in one place, trapped there, like the three sisters, who repeated over and over again that they wanted to leave, but whose lives never changed, never moved anywhere, never actually made leaving happen. And then there were those always leaving, always moving on, the army with its constant march and parade of new towns and new women to seduce and desert.

She wondered how Mr. Ghazi was doing, and if the map store was staying clean and if he was remembering to switch to decaffeinated tea in the afternoons for his heart. Seeing people onstage that she cared about made her think about the people she cared about in life. She wished there were more of them.

When the lights came up after the first act, Satya ran out of his seat to use the facilities, as he had called them, and because of the line there and at the concession stand, did not return more than thirty seconds before the lights dimmed. After the second act it was Rebecca who had to use the restroom, and while she waited in line she looked over the playbill again. She was surprised to learn how many of the cast were local actors. She had known there was theater outside of New York, had heard about select companies making work all over the country, but it had always seemed a little unreal to her. Now, confronted with the actuality of these people and their résumés filled with plays and movies and even television, sadness began to sink in. It followed her back into her seat and left her sobbing at the end of the third act. She didn't cry because the play was sad, although it was, but because she wished she could be in this production and that this production were in New York. Wished she were inside something, not outside, watching it happen.

Wiping her eyes as the lights came up for the final intermission, she looked over at Satya, who was looking away from her, uncomfortable with her display of emotion. Well, at least he wasn't sleeping.

"What do you think so far?" Rebecca sniffed out, looking through her pockets for a tissue. Suddenly a hand holding a handkerchief popped in front of her face, and she turned to see Satya offering her this piece of cloth that belonged more to the world of the play in front of them than their own. She smiled a watery smile and took the offering, blowing her nose loudly. She looked at the handkerchief and then back at Satya, who was still looking away from her, unwilling to see her cry.

"I'll wash this and give it back to you. Okay?" He shrugged. "So, what do you think? Of the play?"

"Is it done?"

"No, not yet. One more act to go."

"I will decide what I think when it is done."

The lights dimmed a final time and the story stuttered to its inevitable conclusion, leaving everyone exactly where they had been when it started. Rebecca did not cry again. Her emotions had been used up in the third act, and she had nothing left for the final moments. Instead of being moved by the ending, as she had been in the past, she was left dissatisfied, angry with all the people who had resigned themselves to things they did not want.

She clapped loudly, however, to drown out her discomfort. Satya, next to her, clapped as well, hesitantly at first and then vigorously, throwing his hands together the way children do, thrilled at the noise they can make.

As they walked out of the theater Satya looked at her, frowning again.

"It was sad, wasn't it? Why couldn't they leave and go to Moscow?"

"I don't know. They just can't." The response struck Rebecca as unsatisfactory, and she wanted to give a different one, but Satya was already nodding.

"It's just like that." He seemed so much more content with this idea than she was, so much more comfortable with things just being, with people being stuck somewhere and refusing to make choices that propelled their lives in different directions, instead preferring to stay where they were, locked in time and space.

"There were things I didn't understand, but I liked it. I like that they have each other in the end. They are a family. It is sad, but there is that." Satya spoke thoughtfully. Rebecca was struck dumb. The family of the play seemed so poisonous to her, so destructive in the way they clung to each other. She had always thought any one of them could have survived better on their own than stuck with all the others. But Satya had seen this family as the preservation of hope, a route to happiness. Part of her was tempted to dismiss him. But she couldn't. Something about the simplicity with which he had analyzed the play struck her as right and true. She had heard a dozen sophisticated academic explanations of Chekhov, but as she watched it, it did seem that simple to her, the people, the way they moved through the world; Satya had seen it.

Disposing of her empty wine bottle in a nearby recycling container, she saw Satya watching her, curious.

"My friend was in the play. She was Irina, the young one. Do you want to meet her?"

Satya's eyes lit up. "She's an actress in the play? You know her?"

"I'm an actress. I know lots of people in lots of plays." Satya didn't notice her sarcastic tone, however, so excited was he at the prospect of meeting someone he had just seen pretend to be someone else. Rebecca wished someone would be as excited to meet her, someday.

"Why are the bins different colors?" Satya was pointing to the blue recycling bins that sat next to the black trash cans in the lobby around them as they waited for Stephanie to finish changing and appear to her loving public.

"Oh, the blue is for things that can be recycled. So, stuff that you can reuse, like paper, which they grind down into pulp to make more paper, and glass, which they remelt to make new bottles and stuff like that. It's good, for the environment."

"We don't have separate bins at home."

"Oh."

"I used to sell bottles from people's trash. I'm glad they don't recycle like this at home. Many people sell the glass and metal. It was helpful, when my grandmother was sick. I could help her, this way. Without it, she would have died sooner." Satya looked self-conscious, but he kept going. "The doctor in the play made me think of her. When he talks about the woman who died."

Rebecca didn't know what else to do, so she nodded and kept her mouth shut, waiting for Stephanie and feeling glad that Bangladesh did not recycle, to give boys like Satya something to do. Weren't there jobs? Something told her that if someone like Satya, someone whose English was good and whose mind was sharp, had been sorting through other people's garbage to help his sick grandmother, there were not, in fact, many jobs at all.

Stephanie emerged a few minutes later, as Rebecca hummed the waltz from the end of the play and Satya ate his third bag of peanut M&M's, which Rebecca had bought to avoid talking about his grandmother and recycling and all the things that made them different from each other. Stephanie looked luminous, high on the energy of the audience, who had given her a standing ovation as the curtain fell. Stephanie had never been all that pretty, Rebecca thought sourly, but right now she looked actually beautiful, confident and sparkling and proud. Rebecca started forward, her arms splayed and ready, her smile pasted into place.

"You. Were. Fantastic!" Stephanie beamed as Rebecca's arms closed around her. Nearby, Satya stood, hovering shyly. Rebecca pulled back and grinned, a real thousand-watt bulb of a grin, just the right mix of pride and admiration and excitement. She motioned to Satya to come over.

"This is Satya. He's, um, the guide, on the trip I was telling you about?"

"Oh, my god, yes, what *is* that? That sounds totally, what?" Stephanie laughed merrily. "Come on, come, there's a place we all drink, come, tell me all about it!"

"Do you want to come?" Rebecca asked Satya, half praying he wouldn't. She didn't know if she could stomach a whole evening of this, of watching Stephanie glow with success while she herself was, what, a paid companion on a ridiculous cross-country trip? Her Bangladeshi colleague in tow like a prop, proving her story was real?

"Will there be food there?"

Sitting at the table with Satya crammed in on one side of her and the rest of the cast of *Three Sisters* on the other, Rebecca didn't know when she had ever been more miserable. Against one arm lay actors basking in postshow hysteria and spilled drinks. Against the other pressed Satya, who was eating his chicken wings with the kind of relish she had seen packs of wild dogs employ when tearing apart a deer on the Discovery Channel.

Stephanie had been holding court for over an hour, describing her process and her preshow rituals with the solemnity of a rabbi explaining the mysteries of Kabbalah. Rebecca hated Stephanie. Everything she said sounded stupid and Rebecca wanted to be the one who was saying it, describing her mystical acting procedures and enjoying the nods and admiring looks passed around the table with the pitcher of beer. As soon as Rebecca saw Satya lick clean the final chicken wing of his third order, she stood, smiling her performance smile again, and announced that they had to go, given their early morning the next day. Stephanie pouted and sighed, whining that they had *barely* gotten to *catch up*, but Rebecca smiled some more and extricated herself with promises to call soon.

Out on the street, Rebecca made sure Satya had followed her through the crowd. They were back at the hotel within fifteen minutes, and it wasn't until she was paying for the cab that she realized that neither of them had spoken the whole time. She looked at Satya and smiled weakly, a genuine smile now.

"Thank you for coming with me."

Satya seemed about to say something in response, but instead, he turned and vomited up the chicken wings into a nearby bush that could have been real or plastic; Rebecca wasn't sure. Straightening, he looked rueful.

"I guess I shouldn't have let you have that beer, right?"

Satya shrugged and wiped his mouth. "The cab, and I eat too quickly when there is so much food."

"Like a stray cat." Rebecca wondered if she should apologize—it was hardly a flattering comparison—but Satya laughed.

"My grandmother used to say that. Thank you for taking me. It was interesting. I think I like plays."

"I'm glad."

"People dressed better in those times. Women wore more, which was better."

"Well, that is certainly an opinion."

"Your friend is not really your friend."

Rebecca smiled at this. "How did you know?"

"You look at her like you want to hit her."

Rebecca laughed. "Yeah. She was good, though. She has that thing, that brightness, that makes you want to look at her."

"Do you have that, as well?"

"If you have to ask—"

"You do, I think."

Rebecca blushed. "Thank you. Thank you for coming. I'm glad I could take you to your first play."

Satya nodded, which could have meant anything, and turned, walking inside and leaving Rebecca alone.

The rest of their time in Philadelphia was less eventful. Satya returned to his more formal guiding the next day, and Mrs. Sengupta seemed recovered, smiling and eating well and asking about their evening. Some unspoken agreement had both of them declaring it was fine, with no further volunteered details, and then off they went to visit the historical sights, from the Benjamin Franklin Museum to Independence Hall, a plethora of America's brief history on display for tourists to enjoy.

Mrs. Sengupta asked why this was all so clean and well maintained, and when Rebecca explained about public works, she was amazed.

"How do things stay clean in India?"

"They don't."

Rebecca couldn't believe that an entire country was simply dirty. But Mrs. Sengupta seemed so very sure.

Women in mobcaps and men in short britches greeted them formally as they stood in line for hours to see the Liberty Bell, which they looked at for approximately five minutes before collectively declaring the need for lunch. Rebecca felt at this point that she had ordered every possible combination of foods on a standard Indian menu, and she wondered how she would survive the rest of the trip if everything was going to taste the same. She'd gotten a thank-you text from Stephanie with a plea to hang out again just as they had started their tour of Independence Hall, and it had taken her until the visit to Benjamin Franklin's grave to respond. Her reply had been effusive but she declined politely, and Stephanie's own text back, a sad face, seemed appropriate.

Their second night in Philadelphia was nothing like their first. Rebecca went directly to her room after her second chicken tikka of the day and lay on her bed, closing her eyes and wondering what she would do if she were onstage right now, acting Irina. She began mouthing the words with her eyes closed, picturing herself in Stephanie's costume and wig. The image lulled her to sleep early, and she was ready for the six A.M. departure to Washington, DC.

She realized as their car, now driven by a friendly Turkish man named Orhan, rolled out of Philadelphia and onto the highway that she hadn't mentioned to her parents that she would be in Washington for two days. *Perhaps it's for the best*, she thought. *If seeing Stephanie has made me feel insignificant, seeing my parents would make me feel completely worthless.* The car drove on, and Rebecca, in the backseat, murmured Irina's lines to herself once again, this time with her face smushed against the window, watching the road speed by.

24

Washington, DC, reminded Pival of the South Park Street Cemetery in Kolkata, a place she had passed many times and never gone into. Kolkata had many Christian cemeteries, and she had never entered one of them, scared to be close to so many dead bodies. Now she was stuck in one.

As they drove into DC the white marble of the buildings around them looked solid and heavy, just like giant tombstones. Pival wondered why people thought bodies should be buried under the ground, to rot with the worms. It seemed barbaric to prefer decay to the clean purification of cremation. Pival wondered if that's how ghosts were made, angry spirits whose bodies had been destroyed by time rather than by fire.

American cities looked nothing like Indian ones, and she viewed them with a mixture of suspicion and delight. She couldn't get over how clean everything was. It excited her, but it also felt strange. All the things she had taken for granted living in Kolkata, the garbage, the beggars, the traffic, it was like another world now. Where did they keep the poor people here? Even the very few homeless people she saw had so many possessions, carried with them in bags or shopping carts.

Their hotel was much the same as the others had been, and Pival was beginning to grow accustomed, or at least resigned, to weak tea and thick white towels. She could not, however, resign herself to the uncomfortable bedding. All the sheets in each bed had felt strange and starchy on her skin, and she had developed a small trail of red bumps along any exposed skin that was left for the bedsheets to rub against. She had taken to sleeping in more and more clothing to avoid this. It left her sweating and feeling like a mummy, wrapped up in layers and layers of cloth. Every night felt like a fever, like when she was a little girl and went through wave after wave of malarial fevers, each one keeping her in bed for weeks. She dreamed strange dreams of drowning herself in the Pacific so that she could wash away in the ocean and some part of her would reach the Ganges.

When she woke up, she considered drowning again. It would be fitting, to drown in tribute to Rahi. He had always loved the sea. When he had left for college in America it had been to study engineering at Stanford, but each time he returned for vacation his stories had been full of biology classes and marine explorations. Ram had been furious when Rahi had suggested he might switch from engineering to another subject, and Rahi had conceded, promising not to. Looking back, Pival wondered if he'd done so. They had only ever had his word on anything and Pival understood now that this had not been a reliable source. Had Rahi visited DC, and liked it? Or had it made him, too, think of death? Had he gone on to study the sea? Would he know, if she died in the Pacific, how long it would take her body to reach India? It was like one of the word problems she had helped him with in school.

Every day, waking up was a mixture of dread and anticipation. Sometimes she woke up gasping with fear, sometimes ablaze with anticipation. Each day she was one step closer to California, and each one of those steps beat the mixture of hope and fear inside her like eggs. With a sudden sharp sense of clarity she missed her cook's omelets, the way she would finely chop green chilies and garlic into them, the spicy bite of them on her tongue. Rahi had loved them, too. She would learn to make him one, if he was there.

"There's the Washington Monument, madam, very tall thing, see?"

Satya was pointing underneath her nose, gesturing out of the side of the large sightseeing bus toward a huge white column reflected on a long rectangular expanse of water. The image in the water shimmered and shook but the one on land held fast, which was good, Pival thought, because otherwise she would never have been able to tell them apart. Everything looked the same here, she thought. All the buildings and monuments were different but they were also, in some essential way, completely the same thing. It looked like nothing she had ever seen before, but exactly what she thought it would be.

After a few more minutes Satya gestured for Rebecca, who was reading, and Pival to get off at the next stop, outside of the Lincoln Memorial. Together they debarked and Pival paused, drinking some of her water from her ever-present purchased bottle.

Satya guided them into a strange white mausoleum-like place, where an enormous man was sitting on an equally enormous throne. She recognized the face, as they grew closer, from her history lessons on America. This was President Lincoln. In front of her, Satya was holding up a five-dollar bill next to his face and grinning.

"Look familiar?"

Rebecca rolled her eyes. She seemed uncomfortable in DC. Satya frowned at her but continued his lecture on Lincoln, the Great Emancipator, only Satya pronounced it *EEE-maahn-cipa-TOOOOR* and as a result it took several minutes before Pival understood what he was saying, and only then because she read a plaque on the side of the statue.

The image of the giant man in the giant chair was awfully frightening, though Pival understood that it was intended to be inspirational. Certainly the things Satya was saying about Lincoln were very nice. This president had freed slaves just like their own Gandhi had ended the caste system. He had also maintained the wholeness of the United States in some way, which was unclear to Pival, but it sounded good. Ram, she thought, would have liked this part. It was nice, for a moment, for once, to think about what Ram would have *liked*, instead of what he had hated.

Pival looked up at the enormous statue in the Lincoln Memorial, marveling at it. The heaviness of the stone seemed to sit on her heart. President Lincoln was so massive and weighed down in this prison of marble. It troubled her to see a real person on such a massive scale, and in such a strange place. She wondered if he got lonely, Mr. Lincoln, as he sat alone here forever. She wondered where Rahi's body was now, if it was rotting under the ground, trapped beneath a large stone slab somewhere. She wondered if that person he had been with, the person who had taken him from Pival, had the body, and if they had buried him, according to their own tradition, or cremated him, according to hers.

"Some people say he might have been gay, you know," Rebecca said, looking up at the statue. Pival couldn't breathe. All the air was sucked from her lungs and she could feel the blood rushing to her face. She looked at Rebecca.

"Who?" she asked, in no more than a whisper.

"Lincoln."

"That's disgusting!" Satya said strongly, his eyes flaring. "Why would you say such a thing?"

"Why is it disgusting?" Rebecca asked, her tone biting.

It just is, it is, it is, thought Pival, trying to breathe, trying to look normal, trying not to cry.

"In Lincoln's day maybe it was unacceptable. But now? It's fine. Gay people can do anything, they can live together, adopt children, get married, get divorced. Be as unhappy as the rest of us. Look, even if he wasn't gay, isn't that what Lincoln would have wanted? A land of equality? Well, now we have it, sort of. Sometimes. Thanks, Abe!" Rebecca saluted the statue. Satya, shaking his head in disgust, walked off to get a water. Rebecca smiled at Pival sheepishly.

"Sorry. I couldn't resist."

"Is it true?" Pival asked, not sure if she wanted it to be or not.

"Who knows? We probably won't ever have a clear answer and they thought of sexuality so differently then—"

"No. Is it true that sometimes things are equal here?"

Rebecca paused at the question. "I guess it depends where you live. But I think generally yes, it's better than it used to be. It can be pretty great, actually. It's legal—*hell,* it's cliché. And I fully support gay rights, by the way. It's not disgusting. At least, I don't think so."

"Where do you have to live for it to be okay?"

Rebecca looked at Pival curiously. "Um, cities, really. Big ones. New York, Chicago, L.A., San Francisco of course, but even here, or some of the Southern cities, places where people aren't so afraid of what's different, you know? Look, I don't know. It's good in New York, I know that much. You see couples all the time, holding hands, kissing in public, going down to city hall to get hitched, and no one cares. Or if they do, they don't say anything. Which is all you can hope for, really, for anything."

Pival nodded. She had so much more to ask, so much more she wanted to know, but she was afraid. L.A. Rebecca had said it was good in L.A. No matter how misguided Rahi might have been, thinking he was a homosexual, calling his father and declaring it as if it was nothing to be ashamed of, she didn't want him in danger. She wanted him to be happy, to be safe. To be close to other people, to love and be loved. Even if it was in the wrong way.

She wished so badly that it had been her, the day the other call came, who had answered the phone and not Ram. She would have no doubts in her mind now if that had been true. She would have asked the person who he was, how he knew her son, if he was happy. She had never been sure who it was who called to tell them, but she assumed it was him, the man Rahi had told them he loved. The man who had taken her son away. But it should have been her on the phone, checking, double-checking. She would have thought to ask for Rahi's body back, to make sure, not just thinking of pride, like Ram. She would have been no less revolted, no less angry with the person who had seduced and ruined their son, who had broken their family apart, but she would have remembered the important things. She wouldn't be living in this agony of doubt.

Ram had not started out a bad husband, she knew. He had done everything for her that his father had done for his own mother. He had fulfilled his duty, fed her, clothed her, kept her safe and comfortable, denied her nothing he did not deny himself. It was only when Rahi failed them, failed himself, that Ram blamed her for the way things had turned out.

She had not protested at the separation after Rahi had told them he was different, that he would not be what they wanted. She had understood the ban. But after the moment that Ram slammed down the telephone and said nothing other than that some son of a whore said Rahi had died, she knew that it was not Rahi who had been wrong all this time, but Ram. If they had welcomed Rahi back into their family, if they had tried to understand him, convince him of the folly of what he was doing, if they could have gotten him back to India at least, it would have all been all right. They could have saved him from himself, from his silly notions and this strange lust he had. They could have tried, at least. That would have been better than nothing.

The tour group walked away from the memorial. Pival looked back several times until it was out of view. Satya tried to take a photograph of her in front of it but she refused. She did not want a record of that moment.

Pival thought that Rebecca was looking rather strange as they walked the streets of Georgetown. This was the first area of the city that Pival

actually truly liked. This part of town was all brick and shorter buildings, smaller streets and trees. There wasn't a trace of white marble or
anything monumental in sight. This was lovely, Pival thought, all little shops and friendly people. She wondered whether this was where
she would do her shopping if she lived here. She looked around for a
decent grocery store but didn't see one, which seemed strange to her.
How did people eat here? Everything seemed so specialized; there
was a cheese shop, a wine shop, a shop for small iced cakes. Did they
not have one big store for everything? When she had been a child in
Kolkata she had followed her mother as she shopped this way, from
one place to another, something here, something there, but now the
grocery stores had everything you could need in one place. Her driver
would take her weekly, and carry all the bags into and out of the car.
It seemed strange that Washington, DC, hadn't developed such a system yet. Come to think of it, she hadn't seen grocery stores or street
markets in New York at all, just little shops. How did people manage
to eat so much in America if there was no food to be had?

It was warmer in Washington, especially by the middle of the day,
and Pival enjoyed the sensation of the sun on her skin. She felt it
warm her, soothing the little bumps left by the sheets. That morning
she had adopted a short-sleeve kurta and loose drawstring pants, not
wanting to bother with a sari. No one had said anything, and Satya
had not seemed bothered, but Pival couldn't escape the feeling that
she was doing something very bold. She looked at Rebecca again, who
wore a loose button-down top layered over a lacy camisole, which
peeped, rather provocatively, in Mrs. Sengupta's opinion, out of the
edge of her neckline, and a pair of tight trousers that ended just below
her knees. Rebecca wore such daring things, with fabrics that floated
around her or clung to her tightly, but she seemed comfortable, free.
Pival wondered what jeans would feel like. Some girls she had known
in school had worn them sometimes. Back then they had been high-

waisted bell-bottoms that had seemed awfully fashionable, and only the wealthiest and most modern girls wore such things, parading around with feathered hair and tall shoes. But most girls had only watched and wished they could wear such things. She had never been daring enough to ask her father for permission, and once she had married Ram, it had seemed like a silly thing, a schoolgirl fantasy, though she still watched other women with something like envy. She wondered if she would ever try on a pair of jeans, or if she would be watching other women until she died. Now that her death might be only days away, it seemed like it was now or never. After all, what was there to stop her?

As they passed by a store with many varieties of denim in the window, Pival opened her mouth to ask if they had the time to stop when Rebecca, whose body had grown tenser for the past several blocks, took her arm and dragged her in before she could even say anything at all. Gesturing wildly for Satya to follow, Rebecca flung them both behind her, and she watched from the window as someone passed by. She turned back to them both, stammering.

"I'm sorry. It's just, I didn't want to see someone I know so I just, I'm sorry, this just seemed easier."

"Why don't you want to see someone you know? And how do you know people here?" Satya asked, looking at her suspiciously.

"I know lots of people," Rebecca retorted, biting the words out. Satya and Pival looked at her, waiting. She sighed.

"I'm from here. I grew up here. You know how it is, your hometown, sometimes you just don't want to deal with people." Pival and Satya looked at each other, confused. Pival had never left the city in which she had grown up. She suspected that Satya hadn't either, before coming to the United States. And this idea of not dealing with people, obviously neither of them understood that. There were people she did not like in Kolkata, but she had certainly never found a way to avoid them. After all, most of them were related to her through marriage. There was no avoiding people like that.

"I'm sorry to derail us, but it's just a minute, okay? Is that okay? Satya?"

The boy looked to Pival, who nodded. She had wanted to see the store. But despite her acquiescence, she didn't know what to make of this. The girl had seemed so calm and confident, and now she chewed the edge of one nail furiously as she waited, her body tense, for whoever it was she didn't want to see to pass.

"Who is it? This person you are knowing?" The words bubbled to her mouth before she could stop them. She was not normally a person who pried into the lives of others, and she felt ashamed. She certainly hated when people pried into her own life. That being said, Rebecca was her employee, her servant. Surely she had a right to ask?

"Oh, it's, nothing, it's just, well, it's my mom." Rebecca said it so quietly that Pival barely heard her. When the word registered, her mouth hung open with shock.

"Your mother is here?"

"Both my parents live here. I didn't tell them we would be coming, since I never thought I would see them. I just—look, it doesn't matter. I apologize."

"You don't want to see your own mother?" Pival's voice rang out clearly and loudly, startling people around them in the store. Rebecca looked at her, shocked.

"No, of course I do, it's only that I'm *working*, obviously, I'm here to be your companion, not to see my parents, right, so—"

"You saw your friend in Philadelphia," Satya commented, looking at Rebecca curiously. Rebecca's face now wore the sour expression of all children caught in their own lies.

"You should see your mother." Pival spoke loudly again, and firmly. More and more people were looking at them, but she didn't care. Rebecca should not pass through the city without her family's knowing she was there. What if Rahi had done such a thing? Perhaps he had, and she hadn't known. The thought felt like a blow.

"I wouldn't want to abandon you like that—"

"I will meet her, too." Rebecca looked at Pival, her eyes wide. "Go. Now. Please."

Rebecca went. For once, Pival had injected the kind of authority into her voice that Ram had always had, and it had worked. She thanked her husband silently.

As she watched Rebecca walk down the street and carefully tap a woman on the shoulder, Pival swallowed deeply and inhaled, checking her throat and lungs. She had not spoken so loudly in a long time. She wanted to laugh. It wasn't the years of coaching that had helped her voice. It was her feelings for another mother.

Now Rebecca was leading a confused-looking woman back toward them. Pival waited with Satya, all thoughts of jeans vanished.

"She looks like her mother, does she not, madam?" Satya murmured to Pival. Satya had grown more familiar with her since they had left Ronnie's care, and while Pival knew she should stop that and impose boundaries, she couldn't force herself to do so. It was very difficult to maintain distance as they traveled. She was equally dependent upon and interested in them. Rebecca and Satya were the first new people she had met in such a long time. They might be the last people she ever met and got to talk to, besides the man in California who didn't know she was coming and wouldn't want to see her. There was no society here to impress, no one to judge how she treated others. She would like to leave the world actually knowing someone who was left behind.

Now Rebecca and her mother were right in front of them. Rebecca was smiling nervously.

"Mom, this is Mrs. Sengupta, the tourist. And Satya Roy, the tour guide."

"And what are you? The entertainment?" the woman asked Rebecca, her eyes laughing. She was a pretty woman still, Rebecca's mother, with silver shooting through her dark hair and wide eyes surrounded by fans of laugh lines, though the skin of her face was taut. She wore a fashionable gray dress suit with simple jewelry in shades of silver and coral, and sensible but stylish shoes. Her face, despite her dancing eyes, was tense, showing she was no more comfortable with this chance meeting than Rebecca.

"I told you, Mom, I'm the companion."

"Of course, the companion. It's all very Regency England, isn't it? Are you going to have an affair with Mr. Rochester or something?"

"Ladies and gentlemen, my mother, Cynthia Greenbaum. If you don't get her jokes, don't worry, you're not supposed to." Pival was sure that Rebecca was destined for an angry remark or a slap after that disrespectful comment but her mother just laughed. Satya leaned down to touch her feet almost automatically but Cynthia stepped back, looking confused. Satya hesitated, his hand hanging in the air for a long moment, and then drew back. Cynthia extended her hand first to Pival and then to Satya, shaking each of their hands firmly.

"I had no idea that you were coming through here, Rebecca."

Rebecca winced. "I wasn't sure if I would have time to see you. You know what these tours are like, something every minute—"

"Still, you should have told me. Well, I suppose you didn't bother to think of anyone but yourself."

Rebecca looked up, hurt.

"That's the problem with being an actress, you know? It's like a job skill to be self-obsessed. What are you doing for dinner tonight?" Cynthia had spoken so quickly Rebecca didn't have a moment to react. Pival watched the thoughts flash through the girl's head before she took a deep breath and opened her mouth to speak.

"Mom, I told you, the trip has all these meals at different Indian restaurants—"

"Oh, god, that sounds wretched. American Indian food every day? Tandoori chicken as far as the eye can see! Come home instead!"

"Mom, I can't just leave. We have to stay together." Pival thought about dismissing her for the evening but realized that Rebecca wouldn't thank her.

"Oh, I meant all of you! Come on over, I'll cook, your father will be thrilled, he's just *in stitches* about this whole thing you are doing, he's going to absolutely die. He'll have no idea, it will be a wonderful surprise. Come at seven. You've still got keys? Pasta is okay, right? Of course, everyone loves pasta! Okay, sweetheart, see you then!" And like a whirlwind, Cynthia was gone, kissing each of them on the cheeks so quickly that neither Pival nor Satya could react and departing in a perfume-scented rush.

Rebecca watched her hurry off down the street. She turned to Pival.

"That is what I meant by 'deal with.'" Pival's voice had abandoned her again, lost in the onslaught of Rebecca's mother, and she could only nod weakly. "My mother is a little aggressive. Do you mind coming?" Pival and Satya shook their heads. "Do you like pasta?"

"I have never tried it." Satya nodded his head in agreement with Pival's quiet statement.

"Then I guess we'll find out." Rebecca started walking again, away from the denim shop. Pival followed her, worried now.

"But if you don't want to, can't you call your mother and say no?"

Rebecca turned to Pival, gritting her teeth a bit. "My plan had been to avoid her completely. But now she's asked us, and it would be rude not to go. Wouldn't it be rude not to go? If it was your mother?"

Pival nodded. "I'll tell Ronnie, don't worry. He'll consider it a trip bonus, a free meal with a real live American family. All part of the package, right, Satya?" Rebecca asked, her tone as bright and brittle as the glass they had seen in the museum. Was that only three days before? It seemed like a lifetime.

Sensing Rebecca's combustibility, Satya wisely declined to answer her question. Rebecca nodded, and smiled again, even more dazzlingly, and then let the expression drop, her face a neutral mask. She started walking, her head down, her body taut, her face smooth with resignation. *Like a prisoner walking to the gallows,* Pival thought, *as if the worst is over, and now it is just death.*

Upon reaching the hotel, Pival decided she ought to send a brief message to Mr. Munshi, as he had implored her many times to "keep in touch." She wrote out an email in the formal language she had been taught at St. Claire's School for Girls, including the obligatory questions about Mr. Munshi's own life, despite having no interest in the answers. She wrote very few letters, so it seemed safest to keep it to the format she knew. She hadn't written letters to anyone except Rahi for years.

She wondered if Rebecca's mother wrote her letters. And if Rebecca read them. She wondered what she should wear to dinner with Americans.

At seven that evening Pival stood in front of the neat and well-maintained house watching Rebecca fumble with her keys. She had decided to dress herself in something simple, a white embroidered kurta with soft comfortable trousers in a white printed silk. She supposed a sari would have been appropriate, but she couldn't face winding herself up in all those layers. For years she had worn a sari daily without complaint, but here it had begun to feel suffocating. There was no one around to judge her anyway, except for Satya, and somehow she knew he wouldn't care.

"Is this where you always lived?" This came from Satya. She saw that he had dressed himself up, in his way. His plaid shirt and khaki pants had been carefully pressed. His hair had been slicked back with scented pomade and he had taken advantage of the hotel's complimentary cologne by liberally dousing himself with it before leaving his room. If Satya got lost at some point this evening they could follow his scent trail to find him.

Rebecca nodded in response to Satya's question. She found the key and inserted it into the lock, but it was stiff, and she could barely turn it. Before she could fight with the door it swung open, and a pleasant-looking man in a sweater and slacks beamed with delight and opened his arms to hug Rebecca tightly.

"Hello, Papa," Pival heard Rebecca murmur as she was closely hugged, but whatever else the girl might have said was lost in her father's chest. The hug lasted a long time. It made Pival uncomfortable to see this display of affection between parent and child.

She couldn't remember Ram hugging Rahi at any point past the boy's fifth birthday. Perhaps it would have been different with a girl, although Pival couldn't imagine Ram hugging anyone, really, including her. He had told her once it was unseemly, the way her family hugged her so much, the way they touched each other. She had taken care to be more circumspect when Ram was with her when she visited her parents, and soon after that, once her parents and Arjun had passed, there was no one left to hug but Rahi, and she never hugged him in front of Ram. Ram would have accused her of babying Rahi, of making him effeminate. Not that it made any difference, in the end.

Now, as she watched Rebecca's father hold her close in front of two perfect strangers, she couldn't help looking around to see who might be watching them from among the neighbors. Finally the man let Rebecca go, but he kept his hands on her shoulders, looking at her like she was something precious. Pival gave a polite smile as the man introduced himself as Morris Elliot and asked their names.

"Please, come in! It's such an unexpected pleasure to meet you."

The three of them were ushered into the house. Pival was struck by the change in Rebecca in the presence of her parents, the way her poise was gone, replaced by a childlike defensiveness. On the other hand, she seemed to fit perfectly into this elegant house well decorated with tasteful furniture and art on the walls. Everywhere else Rebecca had seemed like a cat, ready to spring away at any moment. Here she seemed a part of the scenery, and that did not seem to make her happy in the least.

Pival understood that, she thought. She had fit into her life in Kolkata, because she had made herself fit, but it was the last place she would want to be now, and she thanked the gods again that she would never have to return. It was not always a good thing, she realized, to fit in somewhere.

Ram had always scoffed at those Indians who had emigrated and on visits back talked about how wonderful it was in Australia or England or America. They had traded home for something else and they had lost their roots. But now she understood them, and hated herself for it. She had expected herself not to fit into this place, and she didn't. But neither, it seemed, did anyone else. This was a world in which you could not-fit-in and still survive. No wonder Rahi liked it.

As they sat down to dinner she thought of the many meals she had eaten in other people's houses, and how she had been brought up by her parents and further trained by Ram. Now she was eating in the childhood home of an American girl she had hired for reasons of modesty and curiosity, and watching her Bangladeshi tour guide try to navigate pasta, a dish she herself was extremely unsure of. She never could have imagined this experience even last month.

Pival watched as Rebecca dug into the pasta with vigor, filling her mouth and avoiding answering any of her parents' many questions about her life. They were asking the sort of things any parent would ask, though as the wine in their glasses disappeared the questions did become more pointed, more suggestions than questions.

"Of course, we are very happy that you're so, so creative," Cynthia said, leaning back in her chair, "but don't you ever want stability?"

Rebecca put down her fork deliberately and met her mother's eyes.

"Mom. Don't you want to talk to Mrs. Sengupta about her travels?" Rebecca's tone, while perfectly pleasant, held a warning. Cynthia narrowed her eyes and then, much to Pival's surprise, seemed to shift all at once, from parent to stranger, turning to Pival brightly.

"This is such an interesting trip, Mrs. Sengupta. Have you traveled much before?" Pival blinked. It was like watching a play and being in it at the same time. Was this the way she and Ram had been to Rahi?

"I have never been outside of Kolkata before now only." She responded carefully and attempted another bite of the strange gummy food. Pasta was unusual. It stuck to her mouth in a strange way, and the cheese liberally sprinkling the dish prickled her tongue. Satya did not seem to be having more luck than she was. She reached for the salad. Salads here had many leaves in them, which was new to her, but the essential contents, the onions and cucumbers and carrots, were familiar, and at least she knew how to eat it. The pasta kept slipping from her fork. The atmosphere felt as gummy as the food. She looked at Rebecca, who was drinking her wine with single-minded determination.

"That's so interesting, that you would take this trip. Have you always wanted to see America?" Cynthia was continuing with her inquiries. Was this being a good hostess here? Ram had always told her not to ask anyone questions about anything.

"No. I wanted to come because my son lived here."

"Oh, are you visiting him? That's nice!"

"He doesn't live here anymore." Rebecca and Satya both glanced at Pival quickly and then looked away.

Morris poured some wine into Pival's empty glass. She hadn't minded the wine Rebecca had given her in New York, but she had thought it would set a bad example, her drinking it. This had not seemed to matter to Rebecca, so she was prepared to try again. She still felt a twinge when she sipped, as if she was doing something bad, but according to whom? So she drank her wine in silence, grateful for it, as the children ate and Cynthia and Morris, parents themselves, sat with her in the quiet.

"What do you think of the country so far? I know that's a ridiculous question, but I have to ask."

Pival considered her words carefully.

"It's so much bigger than I thought it would be."

Morris smiled at her and nodded. "It does feel enormous, doesn't it?"

"Or maybe it is only that my home felt very small."

Cynthia looked confused but recovered quickly. "Well. At least you're doing some traveling. I hope Becky's been a good *companion*. Although I think it's hilarious that she's traveling with you; she never leaves New York."

"You never have to leave New York. It has everything."

"I hope she hasn't been a diva," Cynthia continued, as if Rebecca hadn't spoken. She was addressing Satya this time. "Making everything a *scene*. She doesn't get to act much so I think she makes drama where she can, if you know what I mean, which may be fine but not when you've got a plane to catch!"

Rebecca flushed deeply at her mother's comment and bit her lip, refusing to participate. Pival's heart swung toward the girl. She understood Rebecca's parents, yes, but she saw the heated look in her eyes and thought of her own rebellions, of the argument that had occurred when she had declared she wanted to marry Ram. She did not know what Rebecca's jobs were like in New York. She had not considered Rebecca's life beyond what she was doing now. She had inhabited more of Ram's worst qualities than she had thought, and she had taken on none of his better parts.

"I don't know why you don't have your own show by now, Becky." This came from her father, who was smiling broadly, though he was sweating, Pival observed, perhaps from the tension. "You should!"

"Sure. I'll let someone know." Satya looked up and caught Rebecca's eye as she murmured this over her wine. He smiled at her reassuringly. Rebecca looked away.

"It is just *such* a nice change for Becky, though, isn't it, Morris? Traveling? Getting out, seeing the world. I've always wanted her to do more of that, haven't I always said that? Of course, she can't afford it. You know, it's amazing, you raise your kids hoping they'll have a better life than yours. You certainly don't think they're going to have a *worse* one. But I think it's all this Internet stuff, the smartphones— god knows I love mine, but it makes people forget about the *future,* you know? This is all fine for Becky now but I'm just waiting for her to get a real job, you know? Tour guide, well, it isn't what I would have expected but maybe it's *something.* Maybe like historic tours? Then she could be in costume. What do you think?"

Cynthia was, Pival realized, a bit drunk. Rebecca herself had refilled her own glass many times, her face red and her throat working with condensed humiliation.

"She's always been such a bright girl, I don't know why she doesn't use that."

"*She's* right here, Mom. I'm in the room."

"Is it so bad to want more for your child? To want them to be successful? In something, you know, substantial?"

"I can't have this conversation with you right now. I don't know why you brought this up."

"Because nothing in your life ever changes!"

"Well, now it has! You see? See all the changes I'm making? I'm traveling the country as a companion. *That's* a change. And when I get back to New York, I'll find something terrible to do so I can be just as happy as you are, right now. Won't that be great? Maybe I'll have kids, too, so I can teach them to be miserable because nothing they want is worth anything. Won't that make you happy, Mom? When I become just like you?"

Cynthia looked stricken as she gazed at Rebecca over her empty wineglass. Rebecca looked at her, her own eyes shining with furious tears. Pival felt faint. Rebecca was wearing the same expression she'd seen on Rahi's face so often. Ram had always said his actions were for the boy's own good, but Pival had seen, as she saw now, this sense of deep injury and pain. It was easier to see from the outside. Cynthia, whose fear had driven her to hurt her child, and Rebecca, whose pain at her mother's judgment had driven her to insult her mother. She wished she could reach into this moment and stop it, soothe them both, but she couldn't. This was not her family. If she had not been able to help her own son, how could she hope to help these strangers? She sat in the freezing-cold moment with the rest of them, watching tears die in Rebecca's eyes.

"None of this is about my happiness, Rebecca. I hope you understand that." Rebecca looked away, barely there anymore. Cynthia's mouth tightened and it seemed that they were about to continue pushing through each other when Morris cleared his throat.

"Your mother has missed you, Rebecca. That's all she means."

Cynthia looked at Morris in protest, but something in his face must have stopped her, for she merely nodded, agreeing.

"She shows it badly," Rebecca said shortly, her voice choked.

"Yes. She does."

There was such tenderness in Morris's eyes as he agreed.

Both women leaned back subtly, taking a breath, like cricketers on a rest after batting. The moment changed from chill to warmth as both women succumbed to the comfort of his moderating presence. Rebecca poured herself a glass of wine, and then one for her mother. Cynthia breathed deeply and thanked her. Time returned to its normal speed.

This was this family, Pival realized. They were not happy, they were still in pain, but they were going on with dinner. She felt like an interloper, watching something she shouldn't see.

Next to her, Satya ate with gusto, having gotten the hang of pasta eventually and deciding to make up for lost time. He kept looking up at Rebecca and her parents, curious but unconcerned. Perhaps the English was moving too quickly for him. Or perhaps he didn't care much beyond the meal.

Pival wondered about his family. Whose son was he? What had his dinner table been like, who had argued with him there? She had not thought enough about her companions and now it was as if something had broken, some seal on their lives, and she was desperately curious. She drank her own wine, wondering if Rahi had liked wine here, if he had liked pasta, if he had missed fighting with Ram, if his lover had asked him about home and what he had said.

Morris leaned forward, subtly breaking through the family sphere.

"So, Satya, you're from Bangladesh? But you're Bengali, Mrs. Sengupta. So what's the difference? I mean, I know there *is* a difference, but I just am not sure what it is, culturally that is, beyond the border. You're both Bengali, right?"

Pival looked around this lovely dining room and the expectant white faces waiting for her reply. She saw that Satya had looked down, his mouth tight, his body tense, as if waiting for a blow. The blow that would come from her, when she explained that his country was the trash her country had left behind.

Ram would have told these people in no uncertain terms that Bangladeshis were not Bengalis at all, that they had no place in the proud and sophisticated world of Bengali culture, that the country of Bangladesh was a provincial, unstable backwater, a cesspool of poverty and ignorance, and no amount of common language could tie them to West Bengal. It was waiting there on the tip of her tongue. She had heard Ram's views so many times that she could recite them by rote. She opened her mouth and replied.

"We're both Bengali." She wondered, looking at Satya's beaming face, how his tilted teeth had become handsome to her in such a short amount of time. For there was no denying, she'd rarely seen a better sight than his smiling at her now. This time it was Rebecca looking in on an intimacy she wasn't a part of, and Pival found she didn't mind one bit.

Later, as their cab pulled up at the hotel, Rebecca roused herself from her solitary unhappiness, which had filled up the vehicle like smoke, and quietly thanked Pival and Satya for coming to her parents' house for dinner. She seemed sad and small now. Pival wondered what it would have been like if things had been different with Rahi, if he had lived and come home to Kolkata and had a life that was encircled by the lives of his parents. Would he seem diminished, as Rebecca did now? Would he look so defeated by a meal with the people who loved him most? Was Rebecca spoiled and ungrateful, or a woman trapped in the expectations of her family? Pival supposed that she could be both.

"I'm really sorry about that in there. All the heated talk. I hope you weren't uncomfortable. I love my parents," Rebecca said, surprising Pival, who, like Satya, looked away at this outpouring of private emotion. "And they love me. And I'm so lucky, I know, to have them. But what they want for me has nothing to do with what I want."

With that, Rebecca paid the cab and slid out, leaving Pival and Satya there, wondering what to do with their experience of someone else's family. Satya turned to Pival. She wondered what he would say. Perhaps some apology from himself and the tour company, or some Mr. Munshi–coined phrase about Americans. As it turned out, he had neither to offer her. He said nothing, and it was she who spoke first.

"Where are your parents?" she asked.

"They are gone. Everyone is gone." Pival nodded. She understood.

Satya gestured for Pival to come and he opened the door of the cab. She slid her body inelegantly along the vinyl seat until she could descend. Satya waited until she was on solid ground again, and then, with great solemnity, he touched her feet. He had not done so since that first day in Manhattan. She wanted to cry, but instead she nodded, and together they walked into the hotel.

Tomorrow they would be in a different city, and perhaps all of this, the untidy swirl of emotion, the amount that she was feeling for these two people who had nothing to do with why she was in America or what she planned to do with the rest of her short life, would be left behind. But for the first time since Ram had told her that Rahi was dead, she wanted to feel more, not less. She should, she thought, feel as much as she could before she could feel nothing at all. Shouldn't she?

25

To: boss@americabestnumberonetours.com
From: satyaroy57@yahoo.com

Boss,
Writing from Washington DC just now. Philadelphia success. Bus tour good. Very much history. Madam slightly overtired following long ride. Rebecca companion helpful.

Second night excellent lamb. Madam happy with baingan ka bharta despite ghee no mustard oil, would not let me return it to the kitchen. Washington very nice. Clean. Bus tour good. Madam commented on white buildings and giant Lincoln. Dinner with Rebecca companion family featuring pasta meal and genuine American evening. Very success. Possible addition to trips with companion?
Satya

To: boss@americabestnumberonetours.com
From: Rebecca.Elliot.74@gmail.com

Mr. Munshi,
Just reporting from DC. Philadelphia went well, although Mrs. Sengupta had a moment of feeling faint, so Satya and I are trying to make sure she stays hydrated. I took Satya to see a play, I hope that's okay, it was

free and Mrs. Sengupta had given us the evening off as she preferred to rest. Satya said it was good but didn't compare to Bollywood. Otherwise Mrs. Sengupta enjoyed the city. She had never seen streets made of cobblestones.

Washington has been fine, the bus tour was very informative and hit all the normal tourist hot spots. Mrs. Sengupta told us the city reminds her of a cemetery but she liked Georgetown, asking if the same person had made the streets in both cities. We had dinner with my parents this evening so that Mrs. Sengupta could experience a genuine American dinner. This was also free.

Flying out tomorrow to New Orleans. Will check in from there.

Everyone is safe and sound.

Best,

Rebecca

To: boss@americabestnumberonetours.com
From: pivalsengupta345@gmail.com

Dear. Mr. Munshi—

Hello, Mr. Munshi, I am Pival Sengupta writing from Washington DC in the United States. How is your health and that of your family? May the blessings and favor of the gods be with you and protect you.

The trip is most satisfactory. It is an excellent experience of America. I have a wonderful companion and guide. I only wish it was not so cold, and that the Indian food was better.

Thank you for your arrangements. Everything that you have done has been most helpful.

Respectfully,

Pival Sengupta

Reading through his emails in his office as milky tea spilled weakly down his shirtfront, Ronnie frowned. A genuine American dinner? That was a magnificent idea. He wished he had thought of it himself. His mind buzzing with ideas, he called Anita. Perhaps she would agree to host it. They could order food from local diners or that restaurant that served only rotisserie chicken, and Anita could wear jeans and he would trot out one of his many American flag T-shirts. They could find some Americans somewhere to bring; it would be perfect.

"Big Nose! I'm glad you called."

That was odd, Ronnie thought. Anita was never happy he called.

"I've booked us a cruise."

Ronnie started to protest. There was too much to do, he couldn't take a vacation, what on earth was she talking about, with what money? He could almost hear her rolling her eyes over the phone.

"Yours. What else? We're going. No excuses." Ronnie tried to explain about the American dinner idea, but Anita started laughing halfway through.

"A genuine American dinner? What would we know about that?"

"We're Americans."

"Fine. I'll host dinner. When we come back from Greece. Relax, Big Nose, they have rice there. I promise." The phone went dead. Ronnie sighed, and then he smiled. She had agreed to the dinners. And after managing so many vacations, he was going to go on one. Plus, on a boat. Win-win-win.

For someone who had lived most of his life in one place, Satya was getting used to waking up in different beds in different cities. Their flight to New Orleans had left DC the morning before at eight A.M., and the sleepy trio, or rather duet, as Mrs. Sengupta regularly woke early and found five A.M. not so different from six A.M., had huddled in the airport waiting to board a flight where they would spend almost as much time ascending and descending as they would flying through the air. This was their first flight together and Pival seemed nervous, while Rebecca had no reaction other than a strong interest in coffee. Satya merely wanted breakfast. He longed for eggs scrambled with lentils and sweet milky tea as he surveyed the doughy items in the glass case of one overpriced airport café with disgust. Why was everything round? He forwent eating anything and trudged back to the gate as their seats were called for boarding.

At home he and Ravi used to visit the same tea stall daily, bartering with the owner to pay less and trying to catch glimpses of his daughter. They would drink their cooling tea and crush the clay cups it came in under their heels as the city awoke. He wondered what Ravi was doing now. Had his mother responded to Satya's letter? He kept trying to write her another, but the words looked stupid on the page. He had settled for a postcard instead, a New York one he had bought quickly before they left the city, and scribbled a few words on it, telling her that all was well. He hoped, by saying that, that it would become true.

Satya's newly minted New York state ID gave him no trouble whatsoever in airport security, though he wondered if that was due to traveling with Rebecca. Rebecca talked to him in a funny way in public places, with more familiarity than she did in private. She touched his arm gently, she made sure to stand with him if ever he spoke to authorities, and she smiled, all the time, at everyone. He knew what she was doing and he hated it, but it did seem to make life easier. It left him feeling torn between annoyance and gratitude.

He wondered what Ravi would have thought of Rebecca. Every day it felt more strange, more surreal, that he was moving farther and farther away from him, that he was seeing so many things Ravi had never seen. In a way that he couldn't understand, it also made him feel good. It made him feel superior to Ravi, worldly and wise. Their lives together were so small in comparison to the falls, or the ancient glass, or the giant statue of Lincoln, or the play.

The play had been wonderful. It was long, and sometimes boring, but he was too well acquainted with Bollywood movies to expect something to entertain him every minute of its duration. There would always be things he enjoyed and things he ignored. Usually it was the love stories he ignored, except when the women were dressed in scantily cut saris. He loved the action sequences, and the details about people's lives. He hated the family moments, the brothers loving and betraying brothers, the mothers torn down by the system but somehow remaining virtuous. Why did mothers always have to be destroyed to be good people? Why did they have to be destroyed at all?

This play had been about family, though, and about love, but in a way he had not ever seen before in any movie. The people had seemed so real to him. Their lives were familiar, and the way they talked reminded him of the hallways of his building back home, when people had talked over and around each other, picking up conversations and putting them down again like plates on and off the table. The characters had been stuck in their lives. He could have been like that, he knew. He could have become one of the men he and Ravi saw every day, drinking cheap liquor until they passed out on the street, until their wives came and helped them to walk home, the women's faces shaded by scarves.

He had watched class after class above him in school succumb to that same cycle, smart boys felled by some invisible blow, something getting stuck inside of them that caught them and pinned them into place. Some of them had briefly struggled, some had just given in. Few of them had ever thought of leaving home. If he had not had

Ravi, if his grandmother had not died, he might even now have been drinking himself into a stupor, content just thinking about America. Now he had America. But no one else. At least the three sisters in the play had had each other, he thought. But maybe that trapped them, too. He was alone, and for the first time he felt free in a way he had not anticipated. If he hadn't taken the job, if he'd left it to Ravi, he never would have seen a play.

He slept on the flight, and when he woke up and looked out the window as they landed in New Orleans, all he saw was muddy expanses of green land and brown water, and for one horrible moment he thought he had been taken back home to Bangladesh. Instead, he was just in another part of America.

Their driver from the airport this time was a white man. Satya had never been driven anywhere by a white man. The driver, Luc, spoke in a deep and melodic voice that Satya could barely understand, although he nodded along in the front seat, assuming that was the polite thing to do. He caught Rebecca's eyes once as he looked up into the rearview mirror, and her expression was horrified. He shrugged and kept on nodding. The only things he had really been sure that the man said were a question about their destination (the Hampton Inn and Suites New Orleans Downtown/French Quarter), which Satya had pointed out to him on his neatly printed and laminated list of all their accommodation destinations, and a question about where Satya was from because *you sure don't look like you're from Louisiana!* Once he had told Luc he was from Bangladesh, the driver had proceeded to make a series of statements in a kind of half English with most of the syllables either chopped in two or lengthened into five. Satya thought he had heard words he knew in between others he couldn't identify, but every time he had opened his mouth to ask a question the stream of monologue had already rushed ahead.

Once they left the car, Rebecca looked at Satya speculatively. He looked down. He had not known quite how to talk to her since the play. She had been so strange that night, inviting him and then taking him to the odd bar filled with loud actors and drinking so much. He had watched her become a different person several times over within the space of a few hours. She had seemed angry, no matter how many wide smiles she had given her friend or the other people they met. And then they had met her parents, who were odd, sharp people, who made her turn both brittle and soft in their presence, but he envied all of them, just for existing. She had seemed like a little girl with them, sullen and spoiled and rebellious, but he had also seen himself. Neither of them was in the place their families wanted them to be. He marveled at how fast he was learning about her. He'd seen so many layers of her built up and stripped away. He still wondered what she looked like naked.

"Did you understand what he was saying to you?" Rebecca asked outside the cab.

"Of course I did!" Satya was annoyed, his empathy for her burning up instantly. He spoke English perfectly, did he not? Conveniently forgetting just how little of the driver's words he had actually understood, he let his swirl of emotions concerning Rebecca transform themselves into anger at her disrespect.

"Oh. Okay. I didn't know you were so against race mixing. That guy was so adamant about reviving the death penalty for marriage between different races, I am surprised you agreed. Also surprised you agreed about the superiority of the white race. I had no idea you thought that."

Rebecca picked up her bag and walked into the hotel. Mrs. Sengupta was staring at him, her eyes wide and her mouth open. He looked at her helplessly, willing her to understand that he didn't feel that way, he simply hadn't understood and didn't want Rebecca to know. The tension strung out between them as Satya grew more and more desperate to make her understand without knowing what words to say.

"Satya?" She sounded like his grandmother. He couldn't meet her eyes. He was more ashamed than he ever had been of a dirty magazine tucked in between his sheets. He felt the way he had felt when Grandmother had soiled herself in her bed when she was sick and he didn't have the courage to overcome his disgust and clean her up immediately and she moaned in pain and shame and he could only listen, knocking his head against the wall until it hurt so badly he couldn't see straight.

"Did you understand anything that man was saying to you after he asked you where you were from?" Satya shook his head slowly, tears coming to his eyes. He was breaking Ronnie's rule, he knew, he was admitting ignorance, which a good tour guide never does. He was debasing himself in front of Mrs. Sengupta. She would reject him now, she would hate him, she would cancel the trip, she would get him fired. It was over now, and he reached for his bag to trudge to the nearest bus station, for he would quit before she could fire him, and preserve himself in some way—

Suddenly Mrs. Sengupta began to laugh. She laughed with a deep throaty chuckle, which was completely at odds with her quiet voice. Her laugh sprang from her chest beautifully and fully, and as Satya looked at her, amazed, tears appeared in her eyes matching the ones of shame in his own. He did not understand what was happening until Mrs. Sengupta regained her breath and spoke again.

"I am so relieved to hear this, Satya. Because, you see, neither did I!" And she laughed again, her eyes dancing. Satya felt a sudden lightness in his chest as his body relaxed and his face lost its hysterical tightness. He would not have to quit in disgrace or be fired in a cloud of anger. Mrs. Sengupta was happy he had not understood. It was something they shared.

Mrs. Sengupta wasn't interested in the bus tour of the day, so instead they spent the afternoon in the hotel, Satya bored out of his mind, flipping from channel to channel on the tiny room television.

The next day, they set out on their tour of the French Quarter after a breakfast in the hotel, which included a soft fried pastry with an unpronounceable name that was a local delicacy. It tasted the way a pillow felt, but Satya ate six, to be polite. Rebecca watched him, smiling. He looked back at her defiantly. What did he care what she thought?

They walked through the French Quarter slowly, following a walking tour from Satya's book and squinting to make out different details as he narrated them in rapid succession. Satya himself was unsure which place was which. The masses of brick and stone and wood, while beautiful, all looked the same to him. There were so many banks. How could he tell the difference between the Old Bank of Louisiana and the Old Louisiana State Bank? They were built almost at exactly the same time, sitting across from each other in the crowded streets of the Quarter. Despite the tiny area, trying to find and identify all the mansions belonging to dead men with French and Spanish names left Satya, and therefore Mrs. Sengupta and Rebecca, hopelessly lost. By the time they reached the St. Louis Cathedral Satya was on the verge of giving up, when he saw another tour group listening patiently to a man speaking loudly over the noise of the street.

Satya sidled up to the other tour. It was hot in New Orleans and Mrs. Sengupta's ever-present water bottle was in constant use. She also had, in the depths of her bag, a paper fan, which she produced now and began to wave at herself. Across the street, a group of African American women about her age were doing the same, walking down the street slowly with large-brimmed hats, fanning themselves intermittently. They nodded and smiled at Mrs. Sengupta, identifying her as one of their own, a proud older woman with a fan in hand. Mrs. Sengupta seemed confused by this, but Rebecca grinned broadly at them.

"Hot today, honey! You tell them *that*!" shouted one of the women cheerfully as they passed by. The other tour guide gave them a wolf whistle, which amused his group to no end. Satya was confused. Ronnie had told him that under no circumstances should he make any kind of commentary about any woman during the course of his time guiding. It seemed odd that someone who was serving others would catcall, let alone at this large black woman who had to be in her fifties at least. Old women should be beyond the reach of that kind of filth, his grandmother had always said. The woman didn't mind, though; instead she swished her hips provocatively and winked at the man, drawing waves of laughter and applause from the larger tour group.

They listened to this guide, while very much pretending not to listen, or at least, Satya pretended not to listen while Rebecca stood rapt and Mrs. Sengupta found a shady bench to guzzle her water in peace. Satya was struck by the casual nature of the interaction. Every time he had ever been taught something it had been with the understanding that he was stupid and the teacher was a god. As a tour guide Ronnie had had Satya incorporate this idea but tempered it with the understanding of his place in the social hierarchy, that is, he was a servant, and his knowledge would always come second to how the client wished things to be. But this tour guide had none of the subservience Ronnie had drilled into Satya. He spoke with confidence, yes, the way that Satya tried to do, but also with a kind of ease, a comfort with mistakes, a self-deprecation. He let people ask questions, he corrected them when they were wrong. He seemed to be a kind of guardian of the city, for he spoke of New Orleans as if it were his mother, his wife, and his child all in one.

They walked from sight to sight along the French Quarter as the guide described the mixes and clashes of cultures that had created the world of the Creoles, the French and Spanish periods, the city during the Civil War, the shifts and struggles that had blended together disparate peoples in the slow hot saucepan of the city until it had served up something delicious. They walked through the French Market and past the many houses of Southern millionaires, each with a more scandalous story and a more opulent building than the one before. It was a wild city, Satya realized, far smaller than New York but much more colorful, because the color didn't come from blinking lights but from people, the way they lived and dressed, the smells and the constant music everywhere, pouring out of houses and cars and living in the air.

He liked this place, he realized. It was the first place on their trip he had actually liked, a place he would want to spend more time in, wander through on his own, even if the driver from the airport had been racist. There were spices in the air he recognized—cumin, chili pepper, saffron—and those he didn't, scents that tickled his nose. His mouth watered for something new. He had never actually liked a city before. Home was home and before he had left Sylhet he hadn't been many other places in Bangladesh. All the places he had been felt the same to him, village or city, because he had nothing to do there. New York had been hard and overwhelming but it had also been all he knew of America. Now he was starting to see that there were more options here, more than the movies showed and more than the streets of Brooklyn, Manhattan, and Queens. He liked it here. For the first time, having an opinion felt important.

Before he knew what had happened, the walk was over, and Satya realized that he and his charges had followed the other tour through its entirety. Rebecca stepped forward and offered the man a small folded piece of paper, which Satya realized was money. As they walked away he scowled at her.

"Why did you do that?" He was angry at himself, furious, in fact. He had been so lost in his thoughts, in his admiration of the city and in his revelation of the expansion of his own mind, that he had forgotten to do his job. He decided it was Rebecca who had dragged them into this. But she was already pointing at a sign that said FREE NEW ORLEANS WALKING TOURS, PAY WHAT YOU WISH.

"You can give something, if you want. Why not? It was interesting."

Mrs. Sengupta seemed struck by the sign. "Pay what you wish? What is this?"

"It is a foolish American custom." Satya cut Rebecca off before she could say anything. "Imagine, madam, all paying what they wish, who would wish to pay at all? It is a way to get nothing for something." But in fact, people were lining up to pay the guide. He smiled and nodded to them as they deposited small and large handfuls of paper money into his hand, and they thanked him for his guiding, looking straight into his eyes and smiling. Those who did not pay were also the recipients of smiles and nods, with none of the shaming Satya would have expected from the group or from the guide.

"I think it's nice. This guy loves his city," Rebecca said.

"Actually, it's not my city," said the guide, who'd overheard them. "I just love it here. I'm from Los Angeles originally, but I couldn't stay. I needed a place with some history, you know?" Satya found himself nodding along, his indignation receding. He could understand completely. He had come from a place with a history that felt worthless.

As they walked back to the hotel, he realized something the guide had said had affected Mrs. Sengupta, but what, he could not tell. She stood apart from them, quiet and still as they moved through the city. Satya felt that he knew the streets now, and that gave him some comfort, where he had been lost before. But Mrs. Sengupta seemed the opposite of comforted. She moved as if walking pained her and clutched her scarf around her despite the heat. Rebecca caught his eye and shrugged. He looked away. She shifted closer to him as they walked.

"It's a nice city, right? New Orleans. I've only been here once before, I don't remember liking it so much. New York is great and I love it more than anything, but it's nice to be somewhere that feels like it's the product of people, not companies. You know what I mean?"

Satya didn't know what she meant, really, but he wanted to. He felt that by liking it here as they walked through the warm, gooey air of Louisiana smelling the salt and water in the wind, he was starting to.

"What do you think of New Orleans?" This was Rebecca again, addressing their withdrawn widow. The woman flinched as Rebecca spoke, and Rebecca drew back carefully. She looked at Satya again. When Mrs. Sengupta had been so tired in Philadelphia they had managed to work together to help her, to keep her comfortable and healthy. But now she did not seem unwell, just distant.

"It is a very nice place. Very colorful. It seems old, like being in a museum, but one that is alive."

"That's beautiful," Rebecca said.

Pival looked at her strangely. "If you will excuse me, I am feeling tired only. I will not eat tonight. I simply want rest."

"Are you sure—"

"I know my own self," the widow snapped sharply at Rebecca. "I do not need you to give me certainty. You are here to accompany me, not to tell me how to feel."

Rebecca nodded quickly, clutching her arms around herself like she was giving herself a hug. Satya watched them both, worried. He never would have challenged Mrs. Sengupta the way Rebecca did, and he understood her anger at Rebecca's presumption, but he also understood now that the girl was just concerned. He saw tears gleaming at the edges of her eyes as she walked slowly behind Mrs. Sengupta. It surprised him that this reproach from a stranger bothered her to the point of pain. What a strange person, to be so affected by the actions of those she didn't know.

Together they silently seemed to agree on a pace behind Mrs. Sengupta, and though Satya and Rebecca walked together they looked in opposite directions as they returned to the hotel. Mrs. Sengupta had made her clothing into a kind of cocoon, wrapping her voluminous shawl around her body and keeping herself protected from the world. They stepped into the elevator together, and Satya pressed the button for their floor without a word. They all looked up together to watch the numbers light up as they ascended, exited as quietly as they had entered, walked to their rooms carefully, and stood in front of their doors all together, like a scene from a movie. Mrs. Sengupta lingered outside of her room and Satya and Rebecca waited politely for her to let herself in before they opened their own doors. Satya looked at her and hesitated. He knew he was not supposed to interfere but something about the day, the city, it made him bold.

"The restaurant for tonight—"

"I am not hungry."

"It will deliver." Satya looked at Mrs. Sengupta, who stared at him. He was not surprised at her arrested expression. This was the boldest he had ever been with someone like her, someone so beyond him in class. But since he had thrown his authority as a guide away on the walking tour of New Orleans, he might as well throw away his subservience, as well. He wasn't in Bangladesh anymore, and neither was she. Their trip would only last a handful of days more. Perhaps taking care of the widow, who was frail and growing frailer as they traveled, would be better than bowing to her every whim.

"I, I suppose—" She was hesitating. He took out his phone to call.

"I'll buy some wine." This came from Rebecca, of course. They both turned to Mrs. Sengupta, who was still dithering, drawn back into herself, standing on the edge of agreeing.

"That would be nice. Thank you," she said, and opened up her door, sliding in, her silk garments moving around her like snakes. Rebecca nodded to Satya and set off down the hall again, leaving him to get the food while she hunted for beverages. He wanted a soda from her, a Coke, if possible, but he would let her purchase what she wanted. After all, he would not be consulting her on the food.

Within an hour they met at Mrs. Sengupta's door. Rebecca, a plastic bag reading WINES AND SPIRITS FROM THE BIG EASY in her hands, knocked on the door, while Satya juggled his bag of food. Nothing happened for a long moment. Then Mrs. Sengupta, her clothing rumpled and her hair loosening from its nighttime braid, answered the door.

"I apologize for myself, I was asleep only."

"It's been a long day," Rebecca agreed, gently nudging past her and into the room. Satya wondered if the widow had changed her mind, and then, as he saw Rebecca preparing the room's small table for dining, dragging it close to the bed, realized that Rebecca suspected this, too, and was not about to let her do so. Rebecca made things happen for herself. Why had he disliked this quality about her that he most needed in himself?

He watched Rebecca's body contort itself to spread out the food, which she had taken from him after setting up the drinks, including a Coke. Some part of him felt cared for in the same way he had when his grandmother made his favorite meal. He popped the can open and sipped, enjoying Rebecca's movements and the soda in equal measure.

"Dinner is served!" Rebecca sat back, announcing it proudly. Mrs. Sengupta was still hovering over her, anxiously clutching her hands together.

"I got many things," Satya mentioned, "but all of this was included, I promise."

Mrs. Sengupta's mouth curved in the ghost of a smile. She finally lowered herself, carefully, onto the bed, and gestured to one of the many containers of thick brown substances. "This is dal?" Rebecca shrugged while Satya nodded. Mrs. Sengupta asked Rebecca to serve her the lentil dish with rice, and Rebecca carefully loaded a paper plate with both and handed it to Mrs. Sengupta. The widow looked around for something, and Satya handed her the foil-wrapped packet of roti wordlessly. She smiled at him again, a real smile of gratitude this time. Satya turned to his own meal but then realized he had not thanked Rebecca for the Coke. He held up his soda with a faint smile.

"I've noticed you like them. You get one at every meal." He was startled. He had not realized she had noticed. It had been a treat at home, and here where it was everywhere, he was indulging. "Wine?" Both Satya and Mrs. Sengupta shook their heads no, but Rebecca sighed heavily and poured them both a measure. "We're in New Orleans. If you don't get drunk here, you're not doing it right."

"The man did not mention such things on the walking tour," Mrs. Sengupta replied stiffly.

"He didn't have to!" Rebecca drank her wine. "This place has more bars per capita than, I don't know, it's some absurd amount."

"Have you been here before?" Mrs. Sengupta asked, curious, hoping to hear about wild adventures.

Rebecca nodded. "With an ex. Nice to be back." Mrs. Sengupta waited for her to go on, but instead of digging into some of the salacious details Pival half dreaded, half longed for, Rebecca just continued eating.

"It was a nice tour," said Mrs. Sengupta, dipping her roti delicately in the dal and trying it. She made a face.

"Don't you like the food?" Rebecca asked, curious. Mrs. Sengupta ate less with each meal, she'd realized. She hadn't thought about it, but now she wondered if perhaps this wasn't what the widow was used to eating.

"Always Punjabi, these chefs are. Too much of everything and so heavy with the ghee." Satya nodded along. Much of the food was different for him, too, and most of it was heavy, nothing like the fish curries and rice he'd eaten so often at home. Still, he liked it.

"What is the difference?" Rebecca asked, her mouth full of a samosa.

"Class," replied Mrs. Sengupta dryly. "No, this is unfair. I say it because it is what my husband always said only." Rebecca swallowed her samosa and poured everyone more wine, although she had been the only one to try hers.

"You must miss him."

"No." Mrs. Sengupta said it with the gentleness of a falling feather and the finality of a bag of lead. "I should, I know. I hope he will forgive me. He was a good man. He was the kind of father he knew how to be, the kind of husband he was supposed to be, but I don't miss him. My son was here."

Satya looked at the widow as she talked. He had never had a father. He had never had anyone but his grandmother, really. What would it have been like to have all that, and then lose it? "Here in New Orleans?" Satya asked.

"Perhaps. I don't know. Here, I meant America. He came here. I do know he went to California." Rebecca's brow furrowed. She seemed to be tucking some piece of information away in her head. Satya wanted to ask more about Mrs. Sengupta's son, like why she was traveling with a guide and not him, but he didn't.

"This is a nice place. I like the way the city feels. It is so open, people are so friendly. It is strange. Everyone is so many different colors, it is nice. It is so old, and it feels like it is haunted, but the ghosts seem friendly," Mrs. Sengupta continued. "Although I don't approve of these things, this kind of drinking, drinking, drinking. It is not good."

"I suppose that depends what you are drinking, doesn't it?" The widow looked at Rebecca, frowning, not understanding the joke.

Rebecca merely smiled and drained her wine, pouring herself more.

"This isn't bad, really. I've had worse. And sometimes, it helps."

"But for how long?" Mrs. Sengupta said the words so quietly, Satya would have thought that they were in his head, only they weren't, he knew, because Rebecca looked up at them as well. She shrugged and sipped.

"I didn't know the food was so different, place to place. I sort of thought it was all the same. So you don't eat this stuff at home?"

"It's not that we don't eat it, it's that, well, the way it tastes is different from region to region. At home, we ate in the Bengali style, different vegetables, bitter gourds and banana flowers, and mustard in everything. That's what my husband and I liked. In general in Kolkata we eat a lot of fish. Although I don't, anymore. Widows are supposed to be vegetarians."

"Why?"

"I don't know. We just are." Satya didn't know either. It was a relief that Mrs. Sengupta was equally clueless.

"So you just go along with this, even though you don't know why? That's . . . wow. I couldn't do that."

"If you lived somewhere where it was hard to do otherwise, you might," Mrs. Sengupta said. Rebecca looked at her, opened her mouth to speak, and then closed it. She drank her wine.

They spent the rest of the meal in silence, eating quickly. Rebecca looked up from time to time, and Satya wondered if the silence of the meal bothered her. He had observed that her family talked throughout their meal, a practice that confused him. How could you possibly eat that way?

Mrs. Sengupta delicately wiped her mouth, signaling that she was done. Satya himself was on his third plate of food and could have eaten more, but the widow's frequent yawns indicated that she needed sleep, and because the food had been a part of her tour package he didn't feel it would be right to request to take it with him. Well, maybe just a plateful, she wouldn't mind, would she? Surely she wouldn't eat it all. He was, he realized, acting like he would have to split his food with Ravi. The habit hadn't left him, despite the absence of his friend.

Rebecca busied herself cleaning and setting the room to rights, and before he had a chance to broach the subject of leftovers all the food was neatly packed away and they were bidding Mrs. Sengupta a good night. Rebecca practically dragged Satya out of the room, while holding the wine bottle, mostly finished, in the other hand. Once out, she put the bottle to her lips and drank up the remaining liquid. It should have looked disgusting, but some part of it was arousing to Satya, her lips curled around the wine bottle opening, her hair flung back. She put the bottle down and looked at him, a glint in her eye that was dangerous.

"You want to get out of here? It's a good drinking town, I told you." She didn't wait for an answer, she just turned and started walking out of the hotel, the wine bottle in her hand swaying in time with her rear. Satya watched her walk. He wasn't supposed to do this, he knew. Ronnie would kill him. Whatever it was Rebecca wanted tonight, it wouldn't be good for the tour, and wasn't that the most important thing right now? The only thing he was certain of was that he absolutely shouldn't go.

He followed her out the door and into the city.

New Orleans was a different world at night. The sun-drenched lazy pond he had seen that day had transformed into a brightly lit sea of open doors, of bars and drunken people rejoicing in the streets. Around them signs proclaimed the discounts of their respective establishments. Five shots for ten dollars, proudly boasted one, while another promised the world's best margarita for $5.99 plus tax. There was so much alcohol, more than he'd ever seen in his life. In Bangladesh drinking was covert, careful, ill-advised for most, and when people like Satya did drink, spending the night soaked in cheap country liquor, it was discreetly. Here, people were stumbling, walking fast, spilling out of bars and sending lush vapors down the streets around them. He'd never seen anything like it. He had thought New York was a wild place, but this, it overwhelmed his senses. He felt drunk on the smell alone. It repulsed him, but he wanted to be a part of it, somehow. Rebecca looked around, grinning.

"I told you it was a fun town. You pick the place." There was something reckless about her now, something dangerous, which had been simmering since that dinner with her family and was now on the verge of erupting. He wondered what would happen when it did. He pointed to a bar nearby that didn't look overly crowded and had music spilling out of it like water. He knew being around too many people would make him self-conscious, drinking with a woman in public. Rebecca looked impressed.

"A dive! Excellent choice, totally in keeping with the expert tour guide you are. Come on." They entered the bar together. Satya was struck by the fact that no one here seemed surprised to see a white woman with a Bangladeshi man. Not many people had raised their eyebrows at them wherever they had gone in New Orleans, unlike on the road and in the airport.

"Congratulations, Satya, in a world of crap I think you've actually found the one decent local bar. Let's get hammered." Rebecca leaned over the bar, the skin on the small of her back showing as her blouse rose up with the movement, and motioned for the bartender to serve them. He walked over slowly, smiling. Satya saw it out of the corner of his eye; his gaze was glued magnetically to Rebecca's back, to that creamy strip of flesh and the twisting body that revealed it. He wished deeply that he was not a virgin. At least if he had seen a woman naked before, a real one, even slightly naked, he would not be staring like an idiot. He tore his gaze up toward the bartender.

"What can I do you for?" the bartender asked.

"Whiskey, please. One on the rocks and, do you like ice?" This was to Satya. He shook his head no. Ice in every drink was still a strange concept for him and he could not get used to it. He avoided it when he could.

"And one neat. Thank you!" The bartender tipped an imaginary hat and Rebecca laughed, a little too loud, but it made people look at her. As they got their drinks, which Rebecca paid for, claiming she owed him one for coming to the play with her back in Philadelphia, a tall man with a scruffy beard walked up to the bar, sitting on the other side of Rebecca. He didn't look at her once, but Satya watched as her body changed, growing aware of the man beside her. The stranger bought himself a drink but didn't return to his seat. Rebecca drank her whiskey quickly. Satya tried his hesitantly. He hadn't had much whiskey, and besides, you could only get a few brands in Bangladesh, and they had all tasted the same to him. This was different, smoky but sweet.

"What is this?"

"Oh, it's a bourbon, actually. I guess down here when you ask for whiskey this is what you get."

"What else would you want?" This had come from the stranger on Rebecca's other side, his voice twangy and deep.

"I can think of a few things," Rebecca murmured, finishing her drink and gesturing for another.

"I've got this one."

"I'm here with a friend." Satya enjoyed being called her friend, even if it wasn't true.

"I'll get his, too. What'll you have, quiet guy?"

Satya shrugged. "This is nice," he said, taking another sip. The man gestured for more drinks.

"That's some accent. Where you from? Australia?" Rebecca was already rolling her eyes. Satya had to stifle his own laughter.

"I am from Bangladesh." The man seemed confused by this response. "It is a country, near India," Satya added helpfully. He had grown used to people not knowing about Bangladesh.

"Oh, you're Indian. That's cool. You like Indians?" This last part was to Rebecca.

"I like a lot of people." She looked at the stranger for a long moment, giving him half a smile, and then turned back to Satya.

"You two from out of town?" The smile on Rebecca's face broadened, but only Satya could see it. She quickly turned it to a stern expression as she glanced back over her shoulder. This was a game.

"I'm sorry, we're just trying to have a drink here."

"Hell, so am I! But what's a drink without a little friendly conversation?" The man slid his hand around Rebecca's waist. Satya's eyes widened. He was torn between interest and concern. He had grown up in a world where people did not touch each other in public, and watching someone he knew be touched in this way by a stranger both fascinated him and upset him, even though he had just been imagining doing the same thing to the same part of Rebecca. He could not tell if Rebecca was enjoying it or not, but he knew he should not let this man be groping her waist so casually.

"Don't you agree, baby?"

"I'm not your baby."

"But you could be. Couldn't you?" While Satya had been deciding how to react, the conversation had continued, and now Rebecca was tucked up under the stranger's arm, his hand heavy on her waist. She did not seem distressed, but neither did she seem interested. It was almost as if she were watching this happen from very far away.

"I like bourbon," Satya said. He didn't know what else there was to say. Apparently, it had been the right thing, because the stranger released Rebecca to clap him, Satya, on the back in drunken agreement.

"I like you, India! I like both of you. Y'all want another round?"

The bourbon appeared before them like magic all evening. Satya stopped counting what drink he was on, or how many Rebecca had had; she seemed to double him constantly, downing two to his one. Still, her eyes were clear, brighter than before, even. Satya had stopped responding to the stranger, whose name, they had learned, was Ted, about three drinks ago, because not only could he not understand anything that was coming out of Ted's mouth, he could barely understand the words coming out of his own. He had never been this drunk before. The first time he had been drunk had been on two beers shared with Ravi and they had thrown rocks at stray dogs and laughed and laughed and laughed at their yelps. His tolerance for alcohol hadn't really improved from there. Now he sat slumped over his barstool, watching Ted paw at Rebecca like one of those dogs finding a piece of meat. He saw them kiss, out of the corner of his eye, and then he watched as Rebecca pulled back, her mouth wet, her eyes hard.

"We have to go."

"Hey, baby, wha, wha, wha y'sayin?" Ted seemed to be swaying, but Satya didn't know if that was Ted or himself.

"We have to go. Sorry. Early morning. Great night. Thanks!" Rebecca slid some money down the bar for the bartender and tried to hop off her seat, but Ted's arms were there, holding her in place.

Rebecca looked at Ted's hand as if it was something disgusting. Her mood seemed to have shifted immediately. When she spoke, it was in a low tone of warning.

"Please get off of me."

"No, hey, baby, no, I been, I been buying you drinks all night, stay here, okay?"

"No. Not okay." Rebecca was now struggling to extricate herself from Ted's grasp while Satya looked on, his mouth open wide. He knew he should be doing something, protecting her in some way, but all he could do was watch. She stamped on Ted's foot and he released her, swearing loudly.

"You fucking bitch! Dumb slut! What the fuck is this, you whore?" As soon as the words hit Satya's ears they exploded, and his body moved almost without his mind's knowing about it. His fist connected with Ted's face before he knew what was happening, though the blistering pain of his hand meeting the idiot's firm jawbone jolted Satya into a more sober state. Ted reeled back, and Rebecca grabbed Satya's hand, the one that had just hit Ted, giving him another nasty shock. She dragged him out of the bar much as she had dragged him into it, thanking the bartender loudly and laughing.

Outside, Rebecca gasped for air and let go of Satya's hand, the hand he had just used to hit someone, the hand now pulsing with pain. She looked at him, grinning, and suddenly he couldn't feel his hand at all. From behind them in the bar he heard a roar, shouts, protests. He looked at Rebecca. Together, without a word, they began to run.

They ran almost until they reached the hotel, and stood against a wall, panting and trying to catch their respective breaths. Rebecca turned to Satya, and before he knew what was happening her lips were on his, kissing him gently. She pulled back, her eyes soft.

"Thank you, Satya."

She was smiling at him. She wanted him. She was happy he had saved her from that man, happy he had saved her for himself. He lunged for her, kissing her so hard her teeth clicked against his. She pushed him away, shaking her head.

"No. Do you understand? No."

He nodded, but he didn't understand. Hadn't she kissed him? Didn't she want him? It made his stomach lurch and once again, after a night out with her in a strange city, he threw up. This time she stayed with him, and helped him into the hotel, clucking at him gently and making sure he made it to bed. He lay awake, trying to touch himself, only to find his hand was in too much pain to do so. He closed his eyes and slept a drunken sleep, dreaming about her lips and her waist and her breasts until her image blended with those of all the other women in his life, with his mother and her pictures and her big sad eyes, and his grandmother, and he was held by them all, held close and cradled and loved. He dreamed she hadn't pushed him away, just held him closer and let him in.

The first question Rebecca asked herself as she woke up the next morning in a wash of sunlight from her open windows, hungover and thirsty, was what had she been thinking, kissing Satya. She knew the why, the why was all the bourbon, but it didn't excuse the fact that it had happened. She stumbled out of bed, brushed her teeth, and gagged at her image in the mirror. The taste of alcohol was still in her mouth as she downed water and Advil and checked the time, seven thirty A.M. She cursed softly. She didn't have to be up much before nine A.M., but she never slept well after heavy drinking. She lay back on the bed anyway, willing her head to stop spinning.

It had been a stupid, senseless night. She had been feeling confined and reckless after seeing her parents. She had a tried-and-true way to cure this: it was drinking and meeting a man and letting him pound away at her while she went somewhere calm and comfortable in her mind, so she could emerge, rested and refreshed, and go back to being herself again.

But bringing Satya with her ruined that. She couldn't leave him in the bar alone, and she refused to have sex in a public bathroom for reasons of hygiene, good taste, and physical comfort. So she had resigned herself to blowing off some steam with bourbon alone, and she had been charmed by Satya's reaction to the drink and by the strange turn her life had taken, drinking with a Bangladeshi tour guide in the French Quarter. But when that guy had shown up, *Ted,* it had condemned the evening to chaos. She shouldn't have talked to him, shouldn't have flirted. She had known from the way he talked to her that he wouldn't get the game; instead he would get drunk and ugly and make a mess.

He had been a senseless pig, as she had known he would be. She had been fully equipped to handle men like him until her white knight of a tour guide had swung his fist. Thankfully she had dragged them out of the bar before there was a fight, comforting herself with the knowledge that things like this happened in New Orleans all the time.

All of that in and of itself would have been fine. But why did she have to compound the evening of drunken stupidity and kiss Satya? She had forgotten that it might mean something more to him than it did to her. He was so young. He was from a conservative country. He probably thought she was a Western whore.

Her hands were shaking again. *Must be a new nerves thing.* She clutched them into the bedsheets lying smoothly under her, burying them in cheap cloth so that they wouldn't be seen. If she didn't see it, it wasn't happening.

She looked at the clock again. It was eight A.M. That was a respectable time to arrive at breakfast. Mrs. Sengupta would, Rebecca knew, already be there. She wondered if the woman was sleeping at all. Each day she seemed more fragile, the dark circles under her eyes the color of new bruises. She wondered again why Mrs. Sengupta was really taking this trip. She wished that they hadn't had dinner with her parents, that her parents lived in Alaska or Italy or New Guinea, anywhere but a stop on this tour. Now there was too much of herself on display, so much for Mrs. Sengupta and Satya to see.

Rebecca rubbed her eyes and went down to breakfast. She spotted the widow immediately upon entering the breakfast room. All the hotels so far had provided breakfast for their guests, but Mrs. Sengupta was surveying that day's offerings, plainly unimpressed.

"Pretty pathetic, isn't it?"

"This country is allergic to good tea," Mrs. Sengupta murmured, provoking a laugh from Rebecca.

"Hang on." A quick Google search revealed a café around the corner whose tea was, to quote a review, "Tea Die For." Rebecca assumed these awful bits of wordplay were par for the course for rampant tea drinkers, and besides, anything had to be better than this. She coaxed Mrs. Sengupta out the door, leaving word for Satya at the front desk, and had her sitting with a cup of delicately scented oolong within minutes. She herself enjoyed a decent cup of coffee and a croissant, willfully ignoring what the pastry would do to her thighs.

Looking down at her phone, Rebecca realized that she hadn't actually checked it for two days, other than to see the time or the battery life. At home in New York she was glued to her phone, constantly checking for updates, catching up on social media, reading audition notices and casting breakdowns, examining entertainment news and emails from her agent. You had to, she knew; if you didn't check your phone you could miss jobs by minutes. It had happened more than once. But she hadn't been doing it, and life had gone on.

Outside, New Orleans was just waking up, the sun illuminating its gorgeous streets. Rebecca saw a drunk stumble out of a bar and wondered what had happened to Ted. He probably had kept on drinking until he passed out. He seemed the type. What was wrong with her? Everything about him had disgusted her but it was only because Satya had been there that she hadn't slept with him. She was sick of sleeping with people she didn't like.

"What do you think?" Rebecca said, referring to the tea in Pival's hands.

"It is a nice city, as I have said."

"No, the tea," Rebecca said, smiling.

Mrs. Sengupta shrugged and wiggled her head from side to side. "Nice."

Nice seemed to be the most popular word in English among Indians, Rebecca reflected, leaning back in her seat and sipping her own coffee.

"Good tea. Different, but good." The moment stretched on, with Mrs. Sengupta carefully sipping after adding equal portions of milk and sugar. Rebecca watched the widow slip bits of her scone into the milky liquid and then fish them out again with her spoon, eating the mush with apparent happiness. Their silence was companionable but careful, making a bubble rise in Rebecca's throat. But Mrs. Sengupta interrupted her thoughts.

"Now. You tell me about yourself. This boyfriend you mentioned last night, was it serious?"

Rebecca almost laughed but caught herself in time. Mrs. Sengupta sounded like a mother—no, like a grandmother, all stern and waiting to hear about Rebecca's romantic past.

"I wouldn't say so, no."

"But you took a trip with him. Surely it must have been—that is, did you have family to stay with here?"

Rebecca looked at the widow, wondering what she meant. "No. I don't have family here."

"Oh. But then, did you, did you stay together? In one room?"

"Yes, we—" Rebecca didn't get to finish her sentence. Mrs. Sengupta's face had become a mask of fascinated horror, and Rebecca suddenly realized the inquiry behind the questions.

"Did you . . . have many boyfriends?"

Rebecca couldn't suppress her smile this time. The widow sounded almost reverential.

"I've had a few. Some better than others. The one I came here with was nice. He's living in Texas now, married a girl from business school."

"I'm sorry."

"That's all right. I'm prettier than her. I checked." Rebecca smiled and Mrs. Sengupta nervously laughed.

"What was it like? Being with, with so many men?"

Rebecca thought for a long moment.

"Freeing," she said gently. "And sometimes very lonely, too. But I wouldn't trade it. And I'm not a prostitute, you know. You don't have to feel sorry for me."

"I don't," Mrs. Sengupta said, looking in her eyes. And Rebecca knew she meant it. It was time, she thought, to ask some questions of her own.

"Why did your son come to America? If you don't mind me asking." She had been rehearsing the words since Mrs. Sengupta had first mentioned him. She wondered where he was, why Mrs. Sengupta spoke about him in such oblique ways.

Mrs. Sengupta looked startled. Rebecca thought to apologize for the question, but then she decided against it. In a few days, Mrs. Sengupta would be gone, and Rebecca would return to New York, never to see either her or Satya again. Rebecca could not spend this much time with people, travel this long a distance, and remain strangers to them. Though she knew that people made journeys with strangers all the time and never thought twice about it, she wasn't wired that way.

Rebecca maintained eye contact, waiting for the widow to talk about her son. After a moment, Mrs. Sengupta seemed to break through an interior barrier and replied.

"He came here to study. And to leave India."

"Do a lot of people do that?" Rebecca wasn't sure if she was asking about studying or leaving India.

Mrs. Sengupta smiled wryly. "Many people want to leave. So many of our young people go, in our community. Bengalis, that is. Some come back. But"—here she hesitated, searching for the right way to say what was on her mind—"for many, there is not such a reason to return. I do not think we make it easy for our young people, sometimes. There are so many ways that people have to be, at home. Here it seems less like that. Is that true?"

Rebecca thought about it for a moment. "Well. You saw my own family, didn't you? I mean, people expect things of their children, everywhere."

"Yes, but. Forgive me, but, it does not seem as if those expectations have affected you that much. Please, do not be offended. It is only, you still live the way you want to live. And you live so far from home. On your own. You are allowed to live alone. You do not need to face those expectations every day, you do not see your mother's face when you come home. There are not people around you, talking about what you are doing and where you are going and what it means with each other and with, with your parents. There are not people watching you, caring what you are doing, changing what you do by their care. Are there?"

"No. I don't know what that would be like at all."

Mrs. Sengupta nodded. "I see now why so many don't return. I did not understand before I was visiting here only. I have never seen people so free in this way, free from each other. It is hard to miss your home, I think, but it must be hard to be here and then return to a place where you are so, so . . ."

"Confined?"

"Something like this. My Rahi came here to study, but I believe he stayed because it was better here, for him. We did not make it easy for him at home. He was different than many are and that is, that is not possible. There are so many things here, ways to learn and ways to be. You said it was easier here for people, in different cities. There are so many places to go. Each city I have visited I have asked people, what is it like? And they say different things. There is only one way, at home, it seems, sometimes."

"What did he study?"

Mrs. Sengupta smiled. "He was a marine biologist. Or, he wanted to be. His father was so angry. Like a little boy, he said, playing in the sea. Rahi couldn't even swim, just make sand castles and look at the snails. His father said this was what his job would be. No income potential, not a good job at all. But Rahi loved it. He would tell me such things in his letters, and on the phone. I am old-fashioned only, email was not easy for me. Too many buttons. I have learned, now. Too late. Rahi would write me letters, like a good boy. All about fish and plants and things living in the water, such nonsense, but he made it seem so wonderful. I did not understand much of his work, only that he was happy. I do think most parents, at the heart, want their children to be happy. It is only that we want our children to be happy in the right way. The way we were taught happiness was. I think this is a cause of much pain, thinking, perhaps, that there is a right way. I thought there was only one way for him to be happy, I did not understand anything else."

Rebecca sat quietly. This was the longest thing Mrs. Sengupta had ever said to Rebecca, and she didn't know, really, what it meant. It was a gift, Rebecca knew, what Mrs. Sengupta had been saying to her, only Rebecca wasn't sure how to open it.

The widow smiled self-consciously and sipped her tea. She did not apologize for her long speech, or her opinions. She simply let them hang in the air between them. Rebecca appreciated this. She had to unpack everything the woman had said, discover its meaning, before she would be able to respond. Their drinks disappeared and were refilled. The silence between them was occupied by Rebecca's mind, working furiously, and Mrs. Sengupta's mouthfuls of milky tea. Finally Rebecca asked the question Mrs. Sengupta had dreaded.

"Where is he now? Your son?" Mrs. Sengupta looked as though Rebecca had slapped her. Rebecca didn't flinch. Mrs. Sengupta breathed deeply and exhaled, her mouth working, trembling. Rebecca wondered what was coming. Would she scream at Rebecca? Would she cry? Would she tell Rebecca that this was, as Rebecca knew, simply none of her business? But she did none of these things. She closed her eyes and breathed deeply again, in through her nose and out through her mouth, the way they always told Rebecca to in yoga class. Her eyes were still closed when she spoke.

"I don't know. I was told that he died. Very suddenly, one day, in Los Angeles. This is in California." She said the words dully, as if she were reciting facts in school. Rebecca had done a report on the state of Iowa for her fifth-grade class and she had described the state in the same way that Mrs. Sengupta now described what she knew of her child.

"My husband has told me that he received a phone call from his, his friend in California. My husband said that his heart stopped. I do not know if it is true."

"Why would he lie about that?"

"We—my husband—we could no longer speak to our son."

"I'm sorry." The words felt painful in Rebecca's mouth, dry as dust and worthless.

"Thank you." More questions bubbled up in Rebecca, but she pushed them back down this time. There was nothing she could say on the subject of this woman's son. Their last stop was Los Angeles. She had wondered why. Now she understood that this trip had not been for the purposes of seeing the United States. They were taking a slow trip across the country to ready Mrs. Sengupta for Los Angeles. She must have wanted to meet this friend, see for herself in person; she must have needed time to prepare, and so she had built that time in, distracting herself with waterfalls and monuments. She wondered if the friend was someone Mrs. Sengupta would not approve of, a girlfriend who wasn't Indian, perhaps. Rebecca understood now. Jews sat shiva. The widow was traveling it.

They returned to the hotel to find a frantic Satya relieved to see them. He had not thought to ask at the front desk if a notice had been left for him, and he was concerned about their flight to Phoenix in three hours. From Phoenix they would take a train to see the Grand Canyon, early the next morning, and then fly to Las Vegas that evening. Apparently the West Coast of the country wasn't worth much time. With the arrogance of an East Coaster, Rebecca could hardly disagree. She herself had never been to the Grand Canyon or Las Vegas, though she couldn't imagine what kind of experience she, Satya, and Mrs. Sengupta would have in Sin City. Perhaps the widow could use that city to sleep. Or think about the stranger she was about to meet and the city her son had lived in without her, without expectations and without wanting to come home.

Did her own parents feel that they had lost their child to a city? Rebecca wondered. She did not often think well of her parents. But then, she had not questioned her devotion to acting, either, and here she was suddenly doing both.

Soon, they were in a cab to the airport. Rebecca could smell three kinds of toothpaste and mints coming from Satya's mouth as he tried to herd Mrs. Sengupta like a sheepdog. He was freshly showered, his hair still wet, and he seemed presentable, but she could see him wincing at the bright sun and she thought he must be at least as hungover as she had been before her coffee. She met his eyes and smiled, but he seemed flustered, and he didn't look her way again. As they waited for their flight, she handed him a coffee she had bought him after the security check, while waiting through an interminable pat-down for Satya. Satya was not destined to go through a security checkpoint without being noticed. Rebecca was past anger and into amusement. She couldn't imagine a more hopeless terrorist. She told him this as he opened the paper cup to see a coffee with so much milk it looked like butterscotch pudding, pale beige and creamy. He took a reluctant sip and smiled at the amount of sugar. Apparently five packets was right. His tentative thank-you was stiff, but Rebecca simply nodded a "you're welcome" and looked out onto the terminal. She would let Satya get over his discomfort on his own. They weren't the first people who had kissed after a night of drinking, and they would hardly be the last. He would learn from her how to move on. It would be a welcome-to-America gift.

"I used to have a friend and he always wanted to see the Grand Canyon."

Rebecca looked at Satya. It was a strange thing to say, she thought, that he used to have a friend. "What happened to him?"

Satya took a long swallow of his coffee. "He is not my friend anymore. But I am thinking of him just now. I would not know what it was without him. He had read about it in a book and told me it was one thing in America worth seeing. And now I will see it, and he will never know."

"I'm sorry." It was the second time she had said that today. Somehow the two losses she was responding to felt equally important, although she couldn't have said why. It was, perhaps, the way each statement had been spoken, as if it were an irreversible truth, indelibly marked on the life of the speaker. What can't be changed must be endured. She had read that on a greeting card somewhere and hated it. She had yet to accept that there were things that couldn't be changed, and meeting people who not only accepted it, who in fact knew it in their souls, vibrated through her with the impact of a shovel meeting a stone. Satya was looking at her intensely. She turned away.

Their flight took just under four hours. Rebecca thought her mind was too full to sleep but woke up just as the plane hit the runway in Arizona with the bright sun gleaming off the tarmac. Phoenix was baking in late September. It was almost October, Rebecca thought as she adjusted her sunglasses and looked out at the city, flat as a pancake and covered in wide roads and wide cars and wide people. It was evening on the East Coast but it was earlier here than Rebecca wanted it to be. She looked at her hands, which weren't shaking at all now. The morning seemed a long way off.

Their hotel, a Best Western, was squat and sandy, overly air-conditioned, with all the charm of a prison cell. Rebecca unpacked nothing but her sweaters and wrapped them around herself as she shivered in the frigid room. The Indian meal that evening at Tandoor Kebab was a particularly bad one. Rebecca supposed that vegetarian curry was unpopular in this land of Mexican food and Southwestern chilies. All the cumin was evidently seasoning meat, not enhancing lentils. There certainly was no flavor in any of the dishes they endured that evening, the soggy sag paneer with soured cheese and sad gooey rice, which managed to be simultaneously under- and overcooked. Rebecca sighed as she poked at a mushy portion of chana masala and regretted not eating more in New Orleans. They should have been swimming in gumbo to make up for this worthless dinner.

She was surprised to see Satya also picking at his food listlessly. This was the first time this had ever happened. She began to laugh. Mrs. Sengupta looked up at the sound of her laughter. The meal had been entirely silent up until this point, with each of them lost in their thoughts, in the exhaustion of travel, and in fighting the cold of the Arizona air-conditioning obsession. Now, though, Mrs. Sengupta stared at Rebecca, who was almost doubled over with laughter, and without warning, joined her, tears forming in her eyes. Satya's face reflected complete confusion. Rebecca simply pointed at his plate and the dishes around them, all of which were still laden with food. Satya looked down and up again, confused, his befuddlement only adding to the laughter at the table.

"What's happened?"

Rebecca tried to catch her breath. "Aren't, aren't you, hungry?" Satya's face cleared in an instant, and his sheepish grin would have spanned a football field if not for the limitations of his cheeks. He sat as the two women laughed and laughed, and Mrs. Sengupta's laughter turned freely from laughter to tears as they sat in the horrible restaurant and ignored the miserable food. The widow wiped her eyes and smiled a watery smile.

"I would wish that I could cook for you, to show you what is better, but I do not cook. You are the one who cooks," the widow reminded Satya.

"I'm not very good. I'm about as bad as this. But my grandmother tried to teach me," Satya revealed, blushing.

Mrs. Sengupta smiled. "I am sure she is proud."

"She was, I think. She is gone now." Satya said it without self-pity, another fact. "She made the best rotis, though. Nothing like this." He held up a cold roti.

"I think they're tortillas," Rebecca joked.

Satya's eyes sparked with indignation. "Bastards! Think they can trick people!"

"Satya, I'm kidding—" But he was already up and screaming at the management. Once he started rattling away in Bengali, however, the faces of their waiter, the host, and a chef who had emerged and was watching from the doorway to the kitchen all purpled simultaneously with rage. They began screaming in Hindi, and soon a cacophony of noise filled the small and desolate restaurant, echoing against the glass windows and reverberating through Rebecca's ears. What she caught was the phrase "Damn dirty Bangla dog" and suddenly she was adding her own voice to this fight, yelling at them for their racism, for their ignorance and her own, for the fact that she hadn't *had* to know anything about any other part of the world before now. Her own self-disgust burst forth in a mudslide of fury. Before she knew what was happening Satya's hand was on her elbow, and it was his turn to drag her out of a restaurant before a fight occurred. Mrs. Sengupta hurried after them, her purse gripped in her hand and her scarf fluttering back in the manufactured air from the wall AC unit. Before they left, the widow turned back and said one word: "Bastards." And then she exited, as graciously as a queen.

The three of them stood in the sudden desert heat silently, the earlier laughter gone.

"It's better this way. I wouldn't have paid for that meal anyway," Satya said, and then he laughed, a short angry pained chuckle.

"It is better. I am an old woman. I should not have had to hear the evil words of such filthy men," Mrs. Sengupta said stoutly. "Thank you for defending my ears, Satya. Very kind of you. You are an excellent guide."

She bowed slightly over her folded hands and walked toward where their driver, a man named Juan who constantly and quietly spoke Spanish into a Bluetooth attached to his ear, was waiting.

Sitting in the car, Satya realized he was still quite hungry. He looked at Rebecca in mute distress. She rolled her eyes.

"Juan? Do you know a good taco stand around here?"

They sat sweltering near the roadside stand, mouths on fire from the extra chilies Satya and Mrs. Sengupta had requested, faces bathed in salsa. Over her corn and mushroom taco, Mrs. Sengupta's eyes were bright and streaming with happy tears.

"I can't feel my tongue," Rebecca said calmly.

"I was just going to ask if they had anything hotter," Satya said seriously, and Mrs. Sengupta laughed, the sound echoing across the desert. It was, Satya realized, one of the happiest moments he had experienced in months. He wished he could hold on to it, but it was gone, and they were back in the hotel, mouths still smarting with spice, before he knew it.

The morning came bright and clear again, but without the aftereffects of alcohol Rebecca did not find the brilliant Arizona sun so aggressive. She woke up stretching in her blankets, bundled up as though it were January in Chicago, enjoying the light if not the warmth.

On their Grand Canyon Railway tour, she watched the beams of sunlight reflect off the miles of Southwestern desert as they plugged and chugged along, eating up the miles of track slowly but steadily. Giant cacti stood in the distance, looking so perfect that they didn't seem real. Arizona was like a cartoon movie set, from the vultures to the tumbleweeds blowing between the dust-covered plants and enormous red rock formations.

There had been a brief period in Rebecca's life when she had been interested in crystal healing and the energy emitted by the objects around her. It had been a trendy belief to have among the artistic set with whom she ran and she figured she would try anything if it might work. It hadn't, though, and it became expensive with all the crystals to buy and sage to burn, and Rebecca soon abandoned it. But during that time she had read that there was a resonance about the rocks out in Arizona, that they emitted an energy that could affect people, heal them. Now, as she looked across the desert stretching out forever, it made her wonder. Did native peoples really believe this, or had it just been the sheer relief at seeing something solid in a world of shifting sand? Were these gargantuan lumps of red rock sending her signals, trying to break through the glass of the train compartment to reach her and help her on her way? It seemed to her the height of narcissism, to think that the natural world was sending out messages to humans, to assume it cared at all. Didn't the rocks have better things to do?

Next to her, Mrs. Sengupta was also looking out the window as Satya slept, soothed by the swaying motion of the train. The widow glanced at him and smiled. Her hand reached out to smooth the hair across his forehead and he mumbled in his sleep but didn't stir. She gazed at Satya like he was her child. As Rebecca turned away Mrs. Sengupta looked up and smiled at her.

"What is your name? Your first name? Ronnie never told me, actually," Rebecca explained.

"My name is Pival."

"Oh. Thank you."

"You can call me that, if you wish."

Rebecca looked at her curiously. "What does it mean?"

"It means 'tree.' What does Rebecca mean?"

"They say it means 'captivating.' But really it means 'a trap.'"

They both returned their gazes to the window, where the cactus arms with their giant yellow spikes were waving a deceptive hello, reaching out to shake the hands of foolish passersby. Rebecca wished the rocks would send her secret signals, telling her what to do with her life.

They reached the Grand Canyon an hour later. As they got off the train and stared out into the expanse of caverns and crevices carved so deeply and securely into the earth, Rebecca's breath caught in her throat. She had always thought that the Grand Canyon would look like a crack in the ground. This was like that, she supposed, but it was beautiful, immense and spectacular with a thousand shades of orange and red and gray. The bright blue of the sky with its tiny clouds hovering above a sunken world of ridges and valleys, with a brown slippery snake, the Colorado River, winding its way through. They all three walked toward the first viewing point like people possessed, drawn in by the majesty of the canyon.

"How did this happen?" It was Mrs. Sengupta, Pival. She had breathed the question lightly, but her face betrayed how deeply she would count the answer. She looked at Satya, who was, for once, actually prepared.

"Water. All of this is from water. As the river has carved through the stone in a few years until all of this has been revealed."

"In just a few years?" This came from Rebecca, smiling wryly.

"A few. Maybe seventeen million."

"A handful, then." This came from Pival. She was breathing her words again, her voice weak, her chest rising and falling quickly. They stood right at the edge of a viewpoint, alone, somehow, despite all the tourists.

"You must be careful, madam. People meet fatalities here often." Satya's voice was concerned as the widow swayed against the safety railing. She smiled, though, at his words, as her eyes drank in the wide and brilliant views in front of them.

"You mustn't worry, Satya. I will not die here. I promise you that." She spoke with a sense of certainty that should have made Satya feel better, but it only disconcerted him. It disconcerted Rebecca, too. She wondered what the widow had meant—that she wouldn't die, or that she wouldn't die *here*?

"We must take a picture, madam. You have none for the trip." This was true, Rebecca realized. Unlike every other tourist Rebecca had ever encountered, the widow hadn't taken a single photograph. She wasn't even sure if Mrs. Sengupta had a camera.

"Here." Rebecca took out her phone and stood away, ready to snap the photo with the Grand Canyon as the backdrop to Mrs. Sengupta standing in her tunic and trousers.

"I do not need a photograph. There is no one who will care to see this."

"Won't you care?" She didn't respond. "I want one, then. For myself." Rebecca realized as she said it that it was true; she wanted to remember this moment. "Here, can you help us?" she asked a family sporting a tripod and a high-tech series of cameras, who looked not just a little disdainfully at the deficient phone camera. "Come here," she ordered Satya, and looping her arm around him she dragged him into the frame and stood him next to Mrs. Sengupta with herself on the other side, framing her as the Grand Canyon framed them all. When the quick photo session ended, Mrs. Sengupta looked at her and smiled, but there was moisture in her eyes.

The train back blended together with the bus and the taxi to the airport and the flight to Las Vegas. The lights from the Technicolor fluorescent city hurt Rebecca's eyes as they arrived, tired and hungry, late that same night. After the wonders of the canyon, the fake city of fake monuments and fake sights seemed like an insult. Rebecca couldn't believe they had come so far in one day. She wanted to go back, but they simply went forward, to the hotel, to another round of Indian food, to their beds.

Tired as she was, instead of sleeping Rebecca lay in bed thinking about the things she had done to herself, the things she had believed that weren't true, the ways she had always wanted to be another person. She tried to sleep but all she could think about was the river pushing through the rock, and the phrase *There is no one who will care to see this* echoed in her mind over and over and over again until she slept and had nightmares she couldn't remember in the morning.

26

Pival's heart was pounding so loud that she was sure everyone in the hotel, a strange place in the strangest city she could have ever imagined, could hear it. She put down the phone, but her heart didn't calm. If anything, its beating grew only more frantic in the silence of her room. She hadn't meant to call him, really. She didn't know why she had. She had taken the name from her phone's display on the day that the call had come, and when she had searched the numbers on the Internet it took her to a website where people rented out their homes for weekends. She had written down the address and kept it tucked away, not knowing what she would do with it. But today she had simply picked up the hotel phone and called. It was like her hands were moving outside of her body's control.

She had hoped, for one wild, desperate moment, that Rahi would pick up the phone. But it was him instead. His voice had sounded like the voice of a normal American person. She imagined him speaking to her son. She felt sick. She had hung up the call and thought perhaps she should kill herself now, right now. The pain throbbing in her body was so sharp that it didn't seem worth trying to bear. She had wanted to talk to him first, to blame him for what Rahi had done, but if she couldn't do it over the phone, could she even manage it in person? The thought that Rahi awaited her in Los Angeles felt like ever more of a delusion, and what would she do if that was all it had been, a delusion? If she ended her life now she could save herself from the certainty. It would leave a mess, but what did that matter? She wouldn't have to clean it up. And if her body didn't make it to the

Ganges, that would be all right, too. She didn't want another life. It would only go wrong, just like this one. She could run the bath and slit her wrists and be gone.

A knock on the door interrupted these thoughts. She straightened her skirts and smoothed her hand over her hair, and went to open the door to Rebecca and Satya, who were ready to take her to the city tour. Something of her thoughts must have shown in her face, no matter how well she had learned to protect herself over the course of her marriage, because Rebecca laughed and laid a hand on her shoulder.

"It won't be that bad. It's just Vegas, right? We don't have to gamble and we certainly don't have to strip. Unless you want to!"

It was a joke, Pival knew, but she couldn't help flinching at the girl's touch. She had never met anyone who touched people as much as Rebecca did. Being touched made her nervous, but it also felt nice. Her body had been so useless to others for so long now.

"She is joking, please, madam." Satya looked worried.

"I understand. I would not, I think, be very good for stripping. Too much cloth." Rebecca snorted with laughter as Pival gestured to her sari. She felt absurdly happy that she had made Rebecca laugh. She was not a funny person, she knew, and this was not a time she had thought she would develop a sense of humor. She was amazed she could make a joke five minutes after considering suicide.

"Shall we?" It was Rebecca, gesturing out the door. "Oh, sorry, Satya, that's your line."

"You are the actress," he said, giving her a small smile. Whatever was growing between these two, she liked it, although she wasn't sure that Mr. Munshi would approve. But it looked like a genuine friendship, not that she would know. After her marriage, her friends had faded away, as they often did at home when a woman got married and her life began to revolve around her own home. After she got married, the closest thing she had had to a friend was Rahi. Ram met his friends at his club, and Rahi had never brought boys home, although Pival wondered now if that was because he hadn't wanted to or because he wanted to far too much.

She followed her guide and her companion out of the hotel and into the baking heat, which felt more oppressive than it had in Phoenix, although she knew the temperatures were the same. Perhaps it was the harsh sun bouncing off every sharp angle, every hard surface and colored sign. Everything was already too bright, and it wasn't evening yet, when every step would be lit up like a fireworks display, as Pival had seen in photographs. She was not comfortable in this city, but it was the opposite of how she had felt in Washington, surrounded by tombs. Here there was too much life, too many people who looked desperate. She could see groups walking and driving, counting their money and staring at the casinos hungrily.

The city tour was not particularly interesting to Pival, as she had no desire to know more about a place she immediately hated. All the buildings looked like blocks of foam. The heat blurred everything in the corners of Pival's eyes, and she blinked them quickly, wincing at the sand caught underneath her eyelids.

The bus jolted to a stop and suddenly Pival, who had been rubbing her eyes fiercely, realized that they were in a small parking area outside of a massive, brightly colored WELCOME TO LAS VEGAS sign. All the other guests were filing off the bus, so Pival followed them dutifully. *Always dutifully,* she thought, and it filled her head like a bitter cloud. She stopped at the doorway of the bus. People were waiting to have their photo taken with the sign, though she didn't really know why. She supposed it was attractive but she didn't think this would be a moment she would want much to remember. If she hadn't wanted photographs anywhere else, she certainly didn't want one now.

Rebecca and Satya stood, looking up at her.

"Are you coming to see the sign?" Rebecca asked.

"I think I would prefer not. I do not like it here," Pival said. Color flooded her face. She had not expressed any kind of opinion about their tourism activities before this point. She had not dictated anything at all, not even in planning the destinations. It was funny, now that she thought of it. The point of the trip, the exorbitant amount she had paid, the stipulations she had made, all of this was to ensure that she was in charge of what happened, and yet she had been in control of nothing. Ronnie had told her what was done, and she had done it. Parts of it she'd liked and parts she hadn't, and she had thought that this was the way things were, but now she knew, it was the way *she* was. Ram had been in charge and she had accepted it. She had never realized that had she not accepted, he could not have remained in charge. Things might have been different. And the reason that they weren't came from no one but herself.

It seemed strange that her first assertion of authority came at such a stupid time, in such a silly way. Pival sat inside the bus, fanning herself, as the rest of the group took turns taking photos. They posed in strange positions, contorting their faces and bodies like dancers on a stage. She watched them, smiling. She was cool and content where she was. A feeling of certainty filled her like honey slowly drizzling into a bowl. The bus departed again, through the sun-baked streets and past building after building coated with opulence and built at an increasingly overwhelming scale. The bus stopped over and over again, at this point and at that, but Pival remained on it the entire time, resting and relaxing against the plush seats and watching the world go by.

As they were deposited back on the curb of their hotel, a Comfort Inn, Pival actually did feel comforted. She was ready to go to Los Angeles. She would inform Satya and Rebecca that she did not plan to see that city, either, that she had other plans entirely. Until now, she had not known how she would do this, but now she did. It would simply happen. It didn't have to be difficult. She would tell them and they would agree. She had never known how easy it was, telling people what she wanted. If only she had done it long before.

It had started in the teahouse with Rebecca. Or had it begun at Niagara Falls, watching the water pour over and all around them? Or back in Kolkata, defying her servants, sneaking out of the house, doing something she had never done? She felt a surge of love and gratitude for Ram. After all, he had had the kindness to die.

They left Las Vegas at first light the next morning. She felt faint on the bus ride to Los Angeles, a long ride through a never-ending desert. It had been quite a while since she had last eaten. Food had made her stomach twist in knots as the mixture of fear and hope bubbled up in her more with each passing mile. It was not as if they had eaten much that was good here, anyway. *What a strange place,* she thought, *with so much space and nothing good to eat.*

She had agreed to a bus and not a plane because she had thought she might need more time to prepare, but now she was impatient. Every bump in the road seemed personally directed at her; every jolt and sway of the bus only served to make her angry. *Good,* she thought. *Better to be angry.* Feeling so inconvenienced renewed her hope, and she prepared to find Rahi with a resurgence of vigor.

Next to her, Satya was sleeping. He could sleep anywhere. Rebecca was looking out the window as the same view kept passing by. She had headphones in her ears and her mouth moved gently with whatever song she was listening to on her phone. Pival had not known that one could listen to music on one's phone until Rebecca had shown her. Rebecca had played a sad song for her, something sweet and slow. The singer was a woman, but her voice was low, and there was so much of her in the music, so much of her pain. The new songs from home were never so simple; they included so many instruments and melodies that chased each other into new places with every verse. This was repetitive, boring almost. It reminded her of the old songs, of the hymns. She couldn't understand English when it was sung. She had felt Rebecca's disappointment when she had described the thing as *nice*. Rebecca had asked her why she used the word *nice* so much, and she had been ashamed at her vocabulary, once so rich in English, now diminishing to a few overused words. She had thanked Rebecca for sharing the song with her. She wondered if she was listening to that same song now.

Rahi had been crazy for music. Every movie that came out had sent him into a new tailspin of devotion, of humming and singing the latest hit, of dancing through the house with the joy of it. Pival had learned many songs without ever seeing the films that they were meant to accompany, just from Rahi's constant repetition. The high piercing voices of female playback singers and their husky male counterparts had formed the theme songs of his life. She had always been so amazed that he could remember so many things, keeping them all in his head at the same time. *It's music, Ma, it's supposed to stay in your head!* he had told her, laughing at her wonder. Sometimes she would be in a store or a cab and start crying and not know why until she realized that there was music playing, something he had loved.

What did Rahi listen to with this man? Had that *person* been like Rebecca, forcing his own music onto her son? Had he banned Bollywood from the house in favor of sad songs with tunes that went in a circle? She forced herself to think about them together in torturous detail. She tried to imagine what they would be like in bed, but there her imagination failed her; she wasn't sure how any of that worked. She had thought about asking Rebecca, who had seemed like she might know when she mentioned Lincoln, but she had lost her nerve, and now it was too late. She thought of the most disgusting thing she could think of and assumed it must be like that. She would tell this man all the things that he was, and she would know when she died that she had done one thing with her life that was right; she would have defended her son's honor.

After encountering traffic jams on the road, they reached Los Angeles by nightfall. The smog in the air hung around the city like a dirty gray halo, making everything look grimy and sad. Good. She needed no affection for Los Angeles.

That night, entering her room in yet another Best Western, she nodded back to Satya and Rebecca, explaining that she would be having room service. Her voice was firmer than it had ever been, giving Rebecca no room to ask if she was sure. She shut the door and turned on all the lights. She carefully unpinned her sari from her shoulder. She gently unbound it, unraveling every layer, everything that shielded her from the world. She remembered the story of Draupadi, the princess who, when about to be stripped and dishonored in public, was saved by a never-ending series of saris, winding away into infinity. She was not that princess. Her sari ended, leaving her bare. She took off her petticoat, her choli blouse, her bra, and her underwear. She unpinned and unbraided her long hair, letting the graying waves hang to her waist. She turned her eyes to the mirror, looking at her naked body.

She always avoided her body. She had ignored it for years as a child, and then as it had begun to change it had scared her, the hair that flourished in between the folds of things, the crevices of her armpits and the world between her legs that no one would ever tell her about. The plumpness of her breasts, and the way men looked at them. The curves of her hips and how they seemed to move without her even noticing. All these evolutions had concerned her, so she had ignored them. She had grown up knowing that her body was something to be covered and concealed, or it would tempt men and doom her to shame. When she had married and her body had become the property of Ram, he had used it and enjoyed it and stopped enjoying it and she had rarely wondered why, because it wasn't hers anymore. It never really had been. When Rahi was born he had needed her body, too, so it had been joint property, food for one, use for another. Now it was truly hers. There was no one left to take possession of it. But it had changed. It had sagged and shifted, it had weakened and thinned. The hair had changed color and density, the breasts had shriveled, and the hips had shrunk.

Still, she thought. *I am beautiful. I am almost done with life and I own myself and that, somehow, has made me beautiful. I am happy to be beautiful before I die.*

She ran a bath as she waited for her food to come, food she would likely ignore. Ram had always encouraged her to be thrifty. It felt blissful to spend his money, to waste it. Slipping into the warm water, she wondered how the Ganges felt to the ashes of a corpse. Was it like this? She hoped so. If she did make it to the Ganges, she would want it to be like this. This was heaven.

She did not sleep that night. She kept herself from sleep, turning the air-conditioning panel down to a number she did not understand, because it was not in Celsius. It did not matter what it was, it made the room as cold as ice, and she lay like a corpse, still and careful, waiting for the morning.

On the horizon she watched the sun as it rose, marveling at its endurance against the smog and smoke of the city. It shone on everything, no matter what it was. It illuminated people, good and bad, kind and cruel, in the same light, with the same clarity. *What a martyr,* she thought with something like contempt.

The planned schedule was a tour of Universal Studios. She wasn't sure what Universal Studios was, but it didn't matter; she wouldn't be going. She wondered when she should say something to Satya as they loaded into the cab to meet the tour bus. The driver was on the phone, and to her surprise, she knew what he was saying. He was speaking in Bengali, not the Bangladeshi Bengali that Satya spoke, but her Bengali. He was from her world. It had been a long time since she had believed in a sign, but belief or no, this was an opportunity and she would take it as she had taken nothing before. She felt the way she had the day she met Ram, the day Rahi was born, that same sense of being on the edge of something, only this time she knew what it meant.

"Hello, boss, we're going to—" Satya began to say, but she was ready.

"Hello, sir. Pleasant to make your acquaintance." She spoke Bengali the way she had been taught, carefully and well. "We are for . . ." She reached for the slip of paper tucked neatly in her purse and showed it to the driver. He nodded, repeated the address once, and started driving, as Pival leaned back in her seat.

"Madam—" Satya began, confused. Pival merely smiled. "Madam, that is not the place we are going."

"Yes. It is. I don't care about the tour. I want to go there, instead." She would say no more. They would go where she wanted to go. It was her trip. The car drove on. She thought she saw them look at each other with questions on their faces, and so she closed her eyes. They were nice, and she cared for them in a way she could not have imagined, but they were no longer important.

It took them longer than she would have thought to get there, but then, she did not know where they were going. And perhaps anything would have felt like an eternity, or too soon.

Eventually, however, she was arriving at a house that looked small and new and flat like a village hut. Everything here was flat, she thought as she looked around. There was so much space here. It was the opposite of New York. She paid the driver with a one-hundred-dollar bill, wrapped up in a roll in her purse. She refused change. She left the car with Satya and Rebecca still in it and walked up to the address. It matched the one on the envelope she'd received long ago, she knew. She rang the bell. It was Saturday. He would be there, she thought. He had to be.

Suddenly she wondered if he wasn't. It had been so clear in her mind; she would ring the bell or knock and he would be there, the bastard who had taken her son, and she would know him by the sin in his eyes. But what to do if he wasn't there? Wait for him? Sit on his lawn, or stand, planted like a tree? Her heart began to sink in her chest and she struggled to feel again the power she had had, the fury, the confidence in herself. Where was her beauty, that great and terrible thing she had seen only the night before? She had felt like a goddess. Now she was a demon, or worse, a ghost.

"What is happening, madam?" Satya stood behind her, with Rebecca next to him. Pival had forgotten anything existed outside of the man's door.

She rang the bell again. The door opened.

27

When they were driving, Bhim would always ask him how he got anywhere, how he knew where things were in a city so large. Jake asked Bhim about Kolkata; didn't he know his home? Bhim laughed. He had never driven before arriving in the United States, and he never looked out the windows of cabs at home. He had never seen most of the city. After learning that, Jake would take Bhim to places "just to see them." They had driven all around Los Angeles together and Bhim never knew where he was. Jake didn't mind; he enjoyed driving. He felt most calm behind the wheel of his car.

But he did want Bhim to know the city, so when driving hadn't helped, he took him running. Running was a way to know a city without a car, and because Bhim drove only when absolutely necessary, and badly at that, Jake thought maybe running would help. Jake wanted Bhim to fall in love with the city the way the two of them had fallen in love, and then he wanted Bhim to move in with him.

They had been together for over three years. Three years of bliss, of long mornings with coffee and the Sunday paper and endless rounds of toast and long nights exploring each other's bodies and knowing they knew each other best of all. Three years of jokes and meals and surprising things in common that they reveled in. Three years of Jake asking for things in ways that made them seem like suggestions, not demands, and living for the weekends, wanting more, dancing around anything difficult. Three years of Bhim trying to open up more, and failing. Three years of Jake trying to accept that about him, and failing. Three years of each of them hoping the other hadn't noticed their failures. Jake knew that it was insane. He knew that his friends and family thought it was a mismatch, that each was under so much strain trying to change for the other. But he didn't care. This was Bhim, this was the one person he wanted in the world, and Bhim was worth any price. They just had to go slowly, which Jake had, and wear away the resistance, which he did. Eventually, inch by inch, they would get somewhere. He would think, as Bhim lay sleeping next to him, what the next step would be, the next incremental push in the next day they would have together. It was a journey, wasn't it? Being with someone?

So he took Bhim running, as part of a grand plan years in the making, and prayed it would work. They ran at night, because Bhim ran like a duck and worried the sleek denizens of Los Angeles would judge him during the day. Together they would run slowly, slowly, down the streets of the city, getting used to this route and to that. Jake, who had been a runner for a long time, was frustrated at first, having to go at Bhim's glacial pace when he preferred his own punishing strides. But at least this way he could now see the elements around him more clearly, noting the changes of leaves and flowers, the urban wildlife that peeped around the corners of Los Angeles and the coyotes that howled at night.

On one such night he turned to Bhim, who was gasping for breath beside him, and smiled.

"I love you," he said.

"I love you, too," Bhim wheezed.

"Move in with me." Jake said it quickly, like it was all one word, shattering the night with his plea. He knew he shouldn't, but some part of him screamed that it had been three years and it had to be now, his life had to start now, or it never would. And Bhim just looked at him, curious, his face confused, a mixture of tenderness and distance. Jake opened his mouth but what he would have said remained a mystery even to him, because it was at that moment that Bhim gently collapsed on the pavement and died.

Later Jake would know that it hadn't been his fault, that it hadn't been anything he did, not even the running. Later he would learn that Bhim's heart attack, random, unpredictable, instantly fatal, was merely one of those things that happen to human beings. But at the time, he was sure, absolutely and completely sure, that his question had killed the love of his life.

Initially after Bhim had died, Jake's friends and family had told him that whatever he was feeling was okay. He had thanked them for this meaningless statement, too dazed to do anything else. For once in his life, he didn't have the time or energy to judge himself for his feelings, a fact that would have amused him if anything could have made him laugh then. The idea that he would spend more time judging his feelings than feeling them troubled him. They must think him so selfish, he had thought, as he covered each mirror in his house.

He was determined to sit a full shiva for Bhim, an act that would have confused Bhim, had he been there to see it. Bhim had been a lax and unobservant Hindu, and Jake's knowledge of Judaism consisted of jokes made in Woody Allen movies and dishes he ate in delis. The memorial service had been entirely secular, with Bhim's ashes enjoying their own seat in the small hall Jake's parents had rented for the event, and friends and colleagues murmuring their condolences as Jake sat, his eyes vacant, tears leaking out of them at strange moments, like when Led Zeppelin's "Ten Years Gone" started playing, or when one of Bhim's fellow PhD candidates recalled Bhim's use of a Bunsen burner to cook fish one night when they were working in the lab. Even Bhim's adviser had come down from Berkeley, explaining Bhim's research to those around him, even to Jake, who knew each component of Bhim's projects so well that he could have done it himself. Hearing someone else describe the biology of Pacific marine life felt so much like so many talks with Bhim that he closed his eyes and let the words wash over him, and opened them, wet and red, when they were done.

That had been almost a year ago. Bhim had died in November, and now it was October. A whole year, without Bhim. Jake hated himself for living through it.

He let himself think about Bhim only when he couldn't control himself, couldn't help it. Which was almost all the time. He had read many books that told him this would get easier, which felt both completely idiotic and also devastating in its own way. He didn't want to feel better. Feeling better would also mean feeling less.

He didn't run anymore. Instead he joined a gym with a pool and would spend hours swimming, and at the end he would float, staring up at the ceiling. After swimming that day in October, the day he realized it would be exactly a year in one month, he tried to drown himself in the pool, but he couldn't and he cried into the chlorinated water. Then he drove home, parked his car carefully, and groaned as he looked at his front door.

There was a cat there, waiting. It was not his cat. He did not know whose it was. But for whatever reason the cat was waiting there, as it had been every evening for the past week, looking at him hopefully with its glinting yellow eyes. He had not fed the cat or petted it once. Why was it there again? He walked warily to his door, and the animal—he didn't know its sex—started meowing loudly. As he opened his door, it rubbed his legs frantically, its body vibrating with purring. It didn't look particularly dirty or sick, but it didn't look perfectly clean like a house cat either. What did it want? He had no cat food in the house and he had no interest in letting anyone in, let alone someone with fur.

"I'm a bad bet," he told the cat as he jerked his key in the lock, letting himself into the house. The animal gave a strange little growl of delight, and before he could stop it the cat had run into his house. He cursed. The thing hadn't been so bold in the days before; it had gained courage slowly. He should have kicked it on the first day. Then the cat would have known where it stood with him. Now he had the vermin-infested fleabag in his home, rubbing up against his furniture and looking at him with love. As he watched, amazed, the animal jumped on top of his counter and sat, cleaning itself with vigor. He shook his head and walked in, leaving the door open behind him. This was outside of enough. He had lost the love of his life to a trick of the human body. Now he had a cat trying to make his clean home its new litter box. He was going to throw this cat out and drink himself to sleep. And the next time he saw a cat, he would kick it, in revenge. He walked up to the counter and explained to the cat in his most authoritative voice, his tone furious, that it would need to leave. That's all there was to it. The animal looked up at him and, Jake could have sworn, smiled.

That had been three days ago. Since then he had not succeeded at removing the cat, which he had learned was female, from his home. He had chased the cat with various things, including a broom, a bag, and, in one particularly low moment, a meat cleaver. The cat seemed to think this was a marvelous game until it got sleepy and bored and looked at him with the superior way cats have, as if everything humans do is for their amusement. It followed him from room to room. It cried for food and ate the cream he poured for it with relish. He had set up a box with sand for it, though he realized that as soon as he gave up the illusion that the cat would be leaving he would have to secure himself a litter box.

Lying in bed that night, alone, as always, he thought about the weight of Bhim beside him. When he closed his eyes, he could almost feel Bhim's warmth there. No, he *could* feel warmth, but a small and fuzzy amount of it. He opened his eyes and saw the cat, curled up next to him, her face resting on her paws. He thought about kicking her off, but when he reached his hand out to push her away, she shifted her body into his palm and purred deeply. With the warmth of her pulsing through his hand and making him feel not alone for the first time in a year, he knew he would be buying a litter box the next morning.

He had to admit, it felt nice to wake up with something alive in the house. It felt nice that there was a pair of eyes watching him. Even when Bhim had been alive Jake had spent more nights alone in his apartment than with him. Jake was not used to seeing something living around him.

He would find her a home, he decided resolutely. That's what he was doing, foster care for a cat until the right person came along for her. He was not going to be a single gay man with a dead boyfriend and a cat. His life was already too pathetic. Still, when the cat curled up to him at night as he waited for his sleeping pill to kick in, he felt a warm feeling that had nothing to do with shared body heat.

It was far too easy to care about things. He hadn't cared about anything, really, since Bhim had died. Nothing new, that was. He would have thought he'd forgotten how, but it was just like anything else. It came right back.

28

Looking at the handsome man in the doorway, Pival's heart broke, and she realized that it never really had, the first time, because she hadn't truly believed he was dead. But he was. Rahi was gone. If he had been alive, he would have answered the door. She was a fool for hoping for anything. But she had been a happy fool, for a few seconds, every day. Now she didn't even have that. She wanted to press her hand to her heart and stop it. She just stood there, looking at the man who stole her son. She would have to kill herself now, after all. But not before she had told him what she thought of him.

The man at the door had brown curly hair and a puzzled frown. His eyes recognized her. He knew who she was.

"Hello," he said, without a trace of inflection.

"Hello," she responded, her voice shaking.

"I'm Jake. You're his mother. I'm glad you've come." He opened his door and let her inside.

The cat had heralded her arrival, Jake thought as he let Bhim's mother into the house. He had never seen the woman before, not even a photograph, but he knew this was Bhim's mother as well as he would have known his own. She stood straight and tall in her pure white sari, and she had his face.

He had hated her for so long, hated her silence. He had hated her for being the person who had made Bhim into someone who would never love him all the way, someone who could never love himself.

Now Jake stood aside and ushered her into the home he had shared on the weekends with her son and the cat that he should have known was telling him she was coming.

There were two people with her. He wasn't sure who they were. One of them was a short man of indeterminate ethnic identity with a handsome but hungry face. Jake was politically correct enough not to simply assume he was Indian. His skin was dark and his eyes were as well. He looked about twenty-one years old, and he looked like a person who had once been painfully thin. The overlay of flesh on his bones was newly acquired and suited him well. His face was firm and young, and would, someday, be awfully good-looking if he kept eating. Next to him was a woman, in her late twenties, Jake would estimate, although he had never been good with women's ages. Her hair was up in some kind of fashionable wavy twist, and he wondered if she was Jewish, too. Her eyes were dark, and they looked at him curiously. It seemed that Bhim's mother had brought reinforcements. At least he had the cat on his side.

He shut the door behind them and watched them walk carefully through his foyer into his living room, a large open space that looked onto the revealed kitchen. It was a good house for parties, not that he'd ever had one there.

"Won't you sit?" He said it automatically, etiquette overriding emotion. She sat. He took a seat across from her, and the cat, after looking between them, elected to sit with Mrs. Sengupta, curling up in her chiffon skirts and dozing, the traitor. A thousand things to say to her ran through his mind, accusations, an equal-rights speech for all people of every sexual orientation everywhere, even a proper introduction, with memories of Bhim, how they met, how they fell in love, but he stayed silent. She was the one who had been quiet for so long, who had said nothing and done nothing. Let her talk.

She was looking around his home, her eyes taking in his interior decorating.

"Rahi must have liked it here."

"Rahi?"

"Rahi. My son, Rahi Sengupta. What did you call him?" She spat it out. He was tempted to shock her, to hurt her, to say, *my bitch* or *my chocolate dream* or *my personal Kama Sutra* or *gay Ganesh,* but he didn't.

"I guess I knew his name was Rahi. But he called himself Bhim."

It was as if he had spoken a magic word, because her animosity fell away, for a moment. She actually smiled, her eyes unfocusing. "Oh, he didn't. No, he didn't, did he?"

"I can assure you he most certainly did." Jake grew formal when he was angry. Bhim had told him he sounded like the solicitors in nineties Bollywood movies, speaking pure truths in a corrupt court. He used his lawyer voice now to lay his claim. Who was she, telling him what he had called the person he had loved?

"This was . . . this was *my* name for him. He was my brave boy, my Bhim, always ready to save me. It is from a story that we tell. He was just like that, always. As he got older I stopped calling him this and forgot why. But he used the name. I never knew." She smiled again as tears leaked out of the corners of her eyes. Then she frowned. "I don't understand why he would have told you my name for him."

"I suppose he thought that people who loved him should use it." He said the words deliberately to upset her, because this, at least, was true and was fair to Bhim and was to make up for everything he could have said or screamed but hadn't.

"It is not right—"

"He and I were in love. We were together. He stayed here with me and he ate here with me and he fucked here with me and he died here, with me, and you weren't there and you don't get to tell me what right is. I don't care what you called him. The man I loved was Bhim."

She didn't blink, even at the profanity. "Love like that is wrong. Bhim didn't understand, he was sick, you made him sick here. It is not like that at home. Love is not like that." She spoke as though she were speaking to a child, carefully, with the absolute authority that she was right. *This must have been what Bhim thought every time he looked at me,* Jake thought. This soft, sweet voice in the back of his head telling him he was sick. Jake felt an incandescent rage fill him and he could have laughed, because it was like light pouring through his body.

"Love was like that for your son. He loved me, Mrs. Pival Sengupta. I know your name, I know about you. I know you are from Kolkata, and that you didn't talk to Bhim once he told you the way love was for him. I burned his body. He told me that's what he wanted, so I did it. Do you want that, Mrs. Sengupta? Your son's dust? Is that why you've come? You can have it. I would have sent it to you months ago. I would have come to India myself to give it to you. Not for you. But for Bhim, because it's what he wanted, and he should get what he wanted because it's the only thing left I can give him. Besides, according to *my* religion, which isn't being *gay*, by the way, it's Judaism, not that you know the difference, these ashes, these aren't important. You can have it. After all, it's all he was worth to you."

He thrust the box of ashes at her almost violently. It was a neat wooden box, made of olive wood from the town of Lucca, in Italy. He would have loved to take Bhim there. His arm mourned the loss as soon as it was out of his hands. He realized giving her the ashes caused the pain of losing Bhim all over again but he gritted his teeth and bore it, knowing it was the only thing to get this woman out of his house. He couldn't listen to her gently spoken hate. If she wanted the ashes they were hers. He had Bhim in his mind and his heart and she could have the dust. Bhim wasn't in there.

She took the box, but she didn't move. She just sat, staring at it, while large tears pooled in her eyes and slid down along the ladder of wrinkles etched in her face, down her cheeks and around her chin, dripping onto the box itself.

Next to her, the two people she had brought with her were staring, but he couldn't care about them, there wasn't space. He looked at her, his face flushed, pumping with blood, and his hands clenched into hard fists, his untrimmed nails biting into his palms.

"You have what you want. Now go," he said, his voice hard and trembling. He hated that quiver in the back of his throat, that weakness. He was already choking up and he wanted to rip the box out of her hands and he wanted to scream at her until she cried harder, until she made the ashes a paste with her tears. But he didn't, he just clenched his hands and his whole body tighter and tighter, pushing everything in and down and together.

Suddenly she stood, and without a word she left, fled the house, running out the door, her white skirts swishing around her like a departing flock of birds. The room was still and silent. The two strangers looked deeply uncomfortable. Well, they were not his problem.

"You're welcome to leave as well. In fact, I must insist that you do." They nodded jerkily, unable or unwilling to speak. They moved their bodies awkwardly out of his home, shutting the door quietly on the way out. The cat moved briskly around his legs, demanding to be fed.

As soon as his body stopped trembling, he looked out of the window as the cat masticated happily, rubbing her entire face in her bowl. He had already fed her once today, he thought vaguely. She would grow fat and no one would love her.

They were still standing there on his lawn, looking lost. He opened his door.

"Excuse me, but who are you?" he asked them, politely, he hoped, trying to remain calm despite his temper still simmering.

The woman smiled crookedly. "We were about to knock on your door and ask you that same question."

"Where is—"

"We don't know." This came from the boy, with something like deep petrified panic soaking his accented tone. Jake hardly thought one rogue Indian widow roaming the streets of Los Angeles should be the inspiration of this much terror; in fact, it almost made him laugh.

"We were giving her a tour. Satya"—the woman gestured to the boy—"is the tour guide and I'm the companion. Don't ask. We started in New York and now we're here. We don't know Mrs. Sengupta very well, but when we got in the cab this morning she gave this address. I'm Rebecca. This is Satya. So who are you?"

Jake couldn't think of a good response to that question. So instead, he asked another one.

"Would you like some coffee?"

Within fifteen minutes, they were seated once again in his living room, sans widow, sans Bhim's ashes, with beverages. Satya, the boy, looked down with an expression of complete despair. Rebecca watched him nervously.

"We'll find her. Don't worry."

"How?" Rebecca shrugged. Satya nodded. "It's not so easy, to find people. They get lost. Sometimes you never see them again. How will I explain this to Ronnie? Just now she was here and just now she is gone. Where did she go? She ran so fast, I could not follow her."

"She has money. She knows the name of the hotel, it was on the emailed itinerary and we printed her a copy, I know she keeps it in her bag. She speaks English, although here Spanish might help more—"

"She doesn't speak Spanish!"

"She's going to be all right, Satya. I was joking. She's survived this long in the world, right?"

"You don't understand what she is like, what these women are like, they are not like you, they can't just *do* things!"

"Maybe not. But she arranged this trip on her own. And she chose to run and I personally would like to know why. Wouldn't you?" He nodded. They both turned to Jake. He was struck by what a strange pairing they were, this graceful woman, poised and well put together, sitting next to this small man, his shirt a loud and violent mix of plaid colors, his pants unfashionably high-waisted jeans, and his face painfully anxious, boyish, with a sweaty brow.

"Well. I guess she left because . . . Look, my name is Jake Schwartz and her son, Rahi, who I called Bhim, we were in love. He was my great love." Satya's face had already begun to shrivel in disgust, and Jake stopped. He would not do this. He didn't have to explain himself to anyone, least of all this odd pair of strangers. Rebecca caught his withdrawal and she hit Satya's arm.

"Stop it."

"He is one of those perverts!"

"Okay, great, he's a pervert. Just shut up. You can deal with that in your own time, okay? You want to hate gay people, great, but keep your mouth shut here. We're in his house and we need to find Mrs. Sengupta. Okay?" Satya pressed his lips together, angry. Rebecca turned back to Jake. "Sorry. Go on?"

"Bhim came out to his parents, and they rejected him. They told him never to come home. So he didn't, and he hadn't told me much about them, and we never talked about them again. And then he had a heart attack and he died and I . . . I called his parents . . . but his father hung up on me. I thought they didn't care. But she showed up today and I knew, well, that's Bhim's mom. Who else shows up in a sari uninvited? And she wants his body so she can dump it in the Ganges or whatever the fuck and pray that the next incarnation turns out straight. So there you go. More coffee?"

They finished their drinks in silence with the purring cat sprawled contentedly on the counter. Rebecca thanked him, and Satya nodded, still meeting his gaze only in short bursts, as if Jake would seduce him with prolonged eye contact. Jake couldn't summon the energy to care. He was suddenly exhausted. He felt as if a weight had been lifted off his chest, but he also felt hollow, like one of Bhim's snail shells. There was one in the box with Bhim's ashes, he remembered. She could have that, too. He had dozens.

As they rose to go, Rebecca turned back to him.

"She's leaving Los Angeles in two days, but if she wants to come back, to apologize or, or anything, could I bring her? Would you allow that?"

Jake shrugged. "She won't want to come back."

"But if she does?"

He shrugged again. A memory flooded him: it was Bhim, lying in his arms on the sofa, slightly drunk, telling him about his mother, about how she had been the only soft thing in his life before he had met Jake. Jake had asked if Bhim was calling him fat and they had laughed and kissed and the night had gone on and Bhim had not mentioned his mother again.

"She can come. But she won't. She got what she came for."

Pival had not run in so long that her lungs burned like mad and her breath came hard and her heart felt like it would give up pumping at any moment. Her skirts weighed her down, holding back her body. She missed the days of her youth when she had run in shorts and a T-shirt and felt weightless and free. Now everything felt like it was pulling at her, and in her hands, her son's featherlight ashes were made of lead.

He had given them to her, *Jake,* the evil person who had taken Rahi, only he hadn't seemed so evil as she sat in the middle of his living room. She had looked around the room because she didn't want to look in his face and all she could think was, *This looks like a place Rahi would like to live,* and then she understood that it was the kind of place she, too, would like to live in, with all its glorious light, and she understood with shocking clarity that she hated her home in Kolkata and she had never known that before. And her words about Rahi's liking the place had jumped out of her. She didn't know why she would say that there was something about this life with this man that her son had *liked,* because clearly he had been manipulated and seduced, hadn't he?

He had had wide large brown eyes, Jake, and she could see how Rahi would have liked those, too. Looking at him, all she could imagine was what Rahi saw, what love had poured from her son like milk onto this man. She wanted to hate him, she did hate him, but she realized she was looking for things to love as well, the things her son had seen. When she had told him their love was wrong she had spoken more to herself than to him, reminding herself. But then he had given her the ashes and she knew that she had never needed to go on this trip and confront him for keeping her son from her. Here Rahi was, hers for the taking. There was nothing that had held her from her son, ever, but herself.

She had suddenly thought that she had done this trip for nothing. She could have gotten the truth about Rahi, gotten his ashes, and killed herself months ago. But she knew that she wouldn't have *wanted* any of that, that she was happy with the way things had been and that she wouldn't have changed it. This epiphany had made her dizzy and nauseated, and she had had to leave. She was crying, she knew, from the new things making space in her head. They pushed out old thoughts, which turned to water and leaked out of her eyes. She was happy she had taken the trip, had come all the way here. She was happy she had been alive all this time to do so.

Pival had run without looking to see where she was going. She had run down sunny streets with small houses and then down cement sidewalks with strange faces that stared at her as she ran, but she clutched the box to her chest and kept running and it was only when she felt that she might collapse and spill Rahi's ashes here instead of at home that she stopped and tried to catch her breath. She found a tree off the road, and under it a large rock, and she sat down, her head tucked between her knees. She held the box inside the curve of her body between her chest and her thighs. Her lungs, so underdeveloped, according to so many doctors and healers, had gotten her quite a long way.

Pival straightened up and felt something shift inside the box. Her heart began to race again. Had he tricked her? Was there something else in here, something to get her out of his house while Rahi's real ashes were somewhere else? Or maybe he hadn't been cremated at all? With shaking hands she opened the box. Yes, it was the ash that came from the cremation of a body. She had seen that enough times in her life to recognize it. Nestled into it was a small plastic bag. She delicately fished it out, making sure that the ashes clinging to the sides were brushed neatly back into their box. She shut the lid and looked at the bag. It was a small shell. This must have been something that mattered to Rahi. It was something precious to him that this man, Jake, had included with his ashes to keep him company. She vaguely remembered something in some letter about snails, about his studies and his work, which he discussed so rarely that she wasn't sure whether her lack of understanding was due to her ignorance or his reluctance to explain. Perhaps this small creature had been Rahi's life, his study, the subject of his doctorate. And she never would have known, if this man had not put it in the box to keep her dead son company.

She could not cry more. The breakneck run with the wind in her face had dried up all her tears. Pival looked around, wondering what to do now. Suddenly she realized that she was alone, which had been, of course, her intention, but the implications of that had not occurred to her until this moment. She was *alone*. Satya and Rebecca were far away and who knew where they had gone. After all, she had been the one to leave them. They could be anywhere by now, looking for her, perhaps, or maybe not. The world around her seemed to be suddenly a very dangerous place, because she was truly alone in it. Surely she should be used to that?

She wondered if she should simply kill herself now. She knew the truth, she had confronted the man and taken back her son. The next step was to die. She looked out onto the hazy mess of traffic in front of her, overlooking the highway. The cars were driving quickly, speeding down the road. She could jump out into them and that would be that. She could wait for a truck, something large, and take her son's ashes and they could go away together, they could take a trip together. She had never gone anywhere with Rahi. Even this trip had been, she realized, with stunning clarity, a wild attempt to be with him, to see the country she had lost him to. When they had sent Rahi away they never knew he wouldn't be coming back. She couldn't blame him, not when she had seen how people were here, how easy it could be to be a person without the rigid structures of duty and the crushing weight of other people's opinions.

She could not survive here, she thought, nor thrive as Rahi had. America wasn't the country for her, but for the first time she did not resent it for taking her child. America had been a much better place for Rahi to be.

The trucks sprinted past on the road. Pival watched them, her body frozen. Why didn't she do it? All she had to do was walk into the path of a moving car and it would be over. She would never have to feel anything, ever again. She couldn't make herself move. And then at last she knew it was because she didn't want to go.

She had thought she wanted to end her life because it was a life not worth living. This was still true. She had no obligations left in the world, no ties pinning her into place. No one she truly cared about who still existed. Nothing about her life had changed, really, since she had come on this trip, but now she was unwilling to end the pain. The pain that had changed, become a hunger. There was more that she wanted now than death.

Pival turned away from the highway and walked toward the street, still clutching the box. People stared at her as they passed her in their cars. There were no other pedestrians on the roads. What a strange place this was, without people in it. She looked out at the road. She stepped toward it and flung her hand up, as she had seen Rebecca do. Her body swayed almost into the path of oncoming cars, but the taxi that saw her stopped and she got into it, and told the driver where she wanted to go.

When they arrived at Jake's house again, Pival realized that little time had passed. The sun was high in the sky, just starting to shift west. It was a very green part of town, she thought, where other things she had seen through the cab windows had looked dry and brown and hard. She paid the cab with money she had tucked into the waistband of her sari. Her mother had carried all her money this way, she remembered, keeping her money close to her body in a gesture of protection. Pival had always done the same, an unconscious repetition.

Here she was, she thought as she once again crossed the infinite expanse of Jake's lawn and with trembling legs returned to the doorway of his home, caught between the little gesture left behind of her mother and the nothing she had left of her son. She rang the bell and waited.

He came to the door warily, like a wild animal. She held the box of ashes out in front of her like a talisman, though whether it was to ward him off or beg him to let her in she wasn't quite sure. He looked at her and took the box, cradling it like it was something precious. This was how he had thought of her son. Something precious. The thought did not disgust her. She still did not understand what had been between them or how Rahi had loved someone in this way, but this was the only person who existed who still cared this way for her son, other than herself. She was not as completely alone as she thought. He stood aside, once again, and let her in.

This time they did not sit on the couch. This time he kept on walking and gestured wordlessly for her to follow. He opened a door to a room and turned on the light. It was packed full of boxes, neat cubes of plastic all labeled.

"This was Bhim's. All of it. I kept it because, I don't know. You can look, if you want. See what there is. There was no one else to take it, so I took it."

"It was not here?"

"It was in Berkeley. That was where Bhim was doing his research. He had an apartment there."

She had not known this. She had not known anything.

"He did not live with you?"

"He came on the weekends. He lived up in Berkeley, though. He was close to finishing his PhD. His professors came down, for the funeral. The service."

"There was a service?"

"There were a lot of things."

They stood, wordlessly, looking at the boxes together. It was a sea, but a carefully organized one. What would have happened to her things, had she died as she was supposed to? There would be no one who cared about her to pack away her life into boxes and keep it safe. Here was Rahi's life, waiting for her all this time.

"Thank you." She said it to Jake, although she meant more. She had never thought she would thank this man, and now it was all she wanted to do. "May I look?" Her voice wavered as she spoke, that tremble that Ram had mocked and hated so. Jake looked at her with something in his eyes like sympathy. What was he seeing in her? She hoped it was Rahi. That was the best of her, after all.

"It is yours to see," he said, and turned away, moving to go. She looked at the expanse in front of her. There was nothing of Rahi left at the house in Kolkata. Ram had made sure of that, clearing his room as soon as he had died and giving all his belongings to beggars on the streets, leaving his prized possessions and childhood treasures out for the rag pickers to harvest. She had watched them scavenge through her son's early life, fighting over his baby clothing and ripping apart his books until she couldn't stand to watch anymore, until she thought she might scream. It had been the right thing to do, Ram had insisted. She wondered what he had meant by *right*.

"May I stay?" Her voice was stronger this time. She didn't want to go back to the hotel. She wanted to stay here, near all the things that were left of her son, including this man. He looked at her and hesitated.

"I don't know."

"Please? I am very sorry for what I said to you and for taking his ashes. But I have brought them back, and if it is not trouble for you, I would very much want to stay. Please." She was not begging, but she would, soon. She would go on her knees to stay here. If she wasn't going to die, she needed to see how her son had lived. He looked at her with so much pain, this man, this boy, really, for he was not much older than Rahi. He was as broken as she was, she knew.

"I'll make up the couch. You can sleep there." An Indian boy would have given her the bed. She didn't care. She would sleep on the floor if she needed to.

"Thank you." She turned back to the room of things.

"Did you call them? Your friends?"

She started. What friends? "Oh. I did not." She had not even thought of Rebecca and Satya. Now she felt ashamed. They would be worried for her, terrified. "May I use your phone?" He nodded. It rang and rang and then a breathless Satya picked up.

"Madam? Is that you?"

"Hello, yes, it is me. I am sorry. All is all right."

"Where are you, madam? I am coming, I am coming just now."

"I am at the man's house, from this morning. I am there only."

"I am coming just now."

"No. I will stay here. Thank you. I am sorry for worries, for giving you fear. But I am all right now. You may come in the morning only, or not at all."

"But, madam, he is a pervert! And the tour!"

"My tour is done. Thank you, Satya. Thank Rebecca. God bless you both."

She thanked Jake and turned back to the room. Like an explorer on the edge of the jungle, she stepped in, desperate to see what she could find.

She never made it to the couch. She fell asleep hours later, clutching a paper on saltwater plants that she had been struggling to read and now let rest against her face as she lay on the floor of the room surrounded by the artifacts of her son's life and felt at home for the first time in years. She felt like she was floating in the ocean, and it was warm, and soft, and it accepted her, and she was not alone.

29

To: boss@americabestnumberonetours.com
From: satyaroy57@yahoo.com

Boss,
Please ignore text of yesterday. Madam enjoying tour very much so.
Recommend to all friends. Happy in California very much. Exactly what
she wanted.
Satya

Sitting in the hotel lobby surrounded by a mountain of luggage,
Satya wondered what had become of his tour, hoping Ronnie wouldn't
see his frantic email from the day before when he was sure he had
lost the widow. The trip had been going so well until they reached
California and she went insane. Or maybe she had been insane the
whole time, and had only just revealed it, which was a bit unfair,
Satya thought. If you are going to be insane you might as well just
be insane from the beginning and not mess about with deception.
Now he was stuck with all her belongings, and the only thing keeping him from panicking was a strange phone call from the perverted
man who had assured him the widow was alive and well. He was not
an experienced tour guide, he knew, but he did believe that keeping
track of his clients was probably an important part of the job. He was
supposed to be the person in charge here.

But that was life. People had lives beyond what he could understand. There were more things that could happen and more ways that people could be. He would have to let his ideas of things go, he thought, thinking of Ravi, and simply let things happen. There did not seem to be another option.

He guarded the bags and waited for Rebecca. The trip was officially ending tomorrow, but he didn't know if Mrs. Sengupta would do any of her activities for the day, which included a tour of the Hollywood Hills and shopping on Rodeo Drive. Over an Indian dinner during which she had shouted at him about why gay people weren't perverts and he had wished she would get drunk so he could kiss her again, he and Rebecca had decided that they would leave early if Mrs. Sengupta wasn't interested in the tour. Or rather, that he would leave early. Rebecca wanted to stay and contact some people in "the industry," as she called it, though he failed to see what was so industrious about acting, a statement that started her yelling at him again. He thought about the feeling of her breasts when he had leaned against them, trying to clutch one in his hand. He could barely remember, but he thought it had been nice.

"What are you smiling about like an idiot?" Her voice was sharp, brittle now, as she walked up to him. She was nervous about Mrs. Sengupta as well, he knew.

"Just like that," he said in response. Rebecca cocked her head to the side in confusion and seemed to be about to question him, so he cut her off. "The man called today. She is still there with him. Will he try to molest her, do you think?"

"*No.*" Rebecca elongated the word so that two letters seemed like twenty. Her eyes were off again, rolling away.

"But he is a disgusting person."

"So are you. Stop looking at my chest. What do we do now?" Rebecca asked him.

"I don't know."

Rebecca sat down next to him. He could feel her warmth through his shirt.

"Is this normal?" she asked.

"I don't know."

"Is this your first tour?" Rebecca asked it in a voice that made it clear she knew what the answer was. He nodded slowly. She sighed. "Should we go pick her up?"

"But what to do with all the bags?"

She looked at their assorted luggage. "We'll have to bring them to her."

In the back of the cab they looked at each other over the mountain of things, overstuffed bags and carefully wrapped glass. He didn't remember bringing this much with them. It was amazing, he thought, the things that people picked up along the way.

They arrived back at the house and Rebecca paid the driver. He let her. He had no money and no reason to be proud. They unpacked the bags and carted them like pack mules up onto the man's lawn.

"What should I do? If she won't come?" Satya asked.

"I don't know."

Well, he supposed perhaps it was her turn to say it. They rang the bell and waited. Of all the traveling they had been doing, all the places they had been to and all the driving they had done around the country, this seemed like the most arduous part of the journey, and the most overwhelming. It was a strange feeling, to be manipulated by his client, to find that she had been guiding him instead of the other way around. The door opened and he saw Jake's newly familiar face. He forced himself to make eye contact for longer than he wanted to. The man smiled at him.

"Much better. You can hardly tell at all," he said, much to Satya's confusion.

Inside the house, the widow was sitting on the couch, as she had been the day before, only this time she was bent over a notebook, looking at something. As they moved into the house, Satya caught a glimpse of what it was, all drawings of snails. Each of their shells curled into itself endlessly, a swirling universe fitting into two inches of space.

"How are you?" he asked Mrs. Sengupta. He hadn't meant to ask it in Bengali, but it slipped out of his mouth. It was amazing how they had spoken in English all this time, he thought. Was it because his Bengali wasn't good enough for her, or because they were both being polite to Rebecca? Or maybe because in some way English seemed more appropriate and neutral than their mutual native tongue? But now he spoke to her with the care and comfort of his own language.

"Thank you for coming," she responded in Bengali. "I am well. I am sorry to have caused you distress." She switched to English for the last part, for Rebecca's benefit.

Rebecca shrugged. "As long as you're all right."

"Madam, about the tour . . ."

Mrs. Sengupta smiled weakly. "I think I am done with touring."

"Of course, madam, understood, understood, it is only—"

"Can you, is there a way to change the ticket? Only, Jake is going to take me to San Francisco."

The man looked startled. "I am?" said Jake.

"I would like that," said Mrs. Sengupta placidly.

Jake exhaled a long breath. "I don't like you," he said, flatly, to Mrs. Sengupta. Satya bristled, ready to defend his charge. She was still his client for another day.

"I understand this. You can change this ticket? To leave from there, in five days?"

"I will ask—"

"It's possible," Rebecca broke in, "but you'll have to pay for it."

"Everything requires this only."

"We've brought your bags," Rebecca said.

Mrs. Sengupta nodded. "Thank you. You are very kind to me. Is tipping required?" Satya started coughing. The widow seemed to have abandoned tact.

"It's not required, but it's appreciated. At least for the medical bills for the heart attack you gave Satya." Rebecca spoke in a deadpan, realizing too late that mentioning a heart attack was inappropriate. Mrs. Sengupta nodded again and reached into her purse. She handed them each a handful of crisp hundred-dollar bills.

"Is this enough?"

"Only you can know that, Mrs. Sengupta."

"It is more than generous, madam, thank you, madam." Satya tried to touch her feet for the last time, but she stood instead and reached out her hand for him to shake it. He fit his palm onto hers. It was the only time they had touched hand to hand, like equals. He looked at his dark hand in her much paler grip. Soon it was over, and his palms felt sweaty. Mrs. Sengupta reached toward Rebecca to do the same thing, but Rebecca hugged her instead. Mrs. Sengupta looked confused and then, for a fleeting moment, sank into the embrace, letting herself be held. Rebecca leaned back and straightened.

"It was nice to meet you, Pival. And good luck."

"You have both been good to me. I came here under false reasons, and I did not tell you of this. I am sorry. I thought if I did not find Rahi, I would die here. I am glad that I have met you, and that I am not dead."

Satya did not know what to say, and so he said good-bye. He would never see her again, he thought. He thought about all the people he would never see again, his grandmother, his mother, Ravi, people he had known for much longer than Mrs. Sengupta. And yet she had affected his entire life. He wondered what her life would look like from now on. He wondered if everyone he had ever known would leave him, too. He wondered if he would get better at it, as time went on, or if it would always feel as it did now, that a part of him was forever lost every time someone who knew him disappeared.

They took their bags, and they left the house, and they said nothing as they hailed a cab and set off for the airport. Satya had changed his ticket, and would be heading off that day, and Rebecca had offered to go with him, ostensibly to keep him company, but really to pay for the taxi. She suspected he would have tried to walk if she hadn't ordered the cab. Satya would go home to New York that very day. Rebecca would stay behind, with a friend. The widow would do whatever it was she planned on doing. And they would never see each other again.

Satya looked out the window as Los Angeles receded from view, not that he had seen much of it in the first place. He wasn't sure if he could do this again, be a tour guide. Perhaps he wasn't suited for so many hellos and good-byes, so many places passing in front of his eyes.

"What do you think she meant?" Rebecca asked him this, before he left.

"I think she was unhappy. Maybe she's happier now, that she has met someone who knew her son."

"Even though he's a pervert?"

Satya shrugged. "Disgusting people can be all right as long as they aren't perverting themselves on you. And maybe he will change. Meet a nice girl. Become normal. She can help him."

"Maybe. Will you stay in New York? Will you keep being a tour guide?"

"I don't know where else I would go. Or what else I would do."

Rebecca thought for a moment. She reached into her bag and grabbed a piece of paper and a pen, and wrote something down. "Here. Call this number, when you get back. I know someone who might help you."

He smiled at her. "Thank you."

"Thank *you*. This has been a very interesting tour of America."

Satya snorted.

"It really has. I promise. Thank you." And she hugged him. He tried to absorb every feeling of her. As she pulled back he kissed her again, hard, sticking his tongue down her mouth as much as it would go. She bit it. Satya reared back, cursing. She looked at him, calm, her face hard.

"Don't say you're sorry. You're not." He shook his head. He wasn't.

They had reached the airport. Rebecca was going to take the cab back to Los Angeles. Satya apologized for having her go out of her way, picked up his small battered bag from the back of the cab, and waved good-bye. She waved at him once, and then put on her sunglasses. The taxi pulled away. Satya felt empty. He wished it had been different, that she had sunk into him the way he had seen in movies and let him do all the things he wanted to do.

He walked into the airport alone, and ten hours later he was on a flight back to New York watching the sun set on California as his plane sped east. From the plane he took a train and a bus to get home. In his exhaustion he almost went back to the place he had shared with Ravi and so many others, but he didn't; he went to his new home and fell into bed, facedown, sleeping before his cheek even hit the pillow.

Two days later he walked into Mr. Ghazi's shop and introduced himself. The man knew who Satya was because Rebecca had already called and prepared him, and when Satya walked out later it was with a job. He would have told Ronnie in person, but Ronnie was on vacation with his wife, the first he had ever taken with her, and wasn't to be disturbed. So Satya left his resignation in a note on the desk.

Satya got an additional job at a bookstore on Union Square, hauling boxes, nothing that required much of his mind. They did give him books at a discount, however, and he was thinking about buying a few of them. Between the map shop and working as a stock boy, he had just enough to pay for his life, as long as he lived cheaply. That was fine for him; he knew no other way. His grandmother would have been proud of him. He lived now in a world of paper.

He had received a letter from Ravi's mother while he was gone. She had thanked him for writing and told him that she was proud of them both. He had read it, over and over again, absorbing the scent and the feeling of home through the words, thinking about where she was when she had written it, what she had been thinking, what of his old life was around her that she had pressed into the page. Then he put it back in the envelope.

He passed the cart in the street on his way to work one day, the one run by the man who he thought knew Ravi. The man flinched as Satya passed and looked at him, but this time Satya didn't yell at him. Instead, he passed him the letters. Included in them was a note, a recommendation for all the things Ravi would need to know to work with Ronnie, all the things he needed to become a guide. He hoped, someday, he would see Ravi again. But even if he didn't, he had given all he could.

A week later, Ronnie told him that a new man had joined the company. Satya didn't ask who he was. He didn't have to. Ronnie told him that the new guide was doing well, training with the other guides, doing New York tours. Maybe someday he would take a group on a tour of the Southwest, Satya thought, and see the Grand Canyon. Satya smiled. One way or another, they would see it together.

He went to work, and studied maps of the world and thought about where he was in it. And when he was sick of that, he dusted, and brought Mr. Ghazi his tea.

30

"I don't understand why you would build a city in a place that has such hills. It is too much up and down and walking everything. They should have made the city in a flat place, shouldn't they?"

Mrs. Sengupta's face was screwed up with annoyance as she surveyed San Francisco. She looked at Jake, as if challenging him to explain it for her. She had done that often since they had met, looked at him, silently demanding that he give her reasons for the things she didn't understand.

"Were you this aggressive with your tour guide?" Jake asked idly, swirling his coffee around in his cup. They sat at a tea shop in the Castro, where Mrs. Sengupta bathed her face in the steam of an expertly crafted Indian masala tea, while Jake had scandalized the establishment by ordering a latte.

"I didn't bother asking him questions. It was clear he knew nothing, and when Rebecca had something to say, she just said it. Such an amazing thing, to be able to do that. To have the confidence. I have never felt such a thing."

Jake looked away. Mrs. Sengupta, or Pival, as she had asked him to call her, had grown both bolder and more contemplative the more time they spent together. He still wasn't sure how exactly he had ended up traveling with her to San Francisco, taking a week off work and spending his time escorting his dead boyfriend's sari-clad mother around the city, but here he was. Somehow she had gotten him there, with her calm statements and her desperate need.

Part of him was happy to do it, really. Part of him had, he knew, wanted to throw it in her face, the freedom Bhim had had in America, the way his life and self had been acceptable here. Why else would Jake have booked them an apartment in the heart of San Francisco's historic gay district? Why did he insist on taking her to gay bars, crashing a gay wedding in the Shakespeare Garden in Golden Gate Park, pointing out every same-sex couple that passed them on the street? But if he had meant to shame Pival, his actions were having the opposite effect. Instead, with every couple they saw, Pival seemed to relax a fraction of an inch.

"Bhim must have been happy here."

Pival was looking at the window as she spoke, a soft smile playing on her lips.

"You can be whatever you want here. He had never had such freedom in his life. He must have been drunk off it."

Jake smiled at her description. "I suppose. He often seemed quite reserved to me. I don't think I would have liked to meet him in India. I can't imagine him even stiffer."

Jake realized as he said it this was true.

"You don't have to. You had him at his best."

Pival spoke without bitterness, mournful, but without rancor, and Jake wondered how he had gone from hating someone to caring for her so quickly. For the last few days, since she'd asked to stay with him, Jake had felt a rising tide of panic, fear that as he lost his resentment there would be nothing left to keep him going. But somehow he woke up every morning, breathing, thinking, worrying about his new cat, wondering if she liked her exorbitantly expensive sitter. Somehow, even without the engine of anger he'd depended on for the past year, he was still living. Living better, even.

"I could not have imagined a place like this where someone could feel so good about who they are and what they want."

"You should have visited him." Jake wondered why they hadn't, at least before Bhim came out. They had the money, he knew, and he assumed they didn't have the time or inclination.

"Yes. I should have. My husband didn't like long trips, you see. And I did not know then how to travel."

"But now you do."

Pival smiled at him.

"I am learning. Every day, it is only about doing it, and suddenly it is happening. I am learning, slowly, slowly. It is worth it. I thought I was too old to learn, but here I am, doing it again. And I am happy, that I am."

So am I, Jake thought.

"Will you take me to where he worked?"

"Of course."

"Is it by the ocean? You know, that is a funny thing about Rahi. As much as he loved water, he never learned to swim."

Jake smiled.

"Funny you should mention that."

They took the train to Berkeley, Pival exclaiming the whole time at how clean it was. That was her first comment, most places she went, *how very clean.*

"Is India so very dirty then?" Jake asked. He had not asked Bhim much about India, not after it became clear this was another dangerous subject, and never after Bhim had come out to his parents. Pival smiled wryly. She had a dry sense of humor that Jake liked. Everywhere in her he was looking for parts of Bhim, but they never were where he thought they would be. Instead, he found them on the edges of things, in a mispronunciation they shared, the number of spoonfuls of sugar in tea, the way they licked their fingertips and smoothed their eyebrows elegantly and disgustingly at once.

"India is often dirty, yes. But parts of it are not. You should come see for yourself."

"You aren't making a strong case for it," Jake teased her. She took him seriously, though.

"No, you should. You would understand Bhim better, being there. I understand him better here. Together, between the two parts, it makes sense."

"I'll have to visit, then," Jake said, not really meaning it.

"Yes. You will," Pival said, meaning every word.

Getting off the train at the Berkeley BART station, they walked the streets of the little suburban town, dry and verdant and teeming with students. They visited Bhim's lab, and Pival shook hands with each of the scientists who'd known and admired her son. They showed her his research, tried to explain its implications, showered her with a downpour of technical terms and excitement for Bhim's brilliance. She touched the pages of his thesis, printed, bound, and carefully stored in the university library, with reverence.

"It is amazing, when the person you made makes something that you never could," she said. Jake, thinking of the way his own mother made sure to drive by as many of his projects in a day as possible, smiled. Pival took the snail shell he had given her out of her purse, examining the whorls with her fingers and her eyes.

"Did they know about him?" she asked Jake, suddenly anxious.

"Bhim never talked to anyone about his personal life much," Jake said, "but when he passed away, many of them came to the funeral and met me. They knew who I was."

"And they, they didn't mind?" she asked, her eyes wide.

"Does it seem like they minded?"

They looked around the lab. One of Bhim's advisers, an algae specialist, was waving them over to look at something amazing that

Bhim had found. Jake put his hand on Pival's shoulder, and they went to look into a microscope at tiny vitally important things that they might never grasp and couldn't wait to see.

Jake took her to Bhim's favorite café, the Indian restaurant that would make him fish curries if he asked in Bengali, the grocery store where they had shopped for organic produce when Jake tried to teach Bhim to cook. He took her to the apartment where Bhim had lived, the soulless place where Jake and Bhim had, together, achieved a little bit of joy. It was rented to someone else now, but they were kind and let them in for a brief visit. She looked around once, and smiled. When they left, she turned back to Jake.

"That was not a very nice place."

Jake laughed. "I was the one who cared about what things looked like. Bhim said he never noticed."

"That sounds like my Rahi. Completely oblivious to the world outside his own mind. And yet you spent more time in Los Angeles, you said."

"We did, yes. His work was mobile, and—"

"Then perhaps he did notice, after all."

They stood out on the street, watching bicyclists speed by; people walking their dogs; a couple, both men, holding hands. The couple walked, unselfconscious, down the street, lifting their joined hands over the head of a child on a bright pink plastic bicycle, forming an arch above her head for a moment before she moved on and they let their arms fall, still holding hands, still walking along. Jake looked over at Pival. She was crying. She reached over and wiped a tear off his own cheek.

"This is a very nice place. Isn't it?"

And Jake nodded, because it was true.

"This was the best place for him, wasn't it. Better than being at home with me."

"The best thing, I think, would have been not having to choose," Jake said. And Pival nodded, and smiled through her tears.

"I'm glad that he had you. I'm glad that he was loved by you." There was nothing for Jake to say to that. So instead he hugged her until their faces dried in the California sun, and then they went back to the train, back to the city, back into the world.

Jake had arranged for her flight to be changed so that she could return to Kolkata from San Francisco, not Los Angeles. They departed on the same day, her before him, and as he watched her be swallowed up by the airplane terminal, a small figure draped in fabric fading into the background, he knew despite everything, despite however he had felt before, he would miss her. Together, they had fit the two pieces of Bhim's life into one. He knew Bhim better because of her, and when she thanked him in the end he knew part of it was for what she now knew, for the memories he had traded with her.

Now he was home in Los Angeles. It had hurt to take her to Berkeley, but it had felt good, like the ache after running or the way stretching makes your body feel better after it feels much worse. He had felt so much less alone, mourning Bhim with her. The cat was still alive in his house and he named her Draupadi. Mrs. Sengupta had explained the origin of the name Bhim, the story of him and his four brothers, brothers the real Bhim had never had, and the princess who had married all five of them, the beautiful Draupadi. His cat was beautiful, and if Bhim had lived she would have been both of theirs. So the name seemed to fit. He was restless and he worked long hours and he ran long distances but Bhim's ashes still sat on the shelf and he watched them sometimes. He had wanted Mrs. Sengupta to take them, but she had refused. So there they were now, waiting for something. He didn't know for what.

31

Rebecca brushed her teeth, looked at herself in the mirror, and spat. Her face contorted wildly in the early morning light.

She was staying with an old friend, an actress she had known in New York who had moved to Los Angeles and kept promising to move back and never did. Her friend, Shana, had a neat and carefully curated apartment with large windows drinking in the California sunshine. Rebecca squinted, feeling like a vampire, annoyed by the rays. New York had made her bitter, she thought, rolling her eyes at her own cliché.

Life in Los Angeles was appealing, she could certainly see that. She had been there for three days, since Mrs. Sengupta had sent them away and Satya had left for New York, three days that she had filled with cold-brewed coffee and yoga classes and meetings over drinks, endless drinks, that everyone sipped lightly, barely tasting before ordering another. Drinks were not objects, they were networking tools, but some part of Rebecca still regretted the waste, no matter how much she told herself it was an investment in her future.

She met with agents and managers, and smiled and chatted and gave her résumé and felt them assessing her, her body, her voice, her smile. She knew if they could they would have cupped her body, man and woman alike, testing that, too, like a melon at the market. She was exhausted, more than she had been in her travels running from place to place. She kept looking up from conversations and from networking over cocktails and coffees and thinking, *What am I doing here? What does any of this have to do with acting, with being onstage?*

Shana had a lovely life, Rebecca had to admit, if a bit brittle. By all rights, she was doing wonderfully. She was working, a few small parts on television shows, commercial work every month or so, with large enough brands to keep her more than comfortable between jobs. She looked fit, and her skin was clear and swelling with moisture, but her eyes were strained and almost hunted. There was something close to breaking around her edges, something mirrored in every friend of Shana's Rebecca met who was *in the industry*. If in New York actors were high-strung and cutting, in Los Angeles they all showed a little wear and tear under the pressure of being so visibly relaxed all the time. It was as if they were boiling under the strain of being so *chill*. Everything was fine, everything was great, everything was so light it could crush you. People drank happiness with their kombucha, but it didn't seem to sit right in their stomachs, from the fear you could see in their faces when they thought no one was looking.

Rebecca told herself this was all in her head, she was being deliberately negative. She left the bathroom and dressed for the day, donning spandex for a hike in the mountains. The air that filled her lungs was clear, and the sun seemed healing, not stinging as it had in the morning, hours before. She watched Shana try to take the perfect selfie, pouting her lips, sucking in her cheeks, jutting out her collarbones.

"It's good marketing, really. I'm up for a part as a trainer in a new movie, someone the main character thinks about cheating on his wife with. The casting director follows me on Instagram." Rebecca nodded as Shana spoke, overwhelmed. Should she be doing this? It was so much work, this place that prided itself on being so effortless.

That night they went to a party, something in the hills with lots of important people. Rebecca wore a tight red dress and danced, and drank vodka and smiled at everyone, and people told her she was *gorgeous* and charming and laughed at her *quick East Coast wit,* and suddenly this trip she had been on seemed very far away. She had been wrong, it wasn't brittle here at all, it was bright and perfect and she should move here forever and be in movies and be happy. Everyone else was, weren't they?

But as she lay in bed at night even the alcohol couldn't help her sleep and she thought about Mrs. Sengupta. She thought about Satya and she hoped he would call the number she had given him, hoped he would work for Mr. Ghazi. She knew that she wouldn't anymore. She wasn't sure what she was going to do, but Satya needed that job. He needed the Ghazis more than she did. She turned over on Shana's couch, trying to get comfortable.

She checked her phone. It was seven A.M. on the East Coast. She didn't know many people who would be awake, but she knew someone. She slipped out of the apartment and dialed.

"Rebecca?" Her mother's voice, despite everything, made her smile. Cynthia had been waking up at six to run every weekday morning since Rebecca was a child. She knew she would be walking home now, stretching out her body slowly. She could see her, on the streets of Washington, sweaty and triumphant. "You're up early," Cynthia said, tentative. She clearly hadn't forgotten their dinner any more than Rebecca had.

"I'm up late. I'm in Los Angeles."

"Has the trip ended?"

"Yes, I'm here for a few days before heading back east."

"Ah. And how is it?"

Rebecca looked around at the empty streets, the flowers blooming, the green all around her, the orderly neatness of Los Angeles, so unlike New York's squalor.

"It all looks great. But—"

"It doesn't feel that way?"

"It's making me tired. Just in a completely different way."

"Of course. It's exhausting, all that healthy living."

Rebecca laughed. She could see her mother's face, visualizing her own expression in it. "It is! How do they do it?"

"Heavy medication," Cynthia quipped dryly.

"I had hoped it might be better here for me," Rebecca confessed. She closed her eyes, the night air cool on her face. "New York has been hard." She held her breath. Would her mother laugh? Scold her, reminding her of how she had told her so? The dinner at her parents' loomed large in her mind.

"I'm sorry, sweetie." Rebecca felt on the verge of tears. When was the last time her mother had said that to her? And really meant it? "I want you to be happy. It's hard for me, knowing that you're not."

"Do you think I will be happy in Los Angeles?"

"I think they kick you out if you're not."

"It's such a strange place, Mom. Everything seems so thin."

"That's because you're spending time with actors. They don't eat."

"No, I mean, nothing feels real."

"I know. Do you know your father and I thought about moving there, a long time ago?"

"You did?"

"Yes. But we didn't. We took a trip, and as we left, your father said to me, oh, thank god we can stop being happy all the time."

Rebecca laughed and laughed, tears rolling down her cheeks. It wasn't all that funny, she knew, but she found it hilarious, and now she was crying.

"Oh, Rebecca. Don't cry."

"This isn't digging ditches or breaking rocks, I know that. But it's still hard, Mom."

"I know it is. I wish you did something else, not because I think you can't do this, but because thinking about all the people who say no to you, it makes me so mad, honey. So mad for you."

"Thanks, Mom."

"That's why you have to say yes, when you can. I'm happy you went on this trip, love. I'm happy you said yes to something." As Rebecca hung up, ending the best conversation she'd had with her mother in years, she realized she was, too.

After a week, she went home to New York. Her check was waiting for her in the mailbox. There was not a word said about losing and regaining their widow, nor a word from the widow herself. She had thought it would be wonderful to be back in New York but it felt strange. She had survived outside of it, and now it did not feel as essential to her as it had before she had left. Nothing was essential, it turned out.

She sat in her apartment and thought about what to do next. Her agent called her with an audition for a job out of town. And for the first time ever, she said yes.

After the audition, which had gone wonderfully, even she could admit, she took the subway to a Bengali restaurant in Queens. All that time on the road and she had never had Bengali food. She looked at her phone. She'd gotten the job. It would be in a theater in Chicago. She ordered fish baked in mustard paste. She thought about calling her parents, Mr. Ghazi, the guy she'd met last night, and telling them she was leaving New York for a bit. She looked at her phone and decided it could wait. She took out a piece of paper. She thought about the widow and the way her son had written her those letters. *Dear Mrs. Sengupta,* she began.

In Chicago everything was built at a massive scale, Rebecca realized. Perhaps because there was just so much more space out there, in the flatlands. The theater company had put her up in a beautiful apartment, four times the size of her studio in New York, and when they had apologized profusely for the tiny size she had struggled not to giggle. On her first day of rehearsals, unable to sleep, she looked out through her window at sunrise, watching the massive sleepy city wake slowly, sweetly. Today she was going to go to a theater and become someone else for a while. And without even trying, she was happy.

32

When Piyal returned to Kolkata the first thing she did was fire all the servants. Well, the second thing, because the first thing had been to drink a good cup of tea while listening to Tanvi scold and wail at her.

She was surprised, frankly, that anyone was still there. She had assumed they would "bunk," as her son used to say—that is, cut out, leave, be gone from the apartment. She had expected all her belongings to be gone with them, had even anticipated with some sense of relief an empty apartment robbed of all its wealth. But then she remembered, her return wasn't so unexpected to *them,* only to herself. And of course, they would fear being charged with theft, no matter how much she had urged them to take things. A few saris, a bangle, would be the most they would dare.

On the drive from the airport, looking out on the city she had thought she would never see again, she assessed Kolkata with open eyes, the ugliness and the rare beauties, cement housing and fading wooden doors. Letting herself into her flat, she interrupted lunchtime, and suddenly both the maids, the cook, and the driver were fluttering around her, crying and touching her feet, treating her like a returned hero, the Pandavas coming back from the forest. She was forced into a chair and served tea and biscuits before she could get a word in, and then the haranguing began, *How could you leave, madam, we were so worried, you must never do this again,* on and on it went, a stream of reproaches and guilt-inducing statements that would have made her shrivel up into a ball a month ago, promising anything just to make it stop. Now, she straightened, put her tea aside, thanked Tanvi politely, and told her she was fired.

She offered her and each of the other servants a severance that was more than any of them typically made in a year, and thanked them for everything they had ever done for her, for Ram, and for Rahi. Most of them nodded, resigned, but Tanvi almost seemed relieved. She wailed and screamed, it was true, but behind it there was the sense of a burden laid to rest. Maybe that was just the weight that had rested on her heart so long; Pival didn't know.

They moved out the next week, taking money back to their villages or going on to other posts. Pival wrote Tanvi a recommendation that stressed her care and downplayed her judgmental nature, and saw her on her way. Sitting alone, in the apartment she had never thought she'd see again, she felt a sense of peace. She packed away Ram's photograph, the fading marigolds around it, the incense and the offerings. She didn't have to pray to him anymore. All the ghosts of her old life were gone now, except Rahi's, and even that one was a ghost of love.

To find new servants, Pival enlisted the help of an organization that rehabilitated women from Kolkata's red-light district and trained them for housework. They were often immigrants, Pival was told, girls from Nepal, Tibet, and Bangladesh, of course, who had been displaced, or come to India for a better life, or been sold as children and spent their lives in brothels or waiting on sidewalks for men to buy their bodies. They often had trouble finding homes for their girls, Pival learned from the head of the organization, a woman with graying hair and a crisp cotton sari and such life in her eyes. People didn't trust these women to be good workers, not to tempt their husbands, not to seduce their sons. They saw them as vamps, willing women, not humans looking for a new life. Pival hired two girls that day, a quiet Bangladeshi woman who almost never talked and who swept the floors, and a cook from Tibet who made wonderful vegetable dishes and never ever cared what Pival did with her time.

She spent her days reading all the poetry she had wanted to explore, the Tagore book she had brought with her on her trip that she hadn't opened once, and books about sea snails. She saw movies on her own, and ate new foods, and bought bottles of wine just to have in her home. She responded to requests from Ram's family, all asking her to come live with them, stay with them, visit them, with clear but firm negative responses, and they soon stopped asking, which was just fine with her. She visited cemeteries and took long walks around the city, first through walking tours, then on her own. She was finally getting to know her own city, after seeing so many foreign ones. She began to teach her maid and her cook English, starting slow, letting them absorb it, watching the fear in their eyes become happiness a little more each day. It was an almost perfect life, and she couldn't believe she had been ready not to have one anymore.

Except that she still wasn't sleeping well. So she kept waiting for something to happen. And then, one day, the doorbell rang, and there was Jake, standing in the doorway, her son's ashes in his hands, his face open, tense, worried, hopeful. She opened up the door and let him in.

Jake sat on her couch in her living room and drank the milky tea served by the new maid. Pival had introduced him as a friend of her son's, and then thought again. She turned to the maid.

"Actually, he was my son's lover," she said, watching the woman carefully. The maid simply nodded and left. This was the first person she had ever said that to, the first person she had admitted the truth to, and it felt beautiful, the way the truth is supposed to be.

"Will you be staying long?" she said to Jake.

"I think that's up to you," he responded.

They took the ashes to the Ganges the next day. They held the box together and let the ashes and the little shell fall into the sacred waters, watching Rahi slip away. He held her hand afterward as the tears from her eyes slipped into the Ganges as well, and she didn't mind at all, even if they were in public and people were watching them. What must they think, watching this old Indian woman with this strange white man, holding each other's hands and crying? Ram would have hated it. A flare of happiness spread through her whole body, a warmth that emanated out from the hand that held hers. As she watched the water take him away, as it had taken so many people away and would take her, too, someday, she wondered, where would she go next? What would Rahi have wanted to see? She rinsed her hands in the water and stood up. And that night, with Jake in the next room, she slept deeply and fully, and she didn't dream of anything at all. The ghosts were gone now, and when she woke, the first thought she had was, *What happens next?*

And she got up, to go and find out.

ACKNOWLEDGMENTS

There are many people who helped support me, encourage me, push me, and laugh with me as I wrote this novel. I would like to thank:

My agent, Julia Kardon, who is probably the best agent I could ever have asked for and saw potential in my early messy, rambling drafts of this story. My editor, Rachel Kahan, who saw this novel far more clearly than I could have and let me add back in all the things I wanted to. My UK editor, Martha Ashby, who shares my love of tapas and sewing and was the first to toast me with champagne for finishing this novel.

Rachel Meyers, my fantastic production editor; Tavia Kowalchuk, super fan and marketing genius; Maureen Cole, publicity guru; Mumtaz Mustafa, cover designer extraordinaire; and all the men and women of the HarperCollins sales team, whose great enthusiasm and tireless evangelism got this book into all the right hands.

My early readers, who gave me so much generous feedback and even said there were good things: Rebecca Gridley, Victoria Frings, Anastasia Olowin, and Emily Holleman, who collectively gave me all the advice I ever could have asked for and all the wine I needed. Natasha Joshi, for setting me straight about Bengali Brahmin last names, among so many other things.

My teachers and mentors at NYU, especially Joe Vinciguerra, who gave me the courage and confidence and just enough criticism to help me learn how to keep myself writing.

My family in the United States: Deborah Solo, Angel Franqui, and

Alejandro Franqui, for putting up with me and loving me always; and my family in India, especially Raj Kummar Narula, Mridula Narula, and Shuchita Jhaveri, whose trip inspired all this.

And of course, Rohan, who, more than anything else, said just go ahead and do it.

Insights,
Interviews
& More . . .

Meet Leah Franqui

Priyam Dhar

LEAH FRANQUI is a playwright and the recipient of the 2013 Goldberg Playwriting Award and the 2013 Alfred Sloan Foundation Screenwriting Award. A graduate of Yale University, she earned an MFA at NYU Tisch School of the Arts. Franqui is a Puerto Rican–Jewish native of Philadelphia, and now lives with her Kolkata-born husband in Mumbai. *America for Beginners* is her first novel. ❧

Behind the Book Essay

When I was in graduate school for dramatic writing at NYU, I met my husband, a tall Punjabi man from Kolkata, a city in West Bengal. My parents are a culturally mixed marriage; my father's parents moved to New York from Puerto Rico just before he was born, and my mother's family is of Russian-Jewish descent. So I was somewhat acquainted with cultural diversity within a couple, although there has proved to be a difference in terms of cultural background versus cultural present.

I met my husband's family for the first time when we had been dating for almost a year. My in-laws haven't had many opportunities to travel outside of India, and most of their travel within the country has been to visit family or for the purpose of religious pilgrimages to Hindu holy sites. Nevertheless, they elected to visit him in New York for our graduate-school graduation.

As part of the trip to the United States, they took a tour of the country. Indians who make a trip to America often do cross-country tours seeing as many places as possible in as few days for as little money, and my in-laws were insistent that this was the thing to do and therefore they must do it. The idea of it—the way it was organized, the ▶

3

guarantee of ten Indian dinners for every night of the vacation, the way it was organized by Indians for Indians, a packaging of America bought and sold—fascinated me. Explaining someone else's country to a tour group just struck me as the most interesting thing, and I knew that was worth thinking about.

It also came at a time when I was reconciling myself to my new in-laws: The way they felt delicate and brittle, more like my grandparents than my parents. The way they had expectations and prejudices that came from a different culture and world. The way they were sometimes people I wasn't sure I liked, no matter how much they seemed to like me. The way my mother-in-law was disgusted by homosexuality, the way they knew very little about America (and why should they, really), and the way they accepted me but didn't really have much interest in my cultural or religious identity.

This novel became a way to learn about India, about Bangladesh, about sexuality and identity and women. It shaped itself in layers: first a Bengali widow with a gay son she'd allowed to be shunned from her home; then a Bangladeshi tour company that pretends to be Indian to lure unsuspecting tourists; then finally the larger world— what it means to be with someone closeted, how it feels to tour America, everything else I could understand and find about immigration, displacement, culture clash. Although my family are the descendants of immigrants, they are very much part of the American cultural landscape, and immigration the way my husband and his family know it and have experienced it is wildly different.

Most of all, personally, there was the way India loomed in front of my life, with a thousand languages and divisions. We were planning on moving to India and have done so since, and the idea of the country, which I had never visited, terrified and excited me. So it started with my in-laws' trip, in a way, and ended with my own move to Mumbai. ❧

Reading Group Discussion Questions

1. "Mrs. Sengupta was traveling scandalously alone, without a husband or a gaggle of women her own age." Many people in Pival's orbit are shocked by her decision to go to the United States by herself. What about a woman—especially an older woman—traveling alone is so alarming to them? Is it really about safety—as Pival's maid insists—or about propriety? Are solo women travelers viewed with the same concern in other cultures?

2. "Nothing would erase the sense of continued shame" that Satya feels for abandoning his friend Ravi and edging him out of a job. How do you feel about Satya's betrayal of Ravi? Is it understandable or unforgiveable?

3. Mr. Ghazi sees Rebecca's "early enthusiasm become a hardened fear, and he worried for her." How do you feel about Rebecca's sadness and struggles compared to the sadness and struggles of other characters in the book?

What does she, the American-born child of an affluent family stand to learn from the journey, and from the other "beginners"?

4. Ronnie Munshi seems to have achieved the American dream: arriving from Bangladesh with no money, building a successful business, bringing over a wife, and employing other new arrivals. What do you make of him? Is he the picture of a "model" immigrant? What about the Iranian immigrant Mr. Ghazi?

5. Bhim calls himself "the ice queen" because he is so painfully unaffectionate with Jake in public. Jake "thought that Bhim was determined to live in a way his parents would approve of, despite the fact that they would never know it." Why can't Bhim just be out and proud in this new gay-friendly country? How do Jake and Bhim navigate Bhim's deep sense of shame and keep it from destroying their love?

6. Pival reflects that "at home Bangladeshis had no status. They did the worst jobs, if they had jobs at all. They were illegal ▶

immigrants with no rights and no names, just men who melted into the background and women who looked hungry all the time." Because of this stigma, Ronnie Munshi is desperate to ensure that none of his Indian clients know he and his guides are Bangladeshi. Does this distinction between Bangladeshis and Indians matter in America? Do "illegal" immigrants in America face the same stigma as those Bangladeshis in India?

7. Pival reflects, "I do think most parents, at the heart, want their children to be happy. It is only that we want our children to be happy in the right way. The way we were taught happiness was. I think this is a cause of much pain, thinking, perhaps, that there is a right way." Would Bhim agree? Would Rebecca, who has her own fraught relationship with her parents?

8. Did you think that Bhim might still be alive and would be reunited with his mother? Why or why not?

9. As a college student before her marriage, Pival describes herself as "young and alive with purpose." Does she regain her purpose by the end of the novel? How does Pival, the widow and bereaved mother in America, compare to Pival, the miserable, voiceless wife in Kolkata?

10. "When she woke, the first thought [Pival] had was, *What happens next?*" What do you think happens next for these characters? Where will they be five or ten years after the end of this novel? ∽